Eau de Café

Eau de Café

Raphaël Confiant

Translated by
James Ferguson

faber and faber
LONDON·NEW YORK

First published by Editions Bernard Grasset in 1991
First published in this translation in 1999
by Faber and Faber Limited
3 Queen Square London WC1N 3AU

Ouvrage publié avec l'aide du Ministère français chargé de la Culture –
Centre national du livre
[Published with the assistance of the French Ministry of Culture, Centre
National du Livre]

Typeset by Faber and Faber Ltd
Printed in England by Mackays of Chatham plc, Chatham, Kent

A CIP record for this book
is available from the British Library

ISBN 0–571–19587–3

2 4 6 8 10 9 7 5 3 1

To Manman Lily

'Dlo kafé: café très léger
(c'est ainsi qu'on le consomme généralement)
Eau de café: very weak coffee
(the usual way of drinking it)'

'And with the Sea itself we shall not concern ourselves,
but with its reign in the heart of man.'
Saint-John Perse, *Vents*

'Only the incomprehensible really lends itself to words.'
Alain Bosquet, *Le Gardien des rosées*

Translator's note

I would like to thank Raphaël Confiant for his kind assistance and suggestions and the following for their help and advice: Richard Burton, Catriona Davidson and Jenny Plocki.

First Circle

In the beginning – or in other words ever since that time of yesteryear when dogs yapped through their backsides – there was the village of Grand-Anse, turning its back on the Atlantic with meticulous, almost neurotic ostentation, preferring to bury its head among the wooded hills and breathe the air of the Volcano beyond, right up in the far North.

The order of desires is as unchanging there as that of the days. Nobody seeks to understand. And so everyone takes refuge in words since they have no flesh and wipe away their own traces and, above all, since they alone can match the stubbornness of the white breakers rolling in from the high seas beyond . . .

1 The Three Deaths of Antilia

So it was that Antilia left as she had come: without an ounce of ill will. Godmother, whom she liked to snuggle up against throughout the night, was woken just before dawn by the tide making a strange rasping noise.

'I swear it sounded like the belly of a woman trying to give birth,' she declared. 'There weren't even waves but the sea's surface was suddenly wracked by a spasm of hiccups . . . I stayed for a good while looking at it all, despite the sand which the wind was lashing against the window, and when I got back to bed, the little one had gone cold-cold-cold just like a rock in the river . . .'

Eau de Café moved slightly away from the lifeless body and waited for the village to shiver before she broke down sobbing. She sent me to fetch the priest who made up all sorts of imaginative excuses so as not to have to deal with people who had so deliberately ignored his invitations to attend church. Then she dispatched me to the town hall in order to inform the secretary, a big-bellied, goateed and smug mulatto, who pulled a sour face and asked me to come back at the end of the morning. We were alone. Rooted in a loneliness without end.

Weighing up our grief (or whatever you choose to call that feeling of emptiness that was surging into our heads), the carpenter, our next-door neighbour, decided to drop the sullen taciturnity that he had adopted since we took in 'that devil's daughter' and offered to carve her a beautiful coffin out of pear-tree, one of the most expensive woods available at the time. Normally it was only the eldest sons of good families who had cradles made of it. I helped him square the planks, which were as hard as iron.

'With this wood, my boy,' he insisted, 'those bloody worms will have to wait at least a hundred and twenty years before they'll be able to feed on her bones.'

Since he'd been sure that Antilia would never again transfix him with her dark butterfly gaze, he had begun to express a sort of feverish tenderness towards her. He would say 'Eau de Café's young lady', 'your humming-bird', 'that sugar-cane arrow that sparkled in the plain' and a whole lot of other syrupy epithets, all constructed at leisure, as in his day no job was complete without its soliloquy.

Upstairs Eau de Café was preparing the water that would be used to cleanse the deceased. She mixed some *diapanna* leaves and some wild thyme with oil from the eternal lamp which burnt under the portrait of Saint Martin de Porres in a nook in her bedroom. She was humming something that sounded like the way Congo blacks' guts rumble and which she couldn't possibly have begun to understand. Annoyed by my curiosity, she told me to polish the floor right under the bed where Antilia was lying. Although it was nearly eleven o'clock in the morning, it was freezing cold in the room, where the shutters looking out to sea had been opened wide. Every so often the girl stood up in her shroud and went in stately fashion to lean at the window. Godmother would murmur in Creole:

'There's no need to start hankering after this life, goddaughter. There's really no need.'

And she took her firmly back to her place, closing her eyelids. Outside, the sea had taken on a malevolent appearance, even fuller of hate than in the hurricane season, and when it was known in the village that Antilia had passed away, there were those who guessed at some connection between the two phenomena. People from hereabouts grasp the most tenuous of connections on the strength of a shiver that runs down their spine and which they normally exorcise by drinking down a full glass of neat rum in one.

The rabble decided to gather on our doorstep. They strung enough words together to make up their own demented account of events, the telling of which contorted even the most amiable of faces. Godmother carefully locked the door, fearing danger at any moment. The carpenter, leaving his work for a moment, made as if

4

to attack the gathering with his saw but only managed to scare away a couple of brats who were already leaping to and fro between the rocks and the roof of our house. At two in the afternoon the doctor came to certify the death, no doubt at the behest of the town hall secretary or even the mayor himself, a sort of little Mussolini whose main, if not only, concern had always been patriotic parades and fêtes. The doctor kept shaking his head dubiously while filling in his paperwork. Stopping after each sentence, his complexion ashen, he would stare at us with comic intensity before turning to look at Antilia. The whole time he asked not a single question. He got Godmother to countersign a document and then was off like someone who has had a nasty scare. His state of agitation stirred the crowd up further and insults began to fly:

'Eau de Café, you peasant negress, you're no bloody virgin and that dead girl of yours isn't a flesh and blood creature either!'

I alone, in my frailty, was quite inexplicably spared such abuse even though I was ultimately just as responsible as Godmother was. Was I excused because they saw some exclusively female evil behind this business? As it happens, Antilia was denied a proper funeral in church. The priest ordered the church doors shut so that he couldn't be asked to commit such sacrilege. In any case, the whole village would never have let him. Hysterical matrons, led by Ma Léonce, were banging their fists on the wormeaten wood of our shop-front; men were sharpening their cutlasses on the off chance, their blank faces impassive and unpitying An old crone in disgusting rags was screaming.

'Away with you and your evil creature! Go far away from Grand-Anse and take with you the curse that you kept here deliberately to bring a jinx on all of us!'

'Who, one wonders, could shay bay, this dead little girl?' joined in Honorat Congo, our barber, with his In France accent.

'She must be one of Myrtha's bastard daughters,' suggested someone.

'Pff! That slut Myrtha may open her legs to all comers, but she's more barren than a male pawpaw tree, my dear!' ruled the old woman.

5

The carpenter, with the coffin finished, called me over to put on a speedy-quick coat of varnish and advised Eau de Café to pack her things and get out through the door which faced the sea, the door that we never opened because we wanted nothing to do with that side. She grumbled while carefully continuing to shine Antilia's skin with her strange yellowish mixture. Holding her by the arm, wrist, ankle or nape, she worked in a slow to-and-fro motion in time with her throbbing lament. Each drop went back into a bowl and, to my serenest surprise, the liquid was becoming crystal clear, almost lustrous in places.

'They're just like fish scales,' was the first thought to cross my mind.

Then Antilia gave me a fond look, a furtive smile on her lips. As death was doing its hateful work, so her face was gradually returning to that of the abandoned angel we had saved a long time before all this started.

'They just won't leave you in peace,' fretted Eau de Café amidst the muffled din coming up from our front door. 'But what have you done to them, eh? It's as if you'd eaten the goat they'd been keeping for their wedding feast, my little black darling.'

The looting of our shop was under way. Bags of France-flour and red peas, crates of Norwegian salted cod, barrels of salt pork, tin cans of red butter, bottles of rough white rum and wine, all of it was smashed open and carted off by the swarming mob amid shouts, yells, crude oaths and even blows. One of the excited participants remembered that we had a storage place just behind the shop, and another outbreak of pandemonium ensued while mounted police, half unable and half unwilling to intercede, looked on. At the bottom of Front Street, the Syrian cautiously lowered the shutters of the shop he had named the Palace of the Orient.

When her laying out was complete, Antilia brushed her hair with castor oil, put on all her clothes and lay down smiling in her coffin. Then her lipsticked mouth spoke.

'Every one of my dreams is a torment. I see the waves swirl and turn, wilder than a cavalcade of zombies setting off for crossroads, cemeteries or shabeens. I hear strange words coming, rising, falling without understanding why the world is heading for disaster. Do you know why? Do you?'

A violent gust of wind rushed in from the high sea and shook the whole house, stopping the crowd's frenzy dead in its tracks. The coffin flew out of the window that looked out over the open sea, as if sucked out by a huge and invisible mouth, but instead of sinking into the waves, it took off towards the surrounding mountainsides, the realm of coco-plum trees and bracken. Eau de Café, hysterical, pissed herself as she stood there, her dress flapping gently against her skinny legs. She had turned into a formidable fighting cock of Calabrian race which fell upon and routed the crowd, slashing their faces with its beak and sinking its spurs into their palms.

'Make a note of today's date,' she cried as she settled on my shoulder, overcome with trembling. 'On 12th January 1955 I defeated evil. I defeated it!'

On the sideboard the 'Courville Rum' calendar did indeed show that date. Believe me, it's the honest truth . . .

There's another version of events, favoured by bush radio, our local rumour mill: the tempest was preceded by a sudden and terrifying silence, which settled over the village of Grand-Anse at nine o'clock in the morning. We caught ourselves listening for something that was late in appearing but whose presence we could already feel in the strange slowness of our movements. Everyone looked into each other's eyes to see if they had guessed; whoever blinked first lost and, both shamed and angry, had to go to ground at home. Mothers were urgently counting their brood, women traders were hammering planks across their shop-fronts. Bogino, the madman through and through, was on his own as he climbed the suddenly empty alleys which all led to Back Street, making heavily threatening gestures at this mysterious force which was about to surround us and poking fun at the anxiety he caught sight of through the shutters of the well-to-do houses.

It was as if the sea had shrunk back upon itself, licking at the blackness of the sand with barely restrained fury. Along the La Cra-bière promontory the sea grapes seemed tortured in their fifty-year-old bark by 'the wind's spitefulness', Eau de Café told me as she knelt with Antilia, busy with her rosary beads. The girl had under-gone a transformation in the space of a few hours: she had become a woman. A woman with full breasts, with vanilla-coloured skin, who was braiding her hair with provocative motions.

'Has she spoken?' I asked Godmother.

'What do you mean, spoken? Why does it have to be today that she does? Antilia will rediscover her memory when she needs to. Nowhere is it said that the curse my mother passed on to us will pursue us to the end of time.'

A third dry season had passed since the foundling girl had taken over our lives, and people had distanced themselves from us, having failed to discover why and how she had come to Grand-Anse. Ma Léonce, the baker's wife, stopped our credit as she was certain that one of these days we would pay for our rash-ness. Those around us weren't entirely wrong.

As midday approached, all coming and going had stopped and a fine rain drizzled over the village, leaving a bitter-sweet smell in the air which unnerved Eau de Café. To calm herself down she began to polish her big wild-cherry-wood sideboard which was covered with cut-glass plates, tasteless statuettes, family portraits and embroidered napkins. Antilia had opened the window look-ing out on to the sea and stood rigidly, her gaze fixed into the dis-tance, a slight smile on her lips. A huge half-stifled groaning was running through the bowels of the water, which had taken on an eerie greyish hue. I went up to her and tried to hold her hand. Her fingers were almost cold enough to burn.

'Antilia,' I began.

She didn't turn around. She was now twice my size, almost as big as Godmother. The latter, fearing that people would notice these strange goings-on, had locked the door and told me to stay upstairs. When the first winds of the storm started to rattle at the corrugated iron of the roofs, Godmother gave a cry like a cat's miaow and held me against her. Her heart pounded wildly in my ears.

'Don't be afraid,' she kept saying, 'this hurricane won't be all that bad.'

Antilia, like a siren, was chanting, unstoppable, her voice high-pitched but sometimes drowned out by the fury of the winds.

'Shut the window, *doudou*, my dear,' whispered Eau de Café timidly to the young woman.

Whirlwinds of spray were coming into the room, making our eyes smart and misting up the mirrors on the wardrobe. A taste of salt settled on our tightly closed lips. The young woman remained motionless, only occasionally tossing back her hair. Front Street was by now deserted and the church roof was swaying alarmingly. Suddenly Antilia burst out laughing and the house shook as if caught in an earthquake. Pictures fell from the walls, the glasses on the sideboard smashed against each other and the legs of the four-poster bed sambaed sideways.

'Antilia,' said Eau de Café, 'we're only a poor lot of black vagabonds in this place. It's not our fault if we came into this world with our brains in our backsides and haven't had the guts to put it right . . . Spare them! They don't really set out to make black mischief, they just do wrong without weighing up good against evil. Darling, I'm begging you, please.'

Suddenly the rain arrived. A multitude of different rains, each more violent than the previous one, astonishingly loud, falling incredibly thick and fast, hammering on the fragile walls of the houses. Then from the sky came a succession of cracking noises and explosions, spaced out with disconcerting regularity. Antilia ripped off her white cotton dress and tossed it into the wind, laughing all the more loudly. Her laughter seemed to fuel the rumbling thunder and red flashes of lightning shot out from her bulging eyes. Eau de Café buried her head under her eiderdown and covered me with her body.

'I have come from nowhere,' cried the young woman in her inimitable voice, 'or, if you prefer, from this very place, from here itself . . .'

'Be quiet!' yelled Eau de Café, more and more terrified.

Antilia continued to hold forth, maintaining that the hurricane

9

was the black man's annual punishment. The high winds from across the sea were meant to clean the filth from their souls, to wash away both their shit and their vegetable gardens. The hurricane would strip the black man naked so that he could see himself in his real loneliness and stop boring us all to death with his tedious old tales. And now, for once, it's true, he has shut up, silent among the continuous creaking of his hut's corrugated iron, no longer posing or boasting, but begging forgiveness from the Almighty, from the Virgin Mary, from the gods of Guinea, from the Indian goddess Mariémen. Snivelling, teeth chattering, shivering, he holds his head in hands calloused by bad luck.

'The black man from these parts has turned his back on dignity!' screamed Antilia, crouching naked on the window-sill. 'He only has time for cheating and idleness, for mischief-making and unbridled fornication. Now the time of reckoning has come.'

And the great apricot-coloured bird launched itself into the eye of the storm with a single majestic flap of its wing, leaving Godmother and me stunned with fear . . .

According to other reports, Antilia was certified mad and the village populace demanded her immediate internment in the Colson Psychiatric Hospital. People half expected the heavens to open at any moment and cast light on the unspeakable secret of their joy and the stone paths fell prey to a countless mob of fanatics, with women and kids all too ready to start plundering. Only the old greybeards, with words as hard as mahogany bark from the heart of virgin forests, only their toothless mouths grumbled some disapproval, quickly transformed into inscrutable grunts.

'Talking too much never did anyone any good,' was the general conclusion.

A century after these happenings (which comes to about twenty years in white-France language), I have decided to ask my folk more. The Oceanic Hotel is perhaps the most neutral place where I can settle in with my piles of empty notebooks, and in any case the 'Golem' bus dropped me off there without giving me the choice . . .

2 The Three Loves of Antilia

Eau de Café, who had only ever been once in her life to the Grand-Anse parish hall to see a film (they showed *Sissi* for months on end by public demand from one and the same audience), had a neat turn of phrase to describe how whites make love: 'spit jam', she called it, thereby winning immense popularity among the common folk who were shocked by such a practice. It's true that the actors in those films, however glamorous they were, didn't use any of our three amorous approaches. They were happy to chat away endlessly until suddenly, it seemed, the hero stood in front of his heart's desire, fixed his blue eyes on hers and moved slowly and deliberately towards her, the whole thing ending up with a mutual sucking of tongues. Thimoléon, who had been around at the time of silent movies, would tell anyone who wanted to listen, especially if they'd been kind enough to buy him a rum,

'Ladies and gentlemen, the white will always have the advantage over the black man since he doesn't need to get undressed to make love!'

If you showed any surprise, he would reel off from memory a whole lot of films from the thirties up to the present day, including impressive lists of actors and 'actesses' mostly with American names, in order to demonstrate that in no film were naked bodies to be seen doing things to other naked bodies.

'That's the black man's way,' he concluded peremptorily.

As his cinematic knowledge was so great and our experience of whites was confined to the four policemen at Grand-Anse, whose wives almost never left the barracks, many of us ended up believing that whites made babies with their tongues and nothing else. Antilia, who would only wear France-dresses, France-shoes, France-rings and France-nail varnish, announced to all her suitors (and there were plenty of them, you can believe me!) that she would only give in to whoever was able to make France-love.

'France-love, full stop!' she snapped at the main contender among them, the half-Syrian Ali Tanin, whose father had left him a hardware and linen shop at the bottom of Front Street.

Everybody laid odds on him, since when it came to elegance, poise and gift of the gab, he far outclassed the little idiots who had never even left, apart from brief trips to some neighbouring *commune*, the village and surrounds of Grand-Anse. As for him, he had travelled in mysterious Levantine countries with his father, from where the latter brought back fabrics so soft to the touch and so beautiful to behold that his stall was never without customers. People only held one thing against him: that he ignored his old negress of a mother who lived in a decrepit shack in the En Chéneaux area. It was a sad sight to see her pacing the pavement opposite the Palace of the Orient, hoping for a glance, perhaps a smile, or even by some miracle a few words from her former husband or her son. She moved along barefooted, with all the heaviness conferred on her by the elephantiasis that was tormenting her left leg, her wrinkled skin showing in places through her much-patched dress.

'None of us knows what mischief the old cow may have got up to, so let's not be too quick to pity her,' said Eau de Café sententiously, as she waited resolutely behind the shop counter for her to come as usual and try to beg half a pound of salt pork.

Nobody, however, blamed Ali Tanin for being the most inveterate lady-killer in the whole of the North, for he was held in awe from the Tartane peninsula up to Grand-Rivière and made no secret of it either. During the dry-season afternoons, when the heat made a point of numbing your brain and the idle sought out the shade offered by a bit of wall to rest or play a quiet game of dominoes, Ali Tanin, as ever impeccably attired in a silk shirt, either green or black, would come and broadcast his latest conquests in public. He wrote them down in a notebook that he hid in his wallet and, in front of his speechless audience, detailed the attractions of many a young girl whom you would have thought blameless enough for Holy Sacrament without confession. That's why he was surprised to get no reaction when he'd shouted triumphantly: 'Cécilia Lafontant had no choice but to do it the evening before last in my car, gentlemen. Yesterday, at midday, I caught Virginie Saint-Laurent, who was on her way to do a load of washing at the river.'

The listeners used to gawp with admiration at such exploits, with Dachine, the municipal dustman whose minuscule intimate dimensions ruled out any chance of amorous success, even adding,

'Hey! My friend! When you next get hold of those girls, give them one or two good thrusts from me!'

But now, for the first time, the bastard-Syrian's speech was greeted with a mocking silence. Whereas before he used to chase away the kids like me who were trying to snatch little titbits of his lectures, he stood rooted to the ground, stiffer than an ox which has drunk cold water, oblivious to the sweat which was forming round shadows under his armpits. The big mouth stood there in the full sun, as if to attention, until someone took it upon himself to pull him out of his strange stance by shouting,

'That's all well and good! Bravo, Mister Ali Tanin, you're a master-cock, all the hens and young fowls hereabouts live in fear of your spurs, but why have you never had a go at Antilia, eh?'

'Antilia, you know, the girl who lives with Eau de Café,' added somebody else with ironic pedantry.

'Antilia, you know who we mean, man, the one whose beauty is enough to make a priest's eyes pop out.'

Ali Tanin looked like a duellist who has just been shot in the back as he gets his weapon ready. His lips twitched as beads of sweat gathered on them, and the pages of his notebook crumpled under his fingers, several of which bore rings (some people maintained that the yellow stone which he sported on his little finger was a charm which open-sesame'd the most stubborn of thighs).

'The . . . the . . . the black girl . . . who doesn't say anything?' he asked.

'Don't pretend you haven't noticed her! You buy your cigarettes at Eau de Café's,' pointed out a domino player, 'and it's not just because she doesn't chatter like the sluts you're used to that she's dumb like she is.'

'But who of you lot knows where the girl comes from? That boy there, he's Eau de Café's nephew, right? Ask him if he knows,' retorted Ali Tanin.

'Don't mix kids up in adults' business,' interrupted Dachine, to my huge relief. 'If you're all you say you are, prove it to us now by charming Antilia! Talk her round, my friend, and I'll be the first to travel the wide world boasting of your conquests.'

We watched the perplexed and nonplussed bastard-Syrian back slowly away from the group of domino players, staring intently at the hot, sticky tar on the road, and then suddenly speed up back to his shop, where he stayed for a good fortnight. The second-rate fops, the bullshitters and other experts in high-flown phrases learnt by heart from some romance magazine, rediscovered their vanity. Whereas a generally observed rule usually stated that nobody should have a go at a girl until Ali had already had her three times (after which he abandoned them to their fate), the village was now invaded at dusk by cohorts of dandies from Macédoine, from Vivée, from Morne Céron, even from Basse-Pointe, all in search of fresh flesh, and it has to be said that the ladies in question were asking for nothing more. But this state of affairs didn't last long, as it was a question of Ali Tanin's honour, and each and everyone here knows how much that word means in the mouth of a Syrian, even a half one. That's how you-know-who made up his mind to confront the virgin, the negress who had come from elsewhere, who rarely opened her mouth, that Antilia whom people distrusted more and more each year without being able to say why.

So Ali Tanin put on a blood-red shirt for the first time, tied a cowboy scarf around his neck and marched towards Eau de Café's shop. News of the event blew like dust around the village, drawing a crowd of pimps, idlers and all other jigger-scratchers. Head held high, Ali Tanin went through the door and made his declaration.

'Mademoiselle, since the moment that my heart began to bleed from that crown of thorns which is love, I have not been able to eat, drink or sleep. I see only you. Agree to come with me and I promise you that the sweetness of my touch on your skin will know no limits as our two bodies become one.'

A round of applause greeted this lyrical outburst, for blacks, however much they like cheap rum, appreciate the beauties of good French more than anyone else, and it's just possible that they issued this challenge to the bastard-Syrian just to have him spout his charming phrases in public. Then a silence filled a long length of time. Everyone looked at each other. Ali Tanin stared at Eau de Café's servant. Even the infernal grumbling of the Grand-Anse sea had ceased. Finally, Antilia relaxed her frown and said:

'I only want France-love.'

And with that she retired into the back of the shop like someone who had been needlessly distracted from an important task. That same evening, Al Tanin climbed down from his pedestal and wandered about in khaki shorts, talking coarse Creole and swigging beer from the bottle in great high spirits with the worst dregs of our village. Once drunk, he started singing, imitating Tino Rossi:

'Fr-r-r-a-a-nce Love!'

'Ali Tanin is a finished man,' insisted Thimoléon the carpenter. 'Finished with a capital F. Don't be surprised when he goes to live with his mother in that pigsty she calls a house!'

Before touching rock bottom, the master-cock who used to talk round the most stubborn girls as easily as one-two-three (and sometimes, he boasted, just by fluttering his eyelashes), resigned himself to trying one of our oldest courting techniques: the discreet chat-up. This requires the subtle art of feinting and an ability to move without even disturbing the air while letting one's presence be felt; skills which far outstripped Ali Tanin's supposed natural gifts. So when we saw him putting his precious behind on the edge of the little wall by Eau de Café's shop, everyone set about studying the body movements and, above all, the mouth movements of the bashful lover.

First of all and to start with, Sire Tanin had traded in his garish garb for a sober shirt buttoned right up to the neck the way the

Adventists wear them. Some sort of hat was covering the front of his skull, hiding the normally ironic glint in his eye. With one leg crossed over the other dangling down from the wall, Ali Tanin was murmuring to Antilia:

'Amidst the fever of my most sleepless nights I have dared to dream that we might go, you and I, to watch September take flight from the vantage point of La Crabière, that promontory feared by one and all. On the last Sunday of the village fête, when people are sadly putting away their rum glasses in their huts lit by a Coleman lamp, we would wait for the last band of kids to take their last ride on the wooden merry-go-round horses. The drummer, scowling under his bushy eyebrows, would grumble while beating his goat's skin mechanically,

Tibolonm, banbôch bout! (Child, the fair is over!)

'Then the final merry-go-round of pink, blue and yellow horses (yes, the ritual colours) would crumble into a heap of silence. Once again Grand-Anse would become two streets: Main Street, where we wait hopefully for the swaying of the overloaded sugar-cane lorries, and Back Street where families which command respectation speculate over who will marry who in the year to come. Only that mad mother, the sea, would fill the silence with the all-too-familiar din that has accompanied each of our actions since that time when the devil himself was a mere infant. She weaves our thoughts together with mottled foam and that is why our simplest utterances seem like the most beautifully eloquent of courtroom speeches. And yet we turn our backs on her, for God's sake! We curse all her offspring, forgetting that this includes God the Father himself. Sacrilege! Sacrilege! But when the falling sickness jolts some local fellow's sanity, who is the first to rush down to the beach at dawn to roll the poor fool's body around in the waves? Who belches, hands clasped together,

"Sea of Grand-Anse, cleanse for me this soul sullied by sin! Free it from the curse of madness!"

'Young woman, agree to come with me and the entire universe shall be yours.'

All he received by way of answer was a splattering of soapy

water from Antilia who took advantage of the time he was talking this gibberish to pretend to scrub the shop-front. We kids were captivated by the bastard-Syrian's incomprehensible words. Straight after finishing his declamation he mimed kisses and caresses in the direction of our servant, his hands making sublime touching motions in the air, but the *câpresse* simply ignored him as she walked away with her feline grace. For what seemed like an eternity but today I think was four days and three nights, Ali Tanin came to try the chat-up technique on Antilia. His face had become a mask of grave intensity and, in line with the stubborn belief of Grand-Anse people, he began to confuse Antilia and the sea itself, the sea that we were taught to hate from the moment we stopped suckling at our mother's breast.

As his failure became obvious, an extraordinary character took over. He went under the name of Julien Thémistocle and, from day to day, either appeared twenty years older or twenty years younger than his real age. Sometimes I didn't even recognize him, especially during his periods of sudden rejuvenation. Wrinkles and scars fell from his face, his gait became friskier and what is more, even without seeing him, I knew when one of his metamorphoses was under way just from the colour in Eau de Café's cheeks. It seemed to me that Julien and she hadn't exchanged a single word since I had been old enough to understand the world, but she had food sent secretly to him by one of her customers from Morne Capot, the back of beyond where the old devil made a habit, if you believe the gossips, of taming lancehead snakes just as his grandfather had done. We realized at once that Julien Thémistocle had decided to try our second courting method: the verbal assault. Unlike the subtle chat-up, you had to peck away frantically right and left, using all possible and imaginable means. So he stormed Eau de Café's shop, while she sought refuge upstairs for as long as it took for the sordid business to run its course. She who normally chased away the pests with her broom, who kicked out the Brylcreamed poseurs who were desperate to flex their muscles in front of Antilia, who emptied chamber-pots full of piss over serenaders, had decided this time to lock herself away, much to the chagrin of the populace who were dying to see (and made no secret of it) a set-to between 'that fine piece of black man Julien Thémistocle' and 'the white folk's psychic'.

Said Julien Thémistocle from beneath the shop window to Antilia, who was leaning on the counter:

'Come with me, young woman, and high on the furthest point of the promontory, where no man from Grand-Anse has ever set foot, we will leave aside any sniggering fantasies and our two bodies will fuse together into the very core of the cold rock. I will try to fathom your secret, Antilia, in the perfumed furrows of your armpits. I will drink your rum-flavoured sweat and will snap up your *coucoune* with a single twitch of my lips. I will exhaust my feverish mouth against the curves of your arms and then legs while you, impassive like a priestess, will let me lose my very being in the tumult of my senses. For my ears will hear the rhythm of your heartbeat, in the place where all life quivers, while my eyes will explore within yours landscapes of both wonder and goodness. I will laugh at the fantasies of the *chabins* from Macédoine who make out that the she-devil hides inside you. I shall mock the malevolence of the Morne Céron yokels who, each time they come to barter their yams for a pint of oil or a quarter of salt cod at Eau de Café's shop, mutter exorcising curses at you between their clenched teeth. As for the Indians who squat down there at Moulin-l'Étang, everyone knows that they beseech their god Maldévilin to make your hair fall out overnight so that they can see on your bald coconut skull the explanation for your sudden arrival among us. Only the big whites couldn't care less, as they're too busy boozing and whoring, their way of forgetting all the troubles that the present century has landed them with. Come with me, please do.'

Antilia ignored the maroon's entreaties. And yet we caught her in the stance she usually adopted when admiring something (her palms clasped to her ears) the day that Julien Thémistocle had brazened it out with a couple of white policemen who were trying to arrest him over some murky business to do with stolen cattle.

'I am a maroon. The last descendant of the maroons who forced you to eat your own souls in a salad in the woods of Morne Jacob. The first one of you to lay his pale hands on me is dead straight away!'

The intimidated constabulary had beaten a retreat and old Thémistocle had joined the pantheon of our local heroes, although quite a few women bore some grudge against him which they preferred not to explain. So it was that the outlaw's verbal assault washed over Antilia like pure dew off the leaf of a dasheen plant. Émilien Bérard, the young schoolmaster to whom nobody could attribute the slightest romantic adventure and whose spectacles grew thicker each year because of his passion for books, thought his moment had come. Neither the chat-up nor the assault was his forte. Our Creole customs only left him the couldn't-care-less role, a technique consisting of feigning total indifference towards the object of one's desires, ostentatiously ignoring its presence and yet making everyone else aware of one's passion with a dose of bombast. The aim of the strategy was to annoy people so much that they would feel obliged to intercede on one's behalf with the girl. When this tormenting procedure had run its course which could last from two days to two months or two years (the couldn't-careless practitioners being, on the whole, patient types), the girl in question had a a simple choice: either to give in to her suitor or to break the spell with a huge display of public anger.

Émilien Bérard's speech went like this:

'I would take your hand moist with emotion in mine and would get under the very skin of your palm the better to immerse myself in the wild rhythm of your heart. I would murmur some delirious declaration, invoking the drizzles of the dry season which stave off April's torpor, the humming-birds and their gem-like vibrations, the swaying and undulating of the *malavoi* cane pieces at Fond Gens-Libre on the eve of harvesting as well as a whole lot of ancient rumours which torment our memories.

'Nothing would be left unsaid in my onslaught on your ears. The only important thing for me, the tireless suitor, would be to call out once more your trade-wind name:

"Antilia! An-ti-lia Oh!"

'Arm in arm, heart in heart, we would skip over the black crystal sand, leaping over the entwined bodies of Myrtha, the village whore, and a fellow with his face unrecognizably contorted by pleasure. I would embrace fragments of the wind – you have to aim for the gentle breezes from the South with their load of emotions born in the deepest depths of dry gulleys – and, suitably under the influence, not to say as drunk as a skunk, I would daub you with strange echoes.

'Each hand's width of the sea holds its secret. This you know. There are places where you must never set foot for fear of vanishing once and for all into an abyss of endless blue. Stand well back in any case as the Sirens' song can take over your mind and reduce you to a snotty-nosed child.

'There are places where, quite frankly, the old men come and hide to shit for hours on end, using their fleshless gums to chew on a cheap cigar. That's how they tame the eternity of the village and our slender shadows in no way disturb their squatting in the darkness. And finally there is a place where I would like to take you if you would only consent to grant me a little of your haughtiness, that haughtiness which has always goaded the old shrews who are so desperate to flush out your whys and whereforths. In the pupil of your eye flows a whole river of untamable lights that sometimes put your godmother into a state of unconfined fearfulness. In this place of wild sea grapes we can see the island of Dominica and, behind its ominous mass, the sails of ghostly galleons. I would ask you to hail some peg-legged captain and I'm sure you would play along with my childishness, since passion can encourage any number of visions and prophecies. Isn't passion in its newness a hawk winging towards the navel of the heavens?

'As we climbed up the jagged sides of the La Crabière promontory, you would read my destiny in a sudden deluge of purple lightning flashes, those that Thimoléon – that old braggart! – claimed were a reminder of the curse that weighs on our village. You would speak in the golden tongue, that of our former masters, since more than ours, it can give shape to wondrousness and tenderness. How painful for those of us with our humble hut language which is rebuffed day and night at the walls of the great houses! And yet our flesh overflows with excesses of unrequited tenderness: you can see it in the fearlessly raised arm of the cane-cutters who, from Fond Massacre to Moulin-l'Étang, are not scared to defy the heat's excesses. Do I need to offer any more proof?'

Nobody came to the schoolmaster's assistance and without delay he bought some rope to hang himself. Only Honorat Congo could be bothered to go over the evidence again, between two snips of his scissors:

'I say and I say again that the black man spakes better French than the white.'

Antilia disappeared for three days running to La Crabière promontory to make clear to her three suitors that she was declining their declarations of love, probably viewing them as too tainted by their desire to uncover the secret of her identity and especially her relation with the sea of Grand-Anse. When she came back, her mouth was closed for good . . .

3

Each time that the island white, Honoré de Cassagnac, parked his paraffin-blue front-wheel-drive automobile outside our door, Eau de Café hurried to send me to play far away. (Normally she would tan my hide at each *drivaillerie* on my part, as she put it in her half-Creole, half-French jargon.)

'Take a crust of bread and a piece of chocolate from the shop,' she shouted to me as she rushed upstairs to make herself presentable.

The *béké* de Cassagnac was a man of imposing stature ('But is his cock as big?' people sniggered behind his back) and equally striking thinness. His white and worn face was cracked by a host of small red spots, which, together with his hooked nose, made him look like a fighting bird exhausted by the hurly-burly of the cockpit. He was the owner of an estate of about two hundred hectares, planted in sugar-cane, at Séguineau, to the south of the village of Grand-Anse, and he lived there with his daughter Marie-Eugénie, who was almost never seen outside, even at Mass. Once a month he sent for the priest to hold a service in his private chapel. He had all the quiet ferocity of island whites, that's to say he could very well swap jokes in Creole with his black workers and the next moment order his foreman to give a don't-bother-to-come-back note to someone or other because he or she was dragging their heels. He was thus universally feared, even by those who didn't work for him, to the great fury of Thimoléon. The carpenter refused even to acknowledge his presence.

'The *békés* are a devilish race!' grumbled the old communist. 'Ever since they arrived in this country they haven't stopped torturing people for a moment. First the Caribs, then us the blacks, and after that the coolies! When is this hooliganicity going to end, eh?'

'You're such an idiot!' retorted Eau de Café. 'God knows what He is doing. If He has put the white on top and the black below, it's because He has His reasons. You're not going to change that with your atheistic litanies.'

That's why as soon as the carpenter saw de Cassagnac extract his daughter from the front-wheel-drive and usher her into our house, he would shut the door and windows of his workshop and start playing the drum with all the virulence of a Guinea black. Maddened by being imprisoned in this way, the heavy sounds of the laghia rhythm rumbled and rattled the walls of the surrounding houses. The strangest thing was that de Cassagnac didn't seem to mind. He maintained an extraordinary dignity and only an imperceptible twitching of his eyebrows betrayed the irritation that was gnawing at him.

'And a good day to you, madame! Monsieur de Cassagnac de Saint-Mérieux has arrived to see you,' he called in an exaggeratedly ceremonial voice.

'Good day, good day, come in, I'm just opening up,' fussed Eau de Café.

Some days, instead of getting lost like she told me to, I hid behind the bags of sugar and France-flour piled up in the corridor joining the drawing-room to the shop and watched the unchanging ceremony enacted by these three people. Godmother and de Cassagnac carefully laid the young girl down on the corner sofa and sat each in a rocking-chair without speaking for what seemed like an infinity of time. Marie-Eugénie de Cassagnac opened her pale blue eyes, lifted herself up a little and ran her hand through her curly, chestnut-coloured hair. Her movements were jerky, almost mechanical. She was like one of those strange dolls with a key in its back that can speak or move an arm.

'Are you ready?' asked her father cautiously.

'Mmmm! Mmmm!' mumbled the girl, her features agitated by a violent tic.

At this point she would undergo an alarming transformation. Her cheeks seemed to be drawn inwards by some interior suction which contorted her face and pulled her skin back to the bone, and then, just as violently, they would blow out again, all this at regular intervals. De Cassagnac would then say to Eau de Café,

'Shall we go up, my dear?'

Upstairs Antilia was sitting on her bed, staring at the wild sea through the shutters and lost in profound meditation. Godmother hurried to close the shutters, which seemed suddenly to return the young woman to her role of obedient and rather stupid servant. She greeted the planter by bowing deeply and waited for Godmother to put her into a trance. She had revealed herself to be an excellent 'sleeper', one of those daytime somnambulists whose speaking dreams map out your destiny when read by a psychic. For Godmother was an occasional psychic, but only on behalf of local whites because, as she grumbled, the blacks can always go and consult magicians or other dealers in evil potions. A psychic doesn't deal with the devil, she doesn't prescribe or use any of those concoctions made from leprous-toad-ground-into-holy-water-stolen-the-day-before-Easter-mixed-with-menstrual-blood-from-a-virgin-over-thirty-years-old. A psychic does seances, which means talk, talk, talk, and her word is revelation. Or sometimes she reads your dreams. Or she might put a sleeper into a trance and translate her babbling into everyday advice.

Godmother attached herself to Antilia like a grey lizard stuck to the mirror of a wardrobe and seized her head in her hands, sweating heavily. Antilia struggled for a couple of seconds with grotesque spasms and then collapsed on to the bed, completely asleep. Eau de Café seemed exhausted by the exertion and had to hold on to her bedposts so as not to collapse as well. De Cassagnac was sitting in a dark corner, his hat on his knees, his expression unusually humble. Extraordinarily humble. Godmother undressed Antilia, leaving only her brassiere and black knickers (black in order to drive away the incubi which swarmed around Grand-Anse). Then she put her palms over her eyes and propped the young woman up with a couple of pillows. She lit three candles, which she put on the ground by the bed; two at its head, one at the foot. Then she too lay down, her eyes glazed, and took on a more masculine voice, a disturbing change which made me shiver as it did de Cassagnac. From outside, the throbbing of Thimoléon's drum reached us, muffled but nagging, which made the heat in the room even more oppressive. From the end of the roof from which I was watching the scene, thanks to gaps in the corrugated iron, I could hear the reassuring hubbub of the village. The idlers of all ages gathered in the church square to gossip about everything and mostly nothing or to play draughts. The women selling vegetables, stopping by every door and crying: 'Who wants me? Doesn't Madame want me today? I've got pumpkin, onions, barbadine, Saint-Martin yams, nice firm cabbages.' And above all, on the other side, the constant soaring of sea birds over the sea (a sort of homage to the volatile grace of the days), the sea whose brooding hatred watched us with vast eyeballs of bronzed foam.

I shuddered as Eau de Café's assumed voice began to fill the room. She was telling Antilia to give her a name, a 'title' she called it. She begged her, implored her to give up this secret and, when the sleeper answered almost hysterically, 'I don't know what you're looking for, I don't know!' Eau de Café became angry and started shouting in French: 'Talk or else I'll pull your tongue out!' De Cassagnac suddenly got up from his chair and began pacing around the room, fanning himself with his white canvas colonial-style hat. Over the years that these seances had been taking place, Antilia had revealed everything without the slightest reserve: the cause of the mysterious barrenness of a section of the Séguineau plantation, called 'My Life's Pain' by the black labourers; the cure for the skin disease that had ravaged de Cassagnac's body; the hiding place of the villain who was regularly poisoning the water buckets brought to the cattle kept at Savana Zicaque; the sordid dealings between two *békés* from Macouba who wanted to ruin de Cassagnac. The fact was that de Cassagnac, as a man of tradition, was innately attached to sugarcane cultivation even though it hardly brought in anything any more and the sugar refinery at Grand-Anse was threatened with closure year in year out.

The seance concluded, Godmother offered him tonic water in

the drawing-room, where as they talked he would always lecture her on the same subject:

'Sugar-cane is a civilization in itself, you see. It gives shape to life from four in the morning to six in the evening. Everyone has their part to play: the foreman who hands out the tasks and makes sure they're done, the cutters who sharpen their cutlasses on the grindstone before setting off to wage war on the ranks of sugar-cane, the women who follow in the fields, binding the canes together. Yes, my dear lady! The gangs of little black boys who pick up the canes left behind. The farrier who looks after the mules, the mule-drivers themselves who saddle and bridle and cart the heaps of cane to be weighed outside the mill. Isn't it a thing of wonder, madame?'

Godmother would smile approvingly, even though in her heart of hearts she must have cursed what this big, bony idiot of a white man called 'the civilization of sugar-cane'. And he was incredibly lucky that she was unfailingly honest, since on several occasions certain *békés*, versed in the more modern civilization of banana growing, had tried to bribe her so that she would persuade de Cassagnac to get rid of his lands and retire to his residence at Plateau-Didier in Fort-de-France with his idiot daughter.

'De Cassagnac spends too much time with his books,' had tried to argue the *béké* Dupin de Médeuil, a filthy debauchee who had been made second-in-command of the militia in the days of Admiral Robert and who never tired of eulogizing Marshal Pétain. 'You should see his drawing-room: books, books and more books! His maid has told me that it's even worse in his bed-room. While he wastes his time reading like an overgrown schoolboy, his estate is going to the dogs, is falling apart, while up in the North, the Conseil Général is refusing us the subsidies we need for our banana plantations because we can't produce the tonnage. All of Séguineau must, madame, be covered in bananas by the end of the year, for God's sake!'

Some maintained that de Cassagnac was too busy digging up his plantation to worry about agriculture. According to them, he was looking for a legendary crock full of gold coins that his grandfather had had buried during the time of slavery.

Godmother had an inexplicable soft spot for him (wasn't he once the lover of her mother, Franciane?) and so protected him from his enemies, especially those of his own race. Perhaps it was because she, as much as he, wanted to know the identity of the swine who one Mardi Gras had dressed himself in an enormous red, horned mask decorated with thousands of pieces of broken glass and had chased (with a grotesque waddling movement) the nubile daughter of the master of Séguineau through the house and along the verandas, taking advantage of the absence of the governess, who was relieving herself under a nearby mango tree. Marie-Eugénie's screams had made her rush back, and the sight she saw had left her aghast: the little girl and the Devil, face to face, him threatening her with his erect organ. The governess grabbed a broom and put him to flight. It was no good expecting anybody to help as everyone had been dancing in the village streets for three whole days. The little girl seemed frozen to the spot, struck down by fear. From that day she stopped laughing and talking altogether, she who used to brighten the great house with her incessant chatter, and her father fell victim to a huge sorrow. He took her to the United States, to Caracas, to Paris to see the most eminent doctors and, finally defeated, forced himself to ask help not just from a common psychic, but from a coloured woman to boot. When Antilia refused to speak, he would beg her,

'If it's a white who committed this crime, tell me! White, black, mulatto, *chabin*, coolie or Syrian, whoever it is will pay. I shall show no pity.'

In these situations the sleeper would ask for Marie-Eugénie to be brought upstairs and there the two of them would begin a bizarre dialogue that Eau de Café confessed herself unable to translate, apart from the following snatches:

'Water woman,' Marie-Eugénie would grumble, 'I don't like the way you smell of the tide. Don't try to stir up the dreams in my head. You'll learn nothing.'

'Remember! I command you to remember!' cried Antilia. 'I can turn over the wrong side of your life and put your anguish out to bleach in the sun.'

'Ha, ha, ha! . . . What game do you think you're playing, daughter of that damned Grand-Anse sea? You know full well that this village's carcass is eternally cursed. You know that these people who turn their backs on the sea have disobeyed and will be punished. What is the point in punishing just one of them?'

'I understand you,' breathed Antilia as her eyes suddenly opened wide, huge and sea-green. 'They are guilty, all guilty. There's not a single innocent in the place. This whole island will be wiped off the face of the earth and only the jelly-fish washed out to sea will be left to mourn its passing. I swear it!'

'Stop it at once!' screamed Eau de Café, who had grabbed a riding-crop made of mahoe fibre and was whipping the sleeper's legs.

She put her back to sleep even more deeply by pressing on her soles and restarted her merciless interrogation. Who? The name? Marie-Eugénie was gurgling like a three-month-old baby, so her father was forced to take her down to the drawing-room to stop her fit getting any worse. Eau de Café, annoyed by the resistance put up by the two girls, took out her fury on Thimoléon. She opened the shutter that looked over his workshop and shouted to him.

'Hey, nigger! I've had enough of your damned boom-boom-boom. If you're an African, monsieur, you only have to say so!'

'Me, an African!' exclaimed the carpenter, as he came out of his lair with his face as crumpled as an old piece of clothing that has been stuffed under a mattress for years. 'Well, well . . .'

He said 'well' over and over again, disbelieving, furious, crushed, vengeful. Every conceivable emotion ran through him in the blinking of an eye and he replied:

'As soon as a mulatto owns a horse, he's quick to say that he didn't have a negress for a mother.'

'A nigger, you can tell, will end up in hell,' retorted Godmother, slamming the shutter in his face.

In the meantime, Antilia had woken up and was splashing rainwater from the butt over her face. De Cassagnac didn't wait for Godmother to come down to the drawing-room. He carried Marie-Eugénie in his arms and gestured at his driver to start the engine. Sometimes it took him four turns of the crank before succeeding, hence attracting a crowd of kids from the neighbourhood. Through the windows of the automobile I could see Marie-Eugénie's blue eyes, which seemed to be fixed on the roof of our house where I was crouching. I tried to shrink against the burning corrugated iron, no doubt pointlessly as the young girl was in a blind daze.

In her bedroom, Eau de Café was changing the sheets on the bed where she had put Antilia to sleep, and took a Holy Saturday palm branch which she dipped in holy water and carefully shook in every corner and recess.

'Dear God, strike me down if it wasn't Julien Thémistocle who drove that white girl mad!' Eau de Café muttered to herself. 'He's rotten through and through.'

Antilia was already back at her shop counter, weighing pounds of lentils or filling cans with paraffin as if nothing had happened. I would have bet that she didn't remember any of it and thought she'd been asleep all afternoon on one of the benches in the corridor.

4

At high tide, if my memory can be trusted at all, the undertow became strangely more subdued or perhaps we were less wary in the evening, less inclined to watch for the slightest surge on the part of the enemy. Some men took the opportunity to go to the beach to meet the two whores of Grand-Anse. One was a negress with a fantastic case of steatopygia and much taller than other women; the other a mulatto woman with oiled hair. Nobody despised them, as they were doing work there which we recognized to be of public service and moreover they were neither vulgar nor uneducated. People would never have permitted themselves the slightest joke at their expense, except Master Ali Tanin who had adopted the most stringent moral code since his failure with Antilia. Boys agonized in secret with unrequited love for one or the other and feverishly awaited the moment when they could first scrape two and sixpence together, then chat one of them up, and finally talk her round and choose a night. It was a ritual, a well-established initiation that no priest had ever been able to discourage. We only lost our love queens when the government set up an agency to help blacks emigrate to Paris.

Well, some say that the curse started with Myrtha, the buxom negress. People whisper this other version of events, as widespread and well-worn as the others, crossing themselves and only to those they totally trust. This is how it goes: Myrtha, like her sister in debauchery – and like all those who have preceded them since long ago – used to come and say confession once a month and take mass at nine on a Sunday morning without it causing offence to the servants of Our Lord Jesus Christ. At the time in question she was young and had just started up in her trade on the advice of her family and her legion of admirers. By an unhappy coincidence, Grand-Anse had also just been sent a new priest, young as well, who almost never wore his cassock and who played dominoes in the afternoon with the regulars in the dingy rum-shops on Back Street. He had little time for the psalm-singers and pious ladies who wanted to force him to spend all day listening to their nonsense, and would rather go fishing than ring the bells to matins. 'It'll end in tears!' they grumbled in purist circles, but, on the whole, the inhabitants of Grand-Anse were fond of this good-natured blond boy, with his skin tanned by the sea salt. He also amazed them with puns he made up in our language, which he had learnt 'chop-chop', as old Adeline, the maid at the presbytery for three generations, comically put it. All this until Myrtha started confessing every day for an hour at a time and Father Michel emerged pale and strangely exhausted. People began to gossip about this event, as it certainly was an event in this village where nothing ever happened. Soon the young priest stopped going out to meet people and playing football with the boys and stayed in his presbytery. Although this was more in keeping with our idea of ecclesiastical life, we still managed to construct any number of hypotheses concerning his sudden retirement. The most commonly accepted was that Myrtha had confessed a horrible sin to him and that he did not know how to absolve her of it. Ma Léonce, the baker's wife, declared:

'Everyone knows about those women who are cruel enough to rip out the fruit of their wombs and throw it into the undergrowth or into the sea. Near Morne Céron lives a certain Doris, who they say is the devil's betrothed and who is familiar with the Mondongo herbs that you have to let soak for three nights running of full moon before you can drink the tea. After, you feel your guts being torn apart, you feel your heart lurching and pounding. You call for your mother, you bite your fingers, gnaw at your hands, you roll around on the floor, and then, out from between your legs trickles down something red and soft. Then you have to summon the strength and nerve to get rid of it before somebody sees you. Afterwards it's two days in bed, if not three, because the blood in your body has slowed down.'

'But it sounds like you've already tried it, my dear,' said another woman, 'the way you talk about it, eh?'

So it seems that Myrtha, horrified by Father Michel's warning of hell, denounced all the women in the village who had resorted to this practice, and there were plenty of them at the time. The poor priest was terrified to learn that he had fraternized with a people who committed infanticide as casually as they knocked back a glass of rum. After scuttling around his presbytery like a mongoose in its cage, so rumour has it, he decided to leave. On the last day he was seen, lost in a dream, pacing up and down the beach, Bible in hand. Eau de Café, as usual bolder than all the others, tried to make him change his mind, but to no avail. The waves were licking at the hem of his mauve and white cassock and the wind was ruffling his golden locks. He was making grand gestures towards the sea as if in conversation with it, so that since that day he's been known locally as the 'sea priest'. He would never fade from our memories after he waved his robes openly, even ostentatiously, in the direction of the water. The day after he left, the Grand-Anse sea rose up in anger at about midday, without warning, and smashed all the boats on the beach. Three boats which had gone out at low tide never came back and after that nobody dared go near the monster. People shut up the windows and doors that looked out on to the sea and turned their backs on it, cursing it softly. When, months and months later, when time had made time, as we say here, a forgetful fisherman tried to go and persecute the fish in the last vessel not to have rotted away, he wasted a whole day out at sea without capturing even a blue jack or a grouper. Another, then others, followed, and they also returned empty-handed, and we concluded that the larder was from now on empty. Of course, we had to look for a guilty party and we found it in that Father Michel and his stupid fuss that had undoubtedly put an eternal curse on our sea. In the meantime, Myrtha had mortified her body with Rubignac, a product which was used to remove stubborn stains from clothes and which was good against sticky banana spots. The other love queen, the mulattress, had fled to the metropole, where, according to our freshly discharged conscripts, her sapodilla-like flesh was causing a sensation on the streets of Pigalle.

But even within this version of events there is an alternative plot to be divulged, just as plausible as the one that has been told and which should be recorded if you want to really grasp our drama. At nightfall, as has been said, the Grand-Anse beach was the sanctuary for the amorous encounters between our two whores and our local males. Do not imagine some pagan bacchanalia under the knowing smile of the moon, some hymn to the gods of debauchery. On the contrary, each of them dispensed to her partners a boundless love, an unheard of tenderness, in which cries, gasps and obscene grunts were forbidden. The clients would emerge from the experience transformed, with the sense of having tasted a fruit which conjugal love could never offer. A fruit of such purity, so free of the usual torments of vice that people overlooked confessing it to the various priests who succeeded each other in our village and – good God! – they fitted in with the arrangement to such an extent that we guessed that they themselves had had a taste. So it wasn't a sin!

Enter Father Michel who got on so well with black folk and who you wouldn't for a minute have thought would cause trouble. He pretended to make light of our nocturnal habits and openly greeted Myrtha in the street as well as the mulattress, Passionise, the one who had left her husband, Julien Thémistocle, only two months after he'd married her. But evil made use of his youth and his blond good looks to climb on to our shoulders and to do us down once and for all. He stole the heart of the mulattress without any black man in Grand-Anse realizing it and without her telling anyone of her trouble. Unusual trouble indeed, since it was socially accepted that she had to distribute the same amount of love to the humblest black navvy as to the smooth-skinned postmaster, to the novice trembling with ardour as to the old timer decayed by decades of hard labour and cheap rum. Even Dachine, the dwarfish dustman, was entitled to the joys to be found in her arms, warmed by the sea spray. Passionise had therefore broken a basic rule and within the narrow confines of our world, with its exacting demands, when one rule is reversed, it has to be said, the whole is likely to come crashing down, and that in truth is what happened.

From that moment onwards, the mulattress locked herself in her bedroom surrounded by her little wicker baskets, her dolls which shut their eyes when laid down, her solid gold chain necklaces, her tins of Brittany biscuits that she collected for their pretty designs, and her gramophone on which for days on end she played a terribly sad refrain by Billie Holiday. To begin with, people were prepared to put it down to an extended stomach upset. Then, as the weeks passed, they managed to concede that she did need to convalesce. But what nobody liked was the fact that Father Michel came every day to hear her confession as if she was in danger of breathing her last at any minute and that he stayed there with her for more than three hours at a time. Rumours erupted and men worked out their frustrations on Myrtha's rapidly ravaged body as she kept saying 'I don't understand! I don't understand!', wiping away her burning and furtive tears.

One evening, it all became too much. Thirty solid fellows surrounded the mulattress's house just as Father Michel was paying his daily visit and started shouting abuse. One of them made up a song filthier than any ever heard around here:

> *Labé Michèl, sa ou ka fè nou an?*
> *Tiré lolo'w nan bonm siwo-a O!*
> *Labé Michèl, Bondyé pa di sa*
> *Tiré djòldou'w anlè tété sik la O!*
> *Labé Michel, mèt kokè, mèt konfésè.*

(Father Michel, what are you up to in there?
Take your cock out of the honey pot!
Father Michel, God is displeased
Take your greedy mouth off those sweet breasts!
Father Michel, master fucker, master confessor.)

And people rushed from all around, as is the custom, to take up the song and add increasingly obscene verses to it as they went along. On such occasions, imagination knew no bounds, helped along by the flasks of cheap rum which tirelessly passed from hand to hand. Soon the whole village was awake, whereas ever since time began the people of Grand-Anse have gone to bed an hour after their hens. Women, children, old folk, paralytics, the half-blind and other pitiable varieties of humankind came to back up the men, carrying saucepans or plates to beat and venturing dance steps or miming gestures that would normally be considered unworthy of civilized black men.

In the morning, to get his own back, the priest went to say his piece to the sea. And so our sea became cursed and, as you are witnesses, Antilia had nothing to do with it . . .

Perhaps I should make up my mind to dive deeper into my memories and to clear out the debris lying at the bottom. Yesterday I
was finally able to chance a short walk on the black sand of
Grand-Anse and was surprised to discover that I no longer feel
that fascination that the sea's sudden rages used to exert on me.
Now I can read its false charm to perfection; it makes as if to
scowl and suddenly you see the waves soften as if parted by some
supernatural comb. You see vast expanses of bluish water sprinkled with white foam. The sea grapes at La Crabière rear up like a
sublime regiment of mounted coastguards. Ancient passions
seem about to set the promontory ablaze but – damned lies! – the
sea now wakes up, its belly swelling, and crashes down again
with an even louder roar on to itself. Grand-Anse sea. Yellow January sea whose spite is never appeased. Dry season sea, thrash-
ing, unending.

By way of preparing for an imminent reconciliation, I have
taken to keeping the two small windows of my bedroom open all
night, only nailing them closed again (with my shoe heel!) at
dawn so as not to spread panic in the Oceanic Hotel. The owner,
an ex-navy man, would never forgive me for such an indiscretion.
As for the chambermaid, she would probably refuse to change
my sheets. So I spend more and more time there, faced with the
sullen hostility that I seem to attract on the rare occasions that I
venture out into the village streets. For the moment, I am my only
company.

I seem to remember that Eau de Café's shop used to give off a
good smell of salt cod cut up in slices and old rum. On a shelf sat
a pile of crumpled 'errand books', in which she scrawled a list of
her debtors' purchases with a schoolgirl's concentration. She
would invariably grumble about the way Antilia swept up,

would seize the broom from her and push the little heap of dust back from the doorstep.

'Someone could pass by and filch my dust, you know,' she shouted. 'You've no idea how mischievous black people can be. It only takes one of them to be messing about inside and suddenly I haven't a single customer! Then the next thing you know, if God wishes it that way, I could be fighting over a stale crust with the stray dogs tomorrow!'

Antilia shrugged and, taking a large cloth, got on her knees to wipe the floor tiles. The rounded contours of her rump and thighs attracted the interest of the bread delivery man, the early morning workers wetting their whistles at the counter before facing the relentless sun, the Royal Soda lorry driver, who unloaded his crates unusually slowly, and even the village priest. Yes, our village priest, who took pleasure in wishing good day to his neighbours before the six o'clock mass, an insidious way perhaps of reminding them of their duties towards the Holy Church. His cassock twirled between the counter laden with jars of multicoloured sweets and the sagging sacks of lentils and red peas, waiting to be emptied by the half pound.

'Take care, Father,' muttered Antilia as her cloth brushed against the side of his black boots that he sported in military style. Or that, at least, is what she would say on those days that she was in half-human mood, but on others she would screech like a harpy: 'Back off! Go on, back off, man!' splattering all around with the water from her bucket. The priest would retreat on tiptoe, flushed with embarrassment and unfulfilled lust.

'That's no way to speak to a priest,' complained Eau de Café.

'What! Isn't he a man like all the others? Hasn't he got a sausage dangling between his legs?' the servant retorted.

'Blasphemy! Blasphemy!' sighed Eau de Café as she made the sign of the cross.

Behind the shop was a labyrinth of cement bunkers, of wooden planks taken from casks, of bamboo slats and red bricks piled up any old how. This was where Godmother had her store-room, a magic place where suppliers from Town piled up the most eclectic range of goods in a chaos that defied any urge to create order. As soon as the dark green tarpaulin of a lorry came into sight at the bottom of Front Street, Godmother used to take Antilia's place at the counter and send her to take care of the unloading. This was a highly complicated operation, consisting of guiding the driver who was backing into the narrow lane leading to the store-room with loud cries of 'Left! To the right now!' and 'Turn, turn your wheels!' Antilia managed the operation with mind-boggling skill, even though to our knowledge she had never been in a car. All these manoeuvres took at least half an hour, and once the lorry was lined up perfectly alongside the store-room a coal-black and bare-chested fellow who travelled alongside the driver would climb on to the load of goods, undo the tarpaulin and start carrying everything inside on his powerful shoulders. For us, the gang of kids I belonged to, every lorry's arrival was a real spree. Under a sort of unspoken agreement, we were entitled to grab anything that the unloader inadvertently dropped on the ground. We excelled at making him stumble with our crossed fingers and one or two magic spells when he was carrying crates of France-apple juice or chocolate bars. In return, we would help him clean up the back of the lorry once it had been emptied. We fought each other to carry buckets of water to him from the municipal fountain. But the best part of it, in truth, was watching the frolics of Antilia and the driver inside the store-room. We used to squeeze behind the hen house belonging to Thimoléon the carpenter, and there, despite the stench, we could peer through the cracks in the wooden partition eaten away by colonies of woodworm. Antilia would lift her dress up to her chin and lie back against a sack of France-flour. They were white sacks and so the only ones you could tell were clean or not. She opened her legs wide, her arms folded under her head, while the driver, who had merely dropped his trousers down to his knees, fucked her as hard as he could, panting comically. His lips fluttered over Antilia's breasts, hardened with pleasure and yet fantastically supple. From the back of the young woman's throat came a monotonous but exciting murmuring, filling the little store-room with a sort of echo which didn't seem to bother the man unloading the goods. He merely took care not to pile up the crates too precariously right next to them. Sometimes we could hear her muttering in our language:

'*Koké koké zòt! Koké avan zòt mò, lébann malkochon!*' (Fuck for all you're worth! Fuck before you drop dead, you swine!)

Antilia burst out laughing, such hysterical laughing that it made half of us jump with fear and the other half scatter like a flock of blackbirds. We could see the driver's swollen cock furiously stabbing between the servant's thighs while their two bodies dripped with sweat. Their faces were covered with an opal-coloured rain. It must have been as hot as an oven inside, since the store-room, as well as having no ventilation, was covered with corrugated iron. But our lovers couldn't have cared less. It took Godmother, who was made up and dressed for the occasion, calling from the shop to put an end to their coupling. The driver asked us, in return for a few pennies, to pour cold water over him and then put on a clean khaki shirt that he kept in the lorry cab. Finally, apart from Antilia, everybody gathered in the drawing-room around a tray of glasses brimming with anisette or Muscadet and we clinked them together. Godmother was in seventh heaven, on first-name terms and intimate with the different drivers who served the region. They called her 'Ma' affectionately and she loved it. She basked in the compliments they paid to her new rings or the freshness of her complexion. She asked for news of their wives and children, whom she would never meet in her life, and when it was time to set off back to the capital she kissed them on both cheeks, giving them the kind of reproachful look normally reserved for prodigal children. To some she whispered mischievously,

'*Koukoun-la té dous jodi-a an?*' (Was the pussy sweet today?)

'*Sa ou ka di a!*' (You can say that again!) they would all reply without exception, congratulating her on the charms of the girl they sincerely took to be her sister.

But as soon as the lorry's exhaust smoke had drifted away into the evening dew, Eau de Café seemed to go mad. She shouted for

Antilia, who, knowing what was going to happen next, crouched as small as she could by the water tub next to the shop that we used for washing-up and showers. As red as a pepper, she would stamp and shout:

'Antilia, come here at once! You little bitch, you slut! I'm going to teach you to open your legs for every Tom, Dick and Harry that the wind blows this way. They'll know about this in Guadeloupe, I swear to you. I'm going to work you into the ground, you'll see. I'm going to tear you apart.'

Miss Antilia would run and hide on the deserted sand of Grand-Anse beach, knowing that Godmother would never dare to pursue her there. Then the young woman would lie spread-eagled, fully dressed, her eyes fixed, her fists clenched, offering the slit between her legs to the gentle lapping of the ocean. That is how the characters who had ventured there to piss under cover of darkness or to chew over some obscure grudge or to fornicate with one of our whores or commit some devilish act, coined the myth that the girl taken in by Eau de Café was not of this world and spread it around the most distant backwaters of Grand-Anse.

'Dlo koukoun fanm épi dlo lanmè ki migannen, sa ka prézonnen latè Bondyé-a ba'w!' (If the water from a woman's pussy is mixed with sea water, it can poison the whole world!) went the prophecies in the dives along Back Street.

Sometimes Godmother managed to block the escape of the girl we called 'our suffering soul' and thrashed her with a belt as wide as your hand. The young woman didn't flinch, even if each blow left a fiery welt on her skin. On the contrary, it was Eau de Café who collapsed as if exhausted by the futility of her exertions and then she would almost beg her to divulge her origins. I could hear a litany of 'But where do you come from, my dear?' from the bed-room upstairs where they slept together. It was a litany that clearly received no response. Sometimes, at any time of day, Antilia decided that the air was too heavy and, laughing out loud, took off her clothes in front of poor little me at the back of the shop. Her body, with its scent of ripe star apple, unleashed an uncontrollable excitement in me. On those occasions I no longer saw in her the frail child she was supposed to be, but a woman, a real mistress of a woman, in other words someone I could only hope to approach one day in my wildest dreams. She softly ran her hand through the fuzzy fleece of her pussy, looking at me mockingly, then hearing Eau de Café's approaching footsteps, she leapt into the tub and started splashing vigorously. Sometimes she asked me to soap her back, and my adolescent fingers wandered over her voluptuous flesh which the effect of sunlight and water made even more overpowering. My mouth came to rest timidly on her shoulder as I sought her musky scent, but she pushed me away kindly but firmly, not at all bothered by such provocations. If Godmother was having a siesta and a customer shouted for someone to come and serve, she would just yell out:

'*Wonm pa ni! Sik pa ni! Loyon pa rété! Ponmtè pa menm palé!*' (There's no rum! There's no sugar! The onions have all gone! Don't bother to ask for potatoes!)

And the customer would have to wait until she was good and ready, especially when it was one of the errand-book regulars with a bill to settle at the end of the month. Hence the animosity that Antilia seemed to attract, particularly among those women who liked to gossip all day long about other people's comings and goings and who couldn't find a single good thing to say about her. As for our neighbour, Chief Thimoléon, he calmly observed these strange disturbances from the window of his workshop, only putting down his plane or saw when Antilia went too far (as when she dared to tell him tartly that his chamber-pot stank and that it was high time to empty it into the sea).

'*Man pa kanmarad ti kapistrèl!*' (I'm no friend of that slut!) he protested to anyone who would listen, although nobody took his wrath seriously; so, peeved, he seized his chamber-pot and the short bamboo broom that he used to clean it and set off unsteadily towards that Grand-Anse sea which he cursed from the bottom of his heart like everyone hereabouts.

He had tried to hire me to do the job, something I'd always avoided, not because I spurned that sort of task (we'd do anything, us little black boys, for a few pennies) but because local opinion had convinced Godmother that his shit smelt as bad as a dead man's.

'Monsieur has wasted all his money drinking rum and gambling rather than raising a family like a true Christian,' was the common verdict. 'God has selected this punishment for him. But He hasn't been too hard on him, since Thimoléon is, after all, a good craftsman . . .'

So it was that nobody ever went into the carpenter's house. People stopped outside at the workshop window to ask him to do jobs. When his loneliness became too much to bear, he came to chat to Eau de Café about the deeds and misdeeds of his youth or the '14–'18 war, all the time glancing venomously towards Antilia. If by chance he managed to get hold of me, he would terrify me by whispering in my ear:

'Watch out for that female with no mother and no name! She can fill your body with such desire that it'll tear your soul into a thousand little pieces of pain. She can ruin your life. Get away from her while you still can!'

12 January 1937

Dearest,

    They have surrounded us. They have left a terrible laceration in our inner depths and over there I can hear the dull thud of the cutlass cutting the dry coconut in two. A familiar action, a famished action. The black kids chew on its white flesh in the backyards of the shacks, not to stave off hunger, not through boredom, not for any such reason. They chew on green mangoes, jujuba fruits, stale bread crusts, caramels stolen from the shop, all the time glancing furtively at the cars as they race frantically past.

    Under the breadfruit trees, crates or disused casks have been put out as chairs and women painstakingly comb their brats' fuzzy hair. The route des Religieuses starts at the Pont Démosthène, which is overrun at dusk by a legion of chattering streetwalkers, then winds over the sinister mass of the Morne Pichevin and loses its way higher up outside the town.

    A man is prophesying the end of the world next year and is urging us to buy an improbable pile of junk hastily piled into a tarpaulin-covered truck.

    We are all wearing ourselves out against the ridiculous. From the window of my room from where I can make out the red roofs of the town and the ballet of the bats which roost there during the day, I get the idea, absurd when all is said and done, to sew my life back together again.

Antilia

SECOND CIRCLE

For three decades, the young have been turning their backs on the village. Between this sea with its useless ('barren' they prefer to say) womb and the refineries and distilleries whose chimneys no longer smoke, hope is as fruitless as a male pawpaw tree. So people from the old times brood over their dreams in the streets held hostage by the sun. From now on, it is hardly worth distinguishing between the dry and rainy seasons, nor following the rhythm of the hurricanes, let alone interpreting the flight of the doves and slender egrets.

And yet the explanation must be somewhere, right in the middle of the Word made flesh.

6

One day, Antilia, the black girl seer whose buttoned-up mouth everyone feared most, started to dance a calenda of such obscenity as has never before been seen on the village square. I had just celebrated my eleventh birthday, I think. She seemed to wrap the grinding movements of her body around an invisible being and rhythmically impale herself on it in a dazzling whirl of foam. People gathered in silence, at a respectful distance from the clairvoyant, waiting for the falling sickness to strike her down. What calamity worse than this Second World War that was already gnawing away at the surface of our lives could she be about to announce? The old men stood there disbelieving and mocking, their clay pipes in their mouths, dismissing it as no more than an attack of brain fever, as they called it, since this can happen, alas, when a woman's *coucoune* itches too much. Just in case you haven't grasped it: because no man from around here had thought to plough her furrow for a good length of time. In any case, their laughter stuck in their throats when Antilia began to spout a frenzy of exclamations which washed over the corrugated iron roofs before reaching the nearby hillsides, stirring the speckled leaves of the prickly pear and gum trees. To begin with, nobody could grasp the meaning of her words, which stabbed like daggers at the most hardened of ears:

'*Lamadòn rivé! Lamadòn kay pwofondé an tjou bonda marenn zòt, bann isèlèp!*' (Words untranslatable into a civilized language to do with the arrival of a Madonna who comes to castrate the men and sew up the women's vaginas, in other words a load of old rubbish which it would be pointless to take seriously.)

Hearing the name of the Madonna, Father Le Gloarnec, a recent arrival among us, abandoned a meeting of the Cadettes de la France at the presbytery, where he was struggling to promote the idea of chastity to some ladies who had already had three or four abortions or a mile-long queue of kids, to arrive at the Bord de Mer, armed, on the off chance, with a censer and holy-water sprinkler. One never knew with these pagans! Although he'd been living in the colonies since the end of the 1920s, he was wary of his parishioners' double-dealing and had not the slightest confidence in their supposed conversion to the precepts of the Holy Gospel, apart from the handful of regulars to whom he gave communion without confession every morning at six twenty-five. Thus for him every Sunday mass was another test of strength, a new fight in the noble and unforgiving task of evangelizing among the pagan blacks and coolies, let alone the freemason mulattos like the lawyer Féquesnoy, who secretly undermined everything he tried to do.

Antilia was completely naked by now as the priest set eyes on her after struggling through the crowd of curious onlookers. Her beauty struck him straight in the heart. He was truly frozen like a statue. He had needed to stumble across a black girl's firm breasts, ample hips and glistening pudenda in order to appreciate that this race, too, was made in God's image. Worse, this beauty had turned into a brutal desire in the middle of his scrawny guts which spread to his groin with an unstoppable downward surge, a motion which resulted in a specimen of an erection, the like of which had not been seen here since the abolition of slavery. This phenomenon, according to local experts, only took place during the torture known as the 'four stakes', when the quartering reached the stage when the victim was at the point of death. So the penis of Paul-Germain le Gloarnec, native of Brittany, began to swell-swell-swell so much and so strongly that it produced a monstrous bulge at the front of his cassock. Luckily for him, all eyes were fixed on Antilia's antics as people scratched their heads trying to understand what she meant by Madonna, as nobody had ever heard the colour of this word before.

'The Virgin of the Great Return will appear in every *commune* of this island of damnation,' the clairvoyant was saying, 'and all of you must fall to your knees as she passes to beg absolution for your black mischief. You should know that God has already sent to you Monsieur Julien Thémistocle as a punishment, just as he made the volcano explode at the beginning of the century or, each September, he decrees a procession of hurricanes. The mother of Jesus will arrive in Fort-de-France in a blazing of lights and she has already begun to . . .'

The sermon was cut short by the sudden collapse of Father Paul-Germain. His swollen cock, over-hardened by desire, cut off his circulation and put an end to the thumping of his heart. He fell backwards, his penis ripping his cassock to the great alarm of the rabble who stampeded away to the streets at the bottom of the village. Alone and majestically, Antilia approached the body and with many an 'Ave Maria' tried by force to bend back the strange field-marshal's baton, but without success. The church bell was already tolling, the siren at the Fond Brûlé mill was already sputtering into life, the people of Grand-Anse, already dressed in black and white, were already gathering in large numbers at the Bord de Mer, and yet the priest still refused to 'relinquish his lubricious aspirations', as the schoolmaster Émilien Bérard wrote later in an article commissioned by a Fort-de-France newspaper. There was never a jollier wake in any black man's memory! The corpse was carried into the empty lobby of the United Family Friendly Society, and people made up tales and songs about the life of the deceased, exposing in the process the many strains which he had put on his vow of chastity. There was much laughter concerning the way he touched the young girls preparing for their first communion to see if their knickers were clean, because 'Mighty God does not receive dirty sluts into His kingdom', or the quick and furtive assaults that he inflicted on certain fifty-year old female parishioners in the waiting-room of the presbytery. Essentially, we were happy to have had a priest who understood so well our natural Creole lasciviousness and Antilia's prediction was forgotten. She took no part in the revelries. She once again retreated into a frightening silence, contenting herself with occasional shakes of the head and reproachful glances at those keeping vigil. She was only seen to smile at the moment when the priest, whose body, God knows why, had begun to rot and thus smell more quickly than a black man's, was put into his coffin.

The town council had to meet at full strength behind closed doors, chaired by *maître* Féquesnoy, as the mayor, in true diplomatic fashion, was suddenly indisposed.

'Ah! That little Mussolini!' grumbled the lawyer, 'never there when important decisions have to be taken!'

Gathered with him were the young Doctor Valmont, Ali Tanin, a newly co-opted member since he had rightly pointed out that the Ottoman Empire had taken the side of the French Revolution, the headmaster who specialized in making his pupils pregnant and several other nonentities, whose identity it would be pointless to reveal (as pointless as putting a zero before a number).

'I propose that his . . . his genital apparatus be . . . be sawn off,' started *maître* Féquesnoy cautiously.

'Seconded!' shouted together nine councillors, who had not understood a damned word of this gibberish.

'It could be complicated . . .' said Valmont, who feared that the operation would fall to him.

'Seconded!' agreed two illiterate councillors, keen to please the doctor.

The headmaster, who was an expert in matters anatomical, expressed surprise that Father Paul-Germain's penis had not subsided several minutes after death. With which Doctor Valmont replied in a Latin phrase which succeeded in shutting him up.

'It clearly means', he continued, 'that in certain extremely rare circumstances a constriction of the blood vessels at the base of the penis can take place if the stimulation has been too intense, a sort of priapism that the stopping of vital functions sometimes does not manage to disperse.'

'Let's throw that bitch Antilia in jail!' shouted one of the councillors. 'What business did she have to get undressed like that?'

'Where is Sergeant Cardont?' asked the deputy mayor suddenly. 'Someone go and find him quickly . . . in the name of the Republic, One and Indivisible . . .'

The policeman's favourite expression unleashed general hilarity among the town council, reminding them of his southern French gift for oratory which had first found expression on the occasion of his so-called arrest of Julien Thémistocle. Since then Cardont had lived in holy terror of the villagers. He often found himself thinking that he would have been happier in a German concentration camp than in this rotten island where people laughed at everything, not least death. He shut himself up in the police station under the specious pretext that sugar-cane alcohol had messed up his jeep's carburettor and that his bad back ruled out long trips on horseback. But under the current circumstances there was no way out: the town hall was only three hundred metres away.

'I'll give you the bloody Republic One and Indivisible!' he grumbled as he adjusted his braces.

Then he hastily rewrote his will just in case. Arming himself with his two 6.35 revolvers, he walked stoically towards the town hall where a tragic end was probably awaiting him. He entered at the very moment that the deputy mayor was again saying the word 'saw' and thought that they were discussing the method of torture which was to be inflicted on him. He at once pulled out his guns and, aiming at the town council, ordered them to stand with their backs to the wall under a gigantic portrait of Marshal Pétain carrying the motto:

LET US SAVE FRANCE
WORK–FAMILY–FATHERLAND

The councillors shat in their pants. *Maître* Féquesnoy wanted to argue but thought about the future and thought it better to say nothing.

'You won't saw me, you gang of savages!' yelled Sergeant Cardont. 'You band of lunatics! I'm going to deal with you one at a time, you'll see. The shit is going to fly, my friends!'

He locked up the town council in a broom cupboard and led the number one suspect, that is to say the bastard-Syrian Ali Tanin, into the mayor's office, where he intended to interrogate him according to the system used by the sailors from the *Émile-Bertin* and *Barfleur*, a foolproof method originating directly, so they said, from the brilliant brain of Marshal Pétain: genital torture. Indeed, while all the police and security forces around the world were wearing themselves out by beating their suspects around the head, on the back or on the legs, only, in the final analysis, to obtain highly indifferent results, a memo from the information service of the navy read as follows:

Our esteemed Marshal Pétain, saviour of the Fatherland and regenerator of our Race, has decided that the interrogation of all individuals apprehended on suspicion of high treason is to take place in accordance with a method established by himself and a commission of experts comprising Catholic psychologists, with effect from 1st March 1943. According to research carried out in Vichy by the personal physicians of the Head of State, it appears that the most sensitive part of the male anatomy is to be found, without possible doubt, in the region of the balls. It is therefore simple to make the most arrogant of so-called resistance fighters, called 'dissidents' in the French Antilles, confess by applying several electric shocks to this region. In the areas of France where electricity is unavailable, or indeed is rationed, a variation can be employed just as efficaciously. It consists of tickling the suspect's balls with the help of a gander's feather until the skin puckers as if with goose pimples. The suspect will normally talk within four and a half minutes, six or seven in the case of a pervert. This method, however, requires a good deal of experience and a steady hand since any ejaculation is to be avoided at all costs.

This notice is to be displayed in all gendarmeries and police stations in those of our American possessions still under the control of our beloved Marshal, the saviour of the Fatherland.
Signed: Ship's Lieutenant Bayle
pp. Admiral Robert

At this point a series of events took place, several versions of which have been conserved by bush radio, with one emerging over time as more credible than all others. Just as Ali Tanin was bracing himself to submit to Sergeant Cardont's cruelties, there was a hammering of fists on the iron gate of the town hall. Voices were shouting: 'To arms! To arms, citizens!' Over-excited men, armed with metal bars, cutlasses, broadswords and antique hunting guns, had taken over Front Street. One of them yelled:

'The Germans are landing!'

In the blinking of an eye, the sergeant pulled out his weapon and climbed on all fours to the top floor of the building where he barricaded himself in, abandoning the half-Syrian to his fate. The poor fellow took the opportunity to flee and found refuge in Eau de Café's shop. Godmother was sharpening a kitchen knife on a grindstone when she saw him arriving all crestfallen and seemingly overwhelmed by fearfulness. She pushed him outside roughly and shouted:

'What? France is under attack and you, you're chicken. Join the fighting or I shall denounce you in public!'

The streets had become the very image of swarming ants' nests. Young men were singing the *Marseillaise* while their mothers, sisters or mistresses applauded from balconies. Ali Tanin had no choice but to take a pitchfork handed to him by a greybeard who hadn't got up from his bed since the celebration of the Tricentenary of our joining with France, in 1935. He made his way to the seaside where the idlers, boozers, dice-players, jobbers and men with jiggers in their feet were at the front of a crowd staring intently and aggressively at the sea's fury. The chap who had given the alarm was explaining for the tenth time:

'I had thrown out my lobster pot not far from La Crabière, you fellows know, when I saw the belly of the sea swell up and make a sort of kind of buzzing noise. It was just like a Latécoère sea-plane, and then a black thing, twice as big as a she-whale, came out from under the water: a submarine! I only had time to shout 'Argh! Argh!' and to leap on to my oars to try and get out of there before it was completely out of the water. Two blokes, paler than christophenes that have ripened under their leaves, came out through a sort of manhole cover and aimed at me. Yes, aimed at me with machine-guns! They were shouting at me in fierce-sounding language. I almost shat in my pants. They kept saying that brigand Hitler's name while laughing, and that's how I worked out they were enemy soldiers. I started shivering like hell, fellows, despite the sun that was beating down on us. So then the Germans fired into the air, still shouting in their ugly language, and then they got back into their submarine and went back under water. They're out there, sitting behind La Roche, waiting for the moment to come ashore . . . probably tonight, when we're not ready for them . . .'

'The Germans always attack in numbers,' someone added. 'That's how they had us in '14 and again in '40. They're more cunning than monkeys since they're steering clear of Fort-de-France and our fleet. The *Jeanne d'Arc* and the *Émile-Bertin* scare the shit out of them, so they come here, to Grand-Anse, where we've got nothing to defend ourselves with . . .'

The valiant defenders of the red, white and blue flag waited for the enemy all night long. In vain. Wooden torches were lit all along the coast and that alone put them off invading the place. War-weary, the men started playing *sèrbi* or blank dominoes, that's to say with no stakes, which is the sure sign of real boredom in these parts. Ali Tanin, whose lucky day it seemed to be, won every game under the mocking gaze of Julien Thémistocle, who was left cold by all these excitements.

On the stroke of midnight, the water's depths started heaving in every direction. The militia was immediately on a war footing, only to see Miss Antilia emerge from the waves, radiant and sardonic at the same time, wearing a dress of phosphorescent seaweed and thundering:

'We are cursed! This sea is cursed! Get away from here if you do not wish to weep all the tears you have. The Madonna is coming!'

Needless to say, one and all beat a retreat. In the meantime, the priest's body, which had been left on display for several days while a solution was found for its erect member, had adopted the normal posture of any honest corpse. And yet a fine specimen of a smile was adorning his lips. Yes, a smile . . .

Yet my childhood memory carried no trace of this fabulous arrival by Antilia at Grand-Anse for the simple reason that it was me, me and me alone, who had been the first to discover the mad girl in her lair of black sand in the middle of the beach. And it was me again who had pulled her body off the rocks when she had drowned herself . . .

7

His scream has buried itself for all eternity in the memory of our bedside tables. It split open our temples like common or garden guava fruits. It caught unawares the road-mender as he was breaking his river rocks, the fishwife slicing up tuna with her big knife at the entrance to the Main Market, the boasting black kids testing the seabirds' agility with their ancient rifles, the woman of easy virtue who waits until ten in the morning before getting out of bed and washing in the lukewarm water of the sink. And more than that, it mummified the sea along with its cohort of mocking echoes. A terrifying scream!

The people of Grand-Anse did their best to gather silence around them. They trod gently on the crunching asphalt, they lowered their voices or spoke to each other with exceedingly slow gestures. After the intensity of the scream everyone felt the overwhelming need for a vast calm, as if to give things the time to get back into place. As if to prevent a permanent break somewhere along their unchanging road. Give me some peace, if you please! That is our litany.

Eau de Café, who had barely been living in the village for two months, acted like a real yokel in this situation and that's why we were treated with condescension for a long time afterwards. The truth is that she leant over her balcony and shouted without thinking:

'*Sa ki rivé*?' (What's happened?)

She went down Back Street in a state of excitement, barefooted, eagerly questioning every passer-by, every face at a window before shutters slammed shut. She tried to stop the chase-race between Grand-Anse's two buses, the 'Golem' and the 'Executioner of the North', but their drivers, already looking forward to the bloodcurdling overtaking with which they would take turns on the interminable, badly surfaced road to Fort-de-France, paid no attention to her. In a state of disarray, she went to look for the priest at the presbytery where there was not even a cat, at the church where a holier-than-thou woman scolded her for what she was wearing and, finally, she understood: he could only be with the person who had screamed that terrible scream. He had obviously helped him to cross over into death for that scream smelled to high heaven of death, it stank of death. Its interminable vibrations had at once surrounded the village from La Cité to the Bord de Terrain neighbourhood, shaking it roughly and filling the hearts of black men with such closely mixed pain and fear that it left them feeling helpless.

A dishevelled Eau de Café set off back home, finding nothing ahead of her but the day's emptiness. Without realizing it, she had disconcerted people with her country negress tactlessness. They were probably waiting for divine retribution to strike her down at any moment in mid step. Eau de Café squatted down on her front doorstep, as she used to at Macédoine, absent-mindedly scratching at her heat rash, and several weeks later rumours were doing the rounds that she had pissed herself all for the sake of an innocent man's corpse. She called me and asked me to sit with her. I was afraid, very afraid, but I couldn't have said why. Perhaps because her heart was beating like a drum against my head and that it made me aware of a great misfortune still to come. Aren't the things that you don't know always bigger than yourself?

Three hours later, everybody had resumed their normal activities and was joking, greeting neighbours, and carrying on as if nothing had ever happened. Eau de Café and I were well and truly flabbergasted. We had never had dealings with a race of men who could swap expression and mood so quickly. She sent me to buy some bread at the shop belonging to Ma Léonce, who, lording it among sacks of France-flour, was saying to a customer:

'Well, I'm no wiser than anyone else, but I always said that he'd end up going mad . . . a little chap I kissed on both cheeks the day he was born, oh yes. And every day on his way to school, I used to give him a *pain au chocolat* or a coconut cake. He was sweet, quiet. I only heard him chattering once, and as for insulting some-one's mother, I don't believe it . . .'

The customer was nodding silently. It was obvious that his mind was on other things. Here we forget quickly. Forgetting begins almost at the same time as the event itself: we cry, we sob to begin to forget because we hate grief, the big troublemaker, the source of endless shittiness. We forget so as to spare ourselves the effort of understanding and it must be said that the incessant din of the sea at Grand-Anse is a great help. We become strange bewildered animals, brutally weaned babies, poor fools feigning complete indifference. The cadence of each wave coming in from the high seas, smashing itself down on to the black sand, fills our hearts so fully that white foreigners who wander here by chance construct all sorts of complicated and daft theories about what they call our 'innate sense of rhythm'. They confuse the swaying arse of a steatopygous negress with the spasms of a woman danc-ing *haute-taille*, surrendering body and soul to the delirium of the drums. They mix everything up, the fools. They don't realize that in our sleep the gentle motion of the sated sea fills our dreams with intangible sweetness, ties us to its ceaseless pendulum and that is how it holds us in its sway. It has taken away both our rea-son and our madness. It governs our desires and our refusals. It forces its sterile splendour upon us and throws down its chal-lenge to us.

Sometimes it provokes us so much and to such a point that there is no way out but to hang oneself without warning one day of intense heat and it takes pleasure in the scream that comes from our throats. Then, the bitch, it pretends to be astonished, huh! That is how Émilien Bérard, schoolmaster, luminary of Grand-Anse and famed philosopher, took his life in the En Chéneaux neighbourhood, further up from the school where every single day he wore himself out teaching the whites' lan-guage to little black kids who had just walked four or five kilo-metres to school wolfing down ripe bananas or windfall mangoes along the way. Ah, that scream! The purity of the scream, the implacable shrillness, which curdled the very light!

Next to him the angry young man had hung up a bundle containing books, two shirts, a pair of trousers, a ruler, a set-square and his spectacle case. The message was clear: my soul and I are returning to the Guinea, from where our forefathers were snatched centuries ago. But in his pocket was found a neatly folded piece of paper on which he had written:

'Let us give thanks to the gods who hold nobody back in this life.' (Seneca)

Eau de Café, who however had known him less well than almost anyone else here, was overcome by a great griefulness and cursed the villagers who hadn't foreseen or done anything to stop his course of action. Yet nobody other than her had made a fuss about it; they knew what it all meant and that nothing could be done about it. The way things happen has been written in stone since the world began in our village. People concluded that Émilien Bérard used to read 'bad books'. But he wasn't just fascinated by the mystery of the sea, by its splendid solitude under the sun and he used to like bathing in it, allowing himself to be taken by the hypnotic to-and-fro of its foam. Alarmed, we would watch him roll among the waves, go out to meet them and be carried back to the shore like a drifting tree trunk. We could hear him reciting poems he had written in Creole and of which we couldn't understand a word.

'He's a tormented soul, that poor little chap,' Eau de Café had inevitably pronounced as she watched him from her window at dusk.

One day, Antilia had brought him to the house, tugging him by the sleeve of his tattered jacket. He was laughing, covered in sand, his bifocal spectacles misted up with spray, which partly concealed the mad glint in his eyes.

He sat down unsteadily on the sofa and kept saying like an automaton:

'Madame . . . Ah, madame! . . . We are going to find the way. We've been looking for an eternity, our feet are worn out with going round in circles but soon we will know which way to go. This village will stop turning round and round like a roundabout, I promise you . . . This country too . . .'

'Can I offer you a sour-sop juice, schoolmaster?' asked Godmother with all the respectation in the world.

'Water . . . some tap water, that will be fine, thank you.'

Antilia had sat at his feet, staring intently at him. You could have sworn that he didn't even see her. He was talking to himself, feverish, passionate, then suddenly trance-like, dejected. And to think that the village gossips swore he was Antilia's lover.

'I'm reading the memoirs of a famous visitor from the last century at the moment,' he remarked to Eau de Café. 'A strange half-Greek half-Englishman by the name of Lafcadio Hearn. He took American nationality. This man had fallen in love with the Creole way of life in Saint-Pierre. He also came this way and in his book *Martinican Sketches* you can find some of the most beautiful pages ever devoted to Grand-Anse. Those twenty pages bowled me over and that's why I resent Hearn a little because I would have liked to have written them.'

Godmother asked him to read her some passages and the two of them wasted entire afternoons in this way. No wonder then that his death shook her very existence. Meanwhile, another rumour, even more convoluted, surrounds the tragic end of Émilien Bérard and once again implicates Eau de Café, the great scapegoat for the blacks of Grand-Anse. Godmother, it is true, had inherited a locust-wood chest from her mother, Franciane, who herself had received it from the *béké* with whom she had shared the raptures of passion. This is the why and whereforth: when de Cassagnac's wife had been locked up in Fort-de-France (as we shall see later – dear reader, please forgive the wanderings of this tale which seem to run around like a mad ant!) and his grief stopped tearing at the hearts of all those who came close to him, especially his servants, Franciane was able to move into the master's house. Without showing the slightest arrogance. Nor ostentation. She strangely refused to take over her rival's crinoline dresses and jewels, utterly frustrating the sharp-tongued gossip which doubled in bitterness in the kitchens and negro huts. Her clothes remained made of simple Madras and she did almost nothing to her thick fuzzy hair other than wet it with water from the bath-tub, in which she splashed around at all hours of the day. De Cassagnac was moved by such simplicity which disproved the Creole proverb 'No money – legs closed', probably coined in relation to the behaviour of the *demi-mondaines* of latter-day Saint-Pierre. One day, when dusting the attic, she stumbled across a chest that was so heavy that she could not move it an inch. A huge rusty padlock prevented any attempt at opening it. A curious Franciane rushed out to meet de Cassagnac who was just returning on horseback from the village of Grand-Anse, where he had made some purchases including a golden ring topped with a silver ladybird. The young woman barely glanced at this present. She fired questions at her lover concerning the mysterious chest. He scowled and remained silent all the way to the house.

'Why are you angry?' she finally asked.

'I beseech you to forget that trunk.'

'I want to open it.'

'No! No, no, no and no!'

De Cassagnac helped himself to several shots of rum straight from the bottle and collapsed into a rocking-chair on the veranda, his face marked by a deep bewilderment. From then on he tried to escape from the house. Many a time he would mount his horse and disappear beyond the edge of the plantation into the thick woods of Morne l'Étoile, only returning as midnight approached. And then he never went near Franciane's bed! Not at all. He would sit among his blacks, on the beaten earth floor of the main yard, listening intently to the adventures of Brother Elephant and Brer Rabbit. People whispered, wrongly, that he was immersed in grief, more bitter than the bitterest orange, for his former wife. They became even more attentive towards him. They brought him the loveliest fruits in season but he didn't even touch the wild cherries that normally he liked so much. His housekeeper, a big fat boss of a negress, had to take the business in hand before the estate fell apart. She pulled Franciane along by the hair and lectured her:

'That chest contains old books. Bad books, in fact, which it is forbidden to read, so stop pestering our master with your stupidities. In any case, can you even make sense of the written word? What use are they to you?'

Relieved, the island white gradually regained his normal equanimity and nobody mentioned the affair for any number of dry and rainy seasons. Only Franciane, unbeknownst to all, used to go up to the attic when there was no one in the house and stroke the chest's smooth wood while sometimes whispering endearments or humming Creole lullabies. Her secret passion lasted until the terrible uprising of 1927 when de Fabrique, the good white (fate is so good at monkey business!) died with his head cut off by sixteen black and coolie cane-cutters. She had to leave the house and settle in Macédoine, where she unearthed an obliging but penniless mulatto who had always carried a flame for her and was willing to put a roof over her head. When she left, she managed to take the chest with her on a cart and she put it in a glory-hole in her new home, where this time she forgot about it once and for all. After her equally violent death (thanks to the maroon Julien Thémistocle), the chest and its bad books were almost chopped up by her man for firewood. He changed his mind for no reason and took it to Doris, the devil's fiancée, in whose charge the orphaned Eau de Café had just been placed. Some fifteen years later, the latter brought the chest with her when she migrated to the village of Grand-Anse. So it was that this mysterious legacy from the early days of colonization drifted from one destiny to another, each more tragic than the previous one, to end up in the hands of Émilien Bérard, who, more stubborn than anyone, wanted to capture its secret at any price and paid for it, alas, with his neck . . .

There's another story about Émilien Bérard. Here it is. The fellow had been torn asunder by the mother of all heartbreaks one day of his life – a Tuesday in the dry season – and he had stood there motionless in the sun, not knowing whether to follow the enchanting creature who had just stolen his heart or whether just to go back to his house and his waiting wife and kids. The wild-eyed creature kept saying to him:

61

'Man, you have two feet, but you can only take one path, not two. Walk at my side or else it will be as if I never existed.'

He could only stammer:

'Two feet, one path . . . two feet, one path.'

But what other fate could await a man who used to say to anyone who would listen,

'I know that ever since the long ago time of childhood I have carried inside me a disaster about to happen. The sham fullness of the sky, its indifferent blueness, the silence that reigns over the mango trees, the bread fruit trees, the banana trees and the guava trees, all that insolence of green and brown, that isn't beauty, that's death, death that's all smiles!'?

7 The Incubus of Grand-Anse

Ali Tanin's father was baptized Syrian once folk had exhausted themselves trying to pronounce his name. Nobody could remember the date that he had arrived in Grand-Anse but as he was accused of having made his fortune by robbing the corpses of the citizens of Saint-Pierre, destroyed two years into the century by Mont Pelée, evidence suggested that he had been around longer than many of us. Syrian hadn't always owned the Palace of the Orient and Eau de Café could recall having seen him crossing hills and dales pushing a hand-cart loaded with clothes and iron-mongery. He cut a sorry figure, all the more so as he had trouble understanding our Creole. So much so that a black woman, who had a headful of little zeros in place of hair, took him into her house and made him her man and then her husband, although Syrian was a Muslim. Through hard slog and conning everybody, our man ended up buying a hovel on Front Street where he kept several bales of linen. From that day, each and everyone learned to speak Arabic since you only had to clear the bottom of your throat and spit out some guttural noises at full speed in order to do it. Not one of us, passing his shop-front, could resist calling amicably to him:

'Hey, Syria! How are you today? *Acham falhad ichtijad boukhed-nuf Allah mahabnahar!*'

First of all his bulging stomach would emerge, covered in sweat whatever the time of day, precariously held in place by a filthy thermal vest and a pair of trousers with enormous pockets. Then would come his hands, hairy, pale, with the soft, slim fingers of a young girl and finally his red face, featuring a Levantine nose 'longer than three black men's noses put end to end', according to Ma Léonce, the baker's wife. Far from being angry about this mock Arabic, Syrian would wax lyrical in salutations and good wishes concerning your health, your finances or your destiny. When his wife gave birth to Ali, he organized the party to end all parties and invited everybody, irrespective of complexion, and from that day on Grand-Anse definitively adopted this foreigner who rolled his 'r's too much. His shop prospered so much and to such an extent that two or three times he was able to go back and taste the delights of his native land, from where he brought us back fabulous materials and no less fabulous tales. But his fortune only became solidified into heaps of hard cash when a scoundrel of an incubus began lifting up the nightdresses of Grand-Anse's young girls. To begin with, we even thought it was an incubus epidemic, since several women were attacked during the same night, but a rapid enquiry, instigated both by the archdiocese of Fort-de-France and our local constabulary, was able to prove that the cunt-hunter was one and the same person. The incubus operated between two and four in the morning, selecting by choice girls in the flower of their virginity on whose bodies he left scratches, bites, saliva and traces of blood. A thanksgiving mass was not enough to put an end to it and as the French penal code stipulated no particular sanction for such acts, the villagers had to resort to black-magic rituals to protect themselves. The fetish merchants, the manufacturers of protective charms and potions, the melchiors who quoted from the Holy Bible which they read backwards, the sorcerers' mentors were all hard at work for many a week. All to no avail! Julien Thémistocle (everybody had unanimously pronounced him guilty) continued with complete impunity to metamorphose into air and pass through locks, walls and partitions to insinuate his re-materialized body between the legs of Grand-Anse's young misses. Ma Léonce, who was an expert in old men's monkey business, realized ahead of all others that the incubus was pursuing some obscure vengeance rather than seeking to satisfy his well-known lust. (Hadn't he raped Franciane, the stuck-up negress, even when she had a bun in the oven called Eau de Café?) The baker's wife had found it odd, she said, that Thémistocle called on no fewer than twenty girls on each of his nocturnal excursions, which left him scarcely a few minutes of pleasure for each victim. We all know that an incubus flies around quickly, but even so!

She confided her suspicions to the two village toughs who, even more strangely, seemed to have been less than their usual selves since the hymen-snatcher first appeared. The first, a carpenter by trade, held the title Chief Thimoléon and his territory comprised the neighbourhood around the hospital, the abattoir district (when it wasn't slaughtering day), En Chéneaux, Long-Bois and all of the village to the left of the church when looking towards sunrise. The rest of the *commune*, Fond Massacre, Morne Carabin, Redoute and, of course, Back Street, belonged to the second, alias Émilien Bérard's elder brother who had forbidden everybody from saying his Christian name (which was his 'strength') so that we had all completely and utterly forgotten it. We simply said Chief Bérard. At the time of the drama in question, that is, just after the Second World War, the two chiefs and their followers scrupulously observed their respective fiefdoms. Otherwise, Back Street, a neutral territory, served as the arena for duels and punch-ups, each more epic than the last. Any follower of Thimoléon who had a woman living on Chief Bérard's territory had to ask his pretty-please permission each time that he wanted to go and see her and these *laissez-passer* were only granted if relative peace had reigned in Grand-Anse for a good stretch of time. Kids, who weren't involved in these adult conflicts, were given permanent right of free passage and were able to earn a few pennies doing errands for somebody or other during periods of outright war. Mostly and increasingly so as the century advanced and French customs encroached on ours, quarrels were resolved around *sèrbi* tables, that formidable game of dice with such mysterious rules and strict ritual that many well-educated minds had given up trying to understand and were happy merely to lose themselves in admiration in the presence of those players who could shout out the magic number: eleven.

Ma Léonce, who exercised a not insignificant authority over the two chiefs, called them together to find out which of them was guilty of bad manners (or worse, had committed a serious act of disrespectation on the territory of Mister Julien Thémistocle, him-self the chief of the country areas: Fond Gens-Libres, Macédoine, Morne Capot and Assier. A crestfallen Chief Bérard admitted that he had cuffed an impudent mill worker who was claiming to own better fighting cocks than his.

'That chap wanted to put one over me so I had to show him what was what. If I hadn't given him a good slap in the face, you would certainly have never let me live it down, eh?'

Syrian, who was happy to observe our uncouth bumpkin argu-mentations without adding his tuppenceworth, rose a step fur-ther in our esteem by suggesting an unbeatable solution. Our eyes stood out as he said:

'All the ladies of Grand-Anse will have to wear black knickers when they sleep. Yallah!'

'Black knickers? Stop talking such balls!' cried the baker's wife.

'Balderdash!' said Dachine, the village dustman, shrugging his shoulders.

'Ballsishness!' somebody added.

'Ball-ocks!' concluded Chief Thimoléon as if to end the discus-sion.

The poor Syrian didn't know where to put himself in the face of this torrent of rebuffs, all the more so because, like so many for-eigners, he was incapable of seizing all the subtleties of our lan-guage, even though after living here for years and years, he spoke Creole easily enough and French after a fashion. It's all because when slavery ended (that was then less than a century ago, oh yes!), the whites hadn't wanted to give our children any schooling and only deigned to teach us a very limited number of words in their language. They thought in this way they would be able to keep us in poverty but that was to underestimate the Creole black man, an old monkey who needs no lessons in how to climb a tree. Not knowing 'nonsense', 'rubbish', 'drivel', 'piffle' and fellow synonyms, he decided to play with the range of suffixes which would render the nuances between these different words, which resulted, to the great chagrin of the Creole whites, in 'balls', 'balderdash', 'ballsishness' and 'ball-ocks'. Or, for another example, 'fib', 'fibbery', 'fibbishness', 'fibbicity'. And so on. And tough shit for anyone who wants to keep the treasures of the dictionary to himself. Ha, ha, ha! . . .

Ma Léonce saved the situation.

'Well, I already wear black knickers, but they were my mother's. Do you think you can unearth a hundred or even a thousand pairs like them, Syria? Nowadays, they only want red, pink or white . . .'

'On the head of my son, Ali, I swear that tomorrow morning, as the pippiree bird sings, I shall flood all the village of Grand-Anse and all the countryside with a profusion of black knickers, my friends!'

'Oh, really? And what about sizes?'

'Do not upset your minds, for I will have them for nubiles as well as menopausals, for the young and the mature, for those with backsides like a parson's nose and those with arses as wide as a salt-beef barrel. Yallah!'

The miracle came to pass. The next day, at about eleven in the morning, a van driven by two Syrians who had come from Town delivered a pile of cardboard boxes with no marking other than 'father and son' (Ali was about sixteen at the time). They unloaded them without asking a hand from the blacks who had drifted to Front Street in the hope that some charitable soul would buy them a drink. Small Balls Auguste, a cousin of Godmother's with a pockmarked face like a ripe banana and of tinier proportions even than Dachine, sat in state behind the counter of his bar where he had never seen fit to put up a sign. Whenever a boozer gripped the arm of a respectable passer-by to beg 'Buy me a little rum, boss', Small Balls would interject:

'Oh, no! It's too early. Buy him a sugar-cane juice instead.'

The ploy fooled nobody but it was part of Grand-Anse's morning ritual and the fellow's business prospered. A second miracle took place the day that the black knickers were unloaded; Small Balls Auguste came and stood, for the first time in decades, at the front door of his bar and shouted to Syrian:

'I'm first in line to buy. I want them in Myrtha's size, please.'

And that is how everyone found out that he, who was thought

67

to be devoid of sexual appetite because of his dwarfism, was a keen and regular customer of one of our public women, Myrtha, the whore, the negress with a big heart and a phenomenal arse, so big that you could safely balance a cup of coffee on it. We discovered that Small Balls Auguste was that mysterious protector whom the sharpest-tongued gossips had not been able to identify despite intensive research. We were proud of him and for him. Nobody dared to make the slightest mocking remark and Syrian rushed to tear open one of the boxes, then another, to dig out the size in question. When he held up the black knickers triumphantly between his two thumbs, an exclamation went round the bystanders, both admiring and pensive:

'*Fout Mirta ni an bèl môso bonda mézanmi*! (What an arse she's got, that Myrtha!)'

'Gina Lollobrigida herself would be jealous of it,' said Thimoléon, our cinematographic expert, approvingly.

At half past eleven, the women of Grand-Anse formed a queue in a back room of the Palace of the Orient, hastily transformed into a fitting room, refusing to let Syrian help them to undress. That task fell to the innocent lad that was Ali Tanin and that is how he acquired his uncommon understanding of the female personality, of her moods and tricks, of the width of her backside and, above all, of her curves and contours. Many years later when he had become a respected skirt-chaser, he never tired of reliving that memorable day in endless detail and every time people would listen, their tongues hanging out. The lucky chap, it seems, was able to touch the pouting and fleecy fannies of the blue-black negresses, the most sublime but also the most terrifying that you can imagine, an experience which sometimes made him mutter:

'You must respect a negress, oh yes!'

He saw the bold *coucounes* of the red-skinned *chabines* with their hair as yellow as golden mangoes, the bronzed and demure slits of the mulatto girls, which only yield completely in the throes of ecstasy, the ticklish fleece of the *câpresses*, and when the wife and daughters of Coolie René arrived, Syrian tugged his son behind a heap of materials and whispered:

68

'Mind your hands, Indian pubic hair is sharp enough to cut.'

So he was also able to admire their sexual charms, as silky as if 'combed by nature' he told us later. Thus Ali Tanin knew what was hidden under every skirt in Grand-Anse, and that is why when the time came for him to play the cock, no female could resist him, for as the women around here say, once your eyes have seen it all already, why bother carrying on with all that simpering and time-wasting, for heaven's sake? Isn't the damage already done? So you see that Ali's talent for seduction wasn't simply due to his soft green eyes, his light complexion or his fine figure, all undeniable attributes, but also and above all to the exceptional experience which had befallen him at the beginning of his adolescence. He only had two regrets: that neither the Creole white girls nor Antilia passed through the fitting room. The former paid no attention to the gibberish dreamed up by black folk and anyway the incubus was careful not to breach the walls of their estates. What is more, white *coucoune* has been reserved for whites only since the beginning of time, not for coloured people.

'Us coloured people, we can only dream about it,' grumbled Bogino, the madman.

Antilia, who at the time wasn't yet Eau de Café's servant and was still wandering on the village beach without family, friends or roof over her head, saw no point in protecting herself against Julien Thémistocle. She slept on the bare black sand and didn't even get up when the sea sent a wave to wash over her.

'That accursed girl has come straight from the accursed bosom of that accursed sea,' people said disapprovingly.

Syrian shifted three hundred and forty-seven pairs of black knickers by half past twelve. Seven hundred and thirty-two by one o'clock. One thousand one hundred and seventeen by three and so it went on until the end of the afternoon. At dusk all the knicker boxes were filled with coins or notes. He and his son spent all night counting their fortune, the extent of which was never revealed (Syrians are not forthcoming on that subject), but which enabled them that same week to start major refurbishment work on what would become the sumptuous Palace of the Orient which we know today. Syrian's wife, the negress with little zeros for hair who had taken him in when times were hard, was ecstatic:

'Ah, thank you, God! Thank you! Bad luck won't point its finger at us any more. The days of sweat and poverty are finished and finished for good.'

She had only forgotten one thing: to find a pair of protective knickers for her own use. That same evening, mad with rage, infuriated by the bitter failure he was meeting everywhere, the incubus screwed her silly for three hours and in the morning she woke up, saying:

'I'm even having pleasant dreams now. Ah, thank you, God! Thank you!'

When she went into the kitchen where Syrian was pondering the ups and downs of fate and was dreaming of his native land, her happiness collapsed at a stroke. He took one look at her well-satisfied physique, stared at her lips, looked deeply into her eyes and exploded.

'You slut-tart-whore-sewer rat! While I was working myself to death all night counting the money, you, you were busy cuckolding me, were you? Don't say anything! I don't want to hear your lies, the marks on your body are evidence enough. The expression on your face says it all.'

The flabbergasted woman looked at her arms, her hips, her thighs and found that no words came to her defence. Her tongue seemed to have frozen solid, and much as the words came, went and ran about in her head she could not utter the slightest thing. The incubus had tied up her tongue, people said. So it was that Syrian threw her out and that she watched helplessly as her paltry belongings were dumped on to the pavement. In all the years that the poor devil had lived with the trader, she had only acquired an enamel wash basin, a small battered case with a broken clasp, a few Sunday rags and an old Singer sewing machine. Nobody had the time to take pity on her for the village was celebrating; Syrian's idea had proved to be a stroke of genius. Not a single miss or matron, apart from his wife, was violated in the course of the night by that evil *chien-fer* Julien Thémistocle. The negress took away her things and walked up to the En Chéneaux neighbourhood where she was fattening up a fine-looking black pig. She chased him out of his sty and took his place, thus joining the brotherhood of blacks known as the lowest order, those who haven't washed since they were born and who fight with the animals over the contents of dustbins. Syrian never tried to find out the truth, for his race doesn't do things by half measures. Just as they can be overwhelmingly generous (Syrian always gave away shirts at the beginning of school term to families who were temporarily hard-up), so they can be as fierce as fierce can be.

He became a figure in Grand-Anse and was offered a seat on the town council, which he preferred to pass on to Ali Tanin. Once the son was in charge of the Palace of the Orient, Syrian had developed the habit of sitting astride a chair at the entrance to the shop and holding forth about his country of origin. He evoked strange and beautiful places, he waxed lyrical over the desert and cloudless skies, he told of wedding feasts and lavish entertainments, punctuated by interminable wars between cousins, and his audience gaped in wonder, dreaming too of the land of Syria. Nobody interrupted. Only once did Dachine ask, expressing a collective worry:

'Tell me, man, is Syria bigger than France?'

'No . . . no, my friends, there's no comparison.'

Reassured, the municipal dustman asked again:

'Is it more . . . more beautiful than France?'

'Oh, no! . . . No country is more beautiful than France, as you all know.'

And so they listened to him like that for years. Only Julien Thémistocle, who had good reason to hold a grudge against him, sometimes came and displayed his maroon bad manners outside the Palace of the Orient. Stinking of the rough rum they gave him free at the Fond Gens-Libre distillery to stop him setting fire to the canefields the day before milling, he would grunt:

'Ha! You're all full of France and Syria, you bunch of idiots, but you turn your backs on Guinea! There's not one of you lot who wants to go back there! Well, I'm just waiting to die. Kill me and you'll see that my body won't be in its tomb the following day. I'm all set for Guinea!'

People mocked him now that they were no longer scared of him. We wanted nothing to do with this Guinea which he kept boring us with, with a country of savage negroes and cannibals, and only the bookworm Émilien Bérard took his side. We heard that the frustrated incubus Thémistocle had resorted to attacking Marie-Eugénie de Cassagnac, the daughter of the *béké* who owned the Séguineau estate. Having become over-bold, he hadn't even bothered to make himself invisible and had jumped on her in broad daylight on the veranda of the master's house, where a servant had left the child on her own. The village cursed him even more and some honest citizens laid complaints against him at the police station since 'these days it is no longer tolerable for maroons of his type to be roaming the streets'. Julien Thémistocle was saved from probable imprisonment for vagrancy and outraging public morals by the outbreak of the Second World War. He had turned into a valiant soldier for France after hearing General de Gaulle's appeal on the English radio from the island of Dominica. He escaped to join the dissidents under the nose of Admiral Robert's militia, was taken to America, then took part in the Normandy landing before coming back to us decorated, clean, taciturn and driven by an urge to work that commanded respect.

Grand-Anse forgot his crimes and he would greet Syrian whenever he passed by his shop. Was it during this period that he became close to Eau de Café? . . .

9

The Oceanic Hotel is neither a brothel nor a family boarding-house. Nor, of course, a proper hotel. The first evening, the owner had seemed put out to have to prepare a room for me himself. In underpants and bare-chested, he had fumbled in a wardrobe in search of clean sheets, grumbling the whole time,

'*Ola i mété sa? Ola tèbè-a mété sa, tonnan?*' (Where has she put them? Where has the stupid woman put them, for heaven's sake?)

My room had the advantage of having a shutter which closed so badly that you could hear the sea roaring down below. As soon as the moaning owner had left me alone (without even bothering to ask whether I might need something to drink), I had tried to open it and had found that two plywood slats were nailed top and bottom against it. A salt-laden wind came in through the gaps in the shutter and even through the roof, where you could see tiles that must once have been red. The tap at the tiny sink only produced a thin trickle of water, which dried up altogether before I had finished washing my face. I started regretting that I hadn't dared to wake up Eau de Café. But old-timers don't like surprises, we've always been told. They don't like the leaps and bounds of modern life. Honour and respect to their wisdom (or rather to their wise madness).

I had an uncontrollable desire to look at the sea although I knew that there would be no light to reveal it to me. Nights at Grand-Anse are terrible, except for those of August which lend themselves to debauchery. Puzzled, I spread out books and papers on my bed.

'How long will you be staying?' asked the owner, now in a better mood.

'I'll decide tomorrow morning.'

'You know I can get a better room than this one fixed for you. If you'd warned us, we could have made arrangements. There's a bad-tempered sort of woman who works for me, but when the hotel is empty she stops work and just takes care of the restaurant downstairs. So let me know.'

I had spent a sleepless night. The sea hadn't granted me a moment's peace. It had rattled at my shutter, scratched at the roof, uttered cries of pain that froze me with terror. I expected at any moment to see it burst into my room and knock me around in one of its time-honoured and ill-tempered punch-ups. I had caught myself whispering to it that I hadn't done anything. I hadn't questioned its rule or mocked its pride. Hasn't it always dominated our dreams? Having been so far away and for so long hadn't freed me from it. I had come back to it wrapped up in the same reverence as any black man from here. If only it would stop intimidating me!

It was late in the morning when, exhausted, I had again tried to open the shutter. To no avail. The owner had sent me his second-in-command. A stiff woman of few words. She had given me a bar of Marseille soap and had told me that the shower was on the ground floor, behind the kitchen. I now had only one desire: to leave this strange place and find my godmother, Eau de Café. To settle back into the little bedroom where, as a child, I used to wait for Antilia to come and tuck me into bed. I had repacked my clothes and books and rushed outside. Front Street had thrown me off balance. A profusion of shimmering dresses, of tenderly inquisitive eyes, of the hoarse voices of white rum drinkers. The blasting horns of lorries overloaded with goods. The squealing of gangs of loitering kids. A massive, ubiquitous heat, whimsical in places. And on the other side of the day, the sea. The sea brooding over its anger. Taking pleasure in holding back its waves of anger.

And there was Eau de Café, on her doorstep, who had expressed neither joy nor surprise but had started talking straight away while I gave in to the unstoppable flow of her words.

Lament of Eau de Café, the fighting woman
Is it because I can't join two words of French together that you try

74

to shut my mouth? Is it because my womb is reputed to be barren and that your seed is wasted inside me, more useless than drizzle in the middle of the dry season? Because I am going to talk my share of talking and you will have no option but to pretend not to hear, but I'm sure that it will cause an awful commotion in your inner self. So much so and to such an extent that some will run to stick their heads in their sinks, others will chew their clay pipes into pieces and even born idiots will stop slobbering over their dreams, suddenly enlightened by my revelations. For I know everything inside out. I know that Mademoiselle Rose-Aimée de Morne l'Étoile only puts on such fine airs and graces because she lives so high up and she's dizzy from not looking down at what's happening below in the plain. She wanders among us sugar-cane gatherers as if the cane pieces were marking a processional route and you would swear in all honesty that the arrows which come into leaf in December act as her crown. So, proud and wild, she doesn't deign to give us a good morning or good evening and barely a tiny 'thank you' when we point out a forgotten piece of cane under a pile of cords. Well, for one thing, that Rose-Aimée isn't the daughter of her supposed father, who scratches away at some tiny piece of ungiving land and exhausts himself growing yams and a few withered hands of bananas, for the simple reason that he has always had bad luck on his back. That man had more or less signed a pact with the jinx itself and draughts blew through his empty pockets. How then could he have fathered that goddess Rose-Aimée? Impossible! I'm quite prepared to believe that he can lay paternal claim to Louis with the crooked foot, to Marcel and Gérard, even, if you close your eyes, to Thérésine, the no-good *chabine* girl who has the island white Marreau Deschamps as godfather (ha, ha, ha!) but as regards Mademoiselle Rose-Aimée, currently tying up the piles of cane by our side on the Fond Gens-Libres estate, I say no, no and no again. If you want to know where she comes from and how she inherited her not-of-this-world manners, you'll have to trust my tongue for I know about her mother's vices and even the vices that she wanted to try out but didn't dare to put into practice since filth

75

has its limits. Her mother, ladies and gentleman, conceived her with that most savage of men, known as Ugly Congo. There you have it!

Who thinks he can stop me speaking out under the sun on behalf of all those women who have been breaking their backs among the sugar-cane for a century of time (my mother used to prefer saying 'since the time of the Marquis of Yore' although she could never tell me who that paragon of age and wisdom was)? If I remain alone in my hut in Macédoine, it's not because I like people calling me a mongoose. The reason is perfectly simple; I don't want to share my peace and quiet. It's the only thing I own, the only treasure that God, who so forgot the blacks on the day of Creation – or who made them the lowest of all races after the horny toads (in fact they're one and the same!) – has seen fit to grant me. That's why no man has ever crossed the yard at the front of my hut or put his jigger-ridden feet on my doorstep to hear me whisper seductively 'Come here on top of me, I need to feel you inside me'. No! Let the first man who claims to have seen the colour of my bed say so here, in front of me, and I'll have him running straight back to the lap of his whore of a mother. Oh yes! You're going to tell me that before the time of Admiral Robert there was that little dog's bollock Dachine who used to hide among the pigeon pea bushes to play me his *bel-air* drum at nightfall, as if I, Eau de Café, was the sort of woman to like his Guinea black music. Huh! If he knew, on the contrary, how much he sowed terror in my heart, he would never have dared, after three months of trying his charm, to ask me whether he could rub his body against mine. It's hardly surprising that he ended up carting the village rubbish around! The only thing that gives me the shivers, I admit it, is the accordion played by that handsome hunk of a black man from Moulin-l'Étang at the village patron saint's festival. Unfortunately for me, he has never told anyone his name and he is never seen apart from when that time of year comes round. He normally stands by the merry-go-round and entertains people between turns, carrying on for the whole afternoon, and at dusk he takes over the dance on the market square. He plays so well that the women want to dance on their own and to get drunk on the motion of his notes but, mark you, I'm the only one who dares to do so. So you rush to damn me with your biting red-ant comments – 'Look at that Eau de Café showing off. You wouldn't have thought butter would melt in her mouth' – and all manner of nastiness like that, just to see whether I'll stop spinning round and round and round by myself like a top and find some partner among the crowd of yokels in their Sunday best. That's because you mix me up with those little perfumed nymphets who've been trying to get a man from the day that blood began to trickle down their thighs and who waste their lives waiting at their windows as the days go by and no shadow ever appears at the path leading to their huts. As for me, pah! I don't need to be weighed down by all those stupid dreams that clutter up your life just to become moodier than a cat who's had her litter drowned when it's all over. Eau de Café's not going to get caught up in your monkey business, ladies and gentlemen! I may not speak much French but my mind's none the slower for that. I see everything, I know everything, I guess everything and above all I talk straight and loud and clear about everything. That's why you're afraid of me and you want to stuff my words back into my mouth. Go and screw yourselves! I won't tie a rope round my talking because even if you don't like it, it happens to delight my companions in sweat and backache on cane-cutting days. It helps them to bear the terrible stiffness that comes from picking up the cane that the cutters chop down with a great show of strength as if they wanted to prove something to the heavens. Or to the island white. Or even to that foreman who has hated me from day one and whom you call, God knows why, Julien Thémistocle. Me, I find that name so ridiculous that I can't say it without bursting out laughing and you expect me to slave away just to get in that bastard's good books or for the few coppers that he hands out every Saturday. Isn't he made of the same stuff as us, despite his grey eyes, isn't he feared for the simple reason that he got the chance to rest his arse on a school bench? I don't play the same games as the other women in the canefields. They moan with faked ecstasy, flat

77

on their backs in the straw with their legs in the air, just to get little favours out of him. That's the truth! He has never interested me, I tell you, and I've never engineered it so that he's alone with me by the Bois-Serpent spring like that slut Rose-Aimée, who would crawl along on all fours if cocks grew out of the ground. As soon as a man tickles her tits, she's away spreading her legs and swooning despite the coarse sweat running down her arms and the red ants and rashes making her back itch. She lies back in her dirty rags to take the hot cock and makes it go soft in the twinkling of an eye with the way she moves her curved hips.

You say: 'She's mad in the head, that Eau de Café!' Pah! Then leave me alone, if that's what you want. I couldn't care less about your bee-sting comments and curses. You're victims of the rubbish spouted by Father Le Gloarnec, who acted like he was stripping me naked in the pulpit before refusing to give me communion. He would have stopped me setting foot in church if he'd been able to, the scoundrel. 'Eau de Café is a hysterical woman!' he screamed in the ranting he used to call sermons, staring in the direction of the holy-water stoop where I've inherited a seat in the pew from my mother, complete with silver plaque. Hysterical! At first nobody had understood that expression and people thought I'd caught a catching disease. They steered clear of me when I was taking a stroll in the village or threw the right money on to the shop counter so as not to touch anything I had touched. Huh! What did it mean, hysterical? The more I ran through my thoughts, the less I understood the reasons behind such a slander. I had confessed the day before and as normal had admitted my sins from the previous week to the priest, to whom I'd always been a good friend.

What had I left out? Nothing, honestly. I've always lived in fear of leaving behind me a trail of unabsolved sins that would give me even more headaches in the next world. To tell the whole truth, our priest is much happier dealing with the hypocritical females who come and kneel before him with their cleavages leaving nothing to the imagination. Take that Passionise whom the foreman married, God knows why, just as she was on her way to joining the whores on the beach at Grand-Anse at nightfall. Her confessions consisted of one single phrase: 'Father, I have not sinned,' and the idiot would give absolution on the spot. Well, I, Eau de Café, heartless-hysterical-uncouth-rum-drinking-slut that I am, I am absolutely certain that Passionise Thémistocle is acting a part. No, madame is not the saint that she'd like you to believe she is and the veil that she wears to mass is not to protect the modesty of her eyes, but a mask to stop us making out the vice that is written in capital letters on her forehead. I assure you and please open your ears as wide as they'll go to hear it: Passionise is fucking the little *béké* who's the manager on the Fond Massacre estate, and if she hasn't been found out yet, it's because her husband and lover have the same first name and there's no risk of her tongue slipping, that's why! And I've told nobody about this, you see, despite knowing. I said to myself, honour and respect for Julien Thémistocle! He's our foreman, he's fair with us, he doesn't treat us like dog shit, so there's no need to ruin his reputation. Moreover, as the proverb says, you can keep sticking your knife in the water, but you won't do it any harm . . . But the bastard exceeded the bounds of arrogance with me the day that he found us, Mathilde, Tertulia and me, wondering how Ma Léna's niece had managed to acquire her big stomach. We'd been working away since dawn, tying together more piles of cane in one morning than in two normal days since we were keen to get out from under the sun which had risen earlier than usual and was beating down on us without pity. The man came by on his mule and treated us to his entire repertoire of boorishness and disdain. We were sheltering in the shade of a pigeon pea bush by what passes for the river that crosses Fond Gens-Libres. We hadn't heard him coming. He's like that, our foreman. He's like the wind; he would appear and disappear from the four corners of the plantation without anyone hearing his footstep or managing to dampen his zeal and suddenly he would be there, telling you to mend the wheel on such-and-such a cart, pointing out the three canes left behind near a pile, a cutlass stuck in a mango tree trunk or a water bottle with its top left off. He would hand out orders and the men would follow them without grumbling because Julien Thémisto-cle never talked for its own sake and as he avoided talking in parables, it was difficult to misunderstand his educated black man's words. Monsieur pretended not to notice me. Whenever he came across me, he would look right over and past me as if he didn't want to dirty his eyes. This strange behaviour had always secretly annoyed me, I have to say, since I know everything that that arrogant man got up to before he married his Passionise.

I know that he was intimate with Rémise from Morne Capot, Hortense Lacher's third daughter, who can't make a child stick in her womb and who, in her rage, offers her body to any male in need of a woman. And then he was involved with Floriane from the La Mancelle estate, daughter of an unknown mother (a very rare thing among us) and who was brought up by her father who was soon to become her lover and give her a crowd of skin-and-bone kids. And afterwards he was with Étiennise from Anse Four-à-Chaud, who used to gather hundreds of coconuts to make oil that she sold for a fortune to the mulattos of Grand-Anse. She was said to be as fidgety as a mongoose which means in common parlance that she couldn't keep still, that she was always off somewhere, in the countryside or especially by the sea where she had built a hut of bamboo sticks on Crown Land, without getting into trouble. I wasn't the only one to think that Julien Thémistocle would never lead any woman to the altar. But that was to forget that no schemer of Passionise's calibre could be found for twenty miles around. Yet who can still believe that the wedding upset me? I have always made sure that my path doesn't cross that of a man of the Thémistocle breed. I don't know why I've been called a fighting woman because, two or three months after he set up home with Passionise, he came to rape me in the canefield. Me, I never provoked him, and if he succumbed to my charms that's his fault. Not mine. I was so, so young and he was so, so old that I didn't feel anything. Anyway, isn't it said that he hastened my birth?

You can call me mad if it gives you pleasure but, please, drop this 'fighting woman', which insults my pride.

10

The sea at Grand-Anse, our sea, is barren. It has never given anyone so much as a fish – in living Christian memory in any case –
and it proclaims its brazen fruitlessness to the trade winds. At the
tip of the La Crabière promontory sticks out a little cluster of reefs
that we call the Rock, where intrepid young black boys, armed
only with a mask, dive for crabs and octopus. When they return
with their catch, the old men snigger as they explain to them how
they have unwittingly been led to underwater caves, far from the
coast, by sirens, terrifying fish-women, and that if they were to eat
their catch, they would go mad at once. And so they throw it to
the wild dogs or give it as a present to their worst enemies.

'What does it all mean?' Eau de Café used to ask me pointlessly
soon after we had moved into the village.

The most commonly accepted explanation is so laughable that
you could dismiss it like swatting a fly: at the beginning of Grand-
Anse's settlement, when the last maroons were still trying to fend
off the blunderbusses and hence a long time before the volcano
erupted, there was a priest who tried to stop people from living
how they liked to live, from pleasuring, as we say, that is, enjoying
the good-natured lechery which is so peculiar to our Creole character. He would bellow from the pulpit, threatening people by
name with thunderbolts from heaven. He even went so far as to
spy on adulterous wives and to catch them in the act. At that time,
the sea was as full of fish as at Fond d'Or or Basse-Pointe and the
fishermen used to weave their bamboo eel-pots in the fierce heat of
the afternoon. They used to sit where the abattoir is now. At dusk
the villagers would gather on the beach in order to barter their
goods for flying fish or swordfish. Once the village was catered for,
higglers would do the rounds in the countryside with dried fish, so
much so that a fine legend became common currency:

'Grand-Anse is a blessed place. Throw down a seed and it will become a tree by the time the moon rises. As for its sea, it is a veritable larder.'

Thanks to this reputation, the region attracted settlers more quickly than surrounding areas. Everybody wanted his little piece of paradise . . . until the arrival of that zealous Jansenist and his daily excommunications. At around the same time, our work- and sun-deadened black heads began to suffer the ravages of falling sickness. It was like a swarm of ants nipping at your forehead, the nape of your neck and suddenly your whole body, and then you would be dancing a demonic calenda, uttering messages that were perfectly audible, extraordinarily simple in structure, but devoid of any obvious sense. Sufferers would come and rub themselves against you in the secret hope of a cure, big-bellied pregnant women would stick their fingers in their ears to stop their babies hearing and your family would roll you like a barrel of salted meat in the early morning Grand-Anse tide so that the Lord would deliver you from the evil. Then people began to look for the cause of this collective brainstorm and reckoned it could only be that rogue in a black cassock.

Unable to give him a beating, subject him to public scorn, make him impotent or stop his hot air once and for all, they devised a plan. Some fishermen invited him one Saturday evening to go with them on to the high seas so that he could see for himself how generous God was. They assured him that he would be back on Sunday before dawn, which would enable him to say six o'clock mass. The priest hesitated, then fancied that he might be able to glean some new insight into his parishioners. In spite of his extreme vigilance, there were always vices that could elude him. One never knows with blacks!

At sea, he was unable to extract a single incriminating word from the fishermen. He found himself holding forth interminably as his companions smiled mockingly, pretending to be too busy pulling in their lines to chat with him. Disappointed, our holy man fell asleep in a corner of the boat in the middle of a small mountain of tuna fish. The two fishermen roared with laughter and carried on working, no longer holding back from swearing in the filthiest fashion whenever they missed a good bite.

The next day, like a yellow and withered calabash, the sun was already rising above the horizon when the exhausted priest awoke. The fishermen told him that it was barely five in the morning, 'because you see the sun earlier here than on dry land'. He believed them and began his morning devotions. Just then, for a moment, they made out a small grey shape, straight ahead of them, which could only be Coco-Assier, the highest point around Grand-Anse and the sailors' traditional landmark. When one of these would mutter *'Nou pèdi Koko-Asyé'* (We've lost sight of Coco-Assier), his companions knew that they were now alone among the immensity of the waves and each of them felt a slight pang in his heart.

After an hour, the priest started to show signs of anxiety. He was going to be late, for sure. Then the two men started a strange conversation:

'Ou kwè i ni dé kon tout moun?' (Do you think he's got two like everyone else?)

'Dé ki su? Hu! ha! ha!' (Two of what? Ha, ha, ha!)

'Anba wòb-la man ka palé'w, ès nonm-lan ni dé grenn ka pann tou?' (Under his cassock, I mean. Do you think the fellow's got a pair of balls?)

'Annou gadé-wè, fout!' (Let's take a look, bugger it!)

The priest, who understood the subtlest nuances of our language (the proof: he knew all the euphemisms for a woman's genitalia and one day condemned from the pulpit those men who were too keen on playing the mandolin), realized that they were going to strip him naked. He called on heaven's saints, he raged, threatened the two fishermen with eternal damnation and tried to put up a fight, but all to no avail. They even removed his stockings and crucifix before heaving him into the water, about three hundred feet from the shore, laughing all the more uproariously.

'A moué! A moué!' (Help me! Help me!) he yelled, using a phrase in our language both old-fashioned and comical.

Barely able to swim, he went under several times, then reappeared, like a fat, white pig set adrift, spitting out foam all around. The people of Grand-Anse, who were mirthful accomplices in this entertainment, had been gathering in their entirety on the beach since well before dawn. Nobody would have dreamt of missing such a spectacle. Master-drummers had formed circles on the black sand and were making the young people dance. The women selling coconut sorbet and pistachios had even abandoned the church square where they had been waiting since the world began for people to come out of mass and set up shop alongside that sea which they would soon learn to hate like every man in the village. A song was improvised about the priest, a lewd one, of course:

> Misyé Labé, tjenbé dé grenn ou fò
> Tjenbé yo fò O!
> Davwè s'ou wè wakawa pasé, i kay brilé yo ba'w
> Tjenbé yo fò O!
> Davwè s'ou wè mè-balawou pasé, i kay dégrennen yo
> ba'w

> (Father, watch out for your balls
> Take care of them!
> For if the electric ray sees them, he'll burn them
> Take care of them!
> For if the sword-fish sees them, he'll cut them off
> Take care of them!)

All the fishes' names and second names had their turn and you should know that there were a couple of thousand of them during Grand-Anse's years of plenty. All that time, the poor priest was struggling to swim to the shore, swallowing many a mouthful of saltwater (our sea is also saltier than elsewhere). As soon as he could touch bottom the crowd suddenly stopped its jeering as if it had just realized the seriousness of the sacrilege. According to some, the church bells rang out the ending of mass by themselves although the service hadn't taken place. People shivered despite the heat of the sun. There were those who crossed themselves and

84

muttered vague prayers without realizing how absurd such appeals were at the very moment when God's representative on earth was being cast down from his pedestal. Somebody even dared to shout a loud and ridiculous:

'God–Father–the Virgin Mary!'

Once on the beach, the priest rose vengefully to his feet, his eyes bulging, before collapsing flat out. Nobody dared to go near him and a dull terror took root in every heart. Three hours or three days passed by like that. The village of Grand-Anse seemed struck down by stupor. Then the priest regained his senses. His face seemed surprisingly radiant for a man who had just been subjected to such humiliation. He was even gleeful, according to some. Pointing an accusing finger at the terrified villagers, he spoke to them as follows, the whole time carefully shaking the folds of his cassock over the waves:

'You have laughed at my expense, dear parishioners, and without you knowing it, your laughter has penetrated into the womb of the sea. Today I curse you and I curse this sea, the accomplice who echoed your devilish filth into my ears. It will steal your children from you, the finest flowers of your youth, and never again will it offer up the abundance of fish of which you boast far and wide. *Never again!* . . . Go in peace!'

With a long, maniacal snigger, he returned to his presbytery and the next day was in the capital, from where he was sent soon after to Guyane. The plain truth is that from that day on the sea at Grand-Anse became barren and as ugly as a horny toad. That is the most commonly accepted thesis and one that I am far from supporting since I have come here to find out and I shall find out. Antilia will not have died (drowned?) for nothing . . .

Dearest,

They have torn us up by the roots. In the midst of each of us they have exposed the vulnerable shoots of despair. Over there I can hear the snapping of the mastic tree trunk which they are cutting down to straighten the colonial road, since the engineer thinks (and the schoolboy recites), 'a straight line is the shortest course between two points'. They have dressed us up in dreams of straightness, purity, clarity and even reason, and that is why the blacks from Morne Pichevin kill one another for no more than a funny look or a word out of turn. On the Friday before Easter, according to the newspaper La Paix, *the Moriot brothers were picking up their crab traps from around the Cross when the two of them, who had always been known to be closer than closeness itself, cut one another's throats with razors without so much as a cry. One of them, the elder, went to expire on the thirty-third of the forty-four Morne Pichevin steps and it was there that the crime was discovered. As for the younger, his hands covering a gaping wound, the blood dripping from his lips, he had the strength and courage to make it to the Dockers' Daisies bar opposite the Transat office and order an old rum.*

As true as true is! It's what the paper reported. To this day, people are wondering about the incredible silence in which their tussle took place. Perhaps they had 'tied up' each other's tongues, as the journalist put it.

I hate those tear-jerking poets who can get to the bottom of unhappiness with a well-chosen phrase that brings tears to your eyes or rage to your heart. They don't know anything. Those around me have never shown pity and I thank them for it . . .

Antilia

THIRD CIRCLE

Town has taught us how to be cynical and we no longer even believe that mango trees flower in May since the supermarkets stock mangoes all year round. We laugh ourselves silly over our delusion.

There are now two races in this land: those who persist inexplicably in grumbling on in the old colonial language born in the sugar-cane fields and those who wear a different tie every time they go out.

So there are those who talk, talk, talk, chatterers of the first order, for whom silence would amount to death, and those who burn out their lives in a limousine with masochistic joy, dumb with pleasure . . .

11

Godmother didn't offer to put me up. It's true that I had trouble recognizing the brand-new shop that she'd had built thanks to a special government grant. At the time, she bored everybody by repeating:

'Anyone who goes around talking fibbishness about the government can go and buy elsewhere or watch his arse!'

Strangely, she had only renovated the shop-front and, inside, legions of woodworm were marching across the beams and wooden partitions from which pieces had crumbled away, allowing the stubborn murmur of the sea to come through. During the first day I spent with her, she only had three customers, two of whom were after rum on tick, and she never stopped talking to herself and talking down to me as if I was still the child of eight she'd brought up. Armed with a napkin, she got up every so often to polish the counter, a habit going back to the good old days when it was there that she would sell her merchandise from the four corners of the universe.

'My old friend, Ma Léonce, died two years after you left Grand-Anse, my dear,' she said again softly.

In the early afternoon a man appeared in his Sunday best and seemed not to notice me. He casually took off his black felt hat, loosened his tie and cleared his throat loudly while settling back into the only more or less decent chair in the drawing-room. Suddenly Thimoléon recognized me and said solemnly:

'Its good that you came on the eve of the fourteenth of July. It's good of you . . . When shortly I take you into the men's world of the Market (but this incursion only lasts one day, our national holiday, for the rest of the time you will only find sturdy fish-wives there), you must try to attract the attention of the few females, that's to say those serving rum punch or preparing black pudding, the sweet-sellers as well as, oh yes!, the dice-players, the 'he-women' as they call themselves. It's an even tougher task than all the others awaiting you if you have vowed to return among us, a major test, since you mustn't speak directly to them as you would if asking them for something. Such ostentation would be unpardonable. You should know that they don't expect to be treated nicely like that. They would be the first to be shocked and they would show you their displeasure through vulgar hoots of laughter which would also alert all the other men (and what is the point?) as to your bad manners brought back from overseas. You must simply snatch a glass of white rum from a tray as it goes by and toss some coins on to it, or hold up a banknote casually if you want black pudding in a crust, and, from your bearing as a man of action, they will judge who they're dealing with. For have you felt the pain of giving birth alone in a hut while a dozen curious but scared kids keep bursting in on you? Have you felt the worth-lessness of your body as your lover packs up his khaki shirts, his trousers, his palm-leaf hat, his tobacco and all his things and leaves home because you've told him that you're going to give birth? Perhaps tonight, perhaps tomorrow, God willing, you don't know . . . and you've still got to get up, feed the grunting pigs, sweep inside and in front of the hut so that it's clean when neighbours and family come, try (in vain) to get rid of the chil-dren you'd wanted to leave with your mother for a few days, just long enough for their little brother to arrive (ah, what bad luck if it's a little wet-the-bed girl!), heat the water and pile the towels on a chair for the midwife. All that, that's a Creole woman's life, all very ordinary, infinitely banal, a misfortune that's bearable because it's always been like that, so don't come and mess up this fine orderation of things with words as big as Guinea's grass savannahs or polite niceties which would make you look like some sort of cissy boy. They don't need you to snatch a little pleasure from time to time. They manage to get together on their own on Sunday afternoon (their only bit of freedom) and chat, tell of the daily drudgery and laugh about it, mock the name of the man who beats them and make fun of the size of his cock, which he's so proud of, and laugh about that too. As for tomorrow, maybe the larder will be empty if the rainy season doesn't hurry along and make the garden bring forth yams and dasheen. There are the dresses to patch, patch and patch again until they're nothing but thread, and you have to laugh about it. You've got to keep track of the young girls who've grown up overnight and who are now opening their legs in the canefields for the estate foreman or the island white and, good grief, you've got to laugh about that as well once the damage is done. To laugh is to stay alive, since the men slap down their dominoes in the rum shop and there's no point in working out fine sounding phrases. Secrets don't remain secret long and pass from mouth to mouth. So the paternity of the latest children born up in the hills is restored to its rightful owners amidst raucous turkey-cock chuckling. And since the kids are allowed to wander in the countryside on those afternoons looking for coco-plums and pigeon peas and we don't have to turn into zombies to speak French – what a headache, Lord! But they really must learn it at school – we can indulge in Creole, make it express things that only a woman's innards can feel, and savour the texture of each witticism like some strange and delicious fruit. Even if you hadn't gone away, you would never have suspected all this until you had reached the age where you no longer want a woman's body. Ah, yes! You might have thought it, but wrapped up in your own affairs, your own man's world, you wouldn't have given it too much attention. It's only as the years race by that men realize with a start how far their wives have managed to live in a separate world, theirs alone, which shelters them from the despair which is suddenly lying in wait for them, the men. That's why some of them start saying in a learned way: 'Our women are strong, by God, yes they are!' as if the women needed such an overdue compliment, having only ever heard them grunt in monosyllables and, more often than not, yell rum drinkers' insults. But don't think it's contentment, it's nothing like that. In any case, they are proudly oblivious to that word, preferring happiment. No, a black woman's life is one that takes on and fights against the world's ugliness, without failing or weakening.

Be aware, too, that a woman's scream can save your skin because it has the power to freeze the hatred of the thug (I'm sure it's him who's coming for you!) who, unbeknownst to you, is about to spill your guts because he can't even win a little thousand-franc note from you, while you insolently wander from table to table, flexing your muscles, not even shouting out the magic 'eleven', mocking the elaborate gestures of the hard men we call 'chiefs' here as well as the dice masters, and spreading the shitless jitters and cold sweats among the poor players who are counting on today to get through the week to come. So do as much and as well as you can so that the women end up saying: 'That *chabin* is a fine man!' and the trick is done. It's tougher to sweeten up the lady dicers, whose Egeria is Doris, the devil's betrothed, who can rip children from their mother's womb, for they can't be bothered with airs and graces and don't laugh, their faces and eyes are closed and inscrutable, and as they're almost all at least of a certain age, they look down on you even more than on their own brattish boys, especially you, who went away and came back. They think, you see, that you don't retrace your tired steps unless you're one hell of a cheat or you've got something evil in mind. They have never gone back to look into the face of the cheeky swine who used to think himself entitled to shout insults at them when they were young, or if some have – and you can be sure that they've regretted it ever since! – it wasn't to take issue with what he said, as all of it – 'ugly', 'fat cow', 'spotty as a ripe banana' – is true, but to insist: 'Say whatever you like, you idiot, but don't call me a woman, do you understand?' So, unable to think of anything clever to say in return, the speechless fool swears to himself not to try that again. What do you know about these women who grasp the dice like they would some bastard's balls that they are about to tear off? What do you know about the thousands of buckets of water that they've been sent to fetch at the village fountain from the age of five? What do you know about those little remarks, so seemingly innocent but which are veritable snake bites: 'Do you think I want a little black girl like you screaming in my ear? Go and cut some grass for the rabbits!' or else 'Your hair's worse than a forest of burrs, my girl! Good God, what a job getting a comb through this girl's hair!' At the annual dance of the village fête which normally takes place in the school canteen, they've never been seen anywhere else than behind the counter serving sodas to the coiffured and light-skinned flirts like Passsionise from Morne l'Étoile as well as to their bouffoned boyfriends. Don't believe that they have time to daydream, to lose themselves in the tumult of the biguine or mazurka while absent-mindedly tapping their feet. Not at all! At three in the morning, when lovers have disappeared on to the village beach by the sea grapes, where the Fond Grand-Anse river comes out, a blessed place where the sand is clean, they are still sweeping the room, collecting the empty bottles, washing the curry plates, helping the musicians to carry their equipment to their van and, at dawn, when their eyes, feet, arms and backs are just one huge ache, they are savagely and unceremoniously fucked (yes, screwed like a hen by a cock on her back) by the janitor, an old man with yaws, by a handful of drunks who'd fallen asleep in a corner, by anybody anyhow. They haven't the strength to utter a single insult or to scratch at the faces of the animals who take turns on top of them before it's over. Nothing more is said. Right! The party's over, the instruments are packed away. It's early Monday morning, to work! And there they are in the fields gathering the sugar-cane or slicing up tuna in the market on a godmother's stall. There they are, bitter without showing it, already aged. No! Hardened rather, as hard as a cassia-tree's roots. They're the same women who can wear jeans without fear of criticism and with whom men aren't ashamed to roll dice. Rose-Aimée Tanin, who doesn't lower her gaze when a man stares at her, is the very embodiment of those warrior women. And so, you see, you've only just realized what their lives are really like, so show a little humility, you who've never undergone such hardships, and don't stand back to let them pass, don't hesitate to shove past them, to speak to them in coarse Creole, to snatch the thousand-franc note from their hands: they will be grateful to you and you will once again be sure of an additional and ubiquitous protection: from them . . .

12   Coolie René's Fall

Every God-given Friday, the two hard men of the village of Grand-Anse, Chief Bérard and the carpenter Thimoléon, surrendered all power and prestige to a single individual who, the rest of the time, inspired nothing but the greatest scornfulness, a tattered wreck of a man, more often than not under the influence of cheap rum, Master Coolie René. On that day he would sport his rags splattered with cow's blood and his long thin knives that he sharpened against one another as he wandered down Front Street, casting occasional evil looks at his most vehement detractors, notably Ma Léonce, who would retaliate by repeating:

'Coolies are only happy in filth. If you ever go into one of their houses, you'd better hold your nose.'

At that time the Indians hadn't yet dared to settle in the village. They were employed by the local whites to raise cattle on the Assier and Moulin l'Étang plantations and only ventured into our streets on the afternoons of the village fêtes, when they revealed themselves to be formidable dice players. Coolie René's father alone had made the break with sugar-cane and had settled with his family on a more or less sandy spot of land between the football pitch, the river mouth and the beach. It was a place where almond trees and long-lived sea grapes grew proudly. There, with the help of wood from salt-cod boxes, bamboo slats, oil drums and corrugated iron, the ex-estate foreman had built himself a dwelling of such surreal architecture that no word in common currency came close to describing it. It had elements of the black man's wooden shack, the palm-roofed hut, the *béké*'s house and the Hindu temple, the last because the man used to hold 'Coolie god' ceremonies there, to the great horror of Catholics and even respectable folk who didn't believe in God. Luckily the place, called Long-Bois, was on the outskirts of the village and the racket made by the sea more often than not drowned out the high-pitched tassa drums and the prayers to the gods of India. Moreover, despite our priests denouncing these practices as nothing less than sorcery, certain desperate cases (those suffering from love sickness or paralysed for life by a stroke) secretly resorted to the powers of Coolie René's father. His prestige was boosted when he succeeded in restoring the use of an arm to a fat mulatto. Such was his resulting renown that people came to consult the *'poussari'*, as they say in their Coolie language, from the four corners of Martinique and, O miracle, from the surrounding islands and even from America. Grand-Anse remembers him as a man whose expression nothing could change. His inscrutable face never smiled, laughed, sniggered or showed any emotion and was lit only by his glowing eyes. When the municipal abattoir was built by the sea, he was a natural candidate for the job of slaughtering the cattle, given that he cut off the sheep's heads with extraordinary dexterity during his Coolie god sacrifices. With a mob of brats to feed, he took the job and since everybody recognized his work to be of public service, he was gradually accepted by the village.

When he wasn't organizing his devil-worship or officiating at the abattoir, Coolie René's father would lapse into madness. Or at least that's what people supposed, since what other explanation was there for the way he used to march up and down the beach, oblivious to the huge waves splattering him, in order to make incomprehensible gestures towards the horizon and shout things in Tamil which made us tremble without knowing why? Sometimes he took little René with him and would point out things or shapes to him that only he could make out on the sea's surface. The truth only came to light many years after his death when one night in Small Balls Auguste's rum shop a group of boozers had started bantering with Coolie René about his father's madness.

'Apa was entirely sane, ladies and gentlemen. It's the government that was unreasonable and broke its word. It had promised to send the repatriation boat to fetch Apa, and Apa waited for it for years and years, all in vain. Look, those of you who can read, come here. I've never had the chance to rest my backside on a school bench, but I know that this paper I've got here is something to do with my father's contract. It's got the date of arrival here or there and the date for going back to India. Look, it's written there, you can at least make out numbers, dammit! The 16th of February 1898. Grandfather waited, Apa waited, but not me, I'm not waiting. I'm going to die and be buried here, like them. And if Apa used to shout into the wind, don't think either that he'd lost his mind. He was simply calling out the thousand names of our goddess Kali so that she would come to our help and take us away as quickly as possible from this land where we're nothing but dog shit, the scum of the earth in short. I can only remember six hundred and thirty-two names, ladies and gentlemen, and perhaps that's why fate has got it in for me.'

Coolie René inherited his father's job without the town council needing to meet in special session. The little Mussolini had settled the issue briefly with four words:

'*Tout kouli sé kouli!*' (All Indians are Indians!)

So on Fridays the cattle-slaughterer strolled through the village, accepting free glasses of rum or gifts of Mélia cigarettes, which he smoked two at a time, provocatively exhaling a thick cloud of smoke. On those days there wasn't a brat in town who would dare to shout:

'Coolie René! Coo-lie-lie-lie! Coo-lie-lie-lie! Coolie's a dog eater!' And not a little black boy who would risk throwing a handful of pebbles or mango stones at him. The noise of his knives clashing together made their teeth chatter under their parents' beds where they had taken refuge. When he judged that he had amply demonstrated his mastery of the streets, he slowly made his way back to the abattoir, his head held high, contemplating the act he was about to carry out. It was said that he was able to tame the spirit of the wild cattle imported from Portorico or Benezuela so that they didn't rear up at the moment that the shining blade slid into their throats. In fact, on the two or three occasions that Coolie René had been ill and unable to work, it had taken no fewer than five big, fat, strong blacks to overpower them. And yet the Indian was no fatter than a piece of string's shadow! The rest of the week he was a mere nothing, utterly dull and devoid of interest, and although he had also inherited the role of *poussari* from his father, people could hardly be bothered to acknowledge his presence. He was so insignificant that he was almost invisible until somebody would ask him to organize a ceremony in honour of Kali, Nagourmira or Maldévilin and then he would become transformed. As if a little of the aura of these gods that he worshipped rubbed off on him.

Some months after the escapades of the incubus Julien Thémistocle and the miraculous solution of the black knickers dreamt up by the cunning devil Syrian, Ma Léonce decided to pull up the seeds of madness which had grown in the head of her son Bogino. She resolved to turn to Coolie René.

'I am a Christian woman,' she said, trying to justify herself before her fellow gossips who were unanimously disapproving. 'I recite the Lord's Prayer and Hail Mary morning, noon and night. I offer thanksgivings. I confess and take communion. Every year I do the pilgrimage to the Virgin of the Délivrande at Morne-Rouge. I pay for mass to be said for the souls of the poor of Grand-Anse. I put my money in the church collection. And what does the Lord God do for my son, eh? Can't you see that he's becoming a bit nuttier every day? You know full well I won't live for ever. Who'll look after him when I'm gone? Which of you will take over giving him something to eat and some clean clothes?'

It was widely suspected that Bogino's lunacy must have some connection with the brutal and unexplained death of Master Léonce, but nobody dared to ask the late baker's wife why her husband had been found half-stuck in his oven and cooked to a crisp. If the constabulary had closed the case, it was better to let the dead sleep but you can bet that Bogino was paying for the rash act committed by his mother and her lover, the maroon Julien Thémistocle. People competed in whispers to recount the filth that they got up to while the baker was ruining his health lighting his wood oven in the hours before dawn. It has to be said that they didn't try very hard to be discreet as the baker was rather deaf.

Sometimes Ma Léonce's squawking woke up the entire neighbourhood and windows shot open angrily, followed by swearing galore which in turn unleashed a chorus of barking from all the dogs in the village. This racket only succeeded in drowning out the noisy frolics of the baker's wife and Julien Thémistocle even more. So, Coolie René accepted the baker's wife's offer, and how did we know? Because before any Coolie god ceremony our man would undertake a twenty-seven-day fast. He gave up hanging around outside the houses of the mulattos just after mealtimes so that he'd be given the leftovers ('It's for your pig,' they used to say), or at the market, where the occasional blue jack or tuna fin might have been left behind. He also gave up going to Small Balls Auguste's bar and the even more sordid ones on Back Street, where people bought him rum punches just to see him stagger about in the street. When this happened, Coolie René would set off at about four in the afternoon on the long, hard road that would take him back to Long-Bois, fortified by several quarts of rum. Just trying to get out of the rum shop he would knock over two or three tables, to the joy of the gleeful customers who shouted:

'*Wop! Wo-o-o-op!*' (Whoops! Whoo-oo-oo-oops!)

He would screw his palm-leaf hat tightly on to his head and stare giddily up Back Street as if to make sure that his usual propping-up points were still in place. He stepped off the pavement and, shaking with hiccups, carefully put one foot in front of the other before slipping on the mud in the gutter and falling flat on his face.

'*Wop! Wo-o-o-op!*' they shouted.

A car horn brought him to his senses and the poor fool crouched with difficulty before getting to his feet to continue his wending way. His second stopping place was outside the window of Passionise, the mulatto woman and whore, who slammed her shutters tightly closed in alarm and fury and would have suffocated if the Indian's stay had been a long one. At this point, there was always a facetious fellow who would shout:

'Hey, darling, the Coolie priest would like a little cuddle, for God's sake!'

Normally, Coolie René summoned up enough strength to make it to the electricity pole opposite the parish hall. There, a group of good-for-nothings would be playing cards or dominoes, protected by its shade. If, unfortunately, Chief Bérard was among them, he would inflict his violent bad temper on Coolie René. Aiming *damier* fighter's kicks into his ribs, he yelled:

'Beggar coolie! Piss-smelling coolie, get out of my sight! I've seen enough coolies for today.'

Coolie René collapsed again on the baking afternoon tarmac without so much as a cry of pain. One of the card-players went up to him, lifted his head and stuck a rum bottle into his mouth, forcing him to swallow enough to knock out four people. Somehow the Indian managed to get back on to his bony feet and reach the church steps, where the village gossips were waiting for six o'clock prayers. They screamed at him (as the church door was still shut):

'Aren't you ashamed, coolie? If you came to Jesus Christ instead of mixing with the devil, you wouldn't be in a state like that.'

He sat down on the bottom step, just long enough to catch his breath, and as the bells rang out he set off again. Hidden behind the war memorial for those who died for France, a gang of urchins ambushed him and bombarded him with anything they could find that was round: pebbles, genip stones fired with a catapult, ball bearings, punctured footballs. An impassive Coolie René climbed the little hill leading to the hospital, where he fell over again. The caretaker said his usual few words as he poured a bucket of water over him:

'*Tout kouli ni an kout dalo pou fè nan lavi yo.*' (All Indians end up one day in the gutter.)

Afterwards, darkness descended to rule supreme and, in any case, he was by now beyond the village. Nobody cared about him any more and it was never known how or at what time he made it back to Long-Bois. So when we saw him neatly turned out (khaki shirt and ironed trousers), clean shaven and combed, sporting sandals rather than his usual bare feet, and, above all, without a drop of rum inside him, we knew that he was preparing his body to receive the gods of India. A sort of respect mixed with terror worked its way under the mockers' skin and they shivered with goose pimples as he went past. Coolie René would agree to officiate on behalf of any race once the person in question, male or female, who wanted the spell made, had deposited the sum needed to buy the animals for sacrifice and the bags of rice that would be used for the collective meal which would follow. As a charitable soul, he even forgave those such as Ma Léonce who scorned Indians since, as he insisted, 'if the person is bad, the gods will turn against him'. When she brought up the case of her son Bogino, the *poussari* at once interrupted:

'Only Madouraïviren can do anything for madness.'

And he then reeled off an impressive list of vital objects and fruits:

'You must bring me fifteen camphor sticks, a metre of green material, red and white cotton, three hands of bananas, seven dry coconuts, a pan, some *vèpèlè* leaves, some powdered saffron, a little paraffin lamp, a litre of rum . . .'

It was common knowledge that the baker's wife had transgressed the strictures of the Catholic, apostolic and Roman Holy Church in her frantic search for those plants known only to Indians. Suddenly less arrogant, she would ask each of her customers in a childish little voice:

'I need some *vèpèlè* leaves. It's for the headaches that are making my life a misery. If you could just bring me some next time you come, my dear . . .'

But no black man could do anything to help her, since the plants to which coolies ascribed magic properties were otherwise considered to be weeds and didn't even have names in Creole or French. Aware of his temporary advantage over her, the cattle-slaughterer came to see the baker's wife every day and taunted her with deliberate cruelty:

'You're the one who set the date for the ceremony. Madouraïviren is waiting. Don't bring his wrath down on yourself. Have you cut the *vèpèlè* leaves yet?'

'I . . . I'll get them.'

'Less of the "I . . . I . . . I . . ." Madouraïviren won't listen to that sort of story, oh no.'

As the date drew nearer, one 10th of June in the year 1954, if you can believe Thimoléon, a shitless fear seized the baker's wife. She quizzed Émilien Bérard, who had just taken his teacher's certificate exams; Syrian, who had once done the rounds in the countryside with his cart and so knew the Indian villages; *maître* Féquesnoy, the lawyer, whose learning earned him recognition from as far away as Town; Small Balls Auguste, who had resorted to the goddess Mariémen to enlarge his proportions without obvious success and, finally, anyone of any standing in Grand-Anse. In despair, she condescended to speak to the women who sell coal and the beggars. To the two whores, the negress Myrtha and the mulatto girl Passionise. To Rose-Aimée, Syrian's ex-wife, who was now living in a pigsty in the En Chéneaux district. Luckily for her, carnival was already over, as otherwise the words 'Ma Léonce' and *'vèpèlè'* would doubtless have featured in some wild biguine that would have wrecked her pridefulness for the rest of her days. With the hurricane season on its way and people's minds on other things, it was enough to nickname her 'Vèpèlè' behind her back. Two days before the date in question, Ma Léonce saw that scoundrel Dachine coming towards her shop, waving his tick book in one hand and hiding the other behind his back in a deliberate way. It took the baker's wife, dazed by sleepless nights and more and more terrified by the deadline that Coolie René had forced on her, an eternity of time to realize that the municipal dustman was offering a swap: the cancellation of his debts for April and May in return for a bunch of *nèpèlè* leaves. She could have wept for joy as she tossed his tick book into her bread oven. It had never crossed her mind to resort to the man of whom it was said in Grand-Anse that by emptying people's dustbins he had ended up fathoming their souls and making himself familiar with their every vice and virtue.

Somewhat disconcerted, Coolie René came that same afternoon

to collect the various ingredients that he had demanded. He declared to Ma Léonce:

'Tomorrow you must lock up your son for the whole day. He must not speak to anyone, look at a woman, wet his lips in a glass of rum or swear at all.'

As soon as things were going her way, looking OK, making her day, Ma Léonce became her usual arrogant self again, a development which pushed Chief Thimoléon, our carpenter, into taking action. The motive for his bitterness (and vengeance) against the baker's wife remains unknown to this very day. He at once dismissed the solution consisting of meeting Coolie René on a lonely path and giving him such a hiding that he would need at least a month to recover. Although age was catching up with him, Thimoléon remained a hard man who was feared for his agility in *damier* fighting, and all knew that he could call on a secret blow which had laid low more than one big-mouth from Grand-Anse, Ajoupa-Bouillon and Basse-Pointe. To follow this course of action would, in any case, merely serve to delay the Coolie god ceremony. What he needed to do was to damage the Indian's very power to intercede between men and gods, to destroy him as a *poussari*. After much thought, he came to the conclusion that only Myrtha and Passionise, the two whores, could help him in his heinous crime since he had developed a devilish plan: to force Coolie René to break his fast and the sexual abstinence which it implied. Like any self-respecting chief, Thimoléon was screwing several women at the same time and held what amounted to life-or-death rights over them. He had only to open his mouth and Justina from Morne l'Étoile or Francelise from Fond Gens-Libres would go and give themselves to the Indian priest, but he was aware that this would be to inflict a humiliation on them that they hadn't deserved and above all that once the deed was done, it would condemn them to social disgrace. For who would want anything to do with a slut who'd let a coolie climb on top of her? Even he, Thimoléon, would have to stop seeing the woman in question, and he liked each one of them too much to allow any to be sacrificed.

'Me?' protested the buxom Myrtha when Thimoléon confided in her. 'Me, do it with that race? You can offer me the seven wonders of the world, darling, and I still wouldn't accept.'

Passionise, the mulatto woman, gave an ugly grin before saying:

'I do it with Congos who are as black as them, so it's not a question of colour. But what about these coolies, eh? It's said they've got pricks like corkscrews and, what's worse, they smell of fish. What's in it for me?'

The carpenter didn't hesitate for a single second. He took the prostitute by the arm and led her to his workshop, where he at once shut all doors and windows. Without offering any explanation, he started ripping up the floorboards one by one, then, taking a fork, he dug with the energy of a man possessed. Passionise thought he was having a fit or had suddenly gone mad and cried:

'Are you going to bury me alive?'

'Not at all, my dear. I'm not of the same breed as those Guinea blacks Julien Thémistocle and Chief Bérard. I've always done good to those around me and that's what I'm doing now. Be patient!'

For hours he dug until he had made a hole so big that he had vanished. Passionise fought against the waves of panic that threatened to overwhelm her. Her dress was drenched with sweat and her eyes were smarting. Suddenly she heard a dull noise from the bottom of the hole and saw a satisfied-looking carpenter climbing out.

'It's yours, my *doudou*, if you agree to make love with Coolie René.'

'What are you talking about?'

'Bend over and look! Go on, come to the edge. Look, I'll light a candle so you can see better.'

The mulatto woman could make out a crock overflowing with gold coins, which were shining despite the layer of mud that had covered them.

'The *béké* de Cassagnac's crock of gold?' she said disbelievingly. 'But how is it here? Isn't it supposed to be buried somewhere in the Séguineau estate?'

'Ha, ha, ha! You foolish creature! Of course, you're so young. Crocks of gold travel underground, my girl, especially the ones next to which the *békés* used to bury slaves who had just tried to escape. For it to have come as far as here, de Cassagnac's grandfather must have sacrificed at least three or four blacks to finish off his dirty deed. Now it's yours, Passionise. Go and find Coolie René and then come back here. I'll wrap it up in a cardboard box, people today are so envious . . .'

The flabbergasted whore was chewing on her hair, unable to put two words together. The carpenter opened a window and calmly began planing the door of a chest of drawers that he had prepared. He seemed to have all the time in the world.

'*Ou . . . ou genyen!*' (You . . . you win!) she shouted as she rushed outside.

Contrary to custom, bush radio only offers one and the same version of what happened next. Passionise made her way to the municipal abattoir, where she at once undressed in front of a blood-stained Coolie René. The Indian, who had never had a mulatto woman, leapt on top of her and made quick work of it among the sticky offal and animal carcasses that littered the place. The whore felt pleasure for the first time in her life and thanked the Virgin Mary for having found more happiness in one day than in twenty-six years of existence. The sadness that she read in Coolie René's eyes after their frolics were finished cut her daydreaming short and put a dull fear in her heart. She rushed back to the carpenter in order to claim her reward. Thimoléon ignored her. He was busy varnishing his chest of drawers, his tongue sticking out with concentration. He gestured irritably at the hole with his chin. Passionise hurried to the edge of it and couldn't make out the bottom. She lit the candle again and held it over the side, but with no more success.

'Where's my crock? *My crock?*' she screamed, dancing with rage.

'It's too bad you didn't take it before, sweetie. I did tell you: crocks never stop moving about. I can't help it.'

The next morning she boarded the 'Golem' and bought a ticket for France. As for Coolie René, who had infringed the rule of chastity essential to the Indian sacrifice that he was preparing for Ma Léonce, he now knew that he was finished. He would never be anything in the eyes of the men of his race. And nothing in the eyes of other men who had used his services. But, above all, he was nothing in the eyes of the gods of India. His temple would be deserted. His statues, brought over on the first boats from Tamil Nadu and Karnataka, would be abandoned to the wrath of the fanatical Catholics and the even more intolerant Adventists. He also thought of fleeing from Grand-Anse, but where could he go, since he had invested all his savings in buying a butcher's shop in Front Street? In any case, he could neither put back nor cancel the date of the ceremony, as it had been decreed to him by Madouraïviren himself. For several days on end he wandered on the beach like his father had done and realized that he had forgotten most of the Tamil prayers that he had taught him. He stumbled over the first few words before a great emptiness settled in his head, which began to hurt. Terrified, on the eve of the ceremony he tried a desperate move; he went to church and begged Christ to come to his aid. The solemnity of its atmosphere brought him a little peace and courage. He felt his confidence returning and prepared Bogino to receive the blessings of Madouraïviren. He washed his body with fresh cow's milk and perfumed it with saffron. Ma Léonce was in seventh heaven: even before the Coolie god's intervention, her son was showing signs of improvement as regards his behaviour with other people. He had stopped insulting the customers at the baker's shop who wished him good day and even helped the delivery man load the sacks of bread into his camionnette. Syrian went as far as to congratulate her on this metamorphosis since Bogino more often than not used to sleep off his rum on the pavement outside the Palace of the Orient, which put off many customers from going in. The lunatic would grab hold of them, splutter into their faces, accuse their mothers of all sorts of filth and finally demand some small change.

On the said day, the temple at Long-Bois received Ma Léonce, her son and a handful of Indian priests. The baker's wife had left the date secret so that busy bodies wouldn't come and meddle in her affairs or big guts come and feast at her expense. As if by a miracle, Coolie René officiated perfectly and intoned his prayers without hesitation, while the incense smoke mixed with the plaintive sound of the tassa drums, the profusion of red flowers and golden statues, combined with the sound of the nearby sea, created an overwhelming atmosphere which merely emphasized the paucity of those people present, waiting for Madouraïviren to come and answer their prayers. Bogino acted like a little child. He went into the temple's inner sanctum, humbly kissed the god's sword, knelt and stammered out the strange words that the *poussari* ordered him to repeat, and allowed himself to be covered in all sorts of Indian oils and perfumes which smelled strangely good. Dressed in white, cleanly shaved by Honorat Congo, he seemed on the verge of recovering his sanity. The drama erupted just as Coolie René was to cut off the heads of the two sacrificial sheep. An anxious silence took hold of the priests who stood well away from him, leaving him, it seemed, to his fate. Coolie René, who until now had been operating in a sort of euphoria, was suddenly distracted by the image of Passionise's intoxicating body and his arm flinched at the last moment, deflecting the knife's blade from the thin line on the sheep's neck where his father had taught him to strike and which he had never missed since he'd replaced the old man. The animal reared up in a spray of hot blood, its head hanging down between its front legs. The priests gave a cry of horror and moved further away. Coolie René stood frozen in the harsh sunlight, his bloody cutlass in his hand, not knowing what to say or do. Suddenly, Madouraïviren descended into the head of Bogino, who began to smash everything around him. He wrecked the temple, flung the statues into the river mouth and grabbed the half-decapitated sheep to attack Ma Léonce and the priests, who took refuge in a nearby banana grove. Coolie René made it back to the village by the beach, eager to die, to be carried far away under the waters of that cruel sea which must, he thought, have had a hand in his disaster. He let himself drift in the water, not fighting against the waves, but they, in their stubbornness, carried him back to the shore, even from the whirlpool, beneath the hospital, where normally there is no escape for the careless.

Several weeks later, Grand-Anse had returned to its usual lethargy. Bogino had become even madder than before and his mother had begged forgiveness from the gods of the Bible for having betrayed them. Coolie René, for his part, lived in constant terror, although his butcher's shop was beginning to do well, for he was sure that sooner or later Madouraïviren would come and settle accounts. And he knew that the millennial god's vengeance would be terrible . . .

Eau de Café can read tomorrow in our dreams.

She tells me: 'Shut that window for me, so that the sea salt doesn't ruin my silver,' as she shivers at hearing the insistent echoes of La Crabière.

Over there, at the end of the Grand-Anse bay, La Crabière is a deserted promontory that makes an extraordinary gesture of defiance towards the flank of the Atlantic. Although the sea grape trees attracted us, we village kids weren't allowed to go there at midday, the supposedly demonic hour.

Sometimes she called over her crony the carpenter, who boasted of having fought in the '14–'18 war, and they settled his account over a good quarter of rum. They were probably trying to forget that sea, that trader in innocent bodies (Antilia's was more innocent than any other) and in amorous transactions, never tiring of gnawing at our lives. They nurtured their fear and taught it to us like a very venerable legend, while we laughed ourselves silly over these old folk's tales.

It's there before me, found again at last, the Grand-Anse, immense in immaculate darkness. I feel the urge to shout at it – although nobody would hear my words, too absorbed as they are in building up their daily delusions:

'I hate you for having reaped so many and such quantities of our fantasies and for not having given them back. What's more, the village has turned its back on you. Our tongues have turned away from you . . . we no longer venerate your name! We've stopped saying: September sea, O sea transported by shivering effluvia, by spindle-shanks dreams . . . or whatever might tickle a poet's fancy. We don't give a shit!'

Eau de Café won't accept my indifference. She tells me: 'If you came here, it was to understand, so understand, damn you!' She insists on regaling me mercilessly with the daring deeds of Julien Thémistocle, 'an old man who has had his finger in a whole lot of lives and deaths that are all worth hearing about'. Hot air! What's it do with me now that I've grown up and Godmother is now an ancestor? The proof: she smokes a clay pipe.

She won't give up. Her Thémistocle, the one she loved, died when he left to join the *dissidence,* or so she says. Ah, the *dissidence!* I imagine it as a dark province beyond La Crabière, between land, sea and hell. Only a gang of more-or-less outlaw coolies tried to scrape a living there and I'm not sure if the old iron bridge that enabled you to get there still exists. Once upon a time, a locomotive loaded with sweet-smelling sugar-cane used to roll along between its thickets, heading for the Fond Brûlé distillery.

Suddenly the carpenter shouts out: 'I want a *coucoune!* Yeah, I want a *coucoune!*' He sounds just like a boar having its throat cut on Christmas day. Eau de Café shakes her head wearily. She starts filling her pipe with the tobacco that they probably make in secret for her at Morne Capot. '*Coucoune!*' the madman shouts again, referring, in the all but obsolete language of our people, to a woman's private parts. For that language had shattered into shining shards which had lodged themselves in heads, bodies and the warmth of hands, veritable kites with broken strings.

He grabs my arm (outside the sea's rage is mounting): 'In any case,' he says, 'when you see the dice stop like it's been thrown off balance in mid course and frozen white, it's because somebody has wanted to silence it. I swear it! Didn't you play, over there, in their white-man country?'

'I played and I lost,' I say with an embarrassed smile.

Godmother is not happy about the way things are going. Perhaps she'd hoped that I would hold her by the arm as we crossed Front Street so that people (and especially the rabble) would at last realize that she wasn't an old forgotten bag of bones and that there will be a gentleman at her funeral who can speak French. As soon as I arrived at the house, she took me upstairs and carefully opened a battered Carib basket to get out a splendid blue poplin dress.

'I want to wear this when I go. Feel it!'

Her face shone with justified pride, the pride of a black woman who had spent her whole life breaking her back amidst the whites' sugar-cane and then on her own patch of ground, and who had fled to the village before she became permanently rooted in the soil, in other words before turning into a savage. I am moved by this and ask her stupidly:

'Are you thinking of dying, Godmother?'

'Ha, ha, ha! . . . Anyway, even if I don't give it any thought, I'm sure it's got me in mind. Look at Ma Léonce! That old girl only thought about enjoying life and when the moment came, we had to have a collection to pay for her coffin. Pah!'

So, she wants me to understand, nothing looks any different here. Still the same square of up-and-down houses mouldering in their distinguished boredomness and encircled by a hateful sea. Sea of Grand-Anse and the secret of its barren womb that I've long sought to work out inside myself, unconvinced as I am by what is said here and there. Like every inhabitant of this place, I am periodically struck down by an unpredictable torment that we call falling sickness. I have searched in a thousand and one allusions, in the drummer's throbbing thunder heaved heavenwards, in the eye-winking or hip-swaying of the women carrying their offerings to the sea at dusk in versatile enamel pots. In the exodus of the wet season's last rains, pursued by January's bad temper. Even in the 'Help!' cried out by souls in distress, caught by the cold current at Morne l'Étoile. So I came back in order to find.

'When the dice tumbles on to the table,' begins the old rum drinker again, 'after it's been rubbed hard and re-rubbed in a palm, and then stops . . . dead! . . . It's because someone's got wind that it's already made up its mind and they want to test it again so that it works by chance alone. Do you follow? . . . In any case, when you see this happen, keep your mouth shut, keep your urge to protest safely in your guts even if it hurts and don't move, don't move away from the others (they would put you back in your rightful place with just one piece of mockery): an event is taking place, a clash between two iron wills. It's not your place to get involved, mosquito turd, or at least speak your mind beforehand, for Christ's sake! Make your position clear by eleven in the morning when mass has been said and the women have cleared away the fish market with comic haste and put the gaming trestles on to their wobbly legs.'

'You, get back to your hammer and nails!'

It's an order from Godmother, who is struggling with him to get her word in and is keen to talk about Julien Thémistocle at any price. She has learnt from an entire existence of sweat and exhaustion that words are not made to be wasted. Speech isn't water dripping from the sky to be lost in the depths of the earth. When she had decided to hitch her life to that red-skinned man's, she had a feeling that she had transgressed and expected someone to come at any moment and give her news that would make her collapse with grief. And, when she heard a hurried footstep outside her house and Thémistocle wasn't already home, she would listen to the beating of her heart in her frail chest before pulling back the bolt.

'You've got me dying on the brain,' he laughed.

'Me?' she replied, cut to the quick. 'What use to me would be the death of a navvy like you who's spent his life scratching away at the soil and to harvest what, if you please? Bad luck!'

Through the window that looks out on to Front Street, the only one always open, you can see the swelling of the hills surprisingly close by. In the street people are strolling about seemingly unconcerned. Women in their shining finery create the unreal illusion of bustle right in the middle of the dry season heat. The tarmac glistens as if polished. I can make out a tiny figure picking up rubbish from around the town hall. It's Dachine, the one and only municipal dustman.

Godmother has made some Macédoine hot chocolate that she gives me in an imitation china cup. Still hanging on the wall – and it's only now that I realize it – is that dreadfully gaudy picture of a deer hunt, behind which a grey lizard used to hide, and on the sideboard stands a bust of a horribly blond crucified Christ.

The carpenter takes hold of my arm. I jump since I'd forgotten him inside his halo of rum. The bulging veins on his hand carry his blood with a jerky rhythm that makes me feel inexplicably ill at ease. I look for Godmother's watery green eyes, but she has already given me up. She is imperceptibly moving in her worn-out rocking-chair, one hand on her forehead and the other holding on to the arm of the chair. In what unfathomable calculation can she be immersed? I then realize that this is the image of her that I would like to keep.

The carpenter is thinking what to say. Outside, I can again hear – as if it's ever been quiet! – the sea somersaulting, down below the house. From Anse Charpentier to Grande-Rivière it never tires of bruising us, of stabbing at our hearts. I wrote about it over there, lost in European greyness, when I was pretending to be a poet: 'September sea, you rot those loves miraculously protected from gossip since the sweetness of the copses is no myth, nor the scent of the plum tree. I run with bare childlike feet on the black sand, O polisher of rare and sonorous rocks that the Seance Master used for his soothsaying!' But I lost my way in such fantasies . . .

'If you want to make an impression at dice, you arrive, your shirt undone, your stomach hairs bristling,' says Thimoléon again, 'and you shout out loud: "This evening, Mr So-And-So, I'll be leaving five hundred thousand francs richer" and you wander from table to table, sneering, so that people get a good look at your face and remember the gist of your words. Your face, that's the important thing! Because nobody bothers with what you're wearing, with your shoes or any of that, but your mother and all her offspring are written on your face and when people start the insults, they like to know what they're talking about. Ah! It's not that they've got it in for mothers in general, but just for yours and yours alone, so that the words make you feel the same damp burning pain as after a whip lash. So much so that you're now the object of the gathering's mockery and you're covered in shame. And you haven't even felt the dice, warmed them up, stroked them. Above all, on no account let them confuse you with one of those callow youths who work in town and think they can do anything just because they can string two words of French together. When, as it's starting, they storm the gaming tables, stupidly yelling "Eleven! Eleven!" and thinking they can sweep the board, you can be sure that by quarter to twelve they'll be as drunk as old skunks, hunched on the steps outside the market and speaking Creole again in order to beg you for enough for a bet and calling you "Boss".'

Eau de Café is smiling enigmatically. She butts in and starts talking again, ignoring her crony.

The tussle between her and Julien Thémistocle had taken root, in a manner of speaking, in Franciane's womb. You see, when she was pregnant with Eau de Café, Thémistocle, who was suffering a thousand torments after the collapse of his marriage to Passionise, caught her in the undergrowth and violently screwed her. The woman passed away the very next day. As a result, Thémistocle was unanimously condemned to take the little girl as his wife as soon as she was old enough to procreate and to bring her up as her foster-father until then. So their life together had begun in the Macédoine district, in the deepest countryside, linked only to the village of Grand-Anse by a bad and stony path that gave people heat rashes and that even the priest ventured upon as little as possible.

'His father was called Jean Thémistocle and he had an incurable sore on his left leg. Jean's father's name was Marceau Thémistocle and when he referred to his own father, he simply said "Thémistocle" since in those days of slavitude a single name was enough.'

Why had she waited so long to tell me this? Did she think that when I came back I would be dying to know the ins and outs of the questions she'd always refused to answer in the past? She was mistaken: I hadn't the slightest wish to hear the history, however remarkable, of the Thémistocle lineage. After eighteen years away, there were more pressing concerns to occupy me. Above all, I didn't want to slip back into the awful torpor of Grand-Anse, of which I'd only kept meaningless bits and pieces within my memory: chipped demijohns in the mules' saddles on the Vivé estate, the animals carefree in their colonial wandering; my green calabash head rolling under the sun's fire; the laugh of the see-see bird gathering honey in the twisted maze of creepers among the skeleton bodies of the ragged blacks in Macédoine and Bon Repos; the rum-soaked speech of the manager at Fond Gens-Libres. And what was she going on about? Ah, yes! Here we go:

'Everything begins with a little seed that the wind or some other movement one day puts in your patch of land, a seed so small that it gets lost in your palm, and suddenly a sapling is born which you can't see between the clumps of pigeon peas and the castor oil tree. But if your eyeballs could see under the ground, they would be good and scared by what they saw: enormous roots as long as cut-down casuarinas, solidly wrapped around each other . . .'

Today I interpret these words as follows: the race of former masters is still living off the daily, yet grudging, toil of our race. Yet I feel it's still well short of making sense. I have come to see the Grand-Anse sea again and to make peace with it. I can no longer accept the absurd proscriptions, the interminable justifications, the repeated excommunications from apprentice clerics nor even the warning issued to me by Small Balls Auguste when I greeted him this morning:

'Don't go swimming whatever you do, eh! You know what you're like.'

As for Godmother, she all but fainted when I suddenly wrestled with the shutter looking out towards the sea and managed to unjam it from a decade of immobility. The harsh wind seemed to scrape at my eyes but at a glance I could see the vast white rollers, indefatigable and ever-changing, which had once disturbed my nights.

'Do you want to kill me, my boy?' the old woman had implored, almost in tears.

'I wanted to make sure it was still there,' I had dared to joke, but she had already carefully sealed the baleful opening, leading me downstairs.

Grand-Anse sea, I thought, nobody has eyes or ears any more for your endless repetitiveness. *You no longer exist*. And yet for all that, it's from your foamy nets that at dawn we pluck out the human flotsam of a lost soul, and may they be damned, the village blacks, for there they are again, blaming you! Bitch of a slut of a sea! Whore of a sea who never stops messing up our children's lives! And names and more names, O much-hated Grand-Anse sea!

This displeasantness always takes place according to the same ritual: three times the municipal siren's strident scream cuts the air's false calm to shreds and we rush from all around. From En Chéneaux, from La Cité, from Crochemort, from Redoute, from Bord de Terrain. We call out our sorrow, we tear out our eyelashes, we bite our lips. Every mother screams in the instinctive language that comes from who knows where:

'Oti yich mwen an?' (Where's my child?)

The watery face of the Anse is trampled by a stampede of terrified feet, challenging the insolent silence of the waves. The most experienced (or the bravest) rush to beneath the hospital, where rockslides accompany the never-ending flash floods of the rainy season. There, right in the bowels of the sea, there is a bottomless abyss which a current constantly fills with whatever passes within reach. Others try further to the North, almost at the edge of the haughty Crabière. In this place the water is deceptively calm and myriads of hermit crabs scuttle away at the slightest squeak from a seabird. And among rocks as sharp as a foreman's cutlass, young men, eager to show off their courage, try, this time well to the south of the Anse, to climb under the waterfall which pours down from the very shoulder of the cliff and whose water is reputed to give you a fierce itch on account of running through fields of Portuguese yams. But nobody finds anything and they start wandering under the sun's delirium, bumping into each other, exchanging harsh, if not filthy, words and sometimes coming to blows. Old women crumple up their headscarves and dip them into the salt water, which they drink down in one. Because if the sea can take, so can man, for God's sake! And nobody will rest until the body is given back.

Then Bogino, the madman, wakes up from his drunken stupor

in the rum shop on Back Street and casually wanders across the tiny church square. It's now been three hours that people have been peering into the monster's maw and they are anxious to know who could have made the sacrifice of his life. Who? Bogino strides along the sand with unaccustomed dignity and approaches Adelise, the maid at the presbytery. He says to her:

'Your brother is lying at the mouth of the Capote. You won't find him here. In any case, he departed this world long ago.'

What a sight to see everybody rush, whether on foot, by mule or in a lurching bus, to the place in question: a little creek to the south of ours, almost uninhabited, where we used to come and eat crabs at Easter. And we find Adelise's brother, gorged with greenish foam that trickles from his mouth, his stomach as swollen as a doubly pregnant woman's.

14 Be Queen Among Us

And the Madonna came.

We who had barely taken notice of Antilia's prophetic words (all the more so since the euphoria provoked by the finishment of the war against that he-pig Hitler was clouding our nights with dreams of happiment) were speechless. The rumour was first started by two alms-hunters from Back Street and we supposed that it was a way of getting their hands on some small change, given how our ears are always open to fantastic tales. Ma Léonce, who was permanently on the look-out for the slightest supernatural help in her effort to cure her son Bogino's cretinism, gave them any number of bottles of rum in a bid to find out more. In between throwing up, our beggars told her that Town had given itself up to boundless rejoicing, that the church bells were ring-a-dinging around the clock and that even those blacks most steeped in roguishness had rediscovered the sign of the cross. They themselves were crossing themselves plentifully and in their eyes a fever was brewing that owed nothing to alcohol.

Soon trustworthy individuals were able to confirm the news. The vegetable-market women seemed the most rapturous and, instead of explaining to others what was going on, were already busying themselves in preparation for the Madonna's coming. At that time, Grand-Anse had been endowed with a grumbling priest, of Flemish origins, who was even more sceptical than our philosopher, Émilien Bérard. When he had been asked to exorcise a house that was visited each night by zombies, he chased us away, muttering:

'Go homes! Go on, go homes!'

After which he was nicknamed 'Go homes', while we fervently prayed that Monsignor the Bishop would send him homes as well. He clearly did not take his parishioners' reports seriously and breathed not a word about it from the pulpit the following Sunday, which made these ladies decide to dispense with his authorization and go ahead with laying flowers around the church and building a platform on which to welcome that being which all and sundry had come to know with the greatest respectation as the Virgin of the Great Return.

The first miracle among the plentitude of miracles which were to brighten our lives for a good month in the year of grace 1948 was the conversion of Master Ali Tanin, who deflowered as easily as he breathed, to the great distress of the mothers of young girls in bloom. He had been to Fort-de-France, as he did each week to stock up the Palace of the Orient, and instead of broadcasting the tittle-tattle of his urban adventures, began prophesying, bible in hand, at the entrance to his shop.

'She has crossed the ocean just to save us from damnationness, ladies and gentlemen!' he shouted. 'She is whiter than cassava flour, purer than a child's tear, more generous than any mother has ever been since the world began. Prepare to receive her! Let those who live in dishonesty make ready to repent!'

From what he said, the immaculate statue had floated on to the calm waters of Town's bay, haloed with a light like no other with the power to bring peace suddenly into your heart. The park at La Savane had been decorated with holy palms, with multicoloured garlands and sky-blue bunting. *Monsieur* the Governor in person, as well as Monsignor Varin de la Brunelière, were on the quay side to welcome the Holy Virgin. So thick were the crowds that the constabulary had no choice but to wield their truncheons in order to clear a passage for the procession to reach the cathedral. Everyone wanted to touch the feet of the Madonna, who had not been lifted out from her boat and who was carried aloft in a tumult of hymns to her glory, feverish prayers, oaths and incense smoke.

'When she came past where I was standing', the half-Syrian told us, 'I felt that until that moment I had been living a life of knavishness, shamelessly abusing anything that wore knickers and a brassiere. A kind of chill ran down my back, I knelt down, sweat soaked the back of my shirt and I felt my lips move to say a prayer of contrition. Yes, gentlemen, me, Ali Tanin, I who have never confessed in my life!'

The Muslim took off his yellow-stoned ring and watch, took out a wad of bank-notes that he always kept in his belt in case a bargain should crop up, and threw the lot into the Madonna's boat. In the cathedral only the big whites, the Governor and Monsignor, were allowed in to be present at her installation. A verger had shut the doors and stood firmly on the steps, holding his silver-handled staff threateningly. When, in the end of all ends, the crowd was let inside – they filed in quietly in two columns, surprise, surprise! – a cry of admiration, amplified by the cathedral vaults, escaped from their lungs: the Madonna and her boat were enthroned right in the middle of the altar, surrounded by a swarm of acolytes holding enormous All Saints' Day candles high in the air. You should have seen the procession of the Creole aristocracy, ladies and gentlemen, the Dupin de Médeuils, the Laguarrande de Chervilles, the Crassin de Médouzes and others of that ilk, their faces filled with such piety that you might almost forget that most of them were bedding their black servants, when not living in sin with them. The prayers they were uttering were so fervent that you could swear they weren't the same lot who paid their cane-cutters in small change. But here they were throwing crisp new bank-notes at the feet of the Madonna, so many and so much so that the boat, perched high in the nave, began to overflow. When the mulattos made their appearance, the priests had to call on the good will of two bare-chested labourers who crammed the booty into big guano sacks which they carried behind the altar. The Fort-de-France mulattos didn't want to be seen to be mean: they rid themselves of purses, jewels and other valuables under the radiant gaze of the Madonna, whose head had been framed with shining light bulbs. Outside, the blacks were waiting their turn and singing:

Be queen among us!
Virgin of the Great Return!

Then the cathedral was filled with strumpets who sell their charms to foreign sailors in the Cour Fruit-à-Pain, big mouths whose only work consists of making up imaginary exploits around the kiosk on La Savane, boozers from Bord de Canal, wretches, wasters and wastrels from l'Ermitage and Trénelle, assassinators from Terres-Sainvilles, in short all the rabble and riff-raff that Town has to offer. Even the formidable Goldmouth, who had been on the run since before the war on account of an impressive number of exceptionally evil misdeeds, made his appearance under the nose of the authorities.

'I, Ali Tanin, I saw him with my seeing eyes begging forgiveness from the Most Holy Madonna. His hands clasped together in prayer, he called out: "Mother of Christ, you who have come from France to save us blacks from brigandage, I am just a little boy in your presence! Until today I admit I have lived in ignoration with those like me, but what other fate was reserved for me? In Morne Pichevin our race lives in the most total dishonouration. When the wind blows, the corrugated iron flies off our houses like a kite and when the sun is beating down, they become hot like ovens. Our children don't have shoes or books to go to school with and their mouths are forced to mangle French. Our women have nothing to fall back on except lewdness, and as for us, if we couldn't steal from the port, we would have starved a century of time ago. Forgive us, O Virgin of the Great Return, but lighten, I beg you, our load! The black man sweated too hard in the days of slavery to put up with any more suffering . . ."'

'I tell you, not one person moved, not a single cop tried to get him into handcuffs, and all this not because they were afraid of his notorious Durandal flick knife, but because the fellow was exuding faith. Faith, ladies and gentlemen! Thanks to faith, Goldmouth had stopped his devious ways and everyone realized that his sins were immediately absolved. He hadn't been cleared by a courtroom of men, but by God's tribunal. And as he was a man without bank accounts, a penniless ruffian, he wrenched out one of his precious golden teeth and put it as an offering into the Madonna's boat. Don't laugh! He did it in front of me and in front

120

of many other eyes and we were all amazed, in heaven's name! From now on, Ali Tanin will serve the Virgin of the Great Return. No more will he utter crude words or act inconsiderately with women. He has become another sort of man.'

Two people listened carefully to the half-Syrian's account: *maître* Féquesnoy and Eau de Café. The former, a freemason since the age of twenty-five and a leading member of the Radical Socialist Party, at first reacted with holy horror to what Ali Tanin was describing. He was already alarmed that reactionaries and Creole whites would take advantage of events to reinforce their positions and – who knows? – win the Grand-Anse town council. But realizing that the next elections were far enough away, he began to think instead of what had been his main torment over the years, together, of course, with his three daughters' failure to marry, that is to say his lack of erections. It had all started quite unexpectedly one evening when he had been to visit Passionise in her home on Back Street. Much as she sucked him, tickled him, caressed him all over and whispered filthy words into his ear, his cock refused to show any time other than half past six. He had resorted secretly to the powers of Coolie René, who had made him drink a concoction of saffron and barbadine and had invoked the blessings of the goddess Mariémen without achieving the slightest result.

'You didn't treat what I prescribed you with enough seriosity,' the Indian had concluded, refusing all payment.

Julien Thémistocle, the maroon, had prepared for him an infusion of stiff-tree bark, cow heel extract and sea-turtle penis without unwrinkling the lawyer's virility and, in desperation, had sent him to an old witch-doctor who at the age of a hundred and twelve was withering away in some godforsaken plain near Morne Jacob. Black experts had no more success than their Hindu colleagues and *maître* Féquesnoy was reduced to giving up his various mistresses, apart from one whom he'd kept since well before his wife's death, their passion having evolved into fondness which involved neither touching nor undressing. Needless to say, his reputation suffered accordingly and this course of

events was put down to his proverbial miserliness. 'He's probably unearthed some France-white for his eldest daughter,' it was
whispered, 'and he has to buy her trousseau. Or perhaps he'd
incurred a terrible gambling debt, knowing his taste for baccarat.'
Although his secret was kept safe by Passionise, the lawyer
refused to accept that a fifty-year-old as handsome as himself
could admit defeat at the very moment of removing a wench's
clothes. Little by little, despite the convictions he espoused at the
lodge, he became convinced that somebody had cast a spell on
him, and not any old spell if you please, since he had done everything to lift it, but to no avail. So he trembled with joy upon hearing the half-Syrian's story and was the first among Grand-Anse's
upper crust to agree that the fellow wasn't talking nonsense.
Maître Féquesnoy resolved to think of the best way to make his
appeal to the Virgin of the Great Return. If he stayed to wait for
her there, he would have no chance of approaching her, even
though he was deputy mayor, for the simple reason that he was
prominent among the ranks of religion's enemies. Just as much as
Coolie René and his Indian divinities. Or Julien Thémistocle and
his African sorcery. Or as much as Ali Tanin and his father who
worshipped Mohammed without bothering to conceal it.

'A damned freemason is a devil!' was the blunt judgment of the
village bigots.

His act of repentance, he decided, would have to take the most
spectacular form possible, however mortifying. Imagine the general surprise when he was seen one early morning climbing
aboard the 'Executioner of the North' bus with his youngest and
middle daughters. His Studebaker, although feeling its age, still
ran perfectly and did less obnoxious back-firing than the island
white de Cassagnac's front-wheel-drive. It's true that the lawyer
only used it once a month to go to Fort-de-France or to some rich
mulatto's house if a matrimonial match-making gathering was
being organized somewhere in the island. He was dressed all in
white and was humbly carrying a Panama hat in his hand. None
of the other passengers returned his greeting, not because they
held grudges against him for his insolent treatment of the poor,

but because they were immersed in conjecture as to the meaning of his current behaviour. You would have to be a true Saint Thomas to believe that a mulatto would happily sit next to those fat black women vegetable-sellers who were speaking the coarsest Creole you could possibly imagine. Master Salvie, the driver, was flattered by it since it would reinforce the idea that his bus carried only respectable people and not louts like the 'Golem'. When the latter, filled as usual well before his bus (what do you expect, good-for-nothing blacks haven't anything better to do early in the morning!), pulled up next to him and Chief Bérard issued the same challenge as he had every day for fifteen years ('If you get to Galion bridge before me, I'm a little nancy boy!'), Master Salvie shrugged it off.

'*Gadé kilès moun man ni abô mwen!*' (Look who I've got on board!) he said triumphantly to his eternal adversary. 'The day you stop carrying just rabble, we'll be able to have a little chat, my friend.'

Creole blacks have a saying 'a word can kill', but they don't really believe it. But Master Salvie's few simple words were responsible for sending a good ten souls to the cemetery on the downhill stretch leaving the village of Fond d'Or, according to the gloomiest version of this story. Chief Bérard, thank God, wasn't part of the carnage and managed to escape with several cracked ribs. He had wanted to better his record of only braking eight times on the journey from Grand-Anse to Fort-de-France and thereby teach yet another lesson to that big-mouth Salvie. The driver of the 'Executioner of the North' avoided any risks that morning, keen as he was to please the lawyer and his daughters whom he watched in his rear mirror. The regular passengers, for their part, remained silent as if the presence of the bourgeois had paralysed their tongues. None of them wanted to risk stumbling in French only to become a laughing stock later. The Féquesnoys uncomplainingly allowed themselves to be pushed into place by Bogino, the chock man of the bus. Once the fool was 'at work' as he said, he used to put his madness to one side and manage perfectly well to arrange the passengers on the wooden benches, to climb on to the roof to stow away their bags and, at each stop which was allowed, to place a chock, a piece of wood planed by Chief Thimoléon, under the rear right wheel of the 'Executioner of the North'. When the three mulattos got off at the *commune* of Gros-Morne, people realized, not without amazement, that they, too, were preparing to follow the Virgin of the Great Return.

'Well, well, well! Now I've seen it all!' one of the vegetable women managed to mutter.

Maître Féquesnoy and his daughters each changed into a sort of chasuble made of guano sacks and, removing shoes, rings, watches and other symbols of wealth, joined the troop of penitents who were waiting on the square in front of Gros-Morne church for the Madonna to come out. The island white, Dupin de Médeuil, dressed up like his baccarat partner, stared at him incredulously from head to foot and pretended not to recognize him. He too had brought his family, who seemed to have no difficulty joining in with the black crowd's fervent devotions. A scar-faced fellow, who seemed to have more than his share of alcohol inside him, was holding forth in front of the mob:

'The Virgin has arrived just in time in Martinique. Without Her, how could we have resurrected our faith after all the wickedness that Admiral Robert inflicted on us? I who am here speaking to you, I had sworn that if ever death came for me, I would give God a couple of "Up your mother's arse!" when I met Him. Oh yes, and why is it the black man, always the black man, still the black man who has to carry the weight of the world on his shoulders while Mister white always seems able to swim clean through the net? But today I am marching behind the Madonna, my friends, and I have relearned my Christian prayers.'

Hands clasped together, kneeling face-down or frozen in postures of ecstasy, the penitents continued to mumble the 'Be Queen Among Us', the hymn to the Virgin of the Great Return. At five in the afternoon, the *commune*'s priest and his acolytes, dressed in white and blue, processed in great pomp into the church, where, after a brief thanksgiving, the boat containing the statue of the Virgin was lifted head high. The honour of carrying the canopy was fiercely contested, some refusing to pass the task over to others despite its considerable weight. The Féquesnoys joined the procession which set off towards Trinité under the relentless late-afternoon sun. The lawyer glanced sideways at his crony, the banana planter, who was carrying in his arms his youngest child, aged five or six. He envied him for still being vigorous, while he, Féquesnoy, although of the same generation as Dupin de Médeuil, was reduced to looking at women's bodies without being able to touch them. It was when he saw the little boy's head loll heavily to one side that he realized that the island white had been a victim of his in-bred marriage. In order to keep plantations together and within the family, it was in fact the normal procedure within the caste to marry one's closest relatives. On the road, local people were putting offerings into the Virgin's boat while asking her for a helping hand, a favour, a grace or the cure for an illness. They fought among themselves to touch the Virgin's feet, nearly knocking the canopy over at each of their onslaughts. Right at the back of the procession, a ten-wheel lorry was following at walking pace, loaded with bags holding the money and jewels that people had donated to the Virgin. Two burly and bare-chested blacks were in charge of emptying the vessel at regular intervals to stop it overflowing.

'Madonna,' said the lawyer silently, 'I'm not asking for the earth. There are those who are needier than me and I have never known a day without food. If I joined the lodge, it wasn't to defy you and your son, but because I was looking for a cult of reason. I was convinced that life could be explained like a simple geometric problem. Now I realize that was all sheer impudence. My wife left me for a young stud in Town, my eldest daughter does precisely what suits her and I'm worried what will happen to the other two. O Madonna, find them two France-Whites who will take them away over there and show them something other than this mediocre and mean universe of Grand-Anse.'

He would have liked to bring up his other most worrisome trouble but he couldn't find the right words to do it. Anyway, he had never spoken of that problem in real French and only referred to it in our language. 'My bamboo won't go up,' he had complained to Coolie René and Julien Thémistocle when he had sought the intervention of their respective gods. Wouldn't the Virgin of the Great Return be likely to take offence at such coarse terms? While he was groping for a Latin translation to express his problem, a blind man in front of him snapped his white stick and started dancing and yelling:

'I can see! I can see! Thank you Virgin, thank you!'

Féquesnoy saw a paralytic get out of his chair, a tubercular old man stop spitting blood, a woman with elephantiasis find her old shapeliness, a lovelorn sufferer overcome his despair and a whole lot of other miracles each more amazing than the previous one. The procession had swollen in size as it went along and the prayers that could be heard rising from it reached such a level of fervour that even the Virgin herself seemed moved. Her gentle gaze settled on each fuzzy head as if she was handing out one by one the amount of blessing that the penitent deserved, except, that is, on to the curly locks of the Féquesnoys and the Dupin de Médeuils. And yet the island white's soles were bleeding from having walked so far in bare feet. His family was confronting the ordeal with remarkable forebearance for people used to luxury since birth. Féquesnoy ended up suspecting that these blacks on whom the Madonna was showering so many graces could probably teach him a thing or two. It was unlikely that they would really be prepared to renounce their old beliefs. Or drink no more rum. Or stop cuckolding their partners. Or give up cheating at dice or even stop playing altogether. Or cease impugning their neighbour's reputation with gossip. No more this, no more that. That was their chorus and they delivered it with such sincerity that the Virgin had no choice but to give in to their wishes. *Maître* Féquesnoy delved into his life to see whether he had a vice he could offer up in exchange for an erection. He only played cards in order to attract new clients among the rich planters, not for pleasure. He wasn't a great drinker and only had, in all modesty, three mistresses, all kept women who would never have screamed insults in the street or laughed raucously. Much as he wracked his brains, he could find nothing very gratifying with which to tickle the Virgin's appetite.

The procession from Gros-Morne now met up with one coming from Trinité in the middle of the Galion bridge, at the precise point where the fierce contest between the 'Executioner of the North' and the 'Golem' was played out every day. The penitents from the neighbouring *commune*, even more numerous, had come to greet the Madonna bearing banners decorated with crosses and religious mottoes. The statue swayed, almost unreal, between two waves of devotees carrying bamboo torches. Sometimes it would wobble so dangerously that it half fell out of the boat, but at the last moment a fevered hand, two hands, ten hands would save it from going under. For a whole week, Féquesnoy and his two daughters subjected themselves to this pilgrimage and its terrible frenzy. And so did Dupin de Médeuil. And yet the divinity patently refused to cast her eyes on the mulatto and the island white as well as their offspring. Forced to seek lodging with locals at exorbitant prices, almost in rags, wild beards sprouting on their faces, the two men kept hoping until they arrived in Grand-Anse, where the very sight of them created a hullabaloo similar to the one which, during the Second War, had gathered the population together in readiness for an imminent attack from German submarines.

'Grand-Anse is a cursed *commune*,' grumbled an overwrought Chief Bérard. 'Even the Madonna can do nothing for us. She has relieved, cured, brought happiness and wealth everywhere she has gone, but who here can boast of having benefited from a single one of her blessings? Who?'

'You're drunk, you wretch,' shouted a churchy woman at him. 'Instead of repenting, you've got nothing better to do than criticize God's mother. Carry on like that and you'll go straight to hell!'

'I don't give a shit! I've given her fifty-three psalms, twenty-seven Hail Marys, six hundred and twelve acts of contrition without even counting all the hymns my throat has struggled to sing all along her path, and look at Chief Bérard, do you see the slightest change in him, for God's sake?'

The statue was carried up Front Street and down Back Street and the other way round, giving the people of Grand-Anse time to make their wishes to it. It then did the honours in the streets going to the post office and the cemetery.

'O Madonna, give us proper men's bodies!' cried Dachine and Small Balls Auguste, whose mothers when pregnant had used a medicine since removed from circulation by the government.

'Most Holy Virgin of the Great Return, cast light into the mind of my son Bogino!' begged Ma Léonce, the baker's wife.

'Mother of Our Lord Jesus Christ, O pure one, ensure eternal prosperity for the Palace of the Orient!' exclaimed Ali Tanin.

And then Rose-Aimée asked for a cure for her swollen foot; Master Salvie good luck for his bus; Thimoléon the extermination of that 'devilish race, the island whites'; the little Mussolini that Pierre de Coubertin agree to his request that the sack and egg-and-spoon races be entered as Olympic competitions; Coolie René that a woman of a race other than his own marry him so that he could have children who would at last escape the ignominy that weighs on the heads of coolies; Julien Thémistocle that he might find the mastic tree by whose trunk his great grandfather was buried so that he could carve his initials on its bark as well as the sign of the three-headed snake; de Cassagnac that his little girl Marie-Eugénie finally rediscover her sanity and gaiety; Eau de Café that Antilia stop plotting with the Sirens on the La Crabière promontory. But whether townies or yokels and for once mixed up together without distinction, the people of Grand-Anse could shout themselves silly as the procession passed and all in vain, as the Virgin of the Great Return remained as ungiving as plaster. They ended up putting her in the church nave and going back to their day-to-day business with heavy hearts. All night long in the church square Chief Bérard bellowed:

'Madonna, make me white, I beg you! Give me that white colour that demands respectation and admiration from one and all!'

Maître Féquesnoy and Dupin de Médeuil found lodging at the same address as the most beggarly of their fellow citizens. The former found no remedy for his flaccid organ, nor the latter a cure for his deformed boy. Nobody in Grand-Anse received anything whatsoever. So the statue was sent off with no regrets to the neighbouring *commune* of Basse-Pointe, but not before people had noted that only Antilia, the wild girl of the beach taken in by the shop-keeper Eau de Café, had declined to make any sort of wish.

'Because it's her fault and the sea that cherished her so long, that cursedness surrounds Grand-Anse . . .' concluded Bogino, to the general agreement of the villagers.

15

Several of my notebooks have disappeared. I think I'm going mad. I look under my mattress, pull out all the clothes that I carefully put away in the wardrobe, make such and so much of a fuss that the owner of the Oceanic Hotel – retired from the navy, he never stops boasting – panics and comes upstairs to the rescue, even though he's short of breath. He has ended up by getting used to me and treats as an additional act of revenge the fact that the godson of Eau de Café, his competitor, lives under his roof. He bends over backwards to be amiable as soon as I ask for the slightest thing. He has only refused one of my requests, when I expressed the desire that he unfasten the shutter in my room that looks out to sea.

'Leave the damned thing in its damnedness! Take no notice of it, it's better for you that way. It's been fifteen or twenty years since I gave it a glance. But hold on! It happens to have been the day it gave back the body of that . . . Anyway, you know what I mean, you were probably too young to remember all that . . . That little wild girl that Eau de Café had seen fit to employ in her shop.'

Before I can open my mouth, he declares that's all he knows about her and that anyway he has no intention of raking over that sort of black magic. Whenever I mention the name Antilia in front of him, he looks away or turns his back on me. It's impossible to pull him out of his silence, even that infamous evening when we polished off a bottle of Clément rum between us and he told me in every detail about the sexual exploits of the two Grand-Anse village whores.

'My notebooks, where are they?' I'm yelling as he opens the door.

'Look again, nobody comes in here apart from you and the maid, and she can't read. Are you sure you haven't left them somewhere outside?'

'I only write in my room.'

He seems genuinely upset. He helps me turn the room upside-down but we can't find any sign of them. The retired naval man shouts for the maid to come in double-quick time.

'*Sa misyé-a fè'w non?*' (What has the gentleman done to you?), asks the owner, glaring at her.

'It doesn't matter!' I say. 'Just let her give me my things back and we'll forget it.'

'No, no . . . I insist . . . She's got to tell us why she did it. I'm not going to put up with stealing. Had you hidden money in them?'

'Not at all . . . I . . .'

Then the woman lifts up her dress without the slightest embarrassment and pulls out from her expansive knickers my notebooks, whose corners have been crumpled. She seems about to break down in tears and then she explodes:

'The gentleman is a *chabin*. All *chabins* are bad. All *chabins* are mischievous. Otherwise, why does a *chabin* never marry a *chabine*? When a *chabin* crosses my path, I get a whole day's bad luck. I know what I'm talking about; I've had three men give me children and all three are *chabins*. The last was the driver of the 'Executioner of the North'. Why did God put *chabins* on this earth? Hasn't the black man already got enough misfortune without that?'

The owner and I are so speechless that we let her go without further ado. The pained ex-navy man is preparing an apology when suddenly he changes tack and tells me reproachfully:

'Your presence in Grand-Anse is upsetting everybody, my dear sir. Your godmother has caused us so many . . . how shall I put it? . . . yes, that's it, unpleasantnesses in the past that we're afraid you might stir all that up again with the strange questions you're asking all around. Thimoléon and Eau de Café are people from another age who delight in their . . . what should I say? . . . in their mumbo jumbo. Watch out, a bamboo hair or a drop of barbadine root juice is easily slipped into your glass . . .'

'I don't want the maid to clean my room any more, if you don't mind. I can do it myself . . .'

Thimoléon is in his usual place in our Back Street rum shop and he laughs at my misfortunes as well as finding in them grounds to philosophize:

'There are those who are predestined to a certain respectation,' he tells me, 'a respectation coloured with terror, and you, you are one of them without knowing it because you're a *chabin*. You will have to play this trump card as a last resort if and when, by some misfortune, your life ends up hanging by a thread or by a word. Look at them, your brothers in race, your brothers in "chabinity", take a long look at their freckled white skin, at their hair as red as ripe apricot pulp, at their often cat-like grey eyes, at their wide nostrils that belong to great grandsons of the Congo, and now look at everyone else and notice the distance that almost naturally separates you from them. Yes, you yourself. Because you know it, even if you ran away over there to forget it; the *chabin* is a being apart, a bad breed, evil, violent, neurotic, epileptic. The *chabin* inspires fear for he has usurped the pale skin of the former masters but doesn't know how to use it (it's one thing to steal a "protection", it's another to master its mechanism, for Christ's sake!). So there he is, the *chabin*, making his whiteness felt all around him, never allowing the blacks' exhausted and hate-filled gaze a moment's rest, but he doesn't know how to give orders, he's incapable of finding that voice which makes the heart tremble and thump like the *bel-air* drum. His eyes, with their colour that he's again filched from the whites, are reckoned to see in the dark and are supposed to look into the most private of affairs. That's why certain people, fearing some revelation in public, avoid annoying them like the plague even though they curse them in secret. But those same eyes can't take advantage of their lightness to order women, like plantation foremen do, to lift their skirts over their heads quicker than a flea leaps and to offer their gaping wombs to a cock as hard as an iron bar. You see, they can't do anything, these *chabins*. Good-for-nothings, apart from the ones who live in town and, according to bush radio, become solicitors, teachers, doctors and all sorts of high-up professions. So the others who stay here in the country, the blacks often mock them, saying: "It wasn't worth your mother making you into a *chabin* if it was just for you to hold a pitchfork in your hand like us under the eleven o'clock hot sun. Ha, ha, ha!"

'Yet they're feared everywhere because they make up for the strange weakness that afflicts them with violent and sudden outbursts of fury. You see them go red in the face, their fists clenched, and wham! There they are lashing out like deaf men at anything within reach and it's pointless defending yourself, hitting them back, cutting stripes into them with your cutlass, nothing works. They just keep coming at you and when they get hold of you, bloody hell! You're finished once and for all. Black and blue. Buggered! There's no such thing as a soft *chabin*. People have worked out that there must be some sort of protection somewhere, since they act like they're invulnerable. What sort of protection? No one knows exactly, but it must exist! Hundreds of people will swear to it on the head of their godmother. What's more, if Chief Bérard free-wheels down all the hills, even the steep one which leads to Anse Charpentier, and if his bus has been baptized "weedkiller", it's because the gentleman is a *chabin*. A don't-give-a-damn-about-death! Given all that, take care to rethink your tactics. You can no longer expect to dismantle the barrier that the years have built up between you and the blacks of Grand-Anse. Or at least you can start on that road but only as far as a *chabin* is allowed to go. In fact, half the road was already behind you without you knowing it, and what is even more incredibly lucky, many of the chiefs gathered around the gambling tables are of your race and, for as long as a black man can remember, two *chabins* have never been seen to fight between themselves. Not in public in any case! If they have some dispute to settle they wait patiently to face each other in the *damier* dance fight and the stronger, that's to say in our current expression "the baddest *chabin*", kills the other one.

'And whether they're winning or losing, they always handle the dice impassively, very discreetly, and don't you think for a moment that they didn't notice you straight away and so admit you into their ranks. While you were scowling over a bitch of a ten (two fives, the worst) and your whole carcass was sweating over it, they were watching you as they played at their own tables, perhaps saying to themselves "That awkward *chabin*, I know him . . . Where is he from? From Dominante or from around our way, from Macédoine?" and, gesturing towards you with their chins, they exchanged views as to who you might be before concluding that you were either a properly foreign stranger – in which case they would have no choice but to defend you if a brawl broke out – or one who'd come back, gone and come back again, and that it was up to you to watch your own arse. By the time the din of the municipal fanfare playing the *Marseillaise* briefly drowns out the hubbub of the market, they have adopted a definitive attitude towards you on the evidence of your behaviour with the maroon blacks, the estate blacks, those from the village, the coolies and, of course, the women. Suddenly they can be seen converging on a single table – the rarest of sights a table of *chabins*! – and debating among themselves with many a gesture, and if you'd known how to read the deep and secret movements which animate your own people, you'd have realized that they were granting you, as a highly exceptional favour, their endorsement. For you must understand that the hand which has roughly pushed you to one side just as a player at your table brandishes his cutlass and hits out all around him, that this same hand has saved you from a moment of murderous madness because even if the death blow wasn't aimed at you but at a rogue who was up to his tricks next to you, you could have ended up like him, legs in the air, bleeding like a Christmas sucking pig, and the women would have rushed over and rinsed the ground with big noisy buckets of water, putting a new gaming table in the same place, and all that would have been left of both of you would have been the wailing siren of the ambulance taking you far away; you must understand that this hand was a *chabin*'s hand, covered with freckles, where you can see the blue of the veins rising under the speckled skin.

'Do you know where that word "*chabin*" comes from? It refers to a kind of sheep with yellow hair to be found in Normandy. Like the word "*mulatto*" comes from mule! Your fathers, the whites, thus condemned the sons they had with their black slave women to the realm of pure bestiality. Make sure you never forget that, my friend, but without harbouring the slightest resentment about it. What is done is done once and for all.

'Last and not least, you must recall that thanks to the powerful alchemy of colonial rape, there are several kinds of *chabins*, depending on how white their complexion is, or how red their hair, or how light their eyes: sun *chabin*, golden *chabin*, white *chabin*, brown *chabin*, dark *chabin*, mulatto *chabin*, etc . . . and each of these types has its own idiosyncracies that everyone knows by heart. You see, it's as if by some strange atavism the blacks on this island had felt the obscure urge to recreate the tribes they are descended from, but you go and tell them that! They wouldn't understand a word of it. We live, we eat, we talk and talk again, we look after our business and that's all there is to it. And for fear that shit-stirrers like you who've tasted the poisoned fruit of travelling might come back with a whole lot of upsetting ideas, they've invented a Creole proverb, a cast-iron proverb that says: "*Chabins* are blacks, OK!" Remember that during wakes when we pretend to be friends with Death, the story-tellers keep saying to our worn-out memories: "You have lived in the redness of your hair the infernal breath of hellfire . . . in the name of the god Legba, in the name of my heart which in all my life has never missed a beat, I baptise and crown you black . . ."

Like that the order of things is safe. So, *chabin*, over to you . . .'

Dearest,

They have slapped us. Each of our faces is a splendid lie and I can hear over there the painful crumpling of our cheeks and lips swallowing their idiom, fashioning well-copied smiles and, by means of contortions, we make very acceptable mokojumbie masks. We emerge the stronger for it, we think . . .

At Trénelle, since the municipal labourers bought themselves colour televisions, there's been no more gathering of people outside their shacks at nightfall. Shacks in which, from a geological point of view, you can make out four successive stages: the cardboard period, the corrugated-iron period, the asbestos period and the concrete period. Homo sapiens can be measured by his percentage of concrete and by the pseudo-French spun to his children so that they go far at school. 'Please don't insult me, monsieur, with your Creole! I speak French, you know,' you hear, like up in Petit-Paradis. And what about the maid back from Barbès for a month?: 'Ooh la-la! I don't feel well at all, I need my bit of winter every year!'

But sometimes the incorrigible still piss openly in the sordid alleys and the throbbing boom-bam-boom of a drum tries to slip with cat-like stealth into the midst of the night, near the legendary Great Rock.

Writing not to give witness, not to decorate the present with balisier wreaths, not to turn the world upside-down either. None of these. I write the story of those around me with my anger calmed.

Antilia

Fourth Circle

For each of us life has moved in stages from countryside to village, from village to town and from town to France. Our parents had only known a short migration, but as for us, our desires have accelerated, our footsteps have gone ahead of our lives and when we think about going back, we realize how far we have gone astray.

We must learn again to talk since memory itself isn't to blame and it isn't prepared to bend itself to our cosmopolitan fantasies. So we fix our mind, frantically, on a little piece of the past and try to climb back up the ladder of days gone by without receiving the slightest help of any sort.

But what's to be done with crumbs of fantasies, with leftovers of aborted epics?

16

Now, Eau de Café didn't see her life as having happened the way rumour has it. She swears she was brought up by the midwife, Ma Doris, with whom her mother had left her when she went to work in Panama where they were building an enormous canal. 'When my mother comes back,' she would tell her guardian and lover Julien Thémistocle, 'I won't give the time of day to a black man like you. You'll be less than a nothing, a piece of dog shit, you will!' But her mother was swallowed up by that Spanish land and the Second Great War caught up with Grand-Anse and the surrounding countryside during the first hot days of the dry season, when the sugar canes were sporting their flower spears like carefully-combed negress hair.

Ma Doris, who had refused to pass the time of day with the aforementioned Julien for ages although his house was a stone's throw away from hers, was drawing death lines on the ground with ashes from the fireplace and was chanting spells 'on the head of that sevenfold cursed race of Germans, strangers to the Lord'. She squawked between two puffs on her pipe:

'Give me a map that shows the shape of their country. If I don't shut its doors at dawn and dusk, my magic won't work.'

Food began to become scarce. Folk from the town, with their strange ways of dressing and speaking, rushed into the countryside, desperate to trade necklaces and rings of pure gold for a sack of yams or a couple of turkey cocks. They no longer looked down on the plantation black, despite the jiggers and rashes that decorated his toes, oh no! And then when meat and vegetables disappeared from the hills and the yards in front of our houses turned to desert, you could have sworn that slavery had come back. At Macédoine they kept talking of 'slaboury' as if to remind themselves that they were dealing with yet another period of unending sweat.

Nobody dared any more to lay out their cassava flour to dry in the sun. The big whites seemed to have gone crazy. You couldn't speak to them nor even steal the tiniest look at them. If they called for you, you would have to get a move on, otherwise you'd feel their whip on your skin. Soon bush radio was announcing everywhere:

'Friends, there aren't any laws as far as blacks are concerned in this country.'

Julien Thémistocle's grandfather was the only person not to provoke the masters' fury. People still went to take him offerings in the depths of the woods near Morne Jacob, where, it was asserted, he tamed poisonous snakes. To each of us he would teach the following lesson while smiling with that piece of shapeless flesh that passed for his mouth:

'The white man is a wild fig tree. Do you know the story of that tree? To begin with, it's a tiny seed, so small you can lose it in the palm of your hand. Then a bird drops it on to your piece of land . . .

'One day', he continued, 'you find that damned fig tree, you slash at it with your pitchfork. A waste of time! A thousand stems grow up again and soon it becomes a majestic tree in whose shade you would give anything to rest. Be careful!' the old man cried suddenly. 'Don't go to sleep there for you might lose your memory for ever!'

'One afternoon', comments Eau de Café, 'I found him in deep conversing with that tree. It was saying to him, not in human words, but in a kind of musical dialect: "Father, I need two and a half lifetimes and more to reach maturity, and whoever looked after me when I was little won't see me stand defiantly against the sun." The greybeard answered like this: "My people have sprawled senselessly in the treacherous caress of your arms, how do you now expect them to wake up, eh? How do you expect them to shake off this weight of forgetfulness from their eyelids?" The tree was surprised: "Father, since the time when the devil himself was a little lad, I have always calmed worries. What do you reproach me for then?" The ancestor replied: "Let us stop these worderies that are leading us nowhere. When I die, my grandson's wife will come and bury my old Guinea negro's carcass at your feet, so then we will be together . . . we will be together again."'

A few days later, Eau de Café, who more often than not volunteered to take him his rations, almost dropped the half-calabash of salt pork and red peas that she had prepared for him. She stared right into his eyeballs, not daring to whisper a word or move an inch. The old man simply said:

'You are mine.'

He took her and then, with one hand on the woman-child's head and the other in the half-calabash, he swallowed his food without chewing it and fell asleep, sitting in the strange posture of the figures that the Congos at Morne Capot used to make out of bracken. He was staring at a spot at the top of a white gum-tree that had recently been struck by lightning. Eau de Café waited patiently without keeping count of the hours. Perhaps she was there for days on end, who knows? She was caught in the rain. The midday heat dried her. She saw things changing before her eyes, sparkling with lights as the darkness of night began to fall. The old man finally emerged from his meditation and announced:

'Time has turned. I am still here, but shall no longer deprive you of each rising sun. Be gone!'

When Eau de Café came back, he had made death welcome and had buried himself at the chosen place. On his tomb he had placed a rock which you don't normally find in these parts, a rock as red as dried blood and which his father, that's to say No-firstname Thémistocle, the slave, had inherited from a pure African. Eau de Café bent down to look more closely at it. The darkness suddenly began to cover the foliage of the big trees. She touched the rock: it was as hot as if it had just come out of a fire. She tore off two balisier leaves and, quickly wrapping it up, slipped it into her bundle.

The weak woman-child told her story to Julien and in return received only a volley of blows with a creeper and the firm promise that she would be thrown out if she ever found herself telling such fibberies again. But when she showed him the rock, he was, in a word, astounded and, the next day as the tweet-tweet dawn broke, he shouted to the neighbourhood:

'I must go! The *dissidence* is no place for cowardly dogs! France, our mother, is occupied by the German foe and de Gaulle is asking for our help, I must go and defend her. Who will look after Eau de Café? She's still no more than a child but the blood will soon be running between her thighs. She can wash, iron, do the cooking. Yes, she's a good child.'

People turned their backs. He, to whom the human race was a matter of supreme indifference, had all but lost the habitude of speaking to other folk. Only Madame Doris, the devil's betrothed, the one who shamelessly opened up for any '*kal*' ('cock' in our idiom), replied:

'I've got room in my house, man. When you return, if you return, you will find a woman and I promise that none of the male-pigs from around here will succeed in lifting up her skirt.'

A fearfulness was about to strike me: that Eau de Café would never stop talking, that she would pour out in front of me in a single day everything she had always held back, because her words force me to rethink altogether that childhood which I have so meticulously mummified in my very depths. I have come back to stir up the embers of my memory and to try to cast light on the hate that Grand-Anse people feel for their sea, and not to turn everything upside-down. Is she going to make me change my quest?

I sneak away from her like a thief. Gently, backwards, trying not to let the floorboards creak. Front Street is a furrow of blinding light. Municipal workers are repainting the primary school and town hall walls ochre, while an electrician is busy hanging up from balcony to balcony garlands of multicoloured light bulbs. A bus, the 'Golem', pours out its flood of country bumpkins, not caring about holding up the traffic behind. Antilia is the last to get off. She chats with the driver, one foot on the road, the other on the step of the vehicle. The height of her heels catches the eye. A breeze makes her skirt flutter up, showing the juicy roundness of her black girl's legs. I cannot breathe, I am a piece of wood, a splinter of rock. My palms are icy cold despite the mountainous heat of the day. I can hear the grumbling of the ocean sea. Two tip-up trucks split the air with their horns and their drivers swap insults. Antilia climbs back on to the step of the bus, which starts up gently. I am running, I can't feel the weight of my body any more. I am flying, lighter than a bit of dried coconut shell. One of the men painting shouts to me:

'Hey, the race is tomorrow. Can't you wait for the fourteenth of July?'

The 'Golem' turns the corner around the linen shop belonging to the half-caste Syrian Ali Tanin who is listening, with his chair outside on the pavement, to an Arab lament sad enough to break your heart. Yet he is smiling gently and helps me to my feet when I trip up because of a hole in the pavement hidden by an old piece of cardboard.

'It's ten days since they should have fixed that,' he says. 'It's as if people don't have to pay them taxes. I'm going to resign from the town council, you'll see, pah!'

I find myself surrounded by voices, hands, straw hats, all full of concern. My ankle is prodded, my knee felt. A handkerchief wipes my brow. Somebody says:

'*Si i pa ka palé, sé ki i trapé falfwèt.*' (If he can't talk, it's because of the shock.)

'He should go to hospital,' a woman insists.

Nobody wants to let me go on my way. I feel a fool, grotesque. To fall over like a naughty kid, to make a show of my towny clumsiness. Too much, it's all too much. Thimoléon comes to my rescue *in extremis* by dragging me off to our rum shop in Back Street. I follow him, meekly. He sings the *Marseillaise* as he marches along . . .

'Once allowed into the dice circle,' he starts again, suddenly and deliriously, 'it doesn't mean that your arse is safe, that all danger is past. No! Don't get that into your skull or else you'll be handing over your life to fate without so much as a fight. You have come to find your death. Their silence doesn't mean in the least that they don't care. On the contrary, the players are very

143

aware of this difference, conscious that you should reduce it little by little and here, there is no set recipe. Nobody can tell you the best way to act. You are free. Now you see where the danger comes from: if at seven in the evening you are still there looking like a stranger that the wind has blown in, you're dead. Or you leave. It's the same thing. Think what it will be like when you have lost face, when nobody will raise their hat as you go by, and that you will have to keep changing the *commune* where you live until the shame is buried in people's memories. The black man can have a long memory when it comes to harbouring a grudge against his brother. So, watch what your body, your flesh, is doing, pay attention to your movements, your voice. The great hall of the municipal market has been yours from the moment you went in, shirt unbuttoned, and the country blacks as well as those from the village discreetly stood on tiptoes to look at you. You pick up the dice, shake them in your cupped palms and defy the gaze of each and every one around the table (Give me what I've asked for, dammit!) and then throw them with all your strength. But before they stop rolling, you suspect their treachery and snatch them back again almost too late, thanks to the dice box, and you rub them together again so that the number you want warms up:

"It's the eleven I asked for! Eleven!"

'This time your number comes up. They politely ask you your name, about your family, where you're from, the work you do with your own two hands and finally everything that people like to know about other people . . . *I want a* coucoune, *yeah, a* coucoune!'

Godmother's shop is more and more deserted and Thimoléon confides in me that several suppliers have stopped delivering to her altogether. Only the paraffin that she sells by the litre for the stoves of the humble allows her to maintain a semblance of activity. She works the paraffin pump with surprising energy for one of seventy years and more. She expresses her tenderness towards me through an old song (a Charles Trenet melody) that she hums to me while stroking the back of my neck with her withered fingers.

Eau de Café wants (finally) to reveal her life to me.

So, when Julien had left for the *dissidence* – which amounted to crossing the Dominica Channel on the sly to join the Free French Forces – Madame Doris took Eau de Café to Morne l'Étoile. She was a midwife and had a heart as tender as a palm's. In the village, the gossips at once set to work: 'Doris thinks God is going to forgive her for all her years of debauchery, huh!' or 'Poor Eau de Café! There's another one who won't be able to sleep at night. Ah, what a shame!' But in the eyes of Julien Thémistocle, she was the only real human being in that neck of the woods and he said so loud and clear in the rum-shop yard. He hated the whole world. His wife Passionise, who had left home without giving any reason. The island white Dupin de Médeuil, who took away his position as estate foreman soon afterwards on the pretext that through drowning his sorrows in rum he was dragging the plantation towards ruin. The blacks who blamed him for having inherited evil powers from his great grandfather and for engaging in sorcerer's spells.

Years and years later, he came back from the war and found his father dead and buried, his mother ill, bewildered, lying all day on a salt-cod box covered with rags (during the Vichy regime, no sheets had arrived from Europe), her mouth babbling some prayer. The world had changed dramatically in the meantime. In the depths of the woods the army bulldozers had flattened the forest where his father had joined the silk-cotton tree and from now on a municipal by-law banned drinking from certain springs. Julien rushed to his garden at Bois-Cannelle, unhinged by a demented fury, but by a miracle, nothing there had been touched. The clearing he had cut out with such and so much love from within the forest was merely overrun with coco-plum trees and brambles. He straight away seized the brand new Santo Domingo cutlass that he'd bought in town and started weeding-weeding-weeding. He sweated away for days and days and people came from all around to gawp at the phenomenon. Even the people from Ajoupa-Bouillon had heard about it and when they told their *béké*, he sent a foreman to give orders to Julien because 'now, since his offspring goes to school, the nigger doesn't want to dirty his hands any more'. Julien didn't give him a chance to open his mouth: he slit him from head to foot on one of the banks of the Fond Grand-Anse river and spat on his corpse, thereby unleashing a sort of civil war. The Ajoupa folk came to demand compensation and they were offered (reluctantly, it has to be said) a *damier* contest, even though the mayor had let it be known that this sort of savagery was from now on proscribed. Pah! It was to be organized on Easter Saturday and the noise of the drums would be dulled with old guano sacks. The toughs from the two *communes* had often clashed over dice or dominoes but now it was the death of a man that had come between them. The people of Macédoine and Morne Capot secretly blamed Julien for having given them this pointless unpleasantness and all this since coming back. Some of them even went as far as to wish that he would be castrated in the process so that no more bad blood would be spilt for this big ruffian who seemed to hold sway over the universe with his merest gaze.

Eau de Café, who was very happy living with Madame Doris, had had a fleeting premonition of her future husband's death. It has left her with an incurable wound:

'I pushed him towards oblivion,' she murmurs to me, 'I had imprisoned his vitality in my mind too long. That's what it is.'

According to her, when Julien Thémistocle's mother passed away, her son had funeral notices sent to his seven brothers and sisters whom various marriages had taken either to Moulin-l'Étang, Hauteur Bourdon, or even further to the unreal city of Saint-Pierre where the way women walk is an invitation to lechery. People, it has to be admitted, who are not like those from Grand-Anse. Even the way they shook hands wasn't the same, not really. A wake was organized which was more extraordinary than Hermancia's whole life had been. The wordsmiths pitted their talents against each other to sing her praises. One of them amazed all present by the beauteousness of his words. His speech was effectively what follows:

'Mother Hermancia lay down one sunny morning and, having

decided that she had lost the taste for living, sent for Death. When he had sat down on a sofa, she brought out her burial dress from under her bed and calmly ironed it while exchanging pleasantries with her guest. Her voice was crystal clear. She had lost her usual feebleness, which used to make us remark that "Hermancia is a sickly little *câpresse*, as weak as a casuarina branch". Death didn't show his teeth. He was waiting for his moment. Then, Mother Hermancia dressed, put on her head scarf, perfumed herself with vetiver and stretched out, rosary beads on her chest, smiling and seemingly proud. Ah! Ladies and gentlemen gathered here, listen to the story of a woman who never lied, who never envied others, listen and open your ears wider. Mother Hermancia smiled a last time and said: "I'm ready at last." It was then that Death relented and whispered: "You are so happy in your life, why not stay there, woman? I grant you a reprieve of three more rainy seasons. What do you say?" Mother Hermancia shook her head to say no and smiling still and lying on her bed, closed her eyes and waited calmly. Ah! My friends, listen to that story . . .'

Julien drank less than he normally did in such circumstances. He didn't touch the dominoes and turned a deaf ear to the revelling laughter and shouting of those keeping the wake. He was oblivious even to the magic of the tales that seemed to weave the very fabric of the night. He patrolled the veranda, making sure that everyone had their share of food and strong coffee. His younger brother from another father, a certain Clémentin, who was almost the spitting image of the deceased, took him by the arm and led him outside:

'Brother, what was the point of looking for war with the villagers from Ajoupa?'

'What do you mean? It was that nonentity who chose to meet his fate ahead of time!' exclaimed Julien.

In the darkness he stumbled over a rock and swore. The noise of the wake by now only reached them like a distant sea swell. Clémentin was weeping.

'Mother, she was . . .' he stammered.

The night took on a bluish lightness. A real March night.

147

'What did she say before going?' he started again.

'What? Haven't I already told you that I was at Bois-Cannelle busy digging trenches for yams when it happened? They came to find me but I told myself she's already dead and I might as well finish the job. Wouldn't you have done the same?'

'Certainly . . .' conceded Clémentin in a tired voice, 'our mother was a good person, a very good person . . .'

'Let's get back now. The blackbirds will be up before long.'

And until dawn, indifferent to the hubbub of the wake, Julien busied himself digging out the jiggers from the soles of his feet with a large, half-bent safety pin. Finally, the exhausted wake-keepers placed the coffin on to a sheet harnessed with two bamboo poles and the bearers set off as if in a Marathon relay race to the Grand-Anse cemetery, skipping along the stony path . . .

Six endless dry seasons had thus gone by since Julien had come back from the war and he hadn't shown the slightest inclination to go up to Morne l'Étoile. Faces began to frown around him but nobody had the nerve, especially after the fate that befell the man from Ajoupa, to remind him of his obligations. He had put a portrait of Papa de Gaulle on a small chest of drawers that he had inherited from his mother and everybody, young and old, would watch him as he went out and slipped behind his house to gaze, through the always open window, at the man who had saved us from oblivion. As for Doris, she avoided Macédoine like the devil steers clear of holy water, taking a long detour via Fond Massacre each time she had to go to the village of Grand-Anse. One day, however, she had to go down there to help with a birth and she was bombarded with questions:

'How's the little one, then? Why have you never brought her to see us, eh?'

'Eau de Café?' she replied with surprise and not without malice, 'but I've made a young lady of her now! She's learning how to make dresses twice a week with a seamstress from Trinité and she can speak the best sort of French, ladies and gentlemen!'

'So now it's over as far as you're concerned . . .' retorted the gossips with their waspish wickedness.

She went off shrugging her shoulders and came back three times that month. On the last occasion, she announced to all and sundry:

'Old Thémistocle has asked me to tell him what his future holds. I will soon be with him in his house . . .'

And so, after she had publicly examined the various shortcomings of those living nearby, she took the track to Bois-Cannelle, which was all but hidden by the undergrowth. When she arrived at the beaten earth yard in front of the house, she called out:

'Man! Hey, my man!?'

No answer. She dared to peep through the window but it was too dark inside. Even so, she could make out the strange wallpaper made of photos of actresses cut out of romance magazines covering the walls that were probably eaten away by woodworm. Maybe he's gone to the Fourniol spring, she thought, I'll wait for him a little bit longer. On one side of the house, the man had built a sort of primitive bamboo kitchen in the middle of which a fire of brushwood was smouldering, sheltered by three rocks. She noticed that one of them was a strange red colour and wondered what it could be used for. As the daylight was fading and he still hadn't appeared, she retrod her footsteps, keen to get out of this place where, suddenly, everything seemed evil. Could he be an *engagé*, a man in league with the devil like his grandfather, the one who tamed poisonous snakes? So why then did he make me come here to tell him things that ordinary folk can't make out? She was almost running, scratching her arms and legs against the branches which looked as if they wanted to strangle her. Where the path came out, Thémistocle, the fourth of that name, was waiting for her, arms crossed and blocking her way. She said, scared:

'It was today, eh? . . . It was today you said, man?'

'Take off your rags, woman!' he commanded her coldly.

'What do you mean?'

'Do it or else I'll have to force you. Go on, hurry up!'

Doris peered frantically around, hoping in vain for some means of escape, and then, claims Eau de Café, there are two versions of what happened next, which I will be kind enough to tell you. In one of them, it's said that she raised her arms above her and spoke some words in a peasant Creole. Her body glowed with a bright interior light which shook her like a tree top during a hurricane and then she took off into thin air, leaving Thémistocle speechless. 'That's what I believe happened,' said Eau de Café. In the other story, the one that's more commonly told as you can well imagine, it is said that the woman undressed slowly, tears in her eyes, and begged her tormentor:

'I could be as old as your mother. When she went to live with your father, I had just had my nineteenth birthday. Respect and honour for my body!'

In reality, she had just passed the age when a woman's body stops bleeding and still had the firmness of a young wench. Her rump was immeasurably wide enough for any living man's desire. Her *coucoune* was a dark chasm where a crystal-clear and intoxicating sweat gathered in beads. So Doris undressed completely and looked at Thémistocle. The chill of the evening made her shiver. He, in turn, removed his clothes and it was then that she realized the nature of his secret, the why and wherefore of his apparent distrust of women. He had a cock of extraordinary length, perhaps six feet, maybe more, that he wrapped with infinite care around his waist. The abortionist immediately stopped snivelling, fascinated as she was by this gigantic beast. And later, she experienced an obscene ecstasy as the beast entered her *coucoune*, her arsehole, her ears, mouth and nose, each time spurting a broadside of semen the colour of sugar-cane arrows, so much so that she was completely covered with it and fell asleep there on the bare ground until noon the next day. Some men carrying bananas discovered here inside her strange cocoon. She rushed to clean herself at the river, a whinnying laugh on her lips, and chanted:

'*Thé-mis-to-cle!*'

The same day, she went back up to Morne l'Étoile, packed up her things and didn't even leave a pin in her house. She grabbed Eau de Café under her wing and hurried down the hill to Bois-

Cannelle where she set up house with our friend Thémistocle. The village was convulsed with frenetic gossiping, dirty laughs, cries of horror, appeals to divine retribution and all sorts of such things. Brother Geffrard, who had been a postman in the village of Sainte-Marie and who was one of the few who could read, repeated to anyone and himself:

'I've got what she needs in Pope Leo's Enchiridion. Pah! You'll see, all that filth won't last long!'

Godmother is waiting for the moment that I mention Antilia's name. She keeps her eyes half-shut, nervously fiddling with her mock gold ring. She knows that I haven't come to hear the shaggy dog stories of her life any more than Master Thimoléon's obsessive ravings. She doesn't yet realize how patient I can be and is anxiously waiting for me to explode. She does know that I will totally and utterly refuse to listen to the explanation that she had ritually served up in her letters at the time when I was a student in France:

'Our suffering soul has now become a real lady. She passed Higher Certificate thanks to private lessons from the headmaster, the same year that you went down to live with your parents in Fort-de-France, and I'm told she became secretary to a very well-known lawyer. After that, she left for Paris where she works in fashion.'

On the wall, nicely framed and dressed in their dark suits or their crinoline best dresses, the family keeps an austere watch over the little room which is too tidy to be comfortable. But I can't be bothered with their fixed smiles: I want to know everything. I'd been told after the incident: it's the sea's fault! So I'd run to spit in its face. I'd kicked out at it like a stupid mule and then had gone back to my games. My pain hadn't yet got the words to express itself. It was coiled up in some recess of my body, ready to spring out at any moment. I was scared stiff by it and when that name, Antilia, started to crack the defences of my Creole student skull adrift in the Parisian cold, I realized that I was lost if I didn't force myself once I returned home to clear up this mystery.

17 The Secret of Julien Thémistocle, the Maroon

For us local-yokels, the village of Grand-Anse was the centre of the world. Of course, we dreamt of elsewhere, of Town, of France, of Syria or India, and some who had travelled dreamt of Panama or America, but most of us had our doubts as to whether these marvellous lands (with the exception of the horrible Guinea-Africa which we'd repressed in our deepest psychological depths) were truly real. Did they have a sun like ours that rose–shone–set? Did their inhabitants nurture their passions, stubborn hatreds and regrets like we do? We weren't too sure about it. And so we only listened to the tales of those who had travelled with a somewhat sceptical ear and we looked into the fire of their eyes for the sudden spark that would prove that they were making fun of us. The most disbelieving of all was, of course, Eau de Café, the fighting woman with the tongue so sharp that she even allowed herself to take issue in public with Grand-Anse's two hard men, in particular Chief Bérard. As long as she confined herself to inoffensive little subjects, she could get away with nothing worse than a stream of threats or a litany of oaths, aimed mostly at her mother, the beautiful Franciane, but she put her life at risk the day that she was impudent enough to mock his supposedly perfect familiarity with France-land. It should be said that the fellow had started building his reputation (and carving out a fiefdom) thanks to the aura that surrounds anyone who had 'done France', as we said in those days. When exactly this extraordinary event had taken place nobody could say with any accuracy, given that we had always known Master Bérard wandering around the countryside to sell second-hand items whose origins nobody had the nerve to ask him, until he'd collected enough to buy himself a bus. And yet the fact remains that his pockets were always overflowing with bank-notes and coins that he handed out according to his whims in order to demonstrate his power. In this way he had bought the neutrality of the various thugs who could well have scuppered his game but who, born idle, needed his meagre hand-outs too much to get in his way.

A regular at the parish hall and almost as great a connoisseur of black-and-white films as his rival Thimoléon, he claimed to be able to recognize the landscapes projected on to the screen, having lived there for many a year. It little mattered that Monument Valley wasn't to be found in the Massif Central or that the Amazon didn't flow in Alsace-Lorraine, all of it was France and anyone foolish enough to say otherwise could expect a razor cut across the buttock or a little slash in the face that would send him flying backwards on to the other spectators, demolishing into the bargain the worm-eaten chairs which the priest, despite the tons of money that these showings brought in, stubbornly refused to mend. Two whole rows had been wrecked in the course of a punch-up caused by an innocent young chap who, proud of being able to read, had corrected the hard man who was in the middle of waxing enthusiastic:

'Zôt wè lanmanyè Pari bidjoul, lëfray!' (Did you see how magnificent Paris is, mates!)

'It's not Paris, monsieur. It's, er, New York they're showing . . .' said a high-pitched voice.

Thereafter the place was to be known as Dien-Bien-Phu. The constabulary counted five missing eyes, three slashed faces and a related number of lost or broken teeth. The projection was stopped and the room emptied amidst the general confusion. A cemetery of chairs, in God's name! From that day on, no spectator would dare to snigger when you-know-who claimed to have courted Judy Garland on the Côte d'Azur or to have beaten Eddie Constantine at arm-wrestling in a Belleville café. The years passed and Bérard settled into his role as undisputed chief of Back Street, Redoute, Fond Massacre and other less known places. Bad men now no longer travelled on any other bus than his 'Golem'. And so there was much trembling when unknowingly, Eau de Café, the negress recently arrived from the country and ignorant of village customs, asked him with the obvious aim of tricking him:

'Tell me, man, in which month of the year does snow fall?'

Taken aback by this vicious thrust, Chief Bérard's tongue quivered in his mouth. His hands were overcome with trembling and some swear to have seen the whites of his eyes turn red. Normally he was only asked easy questions in a respectful murmur or people put up with listening to his lectures for hours on end. Affected by a slight discoloration of the skin, he had insisted that the black man could become white by rolling in snow, ' . . . the same as the white who stays out under the sun too long becomes almost black,' he added in order to convince the disbelieving.

'If I'd wanted to betray my race, believe me, I would have spent longer wallowing in the snow! I'm not ashamed of being black like you are. OK, black isn't a beautiful colour, but if the Good Lord made us like that, my friends, why criticize his handiwork? Yes, yes, yes, I do sometimes think that he could have given to each and all the same hair, the same nose and the same colour and we wouldn't have to spend our time fighting one another. The white wouldn't have been able to put one over the black. The mulatto wouldn't look down his nose at the Indian. The Syrian wouldn't be considered by all and sundry as a filthy breed. No! And what's more, here at Grand-Anse we're lucky enough not to have any Chinese, but if you knew Town, you'd see them piling up penny upon penny on the back of the stupid blacks, and the next day the blacks are the first to complain when Mister Chinaman turns up his nose at their bare feet.'

If Eau de Café had had the effrontery to embarrass Chief Bérard, it was because, by the purest of chances, she had discovered the secret of this black-who-has-done-France. What happened was that she had gone looking one day for her servant, the elusive Antilia, through the streets of the village during the siesta hour. Godmother was going along on tiptoes in order not to disturb anyone, whispering the girl's name at the street corners, when she stumbled across Chief Bérard busy spying on the Féquesnoy home from the balcony of an abandoned house. At first she continued on her way, but, a nosy rummager at heart, she wanted to know what the Guinea black was finding so interesting. Piano notes, soft notes wafted away by the sea breeze, were coming from the red-tiled inner court belonging to *maître* Féquesnoy, celebrated lawyer and deputy mayor. He, the lawyer, was walking up and down, reading aloud from a book to two of his daughters lying in deck-chairs. The eldest, the most radiant thanks to her abundant hair and melancholic eyes, was leaning over a piano, an instrument that neither Eau de Café nor Chief Bérard had ever seen in real life. A dull sense of jubilation took hold of Eau de Café, once she had got into the habit of hiding behind the chief's back, at the idea that she was spying twice over.

Black folk had never had the honour of being received into the Féquesnoy family. Christenings and birthdays were celebrated within the closed circle of a few grand mulatto families, a state of affairs which set imaginations to work, gnawed at, it's true, by jealousy. Dachine, the municipal dustman, was adamant that the lawyer had been acting as a husband to his daughters since his wife, a good deal younger than him, had gone off with a silver-tongued fellow from Town. Didn't the three girls always go out together, hand in hand, their gaze lowered and duly chaperoned by their father, to take mass? As for Ali Tanin, he affected a deep disgustance for their flesh, which, he assured us, was young and yet already soured by confinement and heat. The eldest still has some beauty left, he added, but for how much longer? Do not forget that the mulatto woman, the opposite of the negress, is born angelic, ages quickly and turns into a harpy at about forty while the negress, the older she gets, the more seductive she becomes. This is one of our mysteries that nobody has ever been able to explain! Besides, nobody in Grand-Anse called the lawyer's daughters by their names. We simply said 'the three Féquesnoy misses' as if they just formed one and the same entity. Everybody remembered the hilarity that had convulsed the lawyer when Thimoléon, all proud in his '14–'18 veteran's uniform, had gone to propose marriage. Féquesnoy had received him on the doorstep and had answered equably:

'But my dear fellow, my daughters aren't for you. I'm reserving them for France-whites. And anyway, you're nearly as old as me.'

'I'm prepared to marry any of them . . . even the youngest who's cross-eyed.'

Then, in front of everyone, the lawyer took a little comb out of his pocket and pretended to comb his hair.

'You're a good chap, Thimoléon,' he said, 'but I don't want grandchildren with barbed wire on their heads. A comb must go through their hair without a snag and it's not with a black man like you that I'll see that happen.'

As France-whites were few and far between in the North of the island, the three Féquesnoy girls set out on the slippery slope to old maidenhood, but without protests since we never heard shouting coming from their house. Soon they didn't go out at all any more and we ended up forgetting that they existed. Newcomers to the village like Eau de Café had only ever rarely seen them. Only one person still nurtured a passion for them – for all three at the same time, with a preference for the eldest with her sombre face – a black man with big toes, untrained and uneducated, who was a trafficker in stolen objects before attaining the pseudo-respectability of a bus driver: Chief Bérard. He imposed his hard man's law on a whole part of the village, notably the area where the Féquesnoy residence was to be found. His clique of flatterers maintained that the two most feared fellows in Martinique were the infamous Goldmouth from Fort-de-France, who had all his teeth replaced with gold, and the driver of the 'Golem'. When anyone was bold enough to put forward the name of Julien Thémistocle, Chief Bérard would shrug his shoulders before declaring:

'Well, I use only natural means.'

But in terms of nastiness, they were an equal match. Chief Bérard had his scapegoats and it was a bad day for him if he hadn't given Coolie René a punch or pushed Bogino into committing some stupid act which would earn him the scorn of the villagers. He was the village's best speaker of mock Arabic and he helped himself free of charge at Syrian's shop without the latter daring to protest. It was if he levied a tithe on the owner of the Palace of the Orient. Whenever he needed a khaki shirt, an elegant charmer's pair of trousers, or even a piece of material for one of his many mistresses, he would burst into the shop with enormous bluster:

'Hey, Syrian! *Maktoub nilsam adjamlik!* Your flannel, where's the pink flannel I saw here yesterday afternoon? *Talham yeddoum bouzhaf iskanhoum!* . . . Come on, the scissors, my friend, move your arse. Here we are, right, you cut me four metres and don't try anything funny. *Allah-ramnèk nilfaz nkoutayeb!* . . .'

Syrian would rush to satisfy his requests without so much as a scowl or a frown. On the contrary, he would stoop forward in a thousand obsequious bows which, far from placating the hard man, seemed to exasperate him. It took some time for us to realize that the Mohammedan had found the best defence against Chief Bérard's depredations. Had he voiced the slightest protestation, the latter would have ransacked the Palace of the Orient. Moreover, as Ali Tanin grew up, Bérard reduced his hold-ups, not that he feared Syrian's son who had nothing of the warrior about him, but because he was afraid that one of his girlfriends, particularly the younger ones, might fall for the green of the bastard-Syrian's eyes and his sugary words.

The mystery of the tough's Carib ancestry, which had bequeathed him prominent cheekbones, slanted eyes and wavy hair, had intrigued quite a few of us, not least his mother, a preening negress of solid stock, particularly as she had no recollection of having erred with one of those most rare specimens of humanity. She had been flabbergasted by the Amerindian features of the newly born child and blamed herself for having continued to wash the laundry at the side of the river until the labour pains had gripped her entrails. She had followed her grandmother's advice by placing a flat stone on her head in the place of the bundle of washing which she left by the roadside. This allowed her to reach her house slowly and calmly, singing a liquid honey song to the approval of the blackbirds that were saying their prayer as they flew in the air. The child was born at the moment when the moon appeared in all its fullness over Morne l'Étoile and the woman felt the overwhelming urge to whisper to him an incomprehensible word that she had heard among the birth-pang groaning of her mother and older sisters, a word that she kept saying for a very long night of time and whose meaning she didn't even think to discover. This word, or rather this short, harsh cry, which seemed to crack the celestial vault and bounce back on to the stars, sounded like 'Anakalinoté'. From an early age, Anakali, as he was nicknamed, was fierce. At the age of two, he bit a snake to death; a year later, he fixed his father's eye with a steady stare for almost a minute; at ten, he had his own cutlass, was looking around for work on his own account and was making more than enough to feed the household. Everyone forgave him everything because, as they whispered to one side:

'He's a black Carib!'

Neither his mother or father nor the constabulary made him go to school. And yet he took his brothers and sisters there although he never went into the yard (some say the opposite, however). All day long, he wandered deep in the woods, where nobody would have dared to follow him, driven by the instincts of his race. He dug up wild yams, carved figures into the cathedral-sized rocks that the volcano had flung there at the beginning of the century and fed himself with unknown or terrifying creatures. In September he worshipped the god Hurakan, the maker of hurricanes which could destroy the universe. Faced with torn-up houses, gutted gardens, mangled trees and drowned animals, the black Carib laughed so cruelly that it pierced your soul. Then, over the years, he rejoined the path of ordinary humanity without anybody knowing quite why. He took a job like anyone else cutting sugar-cane and spent his wages on Saturday evening in the rum shop or on the young ladies who were attracted by his wavy hair and almond eyes. He enjoyed great celebrity when three white archaeologists decided to measure him from head to foot and photographed him from all angles. His picture even appeared in a Fort-de-France newspaper on that occasion. When he was thirty, he went down to live in the village of Grand-Anse where he carved himself out a fiefdom as a formidable chief. He managed to win the respect of Thimoléon, the carpenter, who was his senior, and they agreed to draw up the boundaries of their respective territories. His mistresses clubbed together to enable him to buy a Dodge truck which he turned into a bus and baptized the 'Golem', being a great cinema connoisseur.

'I have no use for brakes on the hills, ladies and gentlemen,' he would warn his passengers as they got on his bus. 'Let those who are afraid of death dismount here and now, dammit!'

He had always shown a certain deference towards Eau de Café although she wasn't one of his customers (she preferred the 'Executioner of the North' which was reserved for the well-to-do). So when he realized that she had been constantly spying on him for the many months that he had been secretly smitten with the eldest Féquesnoy girl, the black Carib became shamefaced. He backed away from the window-ledge of the derelict house from where he could see into the mulattos' courtyard, stumbled over the window-frames and pieces of rubble which littered the ground and stood in front of Eau de Café, his head bowed and silent.

'I like hearing the music she plays on the piano,' murmured Eau de Café.

'It's . . . it's true, her hands are like, you could say, feathers from a . . . humming-bird . . .'

'And yet it's music for whites!'

'She doesn't know the meaning of happiness, her face has sadness written on it,' said Chief Bérard.

They walked together in the evening gloom of the narrow streets like two people who had known each other for a very long time even though their friendship was just born. Each of them felt lighter, more prepared to accept the world's injustices, even to laugh at them. He told her how his first and last schoolmaster had put him off studying once and for all when he had caught him speaking in Creole to his classmates and had ordered him as punishment to learn *Andromaque* by heart. Every morning, before lessons started, he was to recite a scene from this play to the teacher and so fled for ever before the end of the second act (hence the legend according to which he had never been to school). She spoke to him about her passionate and chaotic relationship with the maroon Julien Thémistocle, guilty of having raped her mother Franciane to death in times so long ago that people mixed them up with those of slavery although a good sixty years must have separated them. He admitted that he had sometimes come across Thémistocle in the depths of the forest without exchanging anything more than a simple gesture of solidarity.

'Two male crabs can't live in the same hole, you know,' he remarked. He made Eau de Café promise not to give away his secret, as it would only take Ma Léonce or some other shrew of the same ilk to get wind of it for him to become straight away the laughing stock of Grand-Anse.

'Do you want me to go and ask Mistress Féquesnoy on your behalf, my friend?'

'No . . . no, thank you,' the black Carib blurted out hoarsely. 'She loves someone else . . .'

And he vanished into the dusk on tiptoes so as not to disturb anybody's sleep . . .

18

In his youth, shortly after the First Great War, the island white
Honoré de Cassagnac had refused to marry his first cousin, which
provoked a sort of hullabaloo across the country. The most eminent figures within the caste made the journey to Grand-Anse to
win him over but the fellow would not comply with their injunc-
tions. He had always displayed a rebellious temperament and
normally chose a strange solitude, broken only by his escapades
to local fêtes, where he rolled the dice in games of *sèrbi* with people of all colours, or to funeral wakes, which he seemed to enjoy.
Black story-tellers appeared to exert a powerful fascination over
him, so nobody was surprised when he treated them favourably
on his plantation. He was only known to have one declared
enemy: the maroon Julien Thémistocle.

'It's because they're too alike, those two!' went the whisper
each time that, tipped off by some informant, he mounted his
extraordinary steed, Icarus, his double-barrelled gun in his hand,
and galloped off through the woods in pursuit of that outlaw
whose frequent incursions on to his land were beginning to upset
him.

In truth, whether among whites like himself or in the company
of black folk, de Cassagnac always seemed to be elsewhere, with
his melancholic expression and bearing suggesting some secret
gnawing away at his soul. His father could reproach him for nothing since he had taken over from him as a natural master and the
Séguineau plantation was one of the most prosperous in Martinique. His main fear was that his son would fall for one of those
mulatto women with the killer smile who could unsettle the mind
of any healthy man with a simple sway of the hips. That Honoré
kept five or six of these wenches, as was the convention in those
days, he didn't mind at all, especially as this practice allowed the

planter bosses to establish their authority among ordinary people, but from there to cohabiting with one of them like that Prévot de Cherville from the *commune* of Lamentin, what a disaster, for fuck's sake! With the greatest discretion the old planter had removed most of the young women who might have been able to turn his son's head, either by lending them to other island whites or by pushing them, with the help of a tidy sum of money, into moving in with the first black man who showed an interest in them. He had only made the mistake of overlooking a haughty *câpresse* named Franciane who always went about in rags and who had built her house apart from the black people's shacks. Since he had passed on the estate and was no longer personally involved in hiring his workers, he no longer knew many of them. They just about managed to greet him when he went by, but sometimes the old man didn't even know their names. If, on the other hand, he knew Franciane's, it was because the savage light in her eyes had struck him one evening as she was sharpening her cutlass on the stable grindstone.

'Why does that negress seem to bear a grudge against the whole world?' he had asked the men without any of them replying.

Then he forgot about her since, after all, she did all the jobs that the plantation foreman gave her with good grace. There were already enough idlers to punish and thieves to winkle out without worrying about good workers as well! When he had had to provide a plausible explanation for the collapse of the wedding arrangements that the de Cassagnac and Dupin de Médeuil families had been planning at length throughout 1921 and 1922, Honoré's father found himself, against his better judgment, forced to take his son's defence by bursting into a pretend rage in front of the gathering of his peers:

'Who is going to cast the first stone, eh? Us Creole whites, we leave our new-born babies in the hands of our negress servants. They wash them, make them pretty, dress them and caress them on the pretext that our wives are too frail for that sort of work and then we're surprised when later we have a taste for coloured women. I challenge each of you here present to look me straight in the eye and to tell me that you wouldn't rather have slept every night next to a black or mulatto woman if the world had been a different place.'

The big whites had grumbled, unable to retort to old man de Cassagnac's outburst and, avoiding the question altogether, had at once decided to find another party for Honoré's cousin, whose dowry was already arranged and who could not have been allowed to become an old maid for obvious financial reasons. In the meantime, if you choose to believe bush radio, our unwilling suitor had fled the plantation, not to escape from what he viewed as time-wasting bargaining, but because a sullen fury was eating away at his guts. His most faithful muleteer, Ugly Congo, had been insulted and pushed off his horse by Julien Thémistocle as he was handing out demijohns of cool water to the cane-cutters. The maroon had boasted:

'I am Master of the Plains, he who possesses the three gifts: invisibility, ubiquity and invincibility. From this moment on, I reign over the whole of the North. It must be written down: Julien Thémistocle, Lord after God of the gullies and canefield paths, shall bring the colony, and then the world itself, to its knees.'

And, in front of the workers gaping with admiration, he had revealed how he had acquired his gifts:

'The first evening of the first night of my sojourn in the middle of the forest, in the hollow of locust-tree trunks struck by lightning, in the tendons of solemn ebony trees, there he was: the Enemy. As the moon waned, he raised his army from the borders of the woods which line the La Capote river and led it amidst a colossal rustling sound up to the breast-shaped summits of our sacred hills, Grand and Petit Jacob. I tried in vain to put some distance between me and them, but it was hopeless. I was surrounded. Surrounded by humans below, in the plain. Surrounded by serpents on the hillsides. I said a few prayers, learnt from my grandfather, who knew how to tame them, without managing to slow the dreadful creeping which bit by bit was closing in around me. The hissing that was coming from their shiny scale-covered bodies froze my legs and I felt the moment approach when I would scream my terror to the face of the night. My cutlass brought down a shower of creepers as I cut myself a way through, but as they fell they turned into lancehead vipers rising up hieratically and seeming to stare at me. In reality, they were showing me the way to Bothrops, the Original Female (who is said to be hermaphrodite) whose resting place for all eternity has been at the place named The Fall on the spur of Grand Jacob. The site is a waterfall encircled by gigantic rocks with, at its foot, a pool of clear water where snakes entrusted with defending the temple swim. In a rugged hollow within the central rock, the rock over which the waterfall glides sublimely, Bothrops watches over the remains of Watanani, the last king of the Carib Indians and Chief Bérard's ancestor, and the skull of N'Songo, the maroon who seized his freedom as they were unloading the slave ship at the quay at Pointe des Nègres in the time of yesteryear.

'Whenever you cane-cutters used to talk to me with reverence of The Fall at the time when, as an apprentice foreman, I was pitilessly hunting down the sons of Bothrops, I laughed at what I took to be the fruit of childish imagination or fantasies fevered by bad rum. Who had ever been to The Fall? Who had ever seen the great she-snake, the subject of so many legendary tales? Nobody, of course. I also had to struggle against the foreman who had convinced old man de Cassagnac that the lanceheads were the plantation's police force. And on what grounds, if you please? Because they ate the rats and discouraged little boys from devouring the ripe cane, both huge scourges suffered by our best cane pieces, I admit. But who had held in his arms the negress Herminia from Fond Gens-Libres as she drooled with a deadly foam after a pit viper had bitten her in the neck? To whom did she leave in her dying moments the task of looking after her twelve needy offspring? To me, Julien Thémistocle, who has never known what goes by the name of family. And, Ugly Congo, I haven't even mentioned your own brother, that giant who spoke only African, a hard worker who had dragged his carcass without snivelling around all the plantations of Grand-Anse. He had taught me how to plant that fragile and beautiful *malavoi* cane so that it resists the flash floods of the rainy season months as well as the storms that interrupt the dry season without warning. What was his undoing was his belief that he was forever immune to pit-viper bites from the day that, by a miracle, he survived one of them. He went around saying cheerfully: "The viper and me, we're two of a kind. Each of us knows where his territory ends, you know . . ."

'But one flaming afternoon in June, the beast in question crossed that border just as the Congo had his arm raised for the downward sweep of his cutlass, and as he brought it down on to the cane's stalk the snake only had to brush against him, for death had already started to seize the man as he stood there, in a caval-cade of sun and sweat. We tried in vain to put a hot iron on the bite and to make him drink an infusion of cure-all herb, but he died right there, in the cane piece, at the feet of the pack-mule which had been startled by the snake's presence. So the sorrow-fulness was mine alone, not the foreman's, nor de Cassagnac's, as neither of them were upset by such a small thing and merely had a few bottles of rum sent for the wake and four planks for the cof-fin. That's why I went against their orders by encircling the vipers in the way that Ugly Congo's brother had taught me. For those of you who are too young to have seen me at work, this is how I did it: I selected a group of cane-cutters known for their courage and positioned them all around the cane piece at Rivière-Feuilles, the thickest and hence the one on the whole plantation most likely to conceal pit vipers. I then told the cane gatherers to stamp on the ground with their heels to wake the filthy beasts and gave the signal to attack. The straw shivered with one great rustling as the first canes collapsed in an avalanche of green leaves that seemed to shroud the daylight.

'"There's one!" a cutter would shout from time to time.

'And before his cutlass could come down, the viper had disap-peared into the middle of the cane piece, no doubt leading its fel-lows in a desperate stampede. I gave orders for the work to stop every so often to make sure that the cutting was proceeding at the same speed on all sides. Otherwise, it would only have taken someone to be cutting deeper than the others at a particular place for a host of vipers to slip out into the shadow of the canes and make it to the nearby woods. As the cutting progressed, the cane piece began to look like a tuft of hair. The furious hissing of the snakes stopped any joking on our part. I first made certain that no pile of straw would spread fire to the rest of the plantation and then ordered four men, positioned at equal distances from the cane piece, to throw in burning torches. The cane immediately caught fire, sending mauve and blue flames skywards. The vipers span around, crashed into each other and tried to find a way out while we showered them with insults, the women even more colourfully than us: "*Lisife! Yich Djab! Mo, bann isalop!*" (Lucifer! Devil's children! Die, you gang of filthy bastards!)

'At Rivière-Feuilles, once the last torch had been extinguished, we would more often than not pick up fifty viper corpses that I was quick to have buried on a stony outcrop where few people ever went. And so, right from the first night of the first day of my wanderings, the viper race had decided to make me pay for the entire weight of suffering that I had been inflicting on them for a century of time. Everything around me became a snake: the branches of the bread-nut trees, the Guinea grass, the stumps and creepers. But none of them attacked me, and instead I was forced to take the one and only path open to me, the one leading to The Fall. It was far from being the imaginary place, whose mention once made me shrug with disbelief. The Fall truly existed. Its waterfall was singing. Its smooth and sonorous rocks enclosed the cave that acted as home to the Original Bothrops. The black snake, which was about twenty feet long, moved so that it was directly beneath the waterfall and stared at me with its strange orange iris. Only the extraordinarily pronounced arches above its eyes twitched with a mechanical movement. I was so frightened that it took me some time to make this plea: "Snake God, what do you want of me? I am nothing more than a poor runaway black with only the forests for a haven . . ."

'Bothrops remained motionless, unflinching, its flattened head pounded by the floods of moon-tinted water. I realized that it couldn't hear my words any more than it could the din made by the waterfall. "The viper hears with its body," Ugly Congo's brother used to say. "Even if you yell next to it, it won't touch you. If you fire a gun, it won't know a thing about it unless it's seen the flash of the bullet. To start a conversation with a viper, you've got to bang the ground and make it shake." I tried gingerly and saw Bothrops rise up, almost imperceptibly at first, then more and more quickly and to my great surprise, I could understand its language. I could grasp the sense of each vibration of its scales! An indescribable joy took hold of me and lifted me clean into the middle of the waterfall where the water was soothingly warm. A cloud covered the moon and the cascade suddenly stopped falling. The hermaphrodite Bothrops unwound itself completely and dived into the water towards me, wrapping itself around me from head to foot. It led me into depths that weren't dark where I could make out fantastic creatures whose existence I could never have suspected in my previous life. Its forked penis entered me from behind, mine slipped between the iridescent scales of its opening and we made love for forty-seven and a half days. At dusk on the last day of our copulation, Bothrops returned to its lair while the water began to cascade down again. My mind was numbed. For the first time I could feel the coldness of the place and I was impatient for the night to come to an end. Bothrops climbed to the top of the waterfall, stretched out on an enormous flat stone and surrendered to sleep. At the same time its tail beat gently against the side of the rock, saying to me:

"Black man Julien Thémistocle! I have made you into a snake-man. From now on, you will be as invisible as we are. You will glide among the thickets without exciting the hatred of the estate dogs for you will have no smell. You will also be everywhere at the same time. You will strike, just like us, in all places at all times and your bite will be fatal. They will accord you such limitless respectation that they will no longer dare to speak your name. Just as they call us *bêtes-longues* so as to magic away, or so they think, our menacing presence, so they will adorn you with all sorts of title: the invisible sorcerer, the invincible maroon, the ubiquitous one and even Mister Immortal! And so you will die the day that you give in to their worship, in other words when you yourself begin to believe in all their mumbo-jumbo. Respect the snake, he will show you the way. Be gone and try to undo this iniquitous world that the whites have imposed upon the universe."

'Had I been dreaming? Had I allowed myself to be carried away by the treacherous caress of the moonbeams? I couldn't have said. What was sure was that I began to get to know my new brothers and noticed that snakes formed tribes just as different one from the other as our various peoples. I got to know the yellow dawn lancehead that waits for daybreak on the arid slopes of Morne Bois and tries to sink its fangs into the sun's head. I enjoyed the company of the yellow-laquered, brown-spotted lancehead which seems to smile as it shows its tongue before falling upon the manicou. I developed a particular affection for the black lancehead from Moulin l'Étang whose pink-spotted belly rivals wild orchids in beauty. When it goes to the spring to slake its thirst, it dawdles along comically before sinking its head twice into the water and disappearing into the long grass. I've sometimes found the lancehead that's wine purple mixed with green and straw yellow warming itself against my chest on evenings when icy winds were blowing over Grand Jacob. But the most amazing is the female of silky grey spotted with black. What a reptilian marvel! I watched her for hours caring for her skin during the sloughing season. She would look for the prickly pear tree against which she would rub herself delicately until a spine became caught under one of her scales and she would then uncoil herself with just as much majesty, leaving her old skin as fodder for the nests of crazy ants. The kohl that circles her eyes was even more intoxicating than the way Franciane-the-proud walks. Ha! That negress is mine. Go and tell your boss as much! I won't tire of tormenting you until she submits to my desire.'

Honoré de Cassagnac was torn between puzzlement and hysterics each time he was confronted with tales of this sort. The black man or the Indian who would relate it to him was always so serious in attitude and so sincere in what he said that he couldn't decently slap him around the ear for making a mockery of him. Many a time the name of that Franciane cropped up and although he had never set eyes on her, he was already prepared to adore her. What strength she must have to resist the spells of that Julien Thémistocle, who was in league with pit vipers! He loved her unusual name. And her 'grand manners' which irritated the rabble so thoroughly. But too busy as he was pursuing the man whom he had come to consider as his personal adversary, and exhausting to death no fewer than five horses in less than a month in the process, he didn't try to encounter her. Oftentimes he was on the point of finally giving up the hunt for the outlaw, especially when he realized that Thémistocle moved at night and slept during the day. It was no surprise, then, that his shadow was spotted at Fond Massacre the day after he had been seen at Rivière Claire. Honoré de Cassagnac had him in his sights in the brightness of midday, while the maroon was slumped among the twisted roots of a wild fig tree. He had purposely had two silver bullets made, alone capable of piercing the protective spell that the maroon boasted of possessing. The island white came so close to him that he could have shot him point-blank. The supreme pride etched into the outlaw's features struck him profoundly. He spent a long while gazing at that black and muscular body, stirred by a light breathing which sometimes gave way to a drawn-out twitching in the arms and legs. Placing the barrel of his weapon next to the sleeping man's temple, he closed his eyes before pulling the trigger. Suddenly he felt his fingers go numb, the metal of the gun freeze between his hands and his eyesight cloud over. Honoré de Cassagnac stumbled quickly out from the shade of the wild fig and felt the midday sun hit him full in the eyes, blinding him for the rest of the day. He had time to force his way into the undergrowth and to wait for nightfall. From there he could hear the maroon call on his grandfather who, Honoré discovered, had placed his tomb at the foot of the wild fig. The two men, the living and the dead, listed the crimes that the whites had committed since they had taken over the island ten man generations before. Honoré learned all that the black man held against the white, listened to the litany of his sufferings and discovered a whole lot of secret wounds to be added to the daily cruelties, amazed that all he expected from him, the master, was a little modesty. He realized that Julien Thémistocle took no pleasure in setting fire to the canefields, in extorting money from the plantation workers, molesting their wives or insulting their ancestors. The fellow wandered because wandering was his only way of existing. His only way of shouting to the world that he existed. Once again he said:

'I want that Franciane, that stuck-up negress for me and me alone.'

The next day, Honoré could only fire his gun into the air; the wild fig and its surroundings were deserted. Not a trace of footsteps or fire. He had no choice but to go back down to the plantation, trotting slowly despite his normal love of galloping. Perhaps it was that unusual pace that allowed him to make out, among the flock of women busy tying the canes into piles, the one who answered to the name of Franciane and who was supposed to be so exceptional. At first sight, she was as grotesquely wrapped in old rags as her sisters in poverty, but everything about her was of a higher order. The way she bent down, took hold of the canes, bound them into piles and weighed them. Just to watch her move, a stranger to all ostentation and naturally divine, was a true spectacle. Honoré called her over in a voice so lacking in its customary impatience that everyone realized there and then that she had just won a place in his heart. For the first time, Franciane allowed herself a smile and set back to work with a vengeance since she would never again have to wear herself out with such toil. When Julien Thémistocle came to prowl around her house a few days later, he could only give a long and terrible moan. The stuck-up negress was by now living in the master's house and was thus irreversibly sullied in his eyes. He came under Honoré de Cassagnac's windows to scream his rage, to call him all the names under the sun, his defeat seemingly giving him every right to do so. The stoical island white put up with this overflowing of sorrow for the best part of a month. He would merely draw the curtains before sitting down at his desk, cluttered with papers, ink wells and pen holders. For almost ten years he had been chained to the task of establishing the genealogy of his family from the moment that his ancestors had left Anjou to settle in the French Isles of America. His father had hired a mulatto tutor for him during his adolescence to prevent him becoming as ignorant as the other planter's children who lived far away from Town. He had abandoned plans to send Honoré to the Colonial Boarding-school after the premature death of his mother, the most beautiful Marie-Anne Dupin de Médeuil. So one fine morning, exploding with irritation, Honoré appeared at the top of the flight of stairs in front of the house and yelled at Julien Thémistocle:

'*Sa ki papa'w? Es ou konnèt papa'w? Epi ès papa papa'w konnèt papa'y menm?*' (Who's your father? Do you know who was your father's father? And then your father's father, would he know his own father?)

'My father's father tamed lancehead vipers at Morne Jacob!'

'That may be so, but his father, where did he come from? Did he even have a name? A family?' said the *béké* heatedly. 'You blacks, you're the sons of nobodies.'

Julien Thémistocle bared all his white teeth to the sun and, walking slowly towards the white man who had tried so long to shoot him down, put his face inches away from his enemy's, his breath hot and moist in the other's eyes:

'You who asks so many questions, do you know where you come from, eh? Do you know whether your great grandmother didn't allow a black man to spread her thighs?'

A crowd had gathered in front of the master's house and the plantation foreman was already getting ready to leap to his defence, when those there witnessed the unbelievable sight of Honoré de Cassagnac taking the dirty and dishevelled maroon by the arm to lead him into his drawing-room. The cane-replanting preparations came to a sudden halt and the workers sat in a circle under the nearby trees, passing around flasks of white rum and chewing tobacco. The speechless foreman had stayed rooted to the spot in the full sun, stammering uncontrollably:

'I don't believe what my two eyes have seen! It's impossible! Men, tell me it's not true, for God's sake!'

Inside, the spectacle was even more comical. Julien Thémistocle walked through the house with a hangdog look, anxious not to damage the carpet or knock over some precious object. Such a profusion of order and serene luxury had seized him by the throat and robbed him of his strength. He had lost all his self-assurance and couldn't even find the words to reply to Honoré's polite questions. The white first showed him a strange arrangement of patterns on a small blue linen cushion hung up in the middle of the drawing-room.

'That is our coat of arms,' he said with no trace of vanity in his voice. 'My family belongs to the oldest nobility of Anjou. Under the coat of arms, if you could read, you would be able to make out the following, although the letters are a little faint: "azur with gold chevron accompanyed by three likewise arrow tips two placed middle chief the other at point". That's the design's description . . . My ancestor, Izaïe de Cassagnac, filed his titles of nobility before the Sovereign Council of Martinique on the ninth of March in the year 1673. He had arrived here in 1667 after, for obscure reasons, he had been sacked from his post as brewer to the King . . . From his marriage to a woman whose name I can't yet manage to find he had eleven children, of whom the eldest, Georges, was born in 1680. As you know, among us noble whites, only the eldest sons are entitled to carry their father's name. The other children attach the name to that of their wife . . . Sit down, don't be afraid, often when I come home exhausted, I fall asleep in one of these chairs with my boots covered in mud and my clothes dripping with sweat. Nanny Ferlise, who's been like a second mother to me, undresses me as I sleep! Nanny Ferlise! O! Ferli-i-se! . . .'

Honoré's black nanny trotted into the drawing-room as quickly as she could and almost fell over backwards when she saw the maroon comfortably installed next to her master. Her eyes bulging with disbelief, she hardly heard Honoré order her to prepare two rum punches and instead came back with a bottle of dessert wine. She served the white, looked the black man up and down while tutting with disgust, and turned on her heels.

'So Georges de Cassagnac in his turn married Angélique Baillardeau, whose father was commanding captain of the Martinique militia and a rich planter at the time. After three stillborn and a daughter, she had François, born in 1712, who married his first cousin Catherine Fermilly de Lavoisière. They had nine children, of which the eldest, Jean-Michel, was born in 1741. His first wife was barren, so in a second marriage he took Marie-Ursule Crassin de Médouze. They were responsible for an unknown number of children but the one who perpetuated the branch of eldest sons – and I can prove it – was Octave de Cassagnac, born in 1771, who married Claire-Eugénie Millaud de Sainte-Claire, originally from Anses d'Arlets. Their eldest son, Richard, was born in 1798 . . .'

While the island white was reeling off the list of his ancestors without taking further notice of him and as if talking to himself, Julien Thémistocle, who had long mocked those blacks who couldn't go back further than a generation in naming their families, felt a slow numbness overcome his limbs. He remembered that the only coat of arms that his grandfather sported was the fleur de lys that had been branded on to his shoulder for having run away from the plantation a few years before Abolition. He could hear again that phrase which tortured the old man's mouth whenever he had finished some task or other:

'*Nan Djinen lwen . . . nan Djinen lwen . . .*' (Africa is far away.)

'In 1808,' continued the implacable owner of the Séguineau plantation, 'Jules de Cassagnac married Reine Bany de Richemont. He was made a Knight of Agricultural Merit. In 1889, his son and my father, Pierre-Lambert, married his first cousin once removed, my mother, Marie-Anne, whose father Augustin was registrar of mortgages. They had an only child: me. And if, my dear Julien Thémistocle, I had to list the junior branches of the de Cassagnac family, the Cassagnac de Savinières, the Cassagnac de Beauvallons and others of the ilk, a whole day and night wouldn't suffice. Our race is gently fading away, it is true, for want of rejuvenating itself, and that's why I have had my wife come over from Anjou. She doesn't go out much, ha, ha, ha! . . . But she'll end up getting used to the sun.'

Since that month of February 1924, in fact, when the de Cassagnac Tilbury had deposited several enormous trunks in the courtyard of the Great House, the appearance of the lady from France had been impatiently awaited. She probably arrived at night since nobody could remember having seen her on the road. She was graceful in the way she took care of the bedrooms and drawing-room and sometimes the kitchens, but never went outside. She became pregnant and gave birth to little Marie-Eugénie without attracting the attention of the gossips. Although nobody made clear the connection between the two events, it seems that she started to make appearances outside shortly after her husband had received the maroon Julien Thémistocle in his home. It's true that the latter had stopped his bragging and was now living apart from any other dwelling, humiliated to the depths of his soul, it was said, by the lesson that Honoré de Cassagnac had inflicted on him. When the fellow was drunk in the village bars or country rum shops, he would grumble:

'One day I'll put an end to the de Cassagnac line, you have my word as a Mondongo-black! '

Did he realize that not a single person from hereabouts believed a word of it? Did he realize or not? . . .

19

I can't believe that the days march past, anonymous and identical, on the endless road of time. Each day has its own colour and dimensions but above all its own portents that we most often forget to interpret. This fourteenth of July will remain for ever engraved in the recesses of my memory. In every fibre of my body. At last I am going into Grand-Anse's market-place where my rendez-vous will take place with those I abandoned so long ago that they perhaps don't remember having enchanted my childhood. And yet, inside me, their larger-than-life images have never stopped giving shape to my existence. Just like the monotonance of our sea's waves, for we insist it's ours as though we wouldn't recognize it as the same mysterious creature if it were a little further away from our village.

Each house is sporting a red, white and blue flag, but none can match the effect of the one on the town hall: thirty by ten feet of linen rising up proudly with each gust of wind. From dawn onwards, a loudspeaker has been playing the *Marseillaise* from the balcony on the first floor, filling the hearts of each of us with a strange sort of exaltation. I try to resist this charm, so insidious that it makes your lip quiver or your gaze uncertain. The ex-navy man has put on a magnificent white uniform and on his cap you can make out, although slightly faded, 'The Terrible'.

'I don't like to boast about it,' he confides in me, 'but just as Hitler got his hands on Paris, our ship managed to get away to the West Indies. In November 1940 we were at Basse-Terre, in Guadeloupe . . .'

The Oceanic Hotel smells sweetly of the polish that the maid has spread all around. From my window I can see Thimoléon helping Eau de Café decorate her shop with bouquets of arum lilies and jacarandas. The entire front of his jacket is pin-pricked with decorations acquired in the service of eternal France during two world wars. On Front Street the buses are disgorging tightly packed groups of country people, stiff and formal because of the ties they are wearing in case of circumstances beyond their control, as they put it. An irresistible euphoria is in the air, contained by a sense of seriousness that can be measured by the quietness of the female chattering outside the church and above all by the good behaviour of their kids. I feel happy somewhere inside me and reject this inexplicable feeling. And first and foremost, today I shall free myself from Thimoléon's omnipresence at my side, from his advice, from his veiled threats. I'm not going to have lunch with Eau de Café just to hear her ask me:

'Have you prayed for France, my boy?'

The parade of the war veterans to the memorial, where the statue of a black infantryman struts under the protection of a great white angel armed with a sword, provides the opportunity for the little Mussolini who leads the *commune* to show off his talent for verbosity. This character is a walking poem in himself. It's said that at primary school he showed an immense enthusiasm for Rome and Julius Caesar. As soon as he had two sons, moreover, he named the first Romulus and the second Remus. He probably didn't make a clear distinction between France and Italy, both in truth distant lands and peopled by beings the colour of cassava flour, as the one and only globe in his school was smashed to smithereens by the cannon-like shot of a budding centre-forward who had stolen it a few days after it had been acquired with great pomp and ceremony. As soon as the Duce started making his mischief, our hero, who had already got himself elected mayor, began to swear by him and stuck up in his office and in the corridors of his town hall big photos taken from Italian newspapers, which he obtained nobody knew where. It was no great surprise that he was one of the very few coloured mayors to be kept in post by Admiral Robert's Pétainist regime. According to witnesses from the period, the little Mussolini accentuated his resemblance with his model by trying to roll his 'r's, a particularly difficult business for a Creole when it comes to the beginning and end of words (in the middle, it's not so bad!). And an extraordinary achievement for a man whose trousers were strangers to the school bench. And yet, he wasn't entirely lacking a sense of humour as you can see from the crest and motto that he had carved above the town hall entrance and above his own front door. This graphic masterpiece represented a Roman pikestaff crossed with a Martinican cutlass, under which was written in red letters 'Veni–Vidi–Vichy'.

Little Mussolini's speech at the foot of the fatherland's altar sounds a first false note amidst the harmony of this day. I can't help but laugh to myself at his gobbledegook that nobody, either old soldier or spectator, tries to follow. His words rise, tumble down and then rise again after many a slip and slide in the heat that is about to settle its halo around the village. Suddenly, his words become clear and he is denouncing 'those strangers who come to destroy the tranquillity of our green meadows and the soft warmth of our heavenly beaches'. People look up and stare at each other questioningly, whispering into one another's ears as our hero is now straying from the speech he'd given last year at the same date and that of the year before last and so on right back to the first day that he had 'climbed the steps of the Pantheon of municipal glory'. It was the undeniable truth that for twenty years the little Mussolini had been giving his assembled people the same bombastic sermon and that everybody knew by heart its most tortuous meanderings. Sometimes, in the evening, when a father was bored, he might ask one of his sons to look in the dictionary for the meaning of words like 'halcyon', 'falcon's flight', 'bolshevism' or 'acquiesce', but no one had ever managed to grasp the meaning of a whole sentence from the said speech. And now, believe it or not, here was *monsieur* the chief councillor adding a whole new passage that was clarity incarnate to boot!

Thimoléon decides to ignore me. He doesn't want any trouble. He observes a truce on the fourteenth of July and forgets his Communist convictions. The rum shops on Back Street joyously welcome the thirsty veterans. Sack races are organized on Front Street, while a duck shoot is advertised 'at the seaside'. I stroke the pair of dice at the bottom of my pocket that I bought the day before at Ali Tanin's. I walk with measured tread towards the market, careful not to irritate any tough with my clumsy city-boy bearing. I'm aware that at the least indiscretion on my part they will be quick to surround me. And to rearrange my face with the help of a razor. Every hard man has his own trademark: sometimes a simple slash across the chin, or an elaborate pattern on the face, or even a hole (because a piece of flesh has been cut away). Rare are the dice-players who don't carry some scar picked up at Grand-Anse itself or elsewhere during *sèrbi* games, the slightest details of which they recount for many years after.

I go into the market building. It's the fourteenth of July. The gestures are serious. The smiles are heavy with hidden meaning. The grumblings are tantamount to whole sentences that are immediately understood. From the entrance I spot the various territories which will be established and disestablished bit by bit as the day, and especially the evening, progresses. I can see the table where the coolie Indians, wrapped in an even vaster silence than usual, throw the dice with a silky movement and pick up their stakes as if they were stroking a horse's neck. The blackness of their shiny hair captures my eye for a moment or two. A woman picks up a sheaf of little tricolour flags which had been badly fixed to the main pillar of the building. A player leaps towards her, kisses one of the flags, goes back to his table and shouts 'Eleven!' His opponents snigger malevolently. He loses, looks desperately in his socks for a last bank-note and finally retreats on tiptoe. The table which he's just abandoned, the one belonging to the Congos, is the most terrifying of all, as the players casually finger either a razor or a flick-knife, and what is certain is that they must have hidden behind their backs, between shirt and skin, an even more fearful weapon. At the mulattos' table, they show off a deliberately ostentatious disinterest, so that people don't go thinking that such well-to-do people have become keen on a game for lawless and godless layabouts. A mulatto can come and rub shoulders with the hoi polloi here once a year, not more.

I know that I've got to start at the tables which are open to anyone, those where the stakes are so derisory that the winner can let you off paying without it being proof of his magnanimity. I go back over the rules of *sèrbi*, as taught to me by Thimoléon, and being far from gifted at mental arithmetic, I shiver at the thought of getting it wrong. There's no place for numbskulls in the market, believe me! I fend off a female player who tries to drag me, hooting with laughter, to the women's table; if you do that, if you throw your first dice against a female, well, you're just a cissy that no serious player will bother about. Dachine, the town dustman, as tall as a policeman's boot, suggests that I take his place.

'Don't worry, old chap! We're just having fun.'

'How much?'

'Thirty francs the stake,' answers one of the players.

'All right!'

'Roll the dice, go on, roll them!' the dwarf encourages me.

But at the very moment that my outstretched arm is about to liberate them from the dice box, a soft, cold hand grabs me by the wrist: it's Eau de Café's. Never, in seventy years of existence, has she been to this place on this particular day of the year. People are well and truly dumbfounded. Games come to a stop at every table except the one where the *béké* de Cassagnac and Ugly Congo the second, the fighting cock breeder, are engaged in a tussle that started three centuries ago. Such is the silence in the market hall that we can now suddenly hear the tinny voice of the town hall's loudspeaker and the crowd cheering the winners of the egg and spoon race, a highly prized contest in Grand-Anse. The contestants' hands are tied behind their necks with a length of mahoe rope and a spoon containing an egg is placed between their teeth. They have to run a hundred metres without dropping it. During each electoral campaign little Mussolini promises to register this sport at the Olympic Games, 'since like this at least, we will have a gold medal to shine with all its flames like a solar star in the firmament belonging to our gallant Grand-Anse youth'.

'Come with your grandmother, come on home . . .' says Eau de Café to me in a voice that will suffer no reply.

I resist. I take her hand and try to reason with her softly. She won't listen. Or understand. She has become deaf. She stamps her foot and threatens to have a stroke if I don't fall into line. I look around for Thimoléon. Perhaps he'll be my lifebuoy. He'll take my side. He'll talk some sense into his old friend. But the carpenter has gone up to the veterans' table and is busy rolling dice, which encourages the other tables to start playing again. I'm now at the mercy of Godmother.

'You won't learn anything in this pigsty,' she declares as if to convince me.

'Oh, yes! So you know what I'm looking for, do you?'

'Don't get on your high horse, young man! Let's go, otherwise tomorrow morning heaven knows what they'll be whispering about poor old me. Eau de Café spends her time with *sèrbi* players! Eau de Café lost a hundred thousand francs against the Congos and tra-la-la and fiddledy-dee . . .'

The afternoon has barely started. The streets have emptied a little as people wait for the sun to turn down its heat. Even the sea seems to sink back on itself. A suddenly merry Eau de Café skips into the road, leaving me the pavement. A sort of joyful calm fills me gradually although I can't tell where it comes from. Perhaps because I've never held Godmother's hand so long in mine. People are smiling at us from their windows.

'I'll tell you everything you want to know about Antilia. Be patient, my boy, patience is God's gift, you know.'

I wait until eight in the evening, the hour at which she gives in to sleep, to make my way quickly back to the market where the dice are rolling and hitting with more rancour. More unbearable rancour . . .

Dearest,

They have tied us up. The belly of our city is a quivering wound. La Savane encircled by its century-old tamarind trees, where you are always surprised by the cold of the marble benches, the sardonic smile of Joséphine, the Empress of the French, and, most fundamentally, by the speechifying that takes place there. Like when that respectable old gentleman in a pure wool suit and fob watch takes you by the arm and tells you:

'I'm from four generations of mulattos. Four generations, do you hear me! . . . My great grandfather lived opposite the cathedral and every evening at five o clock he came here to read his newspaper. Where would you see someone doing that now, eh? The blacks have taken over these days! '

At the heart of La Savane is a kiosk that the children gladly leave to the gentlemen when the urge takes them to discuss the latest news from Haiti or Germany in their emasculated French. The Great War is still fresh in their memories. The old gentleman is a poet.

'You should have guessed from my gold watch,' he says reproachfully and this is what he recites for you . . .

The blue sea spells out letters of love
On the enchanted shoulder of Sirens.

He is a great poet, a member of the Lutetian Academy and several times laureate at poetry competitions. And a mulatto as well. A mulatto, if you don't mind! A word which cannot be said without the gentlest of pats on the head and an imperceptible swelling of the chest.

'I was on the steamship Colombia *when she made her last crossing to the Metropole, you know, well perhaps you don't know, you're too young . . . She was a famous ship, I can assure you! When she was casting off, her fog-horn would send shivers down the back of everybody in this town, my dear young lady, it was a veritable knell . . . and you should have seen the families of the departing passengers crowded at the bottom of the gangways. You should have seen the intensity of a look, the trembling of a handshake . . . Oh, yes! Now-*

adays you take the plane and woosh! There you are in the mother-
land and the following evening you can already be back again.
There's no more room for memories . . .'

The old mulatto gentleman seems to be as fragile as porcelain. He
tells me that his eldest daughter, a mulatto girl it goes without saying, plays the piano.

This town (this life) is wretched.

Antilia

FIFTH CIRCLE

We mustn't look for the vitality of things in the fine orderation of their schoolbook logic. Our life has always been heavy with sudden fractures quickly patched together again, with interminable ejaculations for want of real love, and the village of Grand-Anse, which keeps an unspeakable secret, or rather a secret that is picked over a thousand times in a thousand different guises, waits.

Perhaps the waiting is the reason for our limitless terror . . .

20 The Death of Coolie René

So *maître* Féquesnoy had three daughters who never went out, determined as he was to preserve their dignity as mulatto women from all contact with common folk. Every Monday, early in the morning, the eldest would make her way to the post office to pick up mysterious parcels or to post a pile of letters to people over there (in other words, France, in our language). The village gossip merchants were at their wits' end at not being able to get to the bottom of this coming and going, and not only Ma Léonce and Eau de Café, but also Ali Tanin's mother before she was thrown out, had besieged the postmistress, encouraging her to open one of these numerous missives. She, for her part, had an elevated idea of her position and was so outraged at the suggestion that it was thought that one of these days she would have a stroke. She resisted for three months and a bit, after which she was discovered paralysed behind her counter, her eyes vacant and her tongue drooling. While we waited for the government to appoint someone to replace her, the little Mussolini cited exceptional circumstances as a pretext for installing one of his mistresses, an easy-going young thing who didn't wait half a second before violating the secret of the Féquesnoy misses.

The news did the rounds of the village, flew through the countryside and, according to some, even reached the adjacent *communes* of Fond d'Or and Basse-Pointe. To tell the truth, nobody knew whether to piss themselves laughing or, on the contrary, to feel sorry. For each of the letters contained a declaration of love and a marriage proposition to a France-white, whose address Miss Féquesnoy had found in the romance magazines that she consumed avidly. As soon as they arrived in the Palace of the Orient, her father would rush there to buy at least half of them. So it was discovered that she had a predilection for *Nous Deux* since most of

185

the addresses she had chosen came from the said magazine.

'*Maître* Féquesnoy's eldest wants to buy a husband,' people concluded round and about with incredulity.

Of course, most of the young black girls of Grand-Anse had day-dreamed, if only once in their lives, over those promises of happiness for life with a fine, blond, blue-eyed man living in the Ardèche or Dauphiné, but none had believed in them enough to sit down at a table and write down this desire in black and white. What amazed the busybodies who had opened the eldest Féquesnoy's mail even more was that the putative husbands were all approaching forty or sometimes even fifty, while the young woman was believed to be barely twenty-five. It didn't take long for people to assume that her choices were dictated by her father, and they ended up pitying her and her two sisters for being subjected to the single-minded will of a lawyer so ruthless in business that even certain island whites feared him. Isn't this why they'd allowed him to join their baccarat table, where the fellow had proved to be a tricky customer if you can believe Dupin de Médeuil, the banana planter from Moulin l'Étang? As for the parcels that the poor soul received, they contained books about deportment, classical music records (she had a soft spot for Verdi), knitting wool and glass tableware. And, stranger than strange, a whole pile of dictionaries of languages unknown in these parts.

The Féquesnoys never suspected for a moment that their intimate affairs were held up for public scrutiny and discussed by the most venomous imaginations in Grand-Anse. Bored with reading the marriage proposals and the answers, all coarse, which came back from over there and were never followed up by the young woman (or her father), the temporary postmistress took her curiosity as far as opening letters addressed to or received from people in Martinique itself. She was disappointed; they only contained condolences sent to Town families, various bills and tax forms. Soon people lost interest in Mademoiselle Féquesnoy's epistolary amours and busied themselves digging up other pieces of tittle-tattle concerning other people, since in this business everybody gets their turn. The postmistress had acquired an infallible technique, perfected over the months, for spotting the young woman's writing, quickly putting her mail aside from the rest in an old shoe box, waiting for the siesta hour to lick the envelope flaps to moisten them before putting the entire envelopes in a little bowl of lemon-scented water and counting up to five, and finally taking them out and gently opening them with the help of a nail file. As for deciphering them, she waited for the first passing gossip-monger because she only owed her position to the stimulating wobble of her hindquarters and not to any special gifts connected with writing. Closing the envelopes again was harder. It required such a deft touch, such skill in applying the glue that more than one of the shrews feared the fateful moment when Town would make an official appointment. Even if she was as understanding as the young one, said Ma Léonce, who can guarantee us that she'll know how to re-glue the letters without the Féquesnoys noticing? The problem isn't the ungluing, that's a matter of patience, it's the re-gluing that's everything. You just have to put the glue on badly, ladies, and a giveaway bulging will show. It was even suggested to the temporary postmistress that she teach the rudiments of her expertise to two or three young women of her own age who still had supple skin on their fingers. Either through laziness or lack of time, this plan was never put into action and these ladies were only rescued from their tedium by the sharp eyes of the temporary postmistress. She had noticed that a little black boy from Back Street brought her at regular intervals beautiful light blue envelopes that stood out against the overwhelming white of the rest of the mail. To begin with, she had believed him when he had said in a high-pitched voice:

'Mama says can you post this for her, please?'

What gradually goaded her along the path of her discovery was the fact that the child always gave her a fifty-franc coin and that he greedily stuffed the change deep into his pockets. She tried to interrogate him subtly, but he was very conscious of his mission and refused point-blank to explain to her why his mother used such beautiful envelopes to send her news to people in Town. For France, I would have understood, she added, but for here it's sheer waste. Then the up- and down-strokes of the addresses intrigued her for a while until she realized that the sender of the letters was disguising his or her writing. Each letter seemed to have been traced with deliberate slowness, the whole thing giving a contrived, even artificial, impression. Too busy removing the Féquesnoy eldest's letters from the rest of the post, she quickly forgot this little mystery until the boy appeared again at her counter. One day, she asked him:

'Where does your mama work?'

'*Sa pa ka gad'e'w!*' (It's none of your business!) retorted the offended child.

'So how come a nice-looking little boy like you is so badly brought up, eh!'

'– . . .'

'OK, I'll give you the stamp today, you can keep the coin.'

The boy's eyes widened and he carefully took the coin and turned away. The temporary postmistress' strategy only bore fruit the following week. As he came in, he declared:

'Mama irons laundry for the Féquesnoy family, madame.'

'I see! But what do they do with themselves all day long, the three Féquesnoy misses?'

'They're nice, you know . . . the biggest, she plays funeral music on the piano, and the others read.'

'Oh good! So if I understand right, only little fuzzy-head black girls like me have to work to earn a living.'

She was itching to know what on earth a humble laundry woman could have to say to people in Town. Opening the blue envelopes turned into a genuine catastrophe. Being dipped into water discoloured them and, when re-glued, they had the inconvenient habit of becoming rumpled. And yet their contents surprised the mayor's concubine so much and so greatly that she overcame her panic in one–two–three. She had to read the first missive, again written on blue paper, ten times over before informing Ma Léonce, the baker's wife whose gossiping had already broken up households, made enemies for life of twin brothers and pushed many people who were above all suspicion to despair. Amazement took hold of her too and her hands trembled on the post-office counter as she stared at the cramped lines in which the eldest daughter of the most illustrious lawyer of Grand-Anse described, without any ingenuousness, the torments of passion inflicted on her by Coolie René. This revelation was so weighty, so pregnant with future storms, that Ma Léonce made the temporary postmistress swear not to whisper a word of it to anybody.

'A Féquesnoy involved with a coolie, can you imagine! *A Féquesnoy, by God!*' she muttered.

She ended up confiding in her dearie-gossip friend Eau de Café, who was just as much at a loss as her. The two cronies managed to keep the secret for two good months, relishing along with the temporary postmistress the empassions so crudely expressed by somebody whom the entire village of Grand-Anse took to be both a virgin and an old maid. Furthermore, the young lady was a mistress of cunning: she disguised her handwriting and had her letters posted by a child, letters that were addressed to women friends in Town who, in turn, were expected to pass them on to Coolie René when he went down to the docks at Pointe Simon to pick up his Porto Rico cattle. Were there any answers and how did they reach the eldest Féquesnoy daughter? Nobody knew, all the more so since it was improbable that the dog-eating coolie could read or write. As far as anyone could recall, he had never set foot in a school and only spoke Creole (and Tamil during his black-magic ceremonies). But one had to admit that his status had changed since the end of the Second World War. He had opened a butcher's stall at the Main Market and had bought himself a Peugeot 403 van that he kept scrupulously clean even though he carried bleeding animal carcasses in it several times a week. While keeping his Hindu temple in the Long-Bois district, he had also had a concrete house built a stone's throw away from the abattoir and was the object of general approval for having protected his numerous family from disasters and need. Like that, people observed, the government won't have to bleed us dry to give them hand-outs and free medicine tokens. Unluckily for him, his concubine never got used to this new life and went back with her children to her home *commune* of Macouba. The gossip merchants naturally used this as grounds to talk nonsense about how 'coolies are only happy when they're living in filth'. As the Indian had given up boozing and was no longer to be seen in the Back Street bars, he shut himself away in an extraordinary state of loneliness that won the sympathy of a good number of villagers. Moreover, people no longer said laughingly 'Coolie René' but 'Monsieur René'.

The eldest Féquesnoy girl's diary was hence a real treat for our three old gossips who combined their modest scholarly gifts to force their way into the young girl's dreams:

6 June 1952
Father is a tortured being. He only has to hear Chief Thimoléon's drum to be overcome with palpitations. His forehead is covered with sweat, his hair stands on end and he gasps for breath until I bring him his pills and a glass of water. He then urges me to sit at the piano and allows me to play whatever I like, even Schubert, of whom he thinks little. The whole time that the drum is beating he feels ill. My sisters snigger secretly, hiding behind their books. Virginie is engrossed in *La porteuse de pain* for the fifth time and I suspect she likes it for the cheap tears it gives her. Émeline and she are just two fools who know nothing about the real world. Thanks to you, thanks to your such rough hands, I am beginning to understand it. Thank you for your compassion. Perhaps it's the beginnings of love.

9 June 1952
I saw you go past early this morning. Where were you hurrying to? Into whose arms? I find it hard to believe that that simpleton Passionise would take you into her bed, even under cover of darkness. She knows the fifteen insults that attack the honour of all Indians. She never holds back from shouting them out even when there is nobody of your race about. Just for the pleasure of upsetting her neighbours. That whore is pure evil. Quite the opposite of Myrtha. And does she never get tired of turning the heads of Grand-Anse's priests?
I wouldn't like to imagine either that you were on your way to that *Mariane-la-peau-figue* Antilia. Don't forget that she came straight

from the entrails of that accursed sea that gnaws at the walls of our houses. What an idea of Father's to put ours right next to it! Sometimes, when sleep doesn't manage to carry me away, I watch the unfolding of its waves tirelessly cutting through the darkness and I start thinking that it will swallow us up one day without a moment's warning.

Your hands have left prints of tenderness on my skin. My hips are still tingling from their touch. It's enough to make me swoon . . .

12 June 1952

I can't spend my whole life in this prison. I'm suffocating with the heat, the noise of the sea, the cackling of my sisters, the sneering of my father. There are only the fleeting moments that you spare me that stop me sinking altogether. Father hardly seems to suspect anything. He goes off happily to his Town Council meetings or his baccarat sessions with the island white de Médeuil. He even hopes that he won't have to drag us along behind him any more when his lawyer's duties take him to Town. My sisters and I are like three candles burning in a wayside shrine in the country. There are few passing travellers to stop and pray. Very few. There was that Thiméléon at the start of the war but Father wanted nothing to do with him because he's black and nor did I because he's a vulgar black. I'm afraid since my candle began burning first. Afraid that it may be about to go out. Help me. I want to leave here and live your life. To have children who will walk like you and have the rage held in your gaze. I hate the mulatto world, its pomp and good works. This year I shan't go to the great ball that they hold in Town on New Year's Eve. I shall take to my bed and Father can get as furious as twenty devils that I'm missing the chance to meet the most eligible men in Martinique, but I won't move.

Virginie thinks she knows everything about love. She told me that it hurts a lot the first time. 'Like burning yourself with an iron' . . .

8 July 1952

Of all the saints you've spoken about, I prefer Nagouloumira. I admire Maldévilin's fierceness, Kali's grace, Madouraïviren's noble bearing and Mariémen's splendour, but Nagouloumira is more ours, more Creole than the others. He protected your people during the crossing from all dangers. Here, he became Nagouloumira, in other words both Muslim and Hindu, both white and black. Black because 'agalou' stands for 'N'goulou' which means 'pig' in

Kikongo. White because 'agalou' comes at the same time from the French 'goulou' which also has the meaning 'greedy'. In the name Nagouloumira I can see the Muslim 'Ra', the French and African 'goulou' and the Hindu 'mira'. Don't laugh at my lexicographic endeavours! When I took my first higher exams I won the merit prize in Greek and Latin. Alas! My father took me out of the Colonial Boarding-school because he was afraid that Town would end up corrupting his eldest daughter. I've kept my passion for words and their roots. I would rather immerse myself in dictionaries than devour rose-tinted novels like Virginie. I have ordered a Tamil dictionary, so I will be able to decipher the meaning of your incantations. May Nagouloumira protect you, my love!

20 July 1952
Father disgusts me. Each night he makes Virginie and Émiline take it in turns to sleep in his bedroom. He's always been afraid of me and as far back as I can remember he's never looked me straight in the eye. Poor Émeline is the very picture of a faded alamanda flower. Sometimes she daydreams at the window while watching the sea, other times she reads passages from the Bible aloud wandering through the house. I beg you, come to my help. I'm so lonely that sometimes I feel the desire to imitate Émilien Bérard's fatal gesture. It's not lack of courage but the thought of you that holds me back.

After several months, Ma Léonce, Eau de Café and a few other members of the gossips' club formed a delegation and went to the lawyer's house. Somebody had to inform him about the disgraceful liaison between his daughter and that Coolie René. Of course, his failure in the case of Bogino had discredited him, but nothing could rule out the possibility that he was still in cahoots with evil spirits. A coolie is even more cunning than a mulatto, and that's saying something! *Maître* Féquesnoy pretended not to be surprised by the visit of these women in their Sunday best in the middle of the week. He showed the greatest politeness, serving vermouth and champagne biscuits. He listened without turning a hair, asked no questions, cast no doubts on their revelations, made a few anodyne remarks about positive progress in municipal affairs and escorted them back to his front door like a true gentleman. Ma Léonce, who could spy on the vast bourgeois Féquesnoy residence from her first floor, reported that not a cat had stirred there. Just one unusual development revealed to the people of Grand-Anse that something serious was about to happen or indeed was already happening: the lawyer had shut all doors, windows and shutters looking out on to Front Street, which, logic dictated, forced him to open those giving on to the sea. Those that nobody here ever dared to unfasten, so quickly did the wind from the high seas ruin your linen, your silverware and the glass in your mirrors. At dusk, the laundry woman and her boy left the house, their faces etched with sadness. Nobody dared to question them. Then the little boy was seen heading towards Monsieur René's butcher's stall and handing him an envelope before running back as fast as he could to his mother. The drunks were silent at Small Balls Auguste's bar. The whole world held its breath. The Indian seemed rooted to the spot, a large blood-spattered knife in one hand, the missive in the other. After a period of time that bush radio has deemed to be unending, he walked to the pavement opposite the Féquesnoy residence and began to yell:

'That young lady is mad! Yes, she's mad! . . . I've never talked to her, I don't even know the colour of her words or the shape of her body. Ask me whether she's a fat-limbed woman or is as thin as a rake, I'm buggered if I can tell you. So what is that mulatto accusing me of, then? . . . The gentleman has summoned me to a duel tomorrow morning! Where am I supposed to find a pistol? Hey, Féquesnoy, step outside for a minute if you please! I want you to say aloud what you're blaming me for. *Come on out, for God's sake!*'

The Féquesnoy house remained stubbornly shut and the former Indian priest carried on with his threats and pleas until well into the night. He swore that he had never strayed with the eldest daughter and called as witnesses anybody who passed in the street. Nobody, not even Chief Bérard, wanted to become involved in his drama, even though he had always been a faithful passenger in the 'Golem'. People ended up by going to bed and the rumour circulated that Monsieur René was flat out in a gutter after sinking three litres of rum. At dawn, two shots in rapid succession quietened the din made by the Grand-Anse sea for a moment. Everyone stayed in bed, some trying to fall asleep again, in order not to have to take part in what must certainly have turned into a tragedy. Grand-Anse's two buses drove through the village without hooting and many children were absent from school. The Indian's butcher shop and the lawyer's residence remained closed all day, then the next day and the day after that. On the fourth day, *maître* Féquesnoy took his old Studebaker out of the garage, packed in his daughters and a few cases and drove off to some unknown destination without speaking to anybody. After a fortnight the little Mussolini let it be known that '*monsieur* the deputy mayor had taken official leave in France', even though Féquesnoy held no formal office. Life resumed its normal course until the day when Bogino, as was his habit, spoke of a man's corpse in the water beneath the hospital, where the sea is so treacherous that we had given up counting the number of France-whites who'd drowned there.

'*Pèsonn lakay mwen pa pèd!*' (There's nobody missing from our house!) was the response he received all around.

Gathering all her courage, Eau de Café contacted the police, who dragged out the body and concluded with no inquiry that it was a case of drowning. She was the only person to watch over the body at the presbytery along with Adelise, the ninety-year-old maid, and the burial was hastily arranged for an afternoon when a football match had attracted almost the whole of the village to the sports ground of the neighbouring *commune* of Fond d'Or. The gravedigger refused to bury Coolie René in the paupers' grave because those who were lying there might have been poor but were at least Christians during their time on earth. So the Indian's corpse was buried in a cursed corner of the cemetery. Where the excommunicants lie along with black magicians, the Muslim Tanin, Ali's father and now that worshipper of the goddess Kali. Again it was Eau de Café who paid for his coffin made of packing cases and who decorated his tomb with a single hydrangea quickly picked from a little garden without a fence.

'*Isiya dwèt modi pou tout bon,*' grumbled the gravedigger. (Here, you're cursed once and for all!)

21

Look at that man falling flat on his face between the dice tables, who seems oblivious to everyone, even you, the troublemaker, says Thimoléon as he grabs me. Listen to his words, listen when he starts shouting: 'Where are they?' (His words are heavier than the hammering of the rain on the tin roof of a house). 'So they've just left like that, ladies and gentlemen, they've just taken off one fine morning like a gang of vagabonds without any of them bothering to tell me anything about it. Nothing! You hear me, not a thing! Yes, one morning, my boys got out their best clothes, dressed themselves up, put on their shoes and off they went! As if they simply couldn't wait. That's what's happened to me, damn and blast it all!'

Don't snigger at him just yet, like the small-fry players are doing, because if you look carefully you'll notice that the chiefs themselves are on the alert and you'll see that all of this makes sense. Everything here makes sense, you already know this. In this holiday drama set in the market-place, all the truth surrounding this, your people, is gathered together, in other words its entire impasse. There's that man shouting: 'Tell me something, go on, get your tongues moving . . . When it's a question of swapping tittle-tattle, everyone's at it, but as soon as there's something serious at stake, lips are sealed. Don't think I don't know what's making you chicken!'

What was bound to happen happens. Perhaps you suspected as much yourself. Monsieur the mayor turns up, his Mussoliniesque hat on his head and swathed in his red, white and blue sash over his fine jacket of pure wool, followed by a curious mob of brats who are already singing a mocking refrain: 'Monsieur Julien Thémistocle, take the bit between your teeth, Monsieur the mayor is galloping after you! O Monsieur Julien Thémistocle! . . .' As if in his drunken stupor, Julien Thémistocle, the leader of Grand-Anse's rum-swiggers, could have heard anything other than his own delirium echoing in his head and, even if he could, the bellowing of a cow that Coolie René was slaughtering in the municipal abattoir would have made him jump like everybody else. And yet, there he goes again on the same theme: 'Where are they? Where the hell has the BUMIDOM taken them? BUMIDOM, you know, the Bureau for Missing Dead Overseas Men, ho, ho, ho! Tell me, gentlemen, you're respectable people, you reckon you speak better French than France-whites . . . What? You're silent, you to whom Father Le Gloarnec gives absolution without confession, so swollen with righteousness are your hearts. Tell me something, for shit's sake!'

Look, here's monsieur the headmaster, trotting along with his bowtie, who comes to stand stiffly next to monsieur the mayor, sweat dripping from his fuzzy hair on to his dark glasses and Légion d'honneur ribbon. Monsieur the mayor taps him on the shoulder and whispers: 'Could you do me two or three words, Mathurin, I've got to give them a little speech in a minute.' Monsieur the headmaster smiles with all his golden teeth: 'On behalf of the Fatherland, monsieur the first councillor!' By now the whole village is gathered at the main entrance to the market, expecting some impromptu official declaration. Busybodies crane their necks to look inside at what's going on and one of them shouts: 'Ha, ha, ha! I think this time monsieur the mayor is going to throw Julien Thémistocle out of the *commune* once and for all. That old idiot of an outlaw has buggered us about long enough . . .' And then you see Julien Thémistocle yelling in his voice as rough as a cassava-grater: 'Gang of God knows whats! Cissy boys! Don't make me utter the insult that withered a priest's balls! So you've sent me the leader of the *commune*, is that all you could think of in your thick black heads? Ha! One day, my sons whom you've sent over there, into the cold, will come back and settle up with you. Yes, that's precisely what your ears heard: settle up! . . . because my family is well known around these parts. Don't take the name Thémistocle in vain, don't open your rat-trap of a mouth to insult my godmother's arse, no, I'm not baptized . . . ha, ha, ha! . . . On the morning I was meant to be christened, my godmother, Floraline Ladouceur, a woman from Morne Bois, suddenly dropped dead on the path to the church with her clothes that smelled of mothballs at ten paces and her France-hat. A stylish death, don't you think? Since then I've been called cursed. Cursed! Ha, ha, ha! I see that all the games have stopped now. The dice have gone back into pockets and the dice-cups have been turned over so that nobody can whisper a magic word into them on the quiet . . .'

My boy, when you hear all this, realize that they're getting ready for a good laugh because from now on the tension is only going to increase as the day goes on. You should laugh as well, and in doing so you'll take another step in your reintegration into the black world. Don't forget that it's laughter (among other things) that has made a single people out of us! And so, strengthened by the presence of Miss Sossionise, the informer from the presbytery, and brother Ali Tanin, the bastard-Syrian, it's almost the whole town council that has come to re-establish law and order in the market-place. Look at monsieur the mayor pulling up the braces on his trousers, dusting down his tricolour sash and fixing his spectacles on his nose even though his eyesight is as sharp as a falcon's. Look, my restless friend, at the headmaster scribbling away on a table as the villagers look on admiringly. Look at this entire circus and spill your laughter all over the floor until the constabulary orders everyone to open their ear-holes.

'Fwenchmen, Fwenchwomen, dear compatwiots,' monsieur the mayor begins, 'if today I am taking the twouble to stand upon this rock of rocks, it is not to tell you a lot of dwivel but to astigmatize the unworthy attitude of Thémistok. This communist swine Thémistok has no respect for our national celebwations because he follows orders from Moscow! Yes, I reitewate loud and clear, from Moscow! Those of us who know that the Seine's source flows from the Mount of Olives, those of us who venewate the virginality of Joan of Arc, those of us who owe our lives to Godefwoy de Bouillon who dwove back the Awabs at Wonceval . . .'

'It was Charles Martel, not Godefroy,' the headmaster and deputy-deputy mayor whispers to him.

'Those of us who are twue Fwenchmen, who wept when Charles Martel was defeated at Waterloo, who followed Genewal de Gaulle into the *dissidence* . . .'

'Yeah! Ye-e-a-a-ah!' roars the crowd approvingly.

'Who swam after Charles de Gaulle all the way to London, we will not tolewate being slighted on this immortal day, the fourteenth of July, by a dwunkard of Thémistok's type . . .' ('Find me a subjunctive,' he mutters in the direction of the headmaster) '. . . Often, often, I told him to stop his aggwavating behaviour but the scoundwel wouldn't listen to me. He insults the sacwed flag of our fatherland, Fwance. I order him to leave at once the tewitory of my *commune*. Go on, shoo! Shoo, Thémistok! . . .'

'We had no choice but to proceed at once to this expulsion lest our children should have imitated the monkey business of Julien Thémistocle,' whispers the deputy-deputy mayor.

'We had no choice to but recede at once,' blurts out the mayor, 'to expulse our children lest they should have intimated the monkey business of Master Thémistok.'

Applaud when you see the wonderment of the crowd awed by this flurry of imperfect subjunctives – imperfect in their construction, of course, ha, ha, ha! – and don't just stand there, your mouth gaping, more speechless than a Congo presented with a glass of barley water. They're your people, the only people you've got and you owe it to yourself to accept them as they are. Alongside their petty concerns, they nurture myths so fabulous as to make the ancient Greeks sick with envy, and the mystery of our barren sea (don't add the story of Antilia's drowning, I beg you!) is just one of them. That's to say that even if your crazy dream of making sense of all that comes to pass, you'll find yourself with a hundred other unknowns that you can torment yourself with all day long, and, like me, you'll say enough's enough and wait for all this stupidity to end. Because it will end, you can be sure of that, and will sweep us all away with an indescribable suffering that even the most erudite words you learnt in Europe will be unable to express. So play while there's still time! Roll the dice and call on the eleven as if nothing had happened. Pretending is our own form of complicity, us Creole blacks . . .

Oh, yes, I know! I know! I'll gladly grind out another piece of this story, as is the custom around here. Here we go: monsieur the mayor adjusts his braces, dusts off his sash and, standing right over the drunkard, declares: '*Veni–Vidi–Vichy!* Citizen . . . Julien Thémistocle, alias *chacha* seed, alias bishop of booze, I must inform you of my great statutifaction in the face of your obstwuction of the republican way and, furthermore, in light of which, I am now beginning pwoceedings against you.'

Julien Thémistocle, not in the least bit concerned, retorts: 'Up your mother's pass!'

Laughter from the crowd, applause. The gang of kids starts singing again: 'Hey, Julien Thémistocle! Get up, old man. The rum will show you the way home.'

Monsieur the mayor swells with rage and resumes: 'Faced with the obscenewation of this gentleman and . . . his refusal to coopewate with the forces of law and order, I resolve solemnly and democwatically to place him in the custody of the Fwench law. Gentlemen of the Law, do your duty!'

'Don't touch me, do you hear! Don't even touch the tip of my toe because I swear I'll cut off one of your heads! Ha, mussieur the mayor, it looks like you're so statutified by my upsetting law and order that you've got out your red, white and blue cloth to . . .'

The prime councillor screams: 'Communist! Be quiet!'

' . . . to lord it over me. Eh? Is that what you want?'

Monsieur the headmaster takes off his dark glasses, takes out his reading glasses this time from his top pocket, opens a book that he was holding under his arm and, with an authoritative gesture which forces silence on the tumult, begins: 'Monsieur Julien Thémistocle, allow me to quote to you before this spontaneously assembled gathering a beautiful and profound page from our great, sublime and visionary poet, in short Albert Samain. The glory, honour and pride of our eternal motherland, mother of arts and letters, as we all know. It is called . . .'

Suddenly a bullock starts bellowing furiously in the municipal abattoir. Monsieur the headmaster takes off his spectacles and, discreetly breathing on one of the lenses, folds his arms and waits for the animal to quieten down. Rage chokes monsieur the mayor: 'Shut that dwatted animal up! Right in the middle of the town council the other day I couldn't make a single polite remark at the reception for the local fire bwigade because of those verminous beasts bellowing, bellowing. Deputy mayor, go and shut the abattoir up!'

The half-Syrian replies: 'Yes, sir, for France, monsieur the mayor!' As he rushes off to accomplish his top-level mission, the kids make up a song in his honour: 'Ali Tanin, my friend, the coolies are going to bleed you dry.'

In the meantime, Julien Thémistocle has, with difficulty, got to his feet, rubbed his eyes and finally seeing all these characters gathered in front of him, moves forward and shakes the hand of each and everyone as they stand there, paralysed with bewilderment. The applause almost raises the roof. The market and the street outside are by now awash with vulgarities. The rum drinker stands in front of monsieur the mayor and recites a poem by Charles d'Orléans, the only thing he's retained from his fleeting attendance at school:

> *Looking towards the land of France,*
> *One day it happened, at Dover on the sea,*
> *That I remembered the sweet delight*
> *That I used to find in that land;*
> *So I began to sigh from my heart,*
> *Although it certainly did me greet good*
> *To see France that my heart must love.*

Suddenly someone shouts:

'All those idiot whites croaked at Saint-Pierre!'

The little Mussolini is maddened by rage and stammers:

'Ar . . . arr . . . arrrrrest that wr . . . rrr . . . wrrrrretch! Gentlemen of the Law, throw that Moscowteer into jail! . . . No, give him a good hiding and leave him there in the corner.'

Julien Thémistocle cuts through the crowd and is off like a flash in the direction of En Chéneaux, towards the nearby countryside, pursued by the mob of kids. But the players have already returned to their tables. The interval is over. Back to serious matters. In the gathering night, you must know that there's a dull fear which grips the skin of the stomach and makes fingers crack for no reason and it's thanks to that fear that we stay on the look-out. Keep yourself ready for the confrontation that awaits you and measure your loneliness. How vast it is! Eleven! Eleven! The number of death. Mysterious symbol of death that we court. Conjure it up! . . .

22

And if I were to kick up a fuss! And if I were to say: 'Godmother, stop your carrying on, that's enough. I've had enough of your rum-drinking Thémistocle and his escapades.' Even before the milk had stopped dripping off the end of my nose, well before we came down to live in the village, whenever I asked you where was your man, you answered irritably: 'Men are nothing but a bad breed, starting with your father, my cousin, who prefers to live in town. Ha, I'm not having any of that!' or inscrutable sentences of the sort. I believed you, I believed every word from your mouth, every gesture of your hand, every movement of your body. When you said: 'I don't want to stay rotting here in Macédoine, I must go and open a shop in Grand-Anse,' I went along with you. I even capered about with joy. When you settled for this tumbledown house, stuck next to the sea, I didn't hesitate to kiss you and, in my sleep, at the very beginning, the surf shaped my dreams. And I was also the first to get up in the morning and would take the chamber-pot of Aubagne enamel bought in haste from Syrian (in the country, we used to shit by the side of the river) and would go and empty it at high tide. I filled it with sand to rub it clean, letting the waves turn it over and roll it round, then I would run to grab it before it was washed away for good. One of those mornings, I had spotted a little girl sitting in the sand as if she'd been left there during the night. It was Antilia. I came back very excited to the house, shouting:

'Godmother, there's a suffering soul on the beach, tell her she can come and live with us.'

At first you smiled at hearing me say 'suffering soul', your favourite expression, then you leaned at the window dubiously. When we'd arrived in the village, everybody had warned us:

'Above all, watch out for the sea salt, it covers everything, it makes your sheets damp, it gives you colds, it dries out your skin, it makes your bedrooms too humid, so shut all the windows that look out to sea.'

Godmother didn't take any notice and that's what was our undoing, she later maintained, because 'what you don't know is bigger than you are'. We had received the torment of the abandoned child, a singular torment for the reason that it never expressed itself through sobbing or screaming, but through a vast reverie, sometimes dumb, sometimes murmuring, right in front of the monstrous maw of the Grand-Anse sea. Godmother and I were bewitched. In vain had she consulted her cards, for she hadn't been able to find the how and why of this appearance, nor the origins or name of the child. She decided to have her baptised Antilia.

Thimoléon, with whom we had just become close, had objected to this sort of adoption, and, in the presence of Antilia, the greyish hairs on his skin seemed to bristle:

'If it was a brat from here or even from Macouba or Grand-Rivière, you can be sure that its mother would already have been round to claim her property. In my view, it can only be a piece of seaweed that's taken on human shape . . . so many of our children have perished in that bitch of a sea! Pah!'

'Not at all,' protested Eau de Café. 'You village people are afraid of your own shadows. This sad little one sleeps next to me at night and I can hear her heart thumping in her chest when the waves become furious. She's not from the sea! She probably came from the South with her mother, who abandoned her here . . . So many people come up this way to find work in the banana plantations. Where they're from, the dry-season drought is unbearable and the land is hard.'

Antilia was never to be seen in the streets of Grand-Anse. It was as if she had her back permanently turned in order to show off that pridefulness that made us lower our voices in her presence. She would sit on Godmother's bed, staring far away into the sea, or moved by some implacable force, she would make her way to the beach, dig herself a hole and stay there until it was time to eat.

Father Bauer, a lobster-red Alsatian, who was substituting for Le Gloarnec while he was obliged to spend some time in a sanatorium, had seen fit to demand explanations from Eau de Café.

'I'm told you're lodging a devilish creature, is this true? I've never seen her at mass, so how can that be if, as you say, she's a nice little girl? How old is she and why don't you send her to school?'

And so on and so forth with a whole litany of questions that merely succeeded in putting Godmother in a Calabrian fighting-cock fury:

'*Man kay koupé grenn ou, wi!*' (I'm going to cut off your balls!) she screamed at the priest, a kitchen knife in her hand.

Panic-stricken flight, gathering of neighbours, jokes, scurrilous remarks, carnival songs.

Godmother forbade me from following Antilia in her wanderings. Quite often she would go away as far as the La Crabière promontory and wouldn't be seen again for several days at a time. When she came back, she would roar with laughter and bring us back bunches of purplish sea grapes or sea-turtle's eggs. On other occasions, she would dress herself up like a princess and escape to Fort-de-France. Eau de Café never asked her anything but, in the evenings, although she was far from being pious, I could hear her in her bedroom reciting thirty or so Ave Marias together with the young girl. Antilia's voice had resonances of depth and sweetness that defied description. It wasn't a child's voice, I swear it! As for me, like the others, she never spoke a single word to me. Not one.

Through the wall, against which I would stick my ear, fragments of speeches would reach me that were, to say the least, strange:

'Black people in Grand-Anse think that it's enough to know that two and two make four in order to survive. They're shackled to eternal damnation and don't even try to unpick the knots in their lives, nor to settle up with God or anything else. Ha! And yet, Godmother, I never lie about the truth: we will all perish on this island if we continue to go round in circles . . .'

I still hesitate to mention Antilia's name for fear of stopping Eau de Café's flow altogether. Just by talking she must end up one day on this subject. Her tongue won't be able to avoid it indefinitely, it's just not possible. I show her the threatening note that an invisible hand had slid under my door in the Oceanic Hotel the other evening. Eau de Café doesn't seem surprised.

'Don't mention it to Thimoléon,' she whispers to me, 'he's capable of accusing anyone, especially the fellows he hates like Ali Tanin or the headmaster, and that could bring us all sorts of unpleasantnesses.'

'Who could it have come from, Godmother?'

'Huh! . . . That's for you to find out. Haven't you wasted your time playing dominoes in front of the church? That'll teach you to associate with good-for-nothings. When they lose, that lot, they hold a hell of a grudge against you since in their eyes you have disrespected their prowess. You have made them look like little boys. You've stripped their backsides naked, as they say. *Sèrbi* isn't a mere game, godson, it's also African black magic.'

Godmother advises me from now on not to shake hands with anyone without saying a second later: 'Beelzebub, you're not fair nor fine, I am stronger than you', an unbeatable formula, if you take her word for it. And if you find yourself in a situation where you have to accept a rum punch, here's a phial of lucky clover water. Pour three drops of it into your glass on the sly . . .

Yesterday, something important happened: one of the two nondescript windows in my room gave in under the incessant onslaughts of the wind. It must have been three o clock in the afternoon since a sort of mottled tapestry was covering the entire expanse of the sea. I took a few timid steps towards this sudden opening of light and spray, but just as I was about to lean at the window-sill, I spun backwards like a fiddler crab. And what if Antilia was prowling naked on the beach! It was with her, moreover, that I'd discovered long ago that nudity didn't exist. An unclothed body always harbours shadows, signs, sources of heat and infinite spaces. Especially a black body.

I took one of my notebooks to add to it what Thimoléon had told me that same morning in the rum shop between two swigs of absinthe. He seems to have aged by twenty years since we've been swapping those ramblings that are incomprehensible to our fellow drinkers, who have stopped paying us any attention. All Grand-Anse's hardened drinkers have been introduced to me, but I can hardly match any of them with his surname without making mistakes. Rum-lovers are easily offended and let their razors speak French for them at the slightest gaffe, if you believe them, for as the proverb has it, a word weighs nothing in the mouth that's saying it.

'Rejoice at the happy coincidence that has caused you to come back to the fold on the eve of the fourteenth of July, young man,' says Thimoléon, the soul of imperturbability, 'because tomorrow, God willing, I shall lead you into the very centre of all extravagances and all most reasonable thoughts: the market-place. At first sight, you won't recognize anybody there. All present have carved themselves out a mask of inscrutable hardness, everyone weighs their words as if the heaviness of each could at any moment upset the course of destiny. The dice rule supreme there. And above all the magic number, eleven, which they call upon either with fury or in an offhand way to bamboozle their opponent, and stand well back if the cursed seven insists on plaguing a dice master. Ah, the seven! Anything rather than that. The three, the five, the eight, it doesn't matter! But that seven-tailed toad, that cat with seven lives, that seven years of bad luck, nobody wants the bloody thing! Pray inside yourself like the other players that it will go away as quickly as possible and that it stops messing up the chief's display of skill, otherwise he may give in to an evil rage and accuse any one of you. Especially you, the stranger who may be responsible for who knows what sordid ploys! Seizing on the opportunity, he will challenge you to a bout of *damier*, he'll test your mettle, pushing away a pile of tables to try out his steps (it's the first one that counts since it's the one which will dictate the dance's unerring course), rolling up the bottoms of his khaki trousers and tossing aside his palm-leaf hat. He'll shout to you: "There you are, here I am!" as he mimes with subtle wrist movements the throbbing of the *bel-air* drum that has begun to beat in a corner of the market. "There you are, here I am!" "There you are, here I am!" "There you are, here I am!", he'll yell incessantly until overwhelmed by dagger-like stares of reproach, you also decide to enter the ring. And, next thing, there you are trumpeting such an unconvincing "Here I am!" that certain women, those of easy virtue, will start snorting with laughter and whispering mad slanders at your expense in each others' ears. Don't suppose that the drum will get tired waiting for you or that it will spare you a second to try out a left-footed kick! Once the *damier* contest is under way, it's the drum that gives the orders and it's up to you two, the fighters, to obey its each and every command. The crowd is excited by rum and by the joy of the fourteenth of July, and their shouting isn't anything more than an accompaniment to the drum and won't have the slightest bearing on the way the fight goes. You'll be alone, facing life or death, and the other man, the big dice master, won't have a crumb of sympathy for your innocence, which in any case he thinks is faked. He'll move around you, marking out his steps with some unknown ancestral skill, he'll stamp the ground like a pure-bred Cuban bull to frighten you, he'll throw his arms forward to grasp you by the waist and pull back at the last minute, leaving you aghast and paralysed with fear. Ah, he'd been thirsting for a good fight for such a long time! Nowadays they've become so rare, the people who know how to swap blows according to the rules of the art. Don't try to grasp at straws, don't protest by saying "I don't want anything to do with these backward nigger affectations. I'm just a spectator like anyone else!" There's no way out, my friend. You've been chosen: the number seven chose you. It's up to you to rise to the challenge and to show him that your body is stronger than all the ironies of misfate. Try to move your hip, yes, your hip, since that's where your bewildering volley of kicks will spring from once the drum gives the order. Turn on your hip, spin around like a falcon that has spotted its prey in a hollow in the plain and when you've found the right posture, let the bottom of your chest belch out the wild cry that will terrify the women and kids: "Abobo!" Make sure that you've got the drummer on your side and that from now on he'll beat the drum for you, thereby undermining the arrogance of your adversary so that he'll be forced to make his follow yours or risk losing his balance at each break in the rhythm. But watch out, things can happen in an altogetherly different way, otherwise life would be as easy to swallow as a bowl of semolina. The drummer may pretend not to notice that you're a novice and that only an unlucky throw of the dice, a fatal number, put you so suddenly into such a tight corner. Men who are a bit older and are hence forced to show some grown-up responsibility will occasionally whisper to the drummer "Slow down for him! Go on, give the young man a little bit of a chance!", but with his wits dulled by the rhythm of the drum, he'll keep crouching over the barrel and forcing the kid-skin to speak French (and, I ask you, how can one resist the extraordinary power of seduction of our former masters' language?). Indecipherable thrills will run through the crowd gathered around your contest. Look as you might for support from any pair of eyes, you'll find none! All you'll find there are eyeballs rolling with pleasure under the drummer's intoxicating blows or transported to some distant region of the soul, somewhere in darkest Guinea, from whence, one day, some of our ancestors were torn away. When the warm-up has reached its climax, the drummer will rap out a harsh sound that will root the two of you opposite one another, bam! There you are stuck there like two pillars! Like two bulls, masters of the plain, held by the horns and stopped in their tracks! A sublime moment, which will force a church-like silence on to the very centre of the market-place, interminable minutes, longer than the Mississippi, that will gnaw at your heart to test you and bring torrents of sweat to your brow. Use this lull to shout inside your head: "Seven, son of a bitch of a number! Seven, dog shit!" because your opponent is calling on his personal saint in words of an unknown language, praying to be transformed into his holy steed in the forthcoming fight. As soon as the drummer gives you the order to restart the dance of death, this time for real, capture your adversary's gaze in your own with as much violence as possible and let the staccato swelling of your heart snatch at you, snatch at you. Let the fellow try the first kick and gracefully feint to avoid his leg, weighed down as it is with talismans of all sorts, and laugh! Laugh right in his face, dammit! Laugh as you prepare your return kick, because you see the gap that he's left open about where his liver is, that's where you're going to have to get through later if you want to see him writhing on the floor once and for all. Women will say: "He's laughing, that's how strong he is, that *chabin*" and will start praying in your favour, their two hands clasping their anxiously oppressed breasts. Ah, young man, just because of a whore of a bitch of a vermin of a seven, here you are straight away dropped into the ordeal of the *damier* dance-fight in front of your own people and you couldn't hope for a better jury. Especially since sudden death has been banned by the new laws, it's the winner's expression that lets you know whether the loser will survive two days or even two months. Everything will depend on the way the fight takes shape; if you have fought fair, your winning opponent will be able to time his kick perfectly so as to spare you endless suffering and himself the police cells in Grand-Anse and then an even worse fate in Fort-de-France. But be aware, in case you'd forgotten, that if you've opted for some underhand tactic like turning your back on your adversary, pretending to change your steps back into time with the drum, only to turn and kick him with all your might in the stomach, well then, my friend, you can prepare your body for a swamp turtle's death agony. There's an invisible point just above your right breast where the thread of all life lies and it's there that the chief will aim for, not to break it but to strain it hopelessly. It's a very difficult spot to reach as it's protected by the swelling of the breast above and the formation of the ribs below. An elusive spot and so much sought after by all *damier* champions since, whenever it's hit – what a daylight miracle! – you feel that you're going, going, going, going. Your head spins like it's being dragged away by an irresistible current, your veins feel swollen by an intoxicating fluid that gives you an amazing sense of lightness, you sense that you could fly in the air were it not for the fact that your buttocks and thighs have become two tons heavier at the same time. This bears no relation to falling sickness and its vaguely obscene convulsions, nor to the spasm that takes hold of the married woman at the moment when they prepare to nail down her husband's coffin. No relation to any of that. On the contrary, it involves a very dignified sort of delirium, so dignified indeed that it impresses all those present who shout: "*Han fil tjè'y pété!*" (Oh look, his heart's thread's been hit!) Now it seems that the drum is gradually changing its tone like a lancehead viper shedding its skin. You realize that it's suddenly mimicking movements of a hitherto unknown gentleness which, depending on the power of the blow you received, will make you speak random words in an incredible soup of Congo, Creole, coolie language, French and Latin. But I'm talking rubbish myself, young man, and you're doing nothing to stop me! Why envisage the worst of possible outcomes, the one in which you approach a table where the number seven is mocking a dice master and he holds you responsible for his inability to roll good dice? He's just as likely to ignore you and settle on the person next to you, if your unfamiliarity hasn't already convinced him of his own invincibility. With somebody he knows well, he at least realizes what he's up against and what sort of fight he has to prepare in his head. At that point, you become an onlooker like everybody else, and now you must be careful not to get carried away like some vulgar passing tourist; clapping your hands has a very specific meaning in *damier*. It amounts to taking the side of one of the fighters and trying to distract his adversary at the very moment that he is getting ready to aim a kick. Generally speaking, anyone who claps his hands is simply sending a message to his favourite's opponent. He's just saying: "My friend, if by bad luck you manage to split my brother's liver, you'll have me to contend with after! Watch your arse!" All this is often nothing but intimidation and the opponent can, if he wishes, pretend to ignore all such provocation and carry on fighting proudly, even nodding his head to make the drum's rhythm speed up. He can shout out with a cheerfulness that may be false or real: "Roll that drum for me, for God's sake! It's not like I'm a young girl who's about to be deflowered." But despite that, don't let the illusion give you a false sense of security; the fellow has taken note of the face of the man who clapped his hands within a fraction of a second and is already saying a prayer to weigh down his arm muscles . . .'

23 Eau de Café, in her Wild Period

Pulled my thighs apart. Got on top of me. Split my *coucoune* to
make the blood stream on to the grass. 'How old are you, you
dirty slut? How old are you?' he kept whispering into my ear as
his hands groped at my breasts in a sort of ticklish to-and-fro
movement. Pulled my thighs apart wide-wide-wide, as wide as
the sea itself. He was horribly strong, the old man, his muscles
were as hard as guava-tree wood. I shouted 'Help me! Help me!
Help me!' but nobody wanted or could be bothered to answer my
cry. Perhaps because the heat was spanking down hard on to the
plain and nobody could lift their little finger. I screamed into his
face: 'I'm younger than Claire-Elise, who calls you grandfather!'
and then the estate foreman burst out laughing. One hell of a
laugh that I could feel running up the length of his worn-out body
and that shuddered around his navel. His almost toothless mouth
was drooling on my neck while his back moved upwards and
downwards on top of me. A fit of giddiness suddenly seized me
and I could hear myself begging, without any words coming out
of my mouth: 'He's going to split me in two, he's like an axe.
Mama! Mama darling, come and pull this wild boar off me!' But
why call to her, as she's been dead and buried since the day I was
born? As for Doris, my guardian, I already know that she'll blame
me for straying outside the Beauchamp plantation and if you did
so, it's because you wanted the foreman to tear you open. So me
too, I've been torn by him, as well as my sisters Éliane and
Ginette, my cousin Marceline, who's got a dimple on her chin,
and of course Mademoiselle Mina and all the little black girls
from here and there. And yet I'd warned you that he deliberately
leaves the rabbit grass on the plantation uncut to attract little girls
who are about to become women. He doesn't fancy them before
or after, just at the moment when they are budding as females.

When Ma Ginette came to make a fuss in the *béké*'s courtyard and demand compensation for her little Armande whom the foreman had just taken, the master had answered:

'No carrying on like this on my land or else you can pack up your things and clear off, do you understand? I've got ten people who can do your job, so leave my foreman in peace, if you please. He opens them up for me, those little ladies, haven't you managed to understand that yet, for God's sake! I don't like the way those nubile black girls smell of mussels.'

All the same, he'd given Ma Ginette a purse full of money and that's why Armande came by two days later to show off to me. She'll be going to school! While me, I'll be staying at home, carrying buckets of water from the spring and peeling bananas for my elder brothers' meals. No dress, no school! No shoes, no school! That's what the Grand-Anse lady schoolteacher said to Ma Doris the other day at the market-place. Even though the midwife had showered her with all manner of flattering remarks about her long mulatto plait that hung down to the small of her back. Even though she gave her a reduction of six and a half *sous* on her okra. She accepted all that with a smile but didn't want to know about the rest. No dress, no school! So my second mother cuddled me against her bosom and, snivelling with burning tears, said to me:

'My poor little girl, you're already as black as a mortal sin, what are you going to do with your life if you can't read or write?'

Pulled my thighs apart with violencity. His rough, skinny hands that were ferreting among the downy hair between my legs. His rum-sodden breath which suddenly covered my entire face, forcing me to close my eyes. The patched rag that hardly covered my body and which he ended by tearing to shreds. The stiffness of his cock inside me, not really painful, but strange, uncomfortable. Then the violent climax in a vast bellowing like a bull whose horns are being sawn, and the sudden death which terrified me. Yes, the foreman climaxed and succumbed to death in broad daylight, one sunny afternoon, at the foot of Morne Capot, in a place where there are only balsam trees overgrown with rabbit grass and rubble. At first, I didn't understand what had happened. I still had the sky in my eyes, all that purple-blue that was itching at my eyeballs and carrying me far away, further than the columns of fair weather clouds playing at racing one another. He wasn't moving. His arms had become as stiff as stone, his mouth half open, the nails of his right hand sticking into the flesh of my hip. Inside me, his penis remained hard. Suddenly I saw that death was there, unmoving and mocking, its grip sending shivers up my spine. So I yelled, I yelled, I yelled. He was much too heavy for me to roll him off me and escape. My voice was much too high-pitched to be heard from the road. I saw the sun's flames begin to sink on the horizon. The crickets were chirping from time to time as if to practise their night-time din. My lips had become dry through shouting to no avail and the coldness of the foreman's body was freezing my blood. I don't know who saved me from this abyss of horror nor how it happened, nor anything at all. Nobody saw fit to tell me, and Ma Doris avoided saying the slightest word to me as if I'd caught typhoid. In the house I'd been laid out on the bare floor, with just a thin bamboo mat under me, and one of my brothers brought me weird potions, always sprinkled with leaves, which gave me back a semblance of vigorousness. But only a short time later my strength abandoned me and I started talking deliriously. I'd become like two persons in one: one who was talking so much that she was ranting, and another, ill, shrivelled up like a caterpillar, who was listening calmly, very sure of her fate and almost peaceful. At dawn, Ma Doris got up before everybody else and came and put her hand on my forehead, murmuring:

'Someone has hurt my daughter, I know.'

One day, there was a great coming and going outside. Horses prancing, loud white men's voices speaking beautiful French from France and the hysterical screaming of my wet-nurse mother who was trying to stop them from coming into our house. One of the gentlemen managed to push her aside and to come to my bedside. Kneeling, he held me by the wrist without saying the slightest word. I was afraid. Very afraid. Pulled my thighs apart. His hairy and France candle-coloured hands on my damp skin.

His fingers that creep gently up to my slit and brush delicately against it, drawing a giggle from me despite myself. His index finger that spreads the pink-purple lips and slides with great gentleness right into the depths of me, moving to and fro as he carefully watches my rolling eyes. Then he takes his finger out, smells the oil that has trickled from my body, ponders inside his yellow mango head and walks out of the house, fanning himself with his Panama hat. Once the whites had gone, Mama Doris rushed in with a bucket of water, the colour of freshly turned earth, and made me sit in it in order to clean me up. I was shivering and again felt death drawing close again. My flesh was as if already taken. I wanted to weep, to say goodbye to my guardian, to get up and go and look one last time at the hedge of poppies that surrounded the yard outside our house but I couldn't even blink an eyelid. Then I fell into a sleep for an unknown length of time, probably days or whole weeks. I was having dreams that were insidiously soft and gentle although dreadful: my body, with its arms amputated, floating in the sky; my wide-open thighs receiving the trunk of a huge tree, sometimes in the proud form of a silk-cotton tree. And then one fine day, all of this came to an end. Ma Doris simply said to me:

'Eau de Café, have a good wash, your grandmother doesn't like little girls with shit in their ears. I've bought you a pair of plastic shoes and a hat.'

She took me to Morne Céron, on the side of that astonishingly high mountain where Ma Nanette had built herself a house made of woven bamboo sticks. Below, you could make out a vast estate covered with sugar-cane fields as well as a large white, two-storey house perched on a small hill: that of the island white de Cassagnac. Ma Nanette looked at me, prodded my arms and legs, opened my mouth to inspect my teeth and finally said:

'You, my girl, you need a good bath to wash off the jinx that's oozing from your body.'

'It's the curse that her mother Franciane passed on to her,' commented Doris.

'Pah! She was good at fine words, that one, but what a handful of a woman! . . . But why have you come all this way to ask me to do a job that you could just as easily do yourself?'

'No . . . no, I don't think I can. This delivery is too difficult for my limited knowledge. I can't claim to be able to cure curses. Stomach aches, yes, mumps, yes, measles, yes, abortions and that sort of thing, yes, but the spell that's hanging over the head of this little girl, no! You're her grandmother, it's up to you to remove it from her.'

Ma Nanette sat there on her little bench for almost a century of time, smelling the wind, with its earthy scent, that blew at this hour of evening dew. She seemed to be listening to the secret messages that it was spreading among the leaves of the surrounding trees. Her eyes were fixed on the trunk of a golden apple tree where a flock of blackbirds had set up home. Oblivious to our presence, Ma Nanette got to her feet, pulling up the edges of her faded dress, and walked slowly towards it. At the edge of the shade it cast, she stretched out fully on the ground and a long piercing cry sprang from her breast. The earth began to tremble under our feet, which seemed to terrify Ma Doris. And to think that she was nicknamed the devil's betrothed! A silence descended on us and all around was frozen by it. Just as the black night opened its wings, my grandmother woke up:

'I've spoken to her mother. Tomorrow, early, we'll go down to the sea at Grand-Anse. Go away now, Doris, I must prepare the child. She's done nothing to deserve this cursedness that has wrapped itself around her life, and it will continue to pursue her if ever she has a child.'

'She'll have no children,' declared the devil's betrothed, 'and if ever it should come to pass one day, rest assured, I shall straight away separate mother and baby.'

'Thank you! Thank you a thousand times for everything you are doing for Eau de Café. You had no reason to be so generous. God who is in heaven, who sees everything, will reward you for that. Now, get yourself out of my house, quickly! I have many things to prepare.'

Dearest,

They have robbed us of what was most precious to us. They have torn open our language with exultant passion, leaving us with mere scraps, foetuses of sentences and oaths, drums thumping dismally in the very depths of our veins. They have strangled the warmth of its sounds in the sinews of our gullets and all that they have left us is derisory, foul and incestuous.

They are jubilant.

They have turned us into torturers of every word, into people contemptuous and complacent about what we say and we've done nothing, said nothing. 'Kal' (cock), 'Koukoun' (cunt), 'Bonda' (arse), 'Koké' (fuck): that's what's left! The tetralogy of fucking and shitting. The Neanderthal jargon of a cluster of natives, extravagantly made up in anticipation of a first-class burial.

Antilia

Sixth Circle

Nobody has taught us how to decipher the landmarks of memory. All we can do is parrot-phrase, endowed as we are with a prodigious laugh but one swollen with too many excesses. Our speech, in its mad steed's flight, intoxicates us and only succeeds in producing a flat display of days and deeds.

Sometimes we imagine that it would be enough to reconstruct the plot of a single life and so here is the path that cuts its way through the red soil of the mountains.

Grand-Anse, Fort-de-France, Martinique, the Antilles, Central America and, on the other side ('on the other shore' in our language), ironic Europe . . .

24 The General's Hand

A great breath of wind passed through the village of Grand-Anse, announcing the advent of a man who held a place in each of our hearts without us knowing him and applying a balm to whatever normally blighted our existence. The first person to broadcast the news was Syrian's former wife, who, despite having fallen into the most extreme discomfiture, still maintained some contact with her relatives who had moved into town. More ragged and beggarly than ever, a half-lit clay pipe in her mouth, she swaggered along Front Street:

'The Madonna wasn't able to cure my elephantiasis, ladies and gentlemen, so strong was the spell that evil men put on me, but may they shit themselves today! I shall be the first to touch him after monsieur the Prefect and then I shall be cured. Cured!'

These words sank the rum-swillers of Back Street's bars into a serious state of perplexity. Some of them put forward the theory that the Pope himself was about to set foot on Martinique's soil; others, more modest, opted for some Monseigneur from France or Navarre. Not one of them thought of Papa de Gaulle, even though most had risked their lives by joining his troops on the island of Dominica during the last war.

'Don't listen to that woman,' chuckled Dachine. 'She's looking to entice a man because it's a good fifteen years since she was last screwed.'

'Hey, who wants a good time with that sow? Come on, be brave, men, you'll just have to soap her down and then submit to her charms,' somebody added.

And yet, the next day, when they discovered that she had done her hair, washed, dressed smartly in a tight-fitting calico dress and, above all, painted her lips with red lipstick, people realized that she wasn't talking nonsense. Ali Tanin didn't recognize his mother and wolf-whistled at her. Ma Léonce was gasping at not being able to put a name to that face which she seemed to know so well. Chief Bérard, one of life's great uncouth, found himself displaying gallantry by offering to carry her Carib basket for her and Small Balls Auguste, visibly excited at the door of his bar, dropped a tray of rum punches. Oblivious to all others, the ex-Ma Tanin made her way to where Master Salvie's bus was loading passengers for Town. The driver, who was polishing the blood-red paintwork of the 'Executioner of the North' while enjoying an argument between two squawking women who had just got on, was the only person not to waste time in idle speculation: he had been in love with her, in the time of yesteryear, when she hadn't yet let herself be seduced by Syrian's siren sounds of hard cash, 'which didn't bring any happiment', as he used to mutter to himself every time their paths crossed. This indelible heartbreak had frozen into his memory the real image of the woman that marriage, middle-class prosperity and then brutal poverty had disfigured.

'Rose-Aimée . . . Rose-Aimée . . .' he stammered as he saw her approaching as if in a dream.

'My dear Salvie, wait for my elephantiasis to vanish and you'll be so surprised by my elegant shape that you'll see that the years have had no effect on me. I was wrong, it's true, to turn you down, but look at my hair, it's still black, and whenever you want I can take the place of the dirty coolie woman you've installed at Fond Gens-Libres.'

'Where . . . where are you going like that?'

'Ha, ha, ha! I'm going to see General de Gaulle, my dear man.'

He thought she was mad. He looked at his passengers, scratched his head and fixing her straight in the eye, tried as firmly as possible to force her to see that she'd be better off going home to En Chéneaux than wandering around in Fort-de-France, where the money-or-your-life brigade were working overtime holding people up. He even offered to take her home, hastily considering her proposition that they live together. One word, just one, would be enough for him to kick out the late Coolie René's sister whom he'd taken in more out of pity than desire. She was as thin as a stick and agreed in sheep-like fashion to everything he said, which only succeeded in irritating him to the highest degree. Had Rose-Aimée meant what she'd said? Or was she beginning to lose her mind?

'Here's my fare, Salvie, in case you think I'm trying to cadge a free trip from you,' she said and held out a big, almost new, thousand-franc note.

Salvie faltered for an instant before grabbing it, his eyes wide with wonder at the woman who was already climbing into his bus. She was wearing high heels despite her elephantiasis and yet no creature in the world could have been more graceful than her at that moment. Without knowing it, the driver had just perceived in the space of half a second what we awkwardly call eternity. He simply felt that the universe had stopped, that he had fallen swooning before the quintessence of beauty. Even the passengers had stopped gossiping, overwhelmed as they were too by Rose-Aimée Tanin, the women whose cruel fate was pitied by the charitable souls of Grand-Anse. Then it was that one of them produced a sublime sentence, a sentence that entirely captured this little piece of reality. Eau de Café called out:

'Every woman is a queen, even if it's only on one little occasion in her life.'

A crowd had gathered in front of the 'Executioner of the North', while an overwrought Salvie seized his bucket of soapy water clumsily and spilled it over a large part of his jacket.

'Do you mean that you're . . . moving?' he said in Rose-Aimée's direction . . . 'That you've found a place to live in town?'

'No, my dear, I'm from Grand-Anse and I'll stay from Grand-Anse whatever happens, but tomorrow I've got an appointment on La Savane with Papa de Gaulle. Go on, go and get changed, otherwise you're liable to catch cold.'

The horn of the 'Golem', which was passing at full speed, made the idlers jump with fright. Its driver yelled at Master Salvie:

'*Sakré yichkôn, man kay dépyèsté'w talè!*' (Son of a whore, I'm going to cut you to shreds in a moment!)

The triviality of the remark broke the spell. In the twinkling of an eye the 'Executioner of the North' was filled with its usual customers. Only Ali Tanin, the half-Syrian, was still pensively gazing at his mother, rejuvenated by some unknown miracle, and so forgot to tease the young ladies who were setting off in search of some little job or other in town. A crestfallen Dachine tugged at his sleeve and whispered to him: 'It's true what she said. I've just heard the news on Radio Martinique . . .'

This confirmation passed from mouth to mouth until it reached the edge of the village, where Julien Thémistocle, the maroon, the indomitable, was making a speech in front of a gathering of men to whom the municipality had allotted the purely symbolic task of trimming the gliricidia hedge surrounding the primary school. He was busy mocking their surnames:

'Monsieur Présent, could you pass me those secateurs, please . . . and you, my dear Placide, steady that ladder so that you don't break your back falling off it . . . Ha, ha, ha! As for you, citizens Ladouceur and Lecurieux, look out for passers-by, if you please. You're so careless that I wouldn't be in the least surprised if you dirtied a passing lady.'

The council workers no longer even bothered to react to his jibes. Not a week went by without him insulting somebody's name while puffing with pride over his own. According to him, the name Thémistocle had been forcibly imposed upon the France-Whites who were responsible for drawing up registry lists straight after the abolition of slavery.

'My grandfather wasn't a chicken like yours, gentlemen,' he would say. 'When the Morne l'Étoile estate blacks were called together and made to queue up in front of a little idiot of a white, sitting at a table with a big notebook open in front of him, he wouldn't let that fellow open his dictionary at random and give him a name. He wouldn't have any of that monkey business. He turned up with his cutlass in his hand and threatened to cut the white's balls off if he didn't write down exactly what my grandfather was going to dictate to him, by God! Ha! You've got to have some nerve to do that, my friends. They wanted to call him "Diligent", but he kicked up such an almighty fuss that the white was forced to write down "Thémistocle" . . . You can laugh, you bunch of uneducated niggers! Thémistocle is the name of a great Greek.'

On hearing Papa de Gaulle's name, Julien Thémistocle shivered. He cut short his lecture and raced off to Fond Massacre, where he had temporarily moved in with a concubine. The 'Executioner of the North' overtook him on the road and the passengers agreed that this time the zombie, to whom he'd sold his soul, had just come to settle accounts. A tear ran down Eau de Café's cheek, according to some. Rose-Aimée Tanin, whom he'd violated many a time despite the fetidness of her rags, gave an evil laugh. Master Salvie, the driver, blew on his horn several times to try to bring him to his senses, but Julien Thémistocle was running, running, running, altogetherly indifferent to the dogs snapping at his heels and the stones scratching the soles of his feet. He ironed the army fatigue jacket that he'd brought back from the war, polished his boots with spit, shaved hurry-quickly with the help of a rusty Gillette razor that was lying on a shelf, and without offering the slightest explanation to his woman, who was huddled in a corner, used as she was to putting up with his orders, raced to the side of the road to wait for the 'Golem'. Its driver, Chief Bérard, slammed on the brakes and stopped dead in front of him, creating chaos in the back of the bus, where market vegetable women, old folk on their way to withdraw their pensions, nubile young ladies as well as boarders heading for the Lycée Schoelcher were thrown one against the other in a single ouch-ooh-ah of oaths, screams of pain and our-father-who-art-in-heavens.

'Bouwo-di-Nô kay pwan douvan nou, wi, Béra. Sa ou ka fè u?' (The 'Executioner of the North' is going to get away from us, Bérard. What do you think you're doing?) yelped one of his more fanatical passengers.

'La . . . ladjè pété, mézan . . . mézanmi . . .' (War . . . war has broken out, my . . . my friends . . .) he managed to stutter.

'Get going, comrade,' said Julien Thémistocle as he leapt on to the running-board of the 'Golem', 'it's nothing to do with a new war. I've put on my uniform to welcome General de Gaulle as he deserves.'

A reinvigorated Chief Bérard set the gears screaming and set off in pursuit of the 'Executioner of the North', an event that normally took place on the bridge over the river Galion between the *communes* of Trinité and Gros-Morne. The passengers would sing to egg him on:

'Get up steam, driver, the car doesn't belong to you!'

To put off the moment of his defeat, Master Salvie drove straight down the middle of the narrow road, only moving over to the right on the corners that were known to be dangerous. Encouraged by his passengers, Chief Bérard, his foot on the accelerator and his right hand pressing down on the horn of his bus, tried the most daring manoeuvres, to the great alarm of the few passing drivers. The narrow road suddenly widened at the approach to the bridge, which hung over a ravine filled with enormous clumps of bamboo. The supporters of the 'Executioner of the North', mostly respectable folk, older in any case than the 'Golem''s loutish customers, would ignore the insults hurled at them by their adversaries, who screamed:

'*Nou sanfouté lanmô! Béra, bay bwa, fout!*' (We don't give a fuck about dying! Faster, Bérard, for fuck's sake!)

And so, as they reached the mouth of the bridge, where the abyss seems ready to swallow anything that would dare to lean over it, Chief Bérard, the driver with the hellfire touch, would wrestle his vehicle on to the left-hand side, which sloped down to the Guinea grass in the drain, put it into reverse as the right-hand wheels left the ground, brake and then accelerate, while turning the steering-wheel to avoid the head of the bridge all the while hooting, intoxicated by the cheering of his passengers. The 'Golem' would briefly kiss eternity's hand before righting itself and, with a terrible grinding of axles, bump into the side of the 'Executioner of the North', which had long ago admitted defeat. At the very moment of overtaking, the 'Golem'-blacks shouted at the Executioner-blacks:

'*Sakré bann makoumè ki zôt yé!*' (You bunch of old women!)

224

Well, on that famous day that Rose-Aimée Tanin had appeared in extraordinary splendour and had maintained that she was going to see Papa de Gaulle, the battlefield was empty. Heavy rain, which had been falling since the previous day, had filled the roaring River Galion beneath the bridge. A silent Chief Bérard brought the 'Golem' to another abrupt halt, ignoring the protests from his supporters who were urging him onwards to try and catch up with Master Salvie before the village of Gros-Morne – 'otherwise we won't have enough handkerchiefs to wipe away the shame that'll ooze from our foreheads'. In truth, the inhabitants of the *communes* separating Grand-Anse from Fort-de-France, that's to say Fond d'Or, Sainte-Marie, Trinité, Gros-Morne and Saint-Joseph, enthusiastically followed the war between the two buses whose drivers were the most couldn't-care-less types in the whole North of the island. Their own buses wisely stayed uninvolved in a saga that had been going on for two decades and was bound to end in great human carnage. Fond d'Or and Sainte-Marie were on the side of the 'Executioner of the North', while hearts in Gros-Morne and the other villages thrilled for the 'Golem'.

'*Lanjèt manman sa! Lundjèt manman sa!*' (Oh, shit!) repeated the barely recognizable Chief Bérard.

'If you allow those queers in the "Executioner of the North" to reach Gros-Morne before us, it's the last time I travel with you, my friend. That'll be it!' said a voice on the edge of hysteria.

'Salvie must have put a spell on him, what else could have happened?' suggested someone else. 'Look at Bérard, who's normally so full of bravado, whose head's going round and round in circles like a fairground horse.'

The driver was leaning on the parapet of the bridge, staring at the thin silver thread that could be seen through the tangle of bamboo and balisiers. Some passengers got off the bus to shake him but couldn't get close to him. A sort of invisible fluid seemed to be protecting him from their irritated hands, dissolving their exclamations into a thousand little fragments of sound which became mixed into the rumbling of the River Galion.

'See what he's got from dealing with the devil!' a woman declared. 'Hasn't he always refused to have his bus blessed on Saint Anthony's feast day?'

'Master Salvie follows the Church's precepts to the letter, my friends. Now everybody can see that white God is stronger than black God,' said another.

Julien Thémistocle wasted no time philosophizing over the sudden silence of the 'Golem''s driver. He grabbed his bag, jumped out of one of the bus's windows and started his running-race again, across the fields this time because colonial roads never go in a straight line and prefer to follow the contours of the hillsides. He was driven by one single thought: to catch up with the 'Executioner of the North' in order not to miss Papa de Gaulle's arrival. His unexpected appearance froze with alarm many workers busy weeding canefields, made a woman who was sweeping her beaten earth yard fall over backwards, gave a funny turn to Gros-Morne's rural policeman who swore never again to down six neat rums before midday, terrorized a gang of little boys who were playing marbles at the foot of a mango tree with spindly roots, sent chickens, ducks and strutting turkey cocks into flight and amazed a painter (France-white in origin) who, sitting in front of his easel, was attempting to reproduce the lofty elevation of the Mount of Olives. According to bush radio, Julien Thémistocle ran faster than a dozen horses going downhill. Faster than a *soukougnan* spirit, which in any case can move at the speed of light. A few yards outside the village he caught up with the 'Executioner of the North', whose passengers were hooting with laughter, happy for once at having shaken off their eternal rival. It has to be said that the presence of Rose-Aimée, returned to her youthful appearance, had galvanized Master Salvie. His regulars could barely recognize him any more as he was now taking all sorts of risks, approaching the descent at Anse Charpentier at a hundred an hour, hardly slowing down on the bends before the village of Trinité. Nobody complained although each and every one was terrified, except Rose-Aimée, who, sitting alone at the front next to him, was humming a Creole mazurka. The driver's face seemed to have taken on a determination and boldness that nothing could have countered. Little by little, the tension lessened, Eau de Café put her rosary away in her Madras skirt and made a joke. When people realized at the Galion bridge that the 'Executioner of the North' had brought off a brilliant victory, they hugged and congratulated each other and passed around a flask of Madkaud rum, the strongest to be had on the island at the time. None of the market women lost their temper when two full basketloads of vegetables fell from the roof of the bus and spread themselves over the road just outside the Dénel refinery.

'It's a present for Papa de Gaulle!' one of them shouted. 'He saved France, so we can at least make a little sacrifice today, for God's sake!'

And yet the laughter froze on their lips when the impeccably shaven face of Julien Thémistocle suddenly appeared at the window of the door where Rose-Aimée was leaning. The fellow had jumped on to the running board and had hung on to the vehicle without even bothering to catch the eye of the driver or the passengers. The 'Executioner of the North' slowed down, as if of its own volition, and a deep silence broke out inside, made even more bizarre by the back-firing from the exhaust pipe. The bus drove through the village of Gros-Morne, provoking no reaction other than disbelieving snorts. Rose-Aimée put her hand on the maroon's with a tenderness that broke Master Salvie's heart. The ruffian who had many times raped her by day and by night (as he had the evil gift of being able to turn himself into an incubus), the filthy outlaw who defied Grand-Anse's constabulary, a sharpened cutlass in his hand, was not the same man as this handsome specimen who, indifferent to death, was now standing on the running board of the 'Executioner of the North'. Indeed, it would only have taken a sudden braking on the part of Master Salvie to send him flying into some gulley where only the lancehead vipers and opossums would have taken care of his tomb. Eau de Café, who was furious even though impressed by the smartness of his military garb, shut her eyes and began her eternal prayers to Saint Martin de Porres. They passed through the village of Saint-Joseph in the same unspeakable silence. As Town approached, Julien Thémistocle brushed his cheeks against Rose-Aimée's hand and said to her loudly and clearly:

'You've been in my heart for such a so long time that I've forgotten to ask you to share my life.'

'Ah! I've had a dog's life, my man.'

'I know . . . I know . . . but now I won't let you go again and together we'll confront all the bitch tricks that existence can throw at us. De Gaulle has come to bring us a better world. He is a great man.'

'A thousand thanks!' the woman murmured.

Master Salvie reached Croix-Mission in a sort of dream. He omitted to drop off certain market women by the Rich People's Cemetery and received a salvo of insults in return. He had already been forgotten in the hustle and bustle of the town, him and the pain he bore in the only place that nobody, whoever he may be, has ever been able to protect. He slumped on to his steering-wheel, not even collecting the fares, and everyone took full advantage to make their escape except Eau de Café and one or two churchy ladies who despised dishonesty. Rose-Aimée and Julien Thémistocle walked, arm in arm, up the La Levée Boulevard, an unusual affectation in a Creole country, which attracted coarse remarks and mischievous whistles:

'Look at them with their France-fashions,' grumbled a beggar as he held out his hand towards them. 'Good grief, I don't know what this country's coming to.'

The streets of Fort-de-France had been tidied up and bedecked with red, white and blue flags that were so new as to seem unreal. A sense of euphoria gripped Town's blacks, of whom those most inclined to take things easy during this siesta hour, the dice players of La Savane, were debating under the bandstand the relative merits of Napoleon and Papa de Gaulle. Goldmouth, one of the most feared chiefs of Terres-Sainvilles, welcomed his Grand-Anse *alter ego*, with whom he'd fought in the same Ardennes regiment, with open arms. He too had put on a military fatigue jacket, but less shiny-new than Julien Thémistocle's and very probably ripped by razor slashes. The man with eighteen golden teeth didn't refrain from eyeing up his girlfriend and from directing ribald remarks towards her.

'I had them pulled out one after the other', he explained to Rose-Aimée, 'and I replaced them with gold, like that, even after I'm dead, my mouth won't go rotten. Ha, ha, ha!'

In the Allée des Soupirs, the gilded youth of Fort-de-France was submitting to the first tremors of love. A vast stage had been erected next to the statue of the Empress Joséphine, at the bottom of which a tramp was busy pissing.

'So have you come to see the General, as well?' asked Goldmouth.

'May tomorrow come quickly,' answered Thémistocle gravely.

They spent the evening boozing in the 'Dockers' Daisies' and in the Transat bars. The common folk were pacing the streets with impatience and had decided not to sleep. The streetwalkers of the Cour Fruit-à-Pain had, on this special occasion, lowered their rates and it was only an idiot who would fail to take advantage of the offer. Philomène, who was once the enchanted negress of Fort-de-France's downtown neighbourhoods, dispensed phenomenal sweetness to all those who were lucky enough to find ecstasy in her arms.

'It's for Papa de Gaulle,' she whispered to them.

In the morning, a stirring sun took hold of Town. Tricolour flags were embellishing the tamarind tress, lamp-posts, wormeaten houses and buses, which were the only vehicles allowed on the road. Goldmouth and Julien Thémistocle carved their way through the crowd gathered on the pavements and their friendship was so solidly forged that they held each other by the hand, forgetting Rose-Aimée who was struggling to keep up with them. They were recalling their exploits of yesteryear, slapping each other demonstratively on the shoulder and passing to and fro a bottle of rum removed from the shop window of a Chinaman on the Avenue Sainte-Thérèse. Their vagabond attire was hardly noticeable amidst the iridescent dresses and black suits. The bandit with the auriferous dentures suddenly noticed a woman who was covered from head to foot with every possible and imaginable Creole jewel – a glittering pin stuck into her *tête chaudière* Madras headscarf, dahlia rings of impressive circumference, rings decorated with fruit designs – but it was the choker of solid gold that stopped Goldmouth in his tracks with amazement. What magnificent teeth he could have had made from it, for God's sake! She was sitting slightly apart from the crowd, perched on an empty Royal Soda crate, princess for a day, an ephemeral princess whose face was painted with rebellious gaiety. The two comrades stopped dead, exchanging looks of stupefaction, one, the towny, thinking of lifting her necklace, the other, the yokel, thinking of lifting her skirt. They approached her from behind, camouflaging themselves with the help of an old newspaper as if they were protecting themselves against the sun. The crowd had swollen and the words 'Papa de Gaulle' were passing from lip to lip. Goldmouth was the quicker of the two; he succeeded in relieving the young woman of her necklace without even dropping it and immediately disappeared into the crowd. Julien Thémistocle, who had tried to stroke her arm, was at the receiving end of a formidable slap which sent him spinning into a group of layabouts. He just had time to feel the force of an onslaught of kicking and spitting before Rose-Aimée, who had been uncomplainingly following him, helped him to his feet. The princess had vanished from her pedestal and a throng of people was now occupying the place where she had been holding sway over the crowd. Julien would have thought he'd been dreaming were it not for a piercing pain stiffening his jaw. He was torn between anger and astonishment.

'*Oti Bèkannô?*' (Where's Goldmouth?) he asked Rose-Aimée.

'*Mi Papa dè Gôl! Wéé-é-é-é, mi li-m!*' (There's Papa de Gaulle! Hoo-r-aaa-ay, there he is!) bellowed the crowd hysterically.

A black open-top DS19, flanked by a host of police motorcyclists, was coming briskly down the Boulevard Sainte-Thérèse. A fleur-de-lys hat, a long nose and a skin the colour of France-flour sat upon a gigantic body that was standing to attention and waving with one hand. Women fainted in clusters or kneeled to pray. Men ran along after the giant, not caring whether they barged into children or peanut-sellers. Julien Thémistocle, the maroon who had defied whites and their orders since the day he was born, found himself caught up in this demonstration of fervour. He heard himself shouting:

'*Dè Gôl, ou sé papa nou! Fè sa ou lé épi no!*' (De Gaulle, you're our father! Do whatever you wish with us!)

He was swept along down to the La Savane park by the delirious mob. To his surprise, Goldmouth was struggling to make his way upwards through the human tide, the mother of all furies raging in his heart.

'*Sa ki ni?*' (What's wrong?) said Thémistocle.

'Where's that bitch from earlier gone? Where is she, eh?' he was yelling, the veins in his neck taut like mandoline strings. 'Come on, follow me, we're going to find that whore!'

The giant in the hat was wearing a magnificent white uniform and there were already arguments over the exact number of medals that were decorating it. He shook hands with a line of black ex-servicemen who were having trouble holding upright their banners that they'd brought back from all the wars where they'd paid the blood tax to our mother France. One woman, pregnant up to the eyeballs, screamed:

'God, make me give birth right here and now, please!'

Then she lay at full stretch on the thick grass of La Savane and started imitating the throes of childbirth without anybody taking the least bit of notice. Goldmouth stepped over her at the moment that the new-born was making his appearance between her thighs. Julien Thémistocle picked the baby up and gently placed it into the arms of its mother.

He didn't understand the fury that was driving the chief from Terres-Sainvilles. Hadn't he just pulled off the sort of trick that only comes along once in a lifetime? Now he could retire or go on a cruise to Benezuela. When they reached the Schoelcher library, they heard the giant's voice exclaim:

'*Mon Dieu! Mon Dieu! Que vous êtes foncés!*'[1]

---

1 My God! My God! How dark you are!

Salvoes of applause cut their way through a low murmur of disapproval. But the rest of the speech soon healed the wound and the audience swooned at the giant's well-chosen words, simple words, it's true, far removed from Creole grandiloquence, but which seemed to emerge ennobled from his mouth. People in the crowd jostled each other to touch his hands, which he held out with generosity. Children were pushed to the front so that he might touch their foreheads and transmit a little of his intelligence to them. Old women were kissing his fingers in the hope of regaining a second youth. A solitary Goldmouth, furious to the pit of his stomach, continued to search out that morning's princess, whose necklace he'd stolen turned out to be a fake. Yes, ladies and gentlemen, a bloody fake! Julien Thémistocle left him to it and forced his way to the barriers just at the moment when Papa de Gaulle was passing by. Moved by his army jacket and his military medal, the giant gave him a lengthy handshake before paying him a compliment amidst the photographers' flashes. He murmured:

'*Mon Dieu! Mon Dieu! Que vous êtes français!*'[1]

A moment later, in his stentorian voice, Thémistocle shouted out to the crowd:

'You misheard! Papa de Gaulle would never have mentioned the colour of our skin! Never!'

And with that, he rushed around to deliver the good news. Around the Maison des Sports. Along the high walls of the Saint-Louis fort. Processing the length of the La Levée Boulevard. Coming back down to the Bord de Mer, via the Gueydon bridge and the Rive Droite Levassor. On the quayside, he ran into Antilia (she was the princess of a thousand jewels) deep in conversation with Goldmouth who was yelling:

'Here, take back your rubbish and next time you'd better wear real gold round your throat or I'll cut it for you!'

Julien Thémistocle wrapped up the hand that Papa de Gaulle had shaken in a white handkerchief and put it in a pocket of his

1 My God! My God! How French you are!

jacket. It was only at the bus station that he noticed that he'd lost Rose-Aimée. She had not been able to keep pace with his frenetic tour of the town, reporting what the giant had really said. He didn't even realize that he was climbing aboard the 'Executioner of the North', the vehicle of the well-to-do. In contrast to the morning, Master Salvie was displaying an enigmatic sort of cheerfulness. He hustled the market women to make a space for the maroon by the window. One of them took pity on what she thought to be his wounded hand but he took no notice of her. The next day, he installed himself behind Grand-Anse's market-place to receive his customers. He carefully unwrapped the handkerchief that was covering his hand, pocketed the sum that he had demanded (a sum proportionate to the problem that he was supposed to cure) and patted the palm of the rheumatic, the spurned mistress, the scholarship candidate or the fighting cock breeder who appeared before him. In this way he managed to reduce Bogino's madness, a miracle that neither Coolie René nor the Madonna had been able to work, and to restore an erection to *maître* Féquesnoy, thereby also demolishing his radical-socialist convictions and his total allegiance to the Fourth Republic. The fame of Julien Thémistocle spread throughout the island when the newspapers published his photo in the arms of the giant. They came from Lamentin, even from Rivière-Salée or from Vauclin to touch his hand and, for the first time in his life, he had so much money that he didn't know what to do with it. Sometimes he found himself thinking of the life of happiness that he might have had with Rose-Aimée if she hadn't disappeared among the exalted crowd on the square at La Savane. He would have cured her elephantiasis with his magic hand. In the mornings he would make his way to the municipal fountain where Master Salvie parked the 'Executioner of the North' to tell him:

'If you see Rose-Aimée, let her know that I'm waiting for her. I know that you likewise carry a flame for her, but no more than I do, dammit!'

Alas, neither Thémistocle nor Master Salvie nor anybody from Grand-Anse ever heard a word from Rose-Aimée again. Some hinted that she had changed identity and joined the painted and scented procession of street-walkers who haunted the Cour Fruit-à-Pain at nightfall. Julien Thémistocle cured all sorts of ills for as long as he didn't wash the hand that had shaken Papa de Gaulle's. Unfortunately for him, he collapsed into a gutter after having spent the whole night playing *sèrbi* at the Grand-Anse village fête and the blessed hand soaked for hours in dirty water. Thereafter it lost all its power and our hero, who had wasted all his wealth, found himself even more beggarly than before. He returned to being an incubus, an outlaw, a hard man, a follower of the gods of Guinea.

'As far as I'm concerned, that man died the day he left for the *dissidence* to fight Hitler instead of taking care of me after he'd killed my mother,' concluded a bitter Eau de Café.

But everyone in Grand-Anse knew full well that she was lying to herself . . .

25

So you see, Thimoléon complains, you didn't have the faintest idea about any of this. While your brothers were in chains, you, you were wandering around the country, down there in the South, the land of manchineel trees where, says bush radio, the sand on the beaches is cassava white and the sea fantastically calm. And then you leapt, legs crossed, over the ocean to find yourself under the Eiffel Tower, taking ingratitude to the point of not coming to kiss your old godmother Eau de Café. I suppose we count for nothing, we're just mangy old dogs, eh! A fellow who abandons his *commune* at the age of eleven and comes back as old as you are now is capable of anything. Especially if he has the supreme audacity of wanting to understand everything in a single day. In a single day, do you hear me? In any case, you've been the subject of non-stop gossip, and news about you has been doing the rounds. Your life story is as well known as ABC. You were expected, in a manner of speaking. That's why on first meeting nobody asked you the slightest question, not even the gossip-mongers (they are bound by the law of silence) and why your continual astonishment has made a bad impression. Even the things that you'd forgotten! So much so that you're perhaps better off not playing the loudmouth today, unless you've brought back an infallible protection with you from your long wandering. Nobody would permit your defeat. Or your death. In any case, not before you explain yourself! For then, you would be erased from every thought and every word, even those exchanged cryptically. Your position is awkward since you can't allow yourself either to come and go between the dice tables like some European traveller, careless and carefree as regards the stakes, unable to interpret the clearing of a throat, aware only of the outward appearance of things. You, you know full well that behind those faces, behind those tireless hands rolling the dice, there is real substance, a sort of furiousness. There's life and death, everything that you've neglected in the past in favour of new horizons, where other races live, strangers to the rhythm of our breathing. You wanted to get away, but you were held back so well that here you are again today. Now it's up to you to invent an acceptable way of snapping your fingers and throwing the dice! But watch out, their demands will be extreme and in your case such extremity will be pushed back, the limits of bravery will be further extended deliberately in your honour. Your life will again be at stake. How? It's up to you to work that out in your fuzzy head and to measure precisely how hard you'll have to fight. If it's too much for you, you'll soon know because nobody will be bothered not to give you a shove amid that noisy market-place crowd. You'll realize where you've managed to end up and how hard it'll be to get out. On the other hand, if all goes well and true, you'll see some of them holding their dice cups towards you so that you can call on the magic number in their place. It's the beginnings of trust. Not that it'll mean that the fight is won, but the evening is off to a good start and you can allow a little bit of relief to sink into your bones.

The coolies from Basse-Pointe will present you with the most heartfelt challenge because their instinct is hidden beneath their long shiny hair that many blacks secretly envy and so, from the very beginning, they will seek to test you to see whether, having left and come back again, you rate them even lower (more 'at the bottom' they would say) than they already are. They'll send their spit flying towards your feet and wipe their fingers, greasy from eating black pudding, on your shirt while pretending to apologize profusely, and you, you'll have to put up with it all. It amounts to a new baptism: the baptism of returning here. You've no right to get angry, you don't even matter for the time being. One more stranger, that's all. That won't be an end to it, far from it. Those coolies have got more than one grudge up their sleeves and they'll carry on right to the end. They'll follow you with their naturally silky step to any table that you're bold enough to approach and, even without you realizing it, they'll stand there opposite your table, watching you impassively, communicating among themselves in their inquisitive eye language. If you start trembling, then you're caught in a lobster pot, so to speak. If you can bear their gaze while not losing sight of the way the dice are falling on the table – you have to be capable of this feat – then don't move. No gesticulations that they might run the risk of mis-interpreting. And above all, don't forget in which language they are experts, for if you do, the blue-black flash of a cutlass can spring out from anywhere, from behind their khaki trousers or from inside their banana-stained shirts, and you'll see the table take a flying leap, the dice scatter for ever and the players beat a nimble retreat. You'll be on your own with the sweeping blade, ready to split you in two like a ripe calabash. And, whatever you do, keep an eye out for the son of René, the ex-cattle-slaughterer!

Restrain your curiosity! Because you haven't lived a life of mis-ery like them. You haven't felt the humiliating weight on your back (your 'shell' they would say) of the endless stones thrown by little boys in the fields shouting 'Coolie! Dog-eating coolie!' Nor taken to your heels when the gossip Ma Léonce blocks the road outside her baker's shop and, a pair of scissors in hand, takes issue with them:

'Shoo! Band of mangy dogs! I don't want to see another dirty coolie move his arse near here. Starting from now, I'm going to cut into pieces the first one who's rash enough to pass this way.'

What can you say? How can you retaliate? You can't. Apart from bringing the wrath of the god Maldévilin down on to her head, but she's stronger than all that mumbo-jumbo. The *béké* Dupin de Médeuil shares her bed and that's probably why she thinks she can block the road like that. So you haven't lived through that, my friend, you have no idea about emotions that have to be swallowed, angers repressed, tears that flow like from an eye disease. You have no idea about the Indian women raped in some thicket or in the river rustling of a clump of para-grass by the *béké* or a dead drunk foreman. Or abused in the village by that perverted mulatto Féquesnoy. All of this is the sort of story from

237

hereabouts that you'd rather – don't deny it – ignore. It's what acts as daily fodder to our minds, which are supposed to be as narrow as a chicken's backside, as if violence and poverty with a capital 'p' don't open wide the high seas in front of you. As if there was more life in your books than in life itself, as if man doesn't think with his body as well as his mind.

And another thing, don't get it into your head that you can go around raising old dust as regards Antilia. We all knew her memory would never stop scatching away at you from the moment the sea handed back her body at the foot of La Crabière. How many times hadn't I warned her: 'Antilia, look out, that sea is treacherous. Just because it pretends to be friendly with you, it doesn't mean that one day its rage won't decide to drag you under the water.' But what did I get back other than insults or sour faces full of scornfulness? Oh, I know, you're not convinced about her death. The authorities never formally identified the body and some people reckon Antilia took advantage of this drama to make good her escape to Fort-de-France. 'Eau de Café treats me like a slave!' she used to grumble when she was scrubbing away in the back of your kitchen. The drowned person's face had been completely torn away by the rocks, it's true, but I can tell you that from the flesh on that body I saw lying there on the sand, from the weight of her breasts, from the black triangle between her legs, I recognized without any doubt the young lady who used to bathe naked in the mornings in your sink. You can carry on doubting and dreaming up some glorious fate for her, but that's just feeding fantasies which can only lead you to the same end as our philosopher, that dear Émilien Bérard . . .

So, you go into the market-place and you look for what you've lost, you climb back up the ladder of unlived days, you take back the ups and downs of your words and you'll see, everything will fall into place . . .

Another of Thimoléon's tirades:

If you'd planned some escape strategy, rants Thimoléon, if you'd thought you'd be able to take refuge in some sort of arrogant superiority, well you'd better get out now: we'd just be left with some stranger's corpse and not even enough people to organize a proper wake. Remember that here no one can get away from anyone else. We all live within earshot of each other, and the moaning of adulterous women (it's not a question of desire, but ritual) fills our verandas at nightfall without anybody feeling slighted. It's all been guessed at already because there has been the slow build-up day after day, that's to say the obscene jokes, the discreet touching, the pinching of taut buttocks, the games of hide-and-seek around the cassava mills under the half-amused, half-indifferent gaze of onlookers. And then the moment comes when, tired of playing, they decide that they deserve to take the next step and the man makes the move towards his neighbour's wife, and so his brother's wife: 'When you've finished doing your washing-up, I'm ready for you.'

You see, you're surrounded from all sides. It's your move! Find the crack, the chink that will allow you to slip into the fragrant intimacy of the market-place and get yourself accepted again as a man from around here. When, on the stroke of half past one in the morning, there seems to be a pause, a 'lull' we prefer to say, because throats are dry and bellies empty, you can sit under the straw roof festooned with red, white and blue flags next to the old soldiers who in enigmatic Creole relive the dice games they played on the fourteenth of July in their youth. They're the ones you must speak to first by pretending to admire their chests glinting with bursts of medals and in so doing you'll avoid causing offence. They'll want to know without delay in what role you're approaching them: as a loudmouth or repentant son. That's why if it's the former, you must speak your suit-and-tie French and if it's the latter, Creole. Once your choice is made, they'll start the slow process that will lead you all to mutual understanding, toasted by many and many a flask of white rum. But look out! Let them speak! They need to talk just like those of your age need a woman's *coucoune*. Don't interrupt them under any circumstances, even if the meaning of such and such a word seems as deceptive as a double-bladed knife or if you want them to clarify

239

some reference to a story from the time of yesteryear.

From time to time they will spout a few fragments of French to help you along the way. You must listen to them, listen to them, open your ears seventeen times wide, as the Haitians say, until they pop. During the time they hold you under their sway, they'll be weighing you up to find out whether you are really worthy of their consideration, and when you hear 'Admiral Robert was a real *chien-fer*!' or 'Ah, France, what a valiant nation!' don't give into the urge to leap to your feet! They wouldn't understand and you would seriously compromise your next move. Once again you'd be putting your life at risk because they wouldn't be able with a gesture to stop the razor that is about to cut into your back or backside. And you should know, you'll be forced to cheat so that you can be punished. The dice will be marked and tampered with in such a way that when you hold them in your already trembling hand, you'll have no choice but to send them spinning towards the edge of the table and – hell's bells! – there they are on the ground . . . and you, you're in the shit, my friend. Dice on the floor is the height of downfall. The bent-over body leaning down to pick them up lends itself of its own accord to the vindictiveness of a kick (but that's uncommon) or a cut from a razor specially sharpened for the event. Or else everything can happen quite differently. In other words, nothing will happen. People will turn away, their mouths marked with disgustance, so you can sink your hands into the dust, humiliated by violent, wheezing laughter, and when you try to play the dice again, a chief will grab you by the wrist and force you to throw them (this time for good) into the gutter that runs round the market. First warning.

So, if you've come in the guise of a loud mouth, head straight away under the straw roof, pull up a chair without waiting for an invitation and make a point of sitting down with the '14–'18 veterans and shout out 'Gentlemen, honour!' and you can be sure that they'll reply 'Respect!', slightly mystified of course, but that doesn't matter: it's your choice and they'll go along with you. It's up to you to show you're capable of carrying it off. You'll be free to interrupt their speechifying whenever you like, you'll be free to snort with laughter or not, to shake your head or to raise your glass to the health of So-and-So. But even in this version of events, don't try to take unfair advantage! They are the rightful owners of language. They've been in charge of it for an eternity of dry and rainy seasons. But you, you left, you came back, so listen. Listen! They will coax you into unrestrained joy with each of their boasts. It's your job to separate what's serious from the frivolous because they're talking to you in person. You, the nephew, the godson, the man belonging to their old sparring partner, Eau de Café, whose family tree they've reconstructed in no time at all, from your great-grandmother Lactitia Augustin, who had a child with a *béké* from Fond Gens-Libres (which raises you in their eyes although this furtive union only brought a temporary 'De Valois' stuck on to the name Augustin) down to you opposite them, a stranger and yet so close, keen to return to the fold even if it means humiliation.

You'll have to put up with the story surrounding each medal gathered by chance from the battlefields of Europe – 'The Senegalese infantrymen are so black they're blue but they're real men. They're not afraid to die for the motherland like those chickens from Marseille!' before they agree to deal with your case, in other words to give you hints as to how to act, how to speak, what to do so that your entire being falls back into conformity with society here. Not that they will let you into every secret. How could they anyway? They won't present you with a manual or anything like that because they suspect that if you came as a hard man it's because you're 'strong', because your body is protected . . . Oh, yes! They'll tell you, you can bet on it, about the strike at Morne Carabin and Fond Massacre. The war-cries of the rebellious blacks, the cutlasses brandished in the air, the scared island whites who when night came evacuated their wives and kids to Plateau Didier at Fort-de-France. The helter-skelter of bamboo torches in the darkness all the way to the master's house. And now, take note, the world has changed! They weren't just dealing with a handful of foremen armed with old muskets and protected by Creole dogs, bad-tempered but essentially not very dangerous except when they bite your calves. No! More important was what was behind them, in the second row, if you can put it like that: a company of the metropolitan militia, hidden in their jeeps and lorries, machine-guns ready to bark out in the strange early morning silence. Then you'll be told that these new-fangled weapons cut down lives. Young lives, old lives, lives full of maturity, lives swollen with rising sap, all sorts of lives, you see! Black men's lives. They'll keep on spinning you this yarn for all they're worth, swallowing half the sentences as if to unload a secret, a pain too heavy to carry inside themselves, and you mustn't push the point, you mustn't look for the why and how of things. Nor people's names, nor what happened next. You'll find out as the years go by, in the course of intimate conversings, once you're re-rooted here for good. But for the moment, what you're told will be quite enough . . . it's even a great honour that they're doing you, because strangers (or those who go away and come back like you: it's the same thing!) are normally faced with stitched-up mouths, like they show to those mulatto journalists who come up specially from town with their big black cameras. You see, they're already showing you a bit of trust. Carry on!

When the old soldiers are altogetherly drunk and they start mixing up the Dardanelles with the Dominica Channel, then you can take your leave with a simple nod of the head and return among the players who will now know what and who they're dealing with. You will get out a few thousand-franc notes that you'll put down casually within reach after you've dutifully smoothed them out (because holding them out all screwed up is an insult that only maroons can get away with). And then, remind yourself that one never knows what might be hidden there. Sometimes, when you're holding out your hand, somebody can 'take' it and when you're taken, there are only two ways out: either tear the note into fifty little pieces and throw them one by one over your shoulder without turning round and without lowering your stare from the middle of your opponent's eyeballs, or discreetly slice into his hand with a razor swipe so that he can't close his hand and so take your luck hostage. You'll get out your own dice, your 'bones' as they prefer to say, and you'll play with them for a moment or two between your fingers so that people can admire your dexterity, because this is how they'll judge whether you've come to sweep away the few crumbs belonging to the needy or whether you prefer, just for its own sake, to take pleasure in seeing the bones roll in their immaculate whiteness.

26

'I would never have thought you'd still be here a whole month later,' says the ex-navy man, who has become increasingly jovial and chatty as he has seen me become a fixture in his hotel, where apparently I am the only real guest.

I discover that people to whom I've never spoken hate me, since in this little village like everywhere else on this minuscule island, the black man nurtures his jealousy of the black man and sometimes holds him in hatefulness. Bad luck, imposed from on high by the former masters and their offspring, has transformed each of us into a seething mass of suspicions and grudges against our nearest neighbours. Touched by my dismay, the retired navy man ends up by quickly whispering to me:

'Tonight, if you've got a moment, after midnight, not before, eh? . . . Not before, if you don't mind, perhaps you could come with me to the beach. I always take a little walk there as it helps me to sleep. Before going off to roam the oceans I knew Franciane, Eau de Café's mother, who hadn't yet had the signal misfortune to walk on the same lonely path as Julien Thémistocle. She was working as a cane-gatherer on the de Cassagnac estate, situated at Morne Capot, on the northern heights of Macédoine. Everywhere you went you'd hear nothing but praise for the local *béké*, who, they said, didn't behave at all like the other blood-suckers. On seeing a big, fat, cheerful black, people would go into raptures and say: "Look, there's one of de Cassagnac's fellows!" Franciane had never known anything other than the ceaseless piling-up of the canes cut at a demented rate by men who seemed to be in a running-race with the sun. The canes' sharp leaves scratched at her arms and bit at her cheeks and furtive tears were lost amidst the sweat on her body. You can stop, but the canes, they won't stop falling! And in the early evening, when the foreman does his rounds to count the piles, he reprimands you unless you've opened up the most secret part of your flesh for him (or in any case promised to do so). Franciane asked pity from nobody. She forbade the muleteers to help her lift up the bundles that she was carrying to her ox because once you accept a hand from a black man, he'll try to take both of yours. It's in his nature. On several occasions, some cane-cutters, drunk from having wasted half their wages by the third day of the week, had tried to force her as she was working but she had fought back like a fighting cock and had screamed at them: "Keep your madness to yourselves! I'm not the same breed as you, I'm not."

'Proud Franciane? Franciane the stuck-up negress. What a lot of names she'd been called! For this was a female who was wearing out her body to no apparent purpose without ever allowing herself the slightest moment of pleasure. And her eyes, you should have seen her eyes, always lit up by a rage without cause that shook even the boldest. People had drawn this conclusion: "She's not a negress from around here. Before, she lived far away, in the South, and perhaps she misses her family or her home. It must be that!"

'In the evenings, when everyone had returned home and the Congos started to beat their sinister drums, she would squat down with the old women around the fire and gossip. The men wondered: "Well, what's she got to say for herself, that one? She who only drinks, eats, girds up her loins to work and sleeps." Soon enough, it became apparent that she was gifted with words, such a surprising thing for a woman. Because if women have the gift of giving birth, men have that of juggling with words and weaving fabulous stories out of them. So, after all, they thought, perhaps she's not really a woman. Until the day that the master, wandering on horseback around Savane-Pois, caught sight of her, superbly bent over in a thicket of canes, and decided (although slavery had been abolished at least sixty years before) to make her his second wife. The following day, Franciane had left the fields and was busy in the kitchens of the master's house. An impressive white building of wood and stone, surrounded on two

245

storeys by ornate verandas and outside by the most striking bougainvillaea hedges to be found in this part of the island. At Morne Capot, the servants had made their own sense of these events and declared: "God is great, He knows what He is doing. That woman was never intended for the likes of us, didn't you notice how graceful her body is!"

'And that's not to say that they really held anything against her since, from day one, our women have shared the beds of the white masters either through force or seduction, and then, it has to be admitted, it was secretly hoped that by rummaging around in the burning darkness of a fuzzy *coucoune*, the whites would become more sympathetic towards us. Anyway, as regards the case in question, as soon as news of all this reached de Cassagnac's wife, she seemed to fade away overnight, she who was so active, so gay in the company of black women, speaking our language all the time with irritating enthusiasm. She made no jibes and barely looked at her rival. In the morning, slumped awkwardly in a rocking-chair and lost in a heart-breaking dream world, she dispensed her orders to the 'nanny', the black governess of her daughter Marie-Eugénie and her two sons. She ceased to set foot in the kitchens and some of the women missed her laughter. Gradually she gave up dressing, and then washing. She moved from her bed to the rocking-chair and from the rocking-chair back to her bed with frightening indifference. The *béké* took some time to notice this transformation, so busy was he in going to visit Franciane in the house that he had had restored just for her by the lake. As for Franciane, she seemed to find all such attentions entirely natural, a little as if she saw in them the just recompense for her past suffering. She made herself available with studied immodesty in the lake, which a spring supplied day and night with fresh water and where the laundry women came to fill their buckets. But her day-time words were as far and few between as ever, and de Cassagnac tried to put a smile on her face by engaging in extraordinary antics on his balcony like a young black scallywag, and all this despite the fact that he was already in the forty-sixth year of his life.

246

'De Cassagnac's legitimate wife slipped into madness when Franciane's belly began to swell. She would make screaming noises right in the middle of the night that even woke people in the huts furthest away from the master's house, those belonging to the Congos. Yet the master said nothing, heard nothing. The night was reserved for Franciane and for her alone. He ate in her house, talking to himself, knocking back the rum, belching freely. "Now he's a real black man," lamented the nanny to herself. But in the end he had no choice but to send for the doctor at Grand-Anse, as his wife had become so pale that you could see all her veins through her skin and, above all, because she was constantly talking gibberish in the blacks' language.

'Into this turbulent state of affairs was born Eau de Café on the de Cassagnac estate, one 12th of January in the year 1903, when Franciane was raped in a field by a man who wasn't even a native of Morne Capot. A man from elsewhere, from down there, which means from that narrow valley called Macédoine, where the people look like nests of manioc ants when you look down at them from the estate. A man who went under the pompous name of Julien Thémistocle . . .

'Come with me on to the beach tonight, my dear monsieur. I have still a great many important things to tell you.'

The man wasn't feeding me fibs: before signing up for life in the merchant navy, he had slaved away in the white's canefields, Thimoléon had told me.

Eau de Café is resplendent with a joy she is trying to keep secret. She thinks I've come to my senses since I stopped asking her any questions and now that it looks as if I'm about to give up my search. She who can read tomorrow in our dreams already knows that I am going to leave, but to tempt fate she invites me to move into the room that Antilia used to occupy long ago, next to hers above the shop.

'Don't you like the food I make?' asks an anxious Eau de Café.

'Yes, yes . . .' I say as I rapidly swallow a spoonful of the ever-present callaloo soup that she would prepare in the midst of the dry season's furnace as well as during the cold of the rainy season.

Thimoléon asks me about my books and is most surprised to hear that I've never had anything published. He insists that I show him my manuscripts 'because I don't want you to write down stories that never happened. A book must tell the truth, nothing but the true truth. I haven't read a lot but I know that the world's greatest writer, Victor Hugo, always wrote what he saw with his own eyes or felt with his own heart'.

He had learnt to read at the ending of the Second World War, when he had become friendly with the teacher from the En Chéneaux school and when this fellow had persuaded him to join the Communist Circle of Grand-Anse. And so he worshipped the book as much as he did rum and sometimes, in the evening, we could hear him reading aloud from an old, almost disintegrating, history of socialism that his new comrades had given him. Suddenly, his workshop would come to life. His planes would torment the mahogany and pear-tree wood until late into the night. We teased him:

'You must be the devil! That's why you're working at night, old friend.'

Although he had always pretended to avoid Antilia like the plague, I always suspected that at those times the little girl from the sea put Godmother and me to sleep with a movement known only to her and that she went to join him among the reddish planks and the sawdust. I don't think they ever exchanged so much as a word but they must have been communicating through song because, more than once, my sleep was broken by the powerful tones of a voice as vibrant as a hummingbird's wing movements. The sea seemed to lessen its din, the wind withdrew to the depths of the darkness to return and hum gently between the cracks in the walls. In the village stunned by sleepfulness, not even the barking of a dog without a master. Not even the downhill race of a ten-wheel lorry loaded with bananas from the great plantations at Basse-Pointe. A silence of conspiracy.

I felt a terrible urge to throw off my sheets and to at last catch

Antilia in a human posture and perhaps extract a smile from her, but my limbs seemed numbed and my eyes struggled against the marble weight of my eyelids. I had no choice but to stay in that half-conscious state and allow myself to be carried away by the frenzy of her singing amidst a universe peopled by chimeras (the ones we called 'soukliyan' in our language), purple butterflies, bamboo flutes engraved with silver, gigantic men peering into the starless heavens as well as vast rocks without shade. Moreover, it was along these lines that I'd decided to attack. Thimoléon, although on his guard, was surprised:

'Do I believe in the existence of another world beyond ours? . . . Another world, eh? . . . Ha! ha! ha! But what are you getting at there, my little fellow? As a Communist and hence an atheist, I only believe in one thing: that!' he declared as he thumped his fist on a locust-wood table.

Godmother looked daggers at him while murmuring a short prayer to Saint Martin de Porres, her favourite. 'I don't want sin to enter into my house' was her obsession since she had earned the enmity of Grand-Anse's priest for having Antilia in her house. She had stopped going to six o'clock mass and had decorated a corner of her bedroom as a vast altar complete with incense-burners and candles, where she said mass to herself with that supreme audacity typical of Creole women in times gone by.

'You see,' says the carpenter again very quickly, 'you mustn't drive yourself mad looking for the hows and whys of things that the human mind isn't made to understand. We've already got quite enough with this jinxed black man's existence, with this work that endlessly weighs down your life, without filling our heads with even more worries about another world, even supposing that it exists, eh . . . Before the '14–'18 war, you were allowed to go to Morne l'Étoile and to cut down as much wood as you wanted. I filled the drawing-rooms of the Grand-Anse, Fond d'Or and Sainte-Marie bourgeoisie with locust wood, red gum tree, *zamana*, cherry . . . good wood, do you understand? Wood that had taken its time to grow. It was a pleasure you never tired of, working with it. Nowadays, I'm forced to buy that dreadful mahogany that grows in no time at all. How do you expect me to work with that? I'm not a stone-breaker.'

Godmother pours me another shot of Socara wine, a foul brew made chemically in Fort-de-France and which everybody was mad about. I overcome the horror it inspires in me by letting it get me drunk bit by bit. My fingers are trembling imperceptibly. She moves over to her balcony and washes her face in a basin placed under the gutter to catch the rainwater. Yet another rustic habit that she hadn't managed to lose despite having lived in the village now for at least twenty years. Overcome by alcohol, I shout:

'You lied to me! Yes, Eau de Café . . . Don't try to make excuses, no, let me have my say. You told me a whole lot of nonsense: Antilia didn't go to town, she didn't become a great lady, she isn't involved in politics. All that's a load of balls! She escaped the confines of Grand-Anse, then she turned her back on the pettiness of Town where you were rash enough to send her, and as we speak, she is pacing the pavements of Paris, like a suffering soul, selling her star-apple flesh to the highest bidder. You lost her! It was you who lost her.'

Godmother and Thimoléon look at each other, speechless. He takes a pair of dice and starts rolling them on to the table without taking any notice of me. Godmother dampens a towel in the water in the basin and wipes my temples as a mother would. Somebody knocks twice at the door below.

'It's Gabriel-no-teeth bringing me some fish,' says Eau de Café. 'Go and see, Thimoléon. If there's kingfish, I don't want any, it can't be fresh. If it's shark, get me a kilo and a half.'

Once the carpenter has gone down, Eau de Café sits opposite me, looks at me for a long moment and finally says:

'Listen to me carefully, godson! I had already buried the story of that devil's daughter in the depths of my memory. Nobody in the village remembers her any more. We've turned over a new page only for you to come back from foreign lands with your head still full of all that. But what do you really want? What does the fate of that human shadow matter to you? What mysterious bond still ties you to her? Me, I'm entering my seventy-third year and I have every intention of having a proper burial. Don't come and stir up all that devilry which will only bring me into disrepute again. What we don't know is bigger than us . . . forget! Forget, I beg you!'

'Who wants to stop me finding out? You? Who had my room searched at the Oceanic Hotel, eh?'

Godmother comes to within a few inches of my face. Her wrinkles are quivering, emphasizing the terrible fixedness of her stare:

'I can reveal this to you, my boy: since the days of slavery, our women have killed their babies in their wombs so as not to provide workers for the masters. Don't make children to become slaves, that was the password! Later, when freedom came, the priests wanted to prevent us from continuing that practice. "It's a crime!" they sermonized from the pulpit, but that never stopped us from snuffing out the untimely lives that were growing in our bodies. Doris's brews always did the trick. So when some of our women became barren, as a punishment, the priests then in turn withered the womb of our sea . . . As for Antilia, I did thirty-twelve thousand things to stop her seeing the light of day, but I still gave birth to her and she was taken away from me as soon as she was born. On top of that, instead of burying the umbilical cord under a tree, like our traditions demand, it was flung into the sea. That's all, godson, now go away, I beg you . . .'

27 Eau de Café, a Woman Uglier than the
Seven Mortal Sins

Breasts are never too heavy for the stomach that supports them even if, like mine, they're more withered than the *Savane des Pétrifications*. Julien Thémistocle, as soon as I went near you, one market day which you don't even remember, I felt that you were for me. The cat-grey of your eyes swept away all the stale air that my heart had been carrying around since the end of my childhood. I brushed against you as you were helping a market woman unload her basket of dasheen and you said to me cheerfully: 'Watch you don't get hurt!' For a long time I carried the weight of those words inside me. At night, they were with me when I couldn't sleep. In my garden, they helped me bear the harsh dry-season sun with endless patience. And so I've always known that you would be mine, even if I can't read among the stars or make sense of the rising wind's rustling among the sugar canes. My passion – for what else could you call that delicious certainty that itched at my temples each time that your name was mentioned in my presence? – wasn't born out of an earth-shattering attraction. It seems to me that it has always been there, in my very depths, as if waiting for you even when I didn't yet know you. That's why our first meeting wasn't a shock for me, but quite simply the confirmation of a feeling – no! more than that – of something deep in my heart, immovable. I didn't shed any tears in public the day you married that flirt Passionise at the Basse-Pointe church. All I remember was the priest-like usher, a big black man decked out in red and blue, brandishing his lance over the church steps, which the bride's train suddenly covered. I always knew that she would cheat on you and drag your honour through the filthiest gutters. You let yourself be dazzled by her mulatto woman's beauty and by the fine words of the people who reckon that there

are three queens in the North: the Creole white Florence de Cassagnac (whose face hasn't been seen since the devil was a little
boy), the negress and whore to boot, Myrtha, and that Passionise,
so proud of her name Belleterre. But all of that is nothing more
than balls, invented by idle women to lessen the weight of time's
passing on the hottest of afternoons. In reality, our North is overflowing with creatures of diabolical succulence. What do you say
of the sun-coloured *chabines* of Macédoine, of the heady brown
girls of Maxime, of the night-blue black girls from Morne Capot?
Your eyeballs were blinded by Passionise because she caught you
in her net with the help of 'send-me-that-man' powder from a
pedlar in evil herbs from the Desmarinières area at Rivière-Salée
who, if he's still alive, must have reached a century plus another
twenty years. I've often made the journey by foot as far as that
commune, which lies next to an impenetrable mangrove forest.
I've seen the sailing boat there that takes the market women to
Fort-de-France, but have never boarded it myself. I've wasted no
time with the capital, why should I go and wander about there
unless it's to end up as a Morne Pichevin street walker like that
fabled Philomène, who the young virgins talk about with fervour? The well-brought-up young ladies who were too ugly to
root out a husband used to send me to swap two flagons of oil or
a piece of salt pork for the charm that would allow them to get rid
of their jinx. If somebody from around here found me doing it, I
had to pretend that I was acting on my own behalf, and as I was
as ugly as sin I had no trouble in making it look convincing. But
nobody ever got in my way to start asking questions about what
was none of their business. Even the money-or-your-life men who
lurked in the streets of Fond d'Or never gave me any trouble even
though I was carrying, well wrapped up in my knickers, the sorcerer's payment: a pair of Creole rings in solid Cayenne gold, a
ring with a shining gem or an amber necklace. The powder he
gave me in return looked so innocuous that one day, when the
rainy season downpours had soaked me to the skin, I simply
scratched the trunk of a bearded fig tree to collect the sap and,
guess what, the charm worked all the same. So I didn't have to

keep wearing myself out over hills and down valleys: I just had to set myself up as the Invisible's go-between. Which is what I did, without anyone knowing in the neighbourhood, as I only worked for strangers. Until the sublime moment when Julien Thémistocle's shadow crossed my life and I decided first to outwit him and then to catch him in my spider's web. At the time I was afraid to look into a mirror. I hated the bluish blackness of my skin, the shape of my lips, my teeth that were whiter than sour sop flesh. As for my peppercorn hair, don't even mention it! My women friends used to spend whole afternoons complaining:

'Bloody hell, why is God so mean? Couldn't he have spared us a little bit of beauty?'

Nobody could find any reason for this flagrant and, above all, unmotivated injustice. What had we done to upset the Lord of Heaven? What's more, those who had disobeyed him, Adam and Eve, weren't they as white as cassava flour? The day that I fell in love with Julien Thémistocle was the same day he gave us the benefit of his views on the question. I'm just a simple plantation black who wields the hoe and cutlass from dawn till dusk, he told us, but I know things that aren't in books. Moreover, just because our kids now go to school, it doesn't mean that they can start showing off in front of us. The other day, I had to whip the backside of my eldest boy because the brat dared to look me right in the eye. What do they teach them on the blackboard: to defy their parents? Ha! I, Julien Thémistocle, son of Jean Thémistocle, in his turn son of the Thémistocle who tamed snakes in the depths of the forest, I say that God isn't wrong. There's no point in staring at me like that, ladies. When He had made the white, the black and the mulatto, God ordered them to come to paradise for a last interview before sending them on to earth. The white got dressed very quickly and rushed to arrive first: God gave him a small box. The mulatto, casual and couldn't-care-less, as we all know, put on his finery, spent ages over his hair, oiled and scented himself, and by the end of the morning managed to make it to paradise, where God gave him a medium-sized box. Mister Black, as for him, he played the monkey as usual! He peeled sugar-canes, drank some cane juice, re-tethered his ox, teased all the women who passed near his hut, sang and played his drum, drank his fair share of rum, took a siesta and at five o clock in the afternoon answered the call from on high. He received as his share an enormous case as the white and mulatto looked on furiously. The black started dancing about, doing a jig and crowing with joy. God remained expressionless and when the black had calmed down, He ordered all three to open their boxes. The white did as he was told, gloomily, a huge frown on his forehead. A miracle: his box contained gold, silver and precious stones. His face brightened with a radiant smile. The mulatto, confused and somewhat annoyed, opened his slowly. It contained an inkwell and a pen holder. The mulatto smiled, visibly relieved. The black was getting even more excited as he looked at his huge case, certain that God had kept the best of the shares for him. So it was with great haste that he opened his. Damn and blast! It contained a heap of pitchforks, hoes, cutlasses and trowels. The black was speechless. His ears were trembling comically. The white, who had received wealth, and the mulatto intelligence both burst out laughing together.

'Now I'm chained to hard work until the end of time,' muttered the disbelieving black.

Ladies, you need look no further for the reasons behind our ugliness and poverty! God gave us our chance and we wasted it. But why despair? As for me, when I look at your bodies, my mouth waters and I would like to screw you here and now. The mulatto and the white are just the same and that's why all of you can boast such a multicoloured brood of children. There's not one of you with just little black ones. Ha, ha, ha! Our revenge is black and fine-grained *coucoune* with its lips as pink as a conch. As soon as any man comes close to the opening between your legs, he is seized by its radiant energy and sticks his tongue eagerly into its pouting slit until he passes out in ecstasy. To be able to say that black woman is sumptuous, to clear your mind of all the litanies of mischief that the white has spread on her account, you first have to suck her *coucoune*. So, ladies, what are you complaining about? Hand over your bodies to all those thirsty fellows and you'll soon see how they sing the praises of your beauty far and wide. Because a black woman's beauty doesn't lie in silky straight hair, in a pinched nose or lips like a knife blade. You can sweep all that sort of balls out of your heads! A black woman's beauty can't be described with whites' words.

From that day on, I knew that I was beautiful and it's thanks to Julien Thémistocle. I shall always be grateful to him, irrespective of what is said about the sexual perversions of the Thémistocle line. Although people never tired of reminding me that he was the murderer of Franciane, my mother, I offered my body to Julien behind the back of my guardian, Doris. On my way to the village of Trinité, where I was taking sewing lessons from a well-to-do lady, I always found the means to take a diversion and go and fuck with him in some gulley on the Fond-Massacre plantation. I heard the jibes that followed my footsteps from the front door of every house:

'There's a negress who would frighten ugliness itself! Hey, mama, hurry and see this!'

I marched on my way, wrapped in an almost military pride, because I knew that shortly I would be beautiful, very beautiful under the expert touch of that man Julien Thémistocle, whose supposed lack of education was a source of much merriment. People judge you on the infrequency or profusion of your words. In the former case, you're an idiot; in the other, a great intellect. It's quite beyond me why the black man worships the word so much and curses silence! Julien had only spoken at length once in his life, but his parable of the white, the black and the mulatto carried, in my view, more weight than a ton of that gibberish that our race is so keen on. It had brightened my life and I no longer felt the hardness of the stones under my feet. I went to meet him as light as the wind that climbs to the highest point of Morne Jacob but happier. More luminous than that wind which sang of secret sorrows: echoes of mad, unrequited loves or the pain of women widowed in the prime of life. We rolled together in the undergrowth and our bodies moulded the earth that seemed shaken with convulsions. We lost ourselves in one another and these moments had the taste of eternity. Black woman, my good friend, eternity is when you feel a sort of itch rising in your womb that breaks you in half up to your neck and when you're clutching on to the man and asking God's forgiveness for encroaching so much on His territory.

I lived five years of happiment like that, interrupted, alas, during the time that our mother France was on her knees in front of that *chien-fer* Hitler. Once he came back from Europe, the dream was bound to dissolve into seven sorrows, which coiled themselves up in the deepest recesses of my body. And all because he had proclaimed loud and clear in the fancy accent of France-whites a phrase that he'd probably heard over there. The rum shop regulars were cast into stupefied meditation for days afterwards by what he said:

'If God made black men,' joked Julien Thémistocle, the last of the name, 'it's because he ran out of hairs to make monkeys with. Ha, ha, ha! . . .'

SEVENTH CIRCLE

The further back we go into the dark forest of words, the narrower the path becomes and the more it winds aimlessly through the creepers. The black man lives two, three, four lives, or some such number, and that is probably the cause of his conspicuous weakness. He believes himself to be the holder of grandiose secrets, whereas he is merely the plaything of grandiloquent symbols.

The being that you imagined you had loved with all your strength had never even noticed it or had never existed. Our island is frequented by shadows to which we give form in order to reassure ourselves over our fate and that's why ridiculousness is so often the banal explanation for so many evils.

Can suffering that now feeds on something intangible carve out a destiny for us?

28 Antilia's Drowning

After the tenderness of Advent, which tries its hardest to upset every day and every night of Christmas month, disarming the most stubborn grudges and softening up certain hearts for the outbreak of love, comes January and its cunning heat. At Grand-Anse we knew full well that it was pointless to blame the sun because it was from rock, from trees and from the sea's skin that sparks of fire seemed to spring. Useless to turn on fans or to sprinkle yourself with water from a hose fifteen times a day. Even the tarmac, softened and sticky, begged forgiveness. It was as if the weather was imprisoned in the shackles of an invisible force that filled you with disgustation with eating, talking and walking, while drinking rum was like asking for a knock-out blow on the head.

In January the fifty-year-old Julien Thémistocle took on the appearance of a twenty-year-old and rivalled Ali Tanin for elegance. He worked playing the mandolin at the Back Street barber shop to earn enough to buy gifts for his conquests of the moment. The crystal-clear notes that he coaxed from his instrument helped Honorat Congo and his customers to bear the suffocating heat of the afternoons. In the shop, wallpapered with photos of Italian actresses and Brazilian footballers, there was only the sound of the scissors snipping, sweetened by melodies of long ago strummed by Eau de Café's lover. The faces of mature men filled with a sudden seriousness, so vulnerable were they to that terrible, irrepressible feeling that we know as nostalgia. The feeling that has nothing to do with some great broken love or ruined dream, but which springs simply, trivially, from the memories contained in the smell of pickles wafting through the window of a house, from an affectionate tap on the shoulder after a job of work shared, or from watching a pink sky as evening approaches, when the day's chit-chat has worn itself out. Or even from the well-being of that tiredness which overwhelms you as soon as your head touches the pillow.

To break the spell, Honorat Congo was telling a filthy story that he had made up, although he adorned the characters with the names of identifiable people from Grand-Anse. On that fateful day, he told his customers the reason why Chief Bérard had started limping (the year of Madonna or Papa de Gaulle, nobody could remember) even though there was no knowledge that he had been in any way the victim of an accident.

'The fellow was fornicating with the wife of Syrian, gentlemen,' he was bragging. 'Yes, Rose-Aimée Tanin, the negress with lots of little zeros for hair. At the time, Syrian hadn't yet made his fortune thanks to the black knickers and used to fall asleep on a chair in his shop for fear of missing some morning customer.'

'As for Bérard, he probably hadn't yet won his title of chief,' prompted the customer whose beard he was trimming.

'He was starting, he was starting . . . Remember that he had already kicked the arses of two great *damier* masters at Basse-Pointe and Macouba and that he'd already thrown down a challenge to the famous Hurard Belgrade from Morne-des-Esses. His left-footed back kick was beginning to earn respect, my friends.'

Now the mandolin was playing softly. The snipping of the scissors became more staccato. Honorat Congo brushed away each fuzzy lock that fell on to his customer's shoulder with an abrupt movement while mopping his forehead. His excitement reached its peak when he realized that he had an unusual audience at his window, a real audience and not just the usual idlers of Back Street. Afterwards, there was much discussion as to what secret magnetism had attracted Small Balls Auguste, Ma Léonce, the baker's wife, Master Salvie, the driver of the 'Executioner of the North', Dachine, the municipal dustman, Ali Tanin, the bastard-Syrian, Thimoléon, the carpenter and even *maître* Féquesnoy, the lawyer, to the surroundings of the barber shop owned by that Congo black, who was 'so black he was blue', according to the contempt-filled expression used by those to whom the vagaries of the colonial whirlpool had granted a *café-au-lait* complexion. Honorat Congo, moreover, had a favourite topic:

'I'm not the son of a slave like you lot are, oh no.'

Indeed, when right in the middle of the previous century, the Creole blacks, helped by Papa Schoelcher, the Alsatian with the big heart, had forced the island whites to put their chains and iron collars away in their sheds. When the whip was merely a status symbol used to make horses gallop. When the sugar-cane fields were abandoned and the distilleries stopped sending out smoke. When this new world settled into its rhythm, the colony imported from the land of India and later from the Congo boatloads of contract workers. Honorat Congo's father, named Massemba, had a part share with five of his countrymen in a former slave hut on the Séguineau estate where the de Cassagnac dynasty, natives of Anjou, had reigned for three centuries. Their arrival led to tumult. The Creole blacks, who in the meantime had taken possession of the hillsides, ignored them and then decided to insult them, to spit in their faces and throw stones at them. Grand-Anse and the surrounding countryside echoed for months on end to the sound of 'dirty Congo!', 'filthy Congo!', 'stinking Congo!' or 'Congo dog!' By the ending of the century, the ire of the aboriginals had subsided without disappearing altogether. Massemba, whom everyone knew by the nickname of Ugly Congo, spent his life trying to prevent it passing down to his son, whom he had conceived with the first Creole black woman who condescended to let him touch her, an event that happened after seven testing years of emotional drought and carnal abstinence. That woman was the mother of Rose-Aimée Tanin and so the latter happened to be the half sister of Honorat Congo, who was thus none other than the uncle of that seducer of young girls, Ali Tanin. Hence the Creole proverb *'Tout nèg sé fanmi'* (All blacks are part of the same family).

And yet Rose-Aimée would never recognize Ugly Congo's offspring as a close relative nor a relative of any sort and instead did her best, not without success, to disabuse people of the belief that she was connected by blood with the man who was to become Grand-Anse's most celebrated barber. Not only did she not speak to him, but she even pretended not to see him, to the point where Honorat Congo used to mock her on the rare occasions that she passed by his shop:

'I'm so black I'm invisible, ha, ha, ha!'

From an early age, Ugly Congo had kept his son away from work in the fields by teaching him the art of shaving the roughest of beards with a broken bottle end. As a child, Honorat never had to find work among the little gangs who picked up the sugar canes left behind by the gatherers. When Saturday came and with it pay day, the entire contingent of Grand-Anse's Congos queued up patiently outside Ugly Congo's house in the shade of a soursop tree in order to get their chins cleaned. Honorat became so expert in his trade that hard-up Creole blacks, swallowing their repugnance, resigned themselves to let him soap their cheeks. In the end, when as the First World War came to a close and the grievances against Congos were forgotten, the young man was able to rent small premises on Back Street, which quickly prospered and without the help of any black magic. He was the only person to welcome Eau de Café when she opened her shop opposite the church. Even the adoption of Antilia didn't seem to shock him.

'*Fonmi fôl ka fè wôl fôl men i pa fôl pyès*' (The crazy ant pretends to be crazy but isn't crazy), he would say proverbially to those of his customers most hostile to the abandoned girl. 'What's more, if I knew how to cut women's hair,' he never hesitated to declare, 'I would have cut hers so marvellously that certainly and by no means perhaps you would be squabbling among yourselves to win her favours.'

In truth, the fellow, who had inherited his father's ugliness and who was despised by the village flirts, had conceived the plan of setting up home with Antilia. Nothing less! He was not unaware that she had turned her back on the advances of Messrs Ali Tanin, the late Émilien Bérard and Julien Thémistocle.

'What she's looking for isn't beauty,' he concluded from this, 'it's really France-love.'

That required first of all mastering France-French and not our usual Africa-tinted gabble. An obstacle that Honorat Congo over-came with a prestidigitator's skill by deciding to speak with his mouth tightly pursed like a chicken's backside. If, by chance, he noticed Antilia coming his way on the pavement opposite, he would puff himself up and with a mannered gesture sharpen his razor on a piece of burnt wood before declaring very loudly the same pompous sentence:

'I cannot comprehend whay monsieur the Mayor has not resolved to co-opt mayself on to the town council. *Maître* Féques-noy and I are after all the most generous donors to good works in the *commune.*'

Still as preening as ever, he would take hold of his customer's chin to give it a brush and, just as the young girl was passing the shop, he would ask:

'Isn't that so, may dear sah?'

This ornate language had no visible affect on Antilia, who probably didn't even notice that the barber was courting her. She would doubtless have laughed with that hysterical laughter that gave Eau de Café goose pimples. But all was not lost since Honorat Congo gained the reputation of being one of the country's greatest mentors in French, after the deputy Lagrosillière it goes without saying. He started selling his stylistic advice to school-boys who were unable to write their essays on the theme of a beautiful winter's day or to tongue-tied lovers who preferred to delegate to the post the task of revealing their souls' torments. He even ended up being co-opted on to the municipal council fol-lowing the death of one of its members, a development that left Antilia even more indifferent. His shop was never empty; people came from Fond d'Or and from Ajoupa-Bouillon to have him cut their hair, not that there weren't talented barbers in the neigh-bouring *communes*, but because of the pleasure taken in listening to his beautiful France-French. Honorat Congo resisted the temp-tation of setting up house with any of the fighting women who were attracted by his situation, hoping that such exemplary faith-fulness would one day or another end up by winning Antilia over. The years went by, his hair whitened, his speech became more refined through contact with the white policemen who were his customers, his shop was modernized. Only his love, which he had managed God knows how to keep safe from the gossip mongers, didn't alter.

Little by little, he began to turn his anger upon himself, refusing to admit that each and everybody, apart from him, Honorat Congo, finally gets at least a little piece of what he has desired for so long. He heaped sarcastic remarks on everyone, which, because they were wrapped up in Creole humour, saved him from probable beatings. And so, on the day that the infamous event that was Antilia's drowning took place, he was venting his spleen on the absent Chief Bérard:

'Rose-Aimée Tanin didn't waste any time opening her legs for him, ladies and gentlemen. Oh, yes, and in the conjugal bed, on Honorat Congo's word! The whole time, that idiot Syrian was chanting his "*Achlam malfik mamdulillah chamsine*" to his God and kneeling on a carpet. Everything was going sweetly for the two lovers, but, bit by bit, the fellow began to suspect something. What? Nobody knows. And yet he managed to fix it so he could catch them at it like two mongooses and, without losing his temper, he placed the barrel of a smuggled pistol against Bérard's head. "Either I blow your brains out or I bugger you: the choice is yours," he stated to his wife's lover without losing his calm. The chief started trembling, tears came to his eyes, he made Syrian a thousand offers, each more astonishing than the one before, like allowing him to fuck his daughters – and he had a hell of a lot of them with thirty-twelve thousand different women. "From Justina who's twelve years old but already has two big tits on her chest to Hortense who lives with a muleteer from Morne Céron," he specified. "I only have to open my mouth for them to obey. I swear to you, Syrian. Don't do that to me!" The Mahometan wouldn't listen. Slowly but surely, he pushed the barrel of his weapon into the arsehole of Chief Bérard, who bit a pillow so as not to make a mooing sound. A naked and terrified Rose-Aimée hardly recognized her husband. She also thought her hour had come. Drops of blood stained the bed as Tanin carried on with his horrible penetration. "If I pull the trigger now, you'll certainly feel it," he sniggered for the benefit of poor Bérard. Then Syrian suddenly pulled out his weapon and buggered the black man with great thrusts, which drew excruciating screams from him. And then he said: "After this, I challenge you to go and spread it about that you fucked Abdelhamid Tanin's wife. Each time you're tempted to say anything, I want you to feel your buttocks burning, my friend."

'It's hardly worth adding, ladies and gentlemen, that the secret of Bérard's limp and Rose-Aimée's adultery has been fiercely preserved by those two individuals who immediately put an end to their affair. Ha, ha, ha!'

The entire village seemed to burst out laughing, with so many people crowding around the outside of the barber shop. Honorat Congo went out on to the doorstep, scissors in hand, and shouted jokingly:

'Hey! All you females! If there are any of you who need your *coucoune* shaving, Honorat's ready to do it free of charge.'

With the sublime unexpectedly following the ridiculous, in keeping with a solidly established Grand-Anse tradition, a series of giant waves, taller than houses, crashed on to the beach. From Back Street, where people were gathered, they could see gigantic frames of melted silver foam containing blue-green sheets of water to wonderful effect. The people of Grand-Anse rushed on to the beach to etch this phenomenon into their memories. The wind, having taken refuge in the middle of the La Crabière promontory, could not be held responsible. Some put forward the theory that it was due to anger on the part of Zemi spirits, whose tombs had been violated by white archaeologists in the place called Fond Brûlé, in the Vivé district. They had hired two hefty Grand-Anse men to help them dig up the area, on the side of the river, and they had reported finding strange carved stones with three points, which plunged the experts into deep perplexity. One of them, who had got drunk one Saturday night at Small Balls Auguste's bar, had bawled all night long in the deserted streets of the village:

'We've got proof that humans lived here 4,000 years before Jesus Christ. Hurrah, citizens! Martinique is older than Europe.'

The villagers moved cautiously down towards the seaside, Eau de Café leading the way. Struck by a sudden intuition, she called out Antilia's name, begged her to return among us living Christians and to abandon to their fate the Amerindian divinities, and, when she received no answer from her protégée, she started ranting and raving. From La Crabière to the bottom end of Redoute, the spectacle was impressive: the water was calm behind the line where the rollers begin, but on the edge of the beach, from top to bottom, on the three miles of shoreline, what pandemonium! Honorat Congo remarked in his most learned tones that the end of the world was nigh. He could see incandescent zigzags across the blueness of the sky.

The offspring of Coolie René were chanting in Tamil while throwing bougainvillaea petals on to the belly of the sea. Ali Tanin, the half-Syrian, remembered that his father worshipped Allah and murmured prayers in that guttural language that nobody would now have dreamt of mocking. Brandishing her rosary, Eau de Café was repeating endlessly:

'Credo in unum Deum.'

Alone, she moved towards the beast. Nobody was surprised, as it had long been predicted that this would be how she met her end. Just as her feet touched the water, the crashing of the water stopped dead. The waves calmed and a sudden boiling from within the depths released geysers, through which the dancing of that memorable day's dying sunlight cast rainbows. She waded waist-deep into the sea without her skin being burnt. Soon she had disappeared altogether and a frenzy of sorrow ran through the crowd. Several women rolled on the ground, tearing at their hair. Julien Thémistocle, who was the guardian and then lover of Eau de Café, the incorrigible incubus, the maroon in perpetual revolt against the colonial order, the decorated war veteran who had joined Papa de Gaulle in London, the hard-man-chief of the furthest flung districts of our *commune* (and, for those who still cared to remember, the rapist and murderer of Franciane, the stuck-up negress and Eau de Café's mother), now looked like a little ten-year-old boy. He stuck his thumb in his mouth and started whining quietly. His eyelids were covered with a yellowish rheum that attracted thousands of flies.

'*Manman, poutji ou pati?*' (Mother, why did you go away?) he said, walking towards that sea of tranquillity that the Atlantic had become.

Then he pointed to the pile of fallen rocks beyond, below the hospital, by the underwater abyss that had taken the lives of so many innocent swimmers. Two bodies were lying there, one sprawled out, the other rigid, on the shiniest of the rocks. The terrified crowd didn't dare to move. The little boy began to walk along the black sand, leaving behind footprints like a horse's hooves. He took the stiff body by the hand and tried unsuccessfully to lift it up. It slithered between his arms, writhing with such strident wailing that the onlookers had to block up their ears there and then. Dachine, the municipal dustman, offered to go and fetch monsieur the priest, but someone reminded him that he had been confined to bed for weeks without anybody, not even Sossionise, the presbytery informer, knowing what was wrong with him. He was replaced at Sunday mass either by the priest from Fond d'Or or by the one from Basse-Pointe, a state of affairs that was beginning to set teeth on edge as the most zealous female followers of the Holy Church were deprived of communion. They refused, in fact, to divulge their secrets in confession to some fellow who had come from another *commune*. As for the police, it was pointless even thinking of them: those gentlemen from France didn't get involved in the monkey business of the good folk of Martinique. Moreover, what could they have done about the revolt of the Zemi spirits, they who on many an occasion had had to protect archaeologists from the active hostility of most Grand-Anse people? Here, whenever by chance one found some fragment of Amerindian pottery, one hurried to bury it again twice as deeply and nobody ever said a word against the dead people. Only sorcerers used their relics in madness potions or the talismans they turned out at exorbitant prices for the well-to-do in Town.

269

Eau de Café sat up on her seat of stone and offered her flat and withered breast to Julien Thémistocle. The little boy sucked greedily at the milk and began to grow-grow-grow, thus regaining his original strength of a man taller than the Mississippi. Each of them took one of Antilia's arms and dragged her towards the crowd as the night settled its shadow over the roofs of Grand-Anse. The only words that Eau de Café uttered were:

'Why didn't you spare my godson such a spectacle of suffering? Where is your heart? Take him to the shop and rub some bay rum on to his forehead. It's time he was in bed . . .'

And they obeyed her . . .

29 Eau de Café's Testament Speech

I have sparred with death for a long time, in fact since the moment I was born since my mother Franciane deliberately closed her eyes so that I might see the light of day. Death has a sour smell. It slides in the twinkling of an eye into the heart of your house and as the black man is a species who can't keep his tongue still, he'll stir up the whole neighbourhood with his snivelling:

'Oh, neighbour, my dear, I've got a sort of dizziness in my head, I feel I can hardly put one foot in front of the other this morning. Ow! I don't know what's wrong with me, for God's sake!'

He'll demand a damp cloth on his forehead so that his thoughts don't fly off into thin air, he'll drink a tea of bitter herbs to stave off his body's collapse, he'll remember God and will pile prayer upon prayer, a rosary rattling between his fingers. He'll engage in any old monkey business, leaping like a goat until the truth sinks in and then, hah! Look at him putting on a tragic face. Send for my children and grandchildren! Let them kneel at the foot of my bed, for I have a whole lot of most serious things to tell them! The black man is a species who dances a jig in front of death, such is his fear of it

As for me, bear in mind that I've always realized the illusoriness of this life. It has been lent to us, one day we've no choice but to give it back. The main thing is to keep your dignity and tenderness. At Grand-Anse we're too inclined to set off with anger in our guts, a snotty sneer all too often distorting our faces. But death isn't pain! Life is pain, sickness is pain, heartbreak is pain, hunger is pain, but not the moment that we pass from light into shadow. Death is – how shall I put it? – as fine as the line of the horizon. You have to let yourself slip into death without putting

271

up pointless resistance and feel rising in each of your limbs the gentle numbness that slowly carries you away from the hardness of the bed where you're stretched out. The wood of the wardrobe softens, the brick wall melts, your nearest and dearest become shadows moving around for no reason, and only the air itself becomes heavier. The moment of death is really the only one when you weigh the air you breathe, that you feel its weight and its power. Don't laugh, my dear godson! Every evening, since Julien went out of my life, I have applied myself to dying. I'm not talking about that common sleepiness that harpoons you like a bag of charcoal when your day has been too hard. I'm talking about the caress that settles on your eyelids in successive stages and closes them while you continue the whole time to see. The daylight stays there behind the cover of your eyes. Every shadow seems to project its own enormity and it's useless to try and stretch an arm or a leg. It's at this point that the sour smell bursts in and tries to impregnate the sheets, the mosquito net, the bedside table, the basin of water and its jug.

Just so that I have told you everything: Antilia is my daughter. I conceived her in secret with several men since, when you stick your foot in an ants' nest, it's impossible to say which one bit you. She had for fathers the old ancestor Thémistocle, Julien, his great-grandson, the Creole white de Cassagnac, Chief Thimoléon – oh, yes, that smelly old sod – a truly rudderless philosopher, and others whose names it is pointless to reveal. As soon as Ma Doris, my wet nurse in that faraway time when the jinx was working away on our ragged black lives, had helped me to give birth, she wrapped up the child without so much as a word and took it away God knows where. Nobody was any the wiser as I had a pregnancy without a big stomach, and people barely noticed that my hips had widened and that I was struggling to lift up buckets of water. At night my dreams were inhabited by the face of my child for whom I hadn't even had time to choose a name. Doris had reassured me:

'She'll carry the name of those pieces of land that shelter our lives and seem to spin on the back of the sea.'

The midwife had always been impossible to understand. She had exceeded by many an extension the limits of the century in the middle of which she'd been born and was shamelessly prepared to cross those of the present century. I asked her:

'Can I go down soon to the village to see my little girl?'

'Hey, woman, keep a grip on yourself! Life isn't one great dream where you go around gratifying your desires. Your child will be given back to you when you're old enough to take care of it, not before.'

And so I had to keep trudging through the plains of Macédoine, Fond Gens-Libres and Morne Carabin, putting on a couldn't-care-less expression despite the fact that inside me my heart was host to dreadful torments. The time of Admiral Robert came and went, the Virgin of the Great Return wandered through the whole island without handing me the slightest favour, Clémentin's son died in the Indochina war and it seemed that carnage had broken out in North Africa. People moaned as they held their heads in their hands:

'What have we got to do with those unknown countries? Defending France is one thing, we've done it on any number of occasions since the time our fathers braved the Mexico war alongside the Emperor Maximilien, but what's the sense in those coffins containing the finest flower of our youth that are shipped back here once a month?'

The world was about to shift. Indeed it was. I owed it to myself to leave as well and to set up on my account. I had waited too long to break the spell of that countryside that makes your eyes crumble without you being able to do anything about it. You discover one day that your feet hurt when you put shoes on them and that you've no desire to put your best clothes on, except on Sundays because then you've got no choice. At that point you've become a real backwoods negress, muttering to herself when she's bent over working in her garden and who knows by name and what they do all the plants that God has put on earth. Little by little, your tongue loses the knack of speaking French, it becomes so heavy that you just answer by grinning at those town folk who

273

remember once a year that they're cousins or godchildren of yours. Creole becomes your only means of communication. That's what I escaped by opening up shop in the village of Grand-Anse, to the amazement of people here. What lies they told about me! How they ranted:

'Eau de Café's on the slippery slope, my friends! A woman like her who you would have thought could take communion without confession.'

From the start, the village was hostile towards me. People couldn't take it that I was able to set myself up like some Ma Rothschild. Where did I come from? Who was my mother? And my mother's mother? To begin with, only the beggars from Crochemord and Bord de Terrain honoured me with their presence at my counter and even then, that was just for a tiny bit of red butter or half a quarter of bread! Salt was scattered on my doorstep to make me give up and go away. Somebody left a horny toad stuck through with rusty nails on my window-sill. Its back legs had been tied with red thread. To make me go back to where I'd come from. I didn't weaken one jot and swallowed my unhappiness without budging an inch. At night I could hear the groaning of the sea so loud that sometimes I got up, scared, and ran on to the beach in my nightdress. Dachine, the municipal rubbish collector, was for a long time the only person here who would deign to speak to me:

'You'll only become a real village woman the day you don't hear that bitch of a sea's double drum any more. Us, we ignore it, we pay it no attention and that's why it turns somersaults, does circus tricks all day long, just to attract our sympathy. The sea at Grand-Anse is nothing but cursedness. Why did you come to lose your soul here, eh?'

In truth, Grand-Anse people seemed oblivious to its charms. They never mentioned it in the long ramblings that rum helped them to construct from the moment they woke up. Women scowled and gathered together all their courage before running to tip their chamber-pots into its waves. The sand looked like black mica strewn with debris from the stars. The waves took on colours with the first ray of the sun, as if ready to take flight up to the summit of the mountains.

'Do you like staring at it, woman?' asked Thimoléon, my next-door neighbour, the second person to break the cage of silence in which the village had imprisoned me.

'It breaks the tedium. I don't have time to think about all the things that mess up my life . . . Why do you hate it so much?'

'You'll learn in time. Be careful, don't go too close! That whore isn't at all to be trusted despite her seductive poses. When she calms down, it's just a bluff and you can be sure that the next roller will be as high as a house.'

Then they forgot about my strangeness. Time grew on time and the tick books flourished on my shelves. They began to become fond of my nickname Eau de Café. I was feared because I could read tomorrow in other people's dreams and because people came from as far away as Rivière-Salée or Morne-Rouge to consult me. I was accorded complete and utter respectation, but that wasn't enough to bring me peace of mind. A void cut through my flesh, sometimes interrupting me in mid conversation or as I worked and I had to wipe the side of my eye with my headscarf as if irritated by a drop of sweat: my daughter – 'She's called Antilia,' Ma Doris had told me – was calling for me. She would come towards me in the heat of the day, light, her feet barely touching the ground, and would stare at me without saying a word. A real heartbreak. The midwife had refused point-blank to tell me which household had taken her in, always under the pretext that when the moment to find her came, nothing could prevent me from taking back my property.

'What's due to you cannot be carried away by the river,' she would say.

There was no point in questioning people round and about, as nobody had heard of a motherless baby adopted by a village family a long time before. While waiting, I sent for you from Macédoine and brought you up, you, my godson, like a son from my own womb. Don't forget how many years you slept against my stomach! The racket made by the sea used to frighten you. And then you too got used to it and started wandering off as far as La Crabière with the gangs of little black boys and wild pigs. As soon as the rainy season had stopped swelling its waters, you swam in the Grand-Anse sea with a recklessness that terrified me. You would get up in the morning, look through the window and declare:

'Today it's going to be rough beneath the hospital, I 'd be better off going to the river mouth.'

What were you looking for there? The Grand-Anse sea denied us any fish, except the occasional sea crab and squid, so sticky that they became glued to your hands. I wasted my time tanning your bottom every evening when you came home dirty and with your clothes in tatters, as you wouldn't listen. But it was through you that the miracle happened. It was you who brought me back my daughter. She had lived alone for a hundred years in a hollow on the beach without anyone noticing. She had fed herself on salt water, on *touaou* birds' eggs, on sea grapes and hermit crabs. And she hadn't learnt to speak human language. She didn't even know how to smile. Nor cry, it goes without saying. She only reacted to hearing her name: 'Antilia!' She looked up, stared into my face and took hold of the bottom of my skirt. I had waited so long for this moment that I faltered before kissing her. My whole body was overcome with trembling, my thoughts were unable to form any sort of order. There I was, suddenly a mother! The village, alarmed at seeing me adopt this little stranger, said I was transfigured, enamoured and God knows what else. Ali Tanin, who owns a linen shop at the entrance to the village, came to tell me a parable:

'My old friend,' he started, embarrassed, 'I hardly ever set foot in the countryside but all the bumpkins come to me to buy their khaki cloth and so I am familiar with the vicissitudes affecting the furthest-flung properties . . . Don't look at me like that, my friend, I am not an enthusiast for speaking ill of others behind their backs nor a shit-stirrer. Nothing suits me better than peace and quiet, but . . . but, my duty is to warn you. Do you know what happened to the Virgin on the Séguineau estate? There was a silk-cotton tree, two centuries old, which grew in the courtyard of the *béké*'s house, a certain de Cassagnac, it seems, perhaps the one whose daughter you treat, that Marie-Eugénie. This tree was so big that four men could barely touch hands around it. The island white was very proud of it and took pleasure in showing it off to all the France-whites who passed through our island. The blacks worshipped the silk-cotton tree, at whose foot were found every Saturday morning black cocks with their throats cut, women's knickers adorned with padlocks, Saint Anthony candles and requests scrawled on wrapping paper with a piece of charcoal. The master barely took any notice of all this monkey business until the day that a foetus was found there. Yes, my friend, an almost formed baby, all pink with big black eyes! De Cassagnac almost collapsed with falling sickness. He called together cane-cutters, cart-drivers, blacksmiths, cane-gatherers and house servants to give them a rousing harangue on divine retribution and the horrors of hell.

'"From now on," he concluded in a furious voice, "I don't want to see any more of your mumbo-jumbo under my tree. The first one of you I catch will get a don't-bother-to-come-back note. Do you understand?"

'The rabble bowed their heads, because you know those plantation blacks, my old friend, they act like sheep all the better to make a fool of you. How many times haven't I caught one of them who was snivelling for a reduction of five *sous* while stealing a pair of knickers in the same breath. Heh, heh! The morning after that memorable lecture, a pair of Spanish cocks were found lying in their own blood on the biggest protruding root of the silk-cotton tree. De Cassagnac wasn't a bad sort and he didn't carry out his threat. You know that yourself, since he was close to your mother Franciane, the stuck-up negress, for a long while. Don't give me that stare, Eau de Café! I've already told you that even if I never leave my lair, with its rolls of material and shoe boxes, I know everything that goes on in this neck of the woods. The island white thought inside his head for a whole day and night, which put the blacks in a state of terror and stopped the cane cutting. What was he planning? Which of them would end up paying for the sorcerer who hadn't bothered to obey the master's orders? The old women were predicting the worst, having known the old times, that's to say the dying fire of slavery. But de Cassagnac reappeared, an unfathomable smile on his lips, and ordered two carpenters to make a box the size of a three-year-old child. A shiver ran through the gathering of blacks. Good God-Lord-Virgin Mary, what monstrosity had taken root in the Creole white's calabash head? What, for heaven's sake? In the early afternoon, when the box was finished, de Cassagnac walked calmly towards the estate chapel and took hold of a statue of the Virgin which he had placed inside the box. Then he had the box nailed into an opening in the silk-cotton tree's knotted and tortuous trunk. He had just had constructed one of those altars that you see so often at crossroads on country lanes.

'"*I la ka véyé zòt* ," he declared. "*Tala ki kwè I pé dérèspèkté Manman nou tout ki la a, enben fè'y non, i ké konnèt wotè konba'y!*" (She is watching you. Let he who thinks himself able to show disrespect to our Mother of all come and defy her, then he'll soon know who he's dealing with!)

'It goes without saying that the wise men, the sorcerers, the bush doctors, the quacks, those who work with their left hand, the incubi, the soothsayers, the spell-makers, the clairvoyants, the faith healers and all their ilk abandoned the shade of the silk-cotton tree. Even during the day, the estate workers gave its powerful branches a wide berth and some of them ended up by no longer looking at it. It was mentioned no more and when somebody was forced to refer to it, he would murmur "*Gran bagay lonng-lan*" (the big, tall thing). Time passed and the tree grew. The opening into which the Virgin had been placed was slowly covered by a confusion of bark, knots and creepers. One day, it had vanished completely from view and the blacks in league with the devil started up their circus all the more actively. De Cassagnac finally decided to have the silk-cotton tree cut down. He procrastinated so much over the date on which it was to be done that a hurricane had the opportunity to topple its great carcass. The din made by it falling over could be heard, so they said, as far as the village of Basse-Pointe. The island white seemed relieved not to have been the executioner of that tree which had sheltered eight generations of whites, blacks, mulattos, *chabins* and Indians. A muleteer whom he trusted completely and to whom he denied nothing nagged him so hard that he agreed that the tree's trunk should be cut open so that the Virgin could be taken out. A gang of woodcutters worked in relay for several days on end, but the silk-cotton tree refused to give up the statue. They found the nails that had held the box in place all right, along with part of the box, but the trunk was completely empty inside, hollow from the top down to the roots. The silk-cotton tree had been dead for a century of time and not a single human being had noticed. That splendid creature which shaded the beaten earth courtyard of the master's residence had been nothing more than a skeleton! There we are, my old friend, now it's up to you to make sense of the colour of my words. Don't say later that I, Ali Tanin, didn't warn you!'

Eau de Café refused to decipher the message. Ha, ha, ha! Don't be surprised that I talk about myself in the royal third person. Here, in the village, I was immediately crowned with the title of 'Queen of the countryside'. Mulatto folk don't like the smell of our sweat, it seems, and our splayed-out toes that give off an odour of stinking feet upset them. Perhaps those people don't shit like everyone else, hah! Bear in mind that Eau de Café has never been impressed by the whisperings that follow her as she passes by or even by the plotting that they organize against her to try and make her leave. I won't reveal my secret to a soul. Not even to you, godson. Despite the fact that you're educated, that you've done France, you're not fit to hear it. You will never be able to understand who Antilia was. Give up your search . . .

30

To make Godmother happy, I've left, not without a pang of regret, the Oceanic Hotel, where each night the sea made me a gift of its loving warmth. My departure from Grand-Anse is in any case only a matter of days, hours even, away. The ex-navy man and the maid were very affectionate towards me as they guessed that I would never again set foot in Grand-Anse in my life. Only Eau de Café and her crony Thimoléon are still trying to sidetrack me, even though they too are already prepared for the inevitable. Who would want to spend a century of time listening to their ancient ramblings and try to work out the plot? Antilia's former bedroom adds to my urge to escape from that stuffiness which, I can't think how, I've tolerated without flinching. It is both empty and clean. Not a spider's web or a speck of dust. And yet Godmother insists that she hasn't aired it since Antilia's tragic end. She puts a mattress on the bare floor and sticks a picture of the Last Supper on to one of the walls. On the first evening, I realize that the young girl lived in a sort of jail. Stuck between Godmother's room and the bathroom, the room doesn't have any opening and you're forced to leave the door half-open so as not to feel that you're suffocating. Worse, you can hardly hear the tide. How could Antilia, daughter of the sea, have borne such a cruel privation?

'Frustration is eating away at you, godson. Don't deny it, your face has unhappiness written all over it,' says Eau de Café to me. 'I shall try to provide you with a lot more explanations, but I can't guarantee the outcome. I'm so old. What is death waiting for to carry me away?'

'No, you've said quite enough,' declares the carpenter, 'but me, I haven't yet exhausted the extent of what I've got to say.'

You want to know about Doris, the midwife, who brought up

your godmother throughout the Second World War? asks Thiméléon. The problem with the black man is that in order to make sense of the pattern of his life, you have to go all the way back to the first one off the boat, or almost. The history of any white of the Isles is much simpler; it starts and ends with his own person as if his grandeur was sufficient in itself. Each master (we continued to accord them this title through habit) seems to be his own ancestor or, in any case, to have concentrated in himself all his qualities and his destiny. On the other hand, the lifeline of the black man is unpredictable and from generation to generation you witness incredible upsets, which in order to be interpreted, have to be linked to the membranes of days gone by. Now, to be precise, Doris never had, as far as we could recall at least, mother, father, nor birthplace. She was, you might have said, somebody without any background although from the liquid glinting of her hair people suspected (like with Chief Bérard) some Carib ancestry. Some were sure that she'd always lived at Morne l'Étoile and that her real age was three times that which showed on her face. 'She doesn't know what death is,' they said behind her back. And it's the plain truth that you could have given her twenty, fifty or even a hundred and twenty-five years depending on her mood on a given day or even the colour of that same day.

Her profession brought her on to most of the region's estates and so, at night, a charitable man had to be found who would open the door of his hut to her, because the women feared her with an irrational fearfulness. When by chance she came back to the same estate, she would call out to nobody in particular with an obvious desire to shock:

'I'm looking for someone to exercise on top of me tonight. Not the same one as last time, ha, ha, ha! . . . He could only manage two little strokes that I couldn't feel, ha, ha, ha!'

Nobody dared to reprimand her since they needed her expertise and above all because she didn't ask for anything in return for her services. If she was rewarded with ten *sous* or some little piece of poplin, she would accept with a broad smile. If she got nothing more than a 'Thank you, Ma Doris', she would still acknowledge it with a nod. Her heart was as big as her *coucoune*. And yet, this woman who helped all and sundry to give birth couldn't have a child herself. A real male pawpaw tree. That was the demon eating away at her which pushed her to abuse her own body. In the countryside, the riff-raff was convinced that she used her wild plants and mysterious potions to destroy the child seeds that men had deposited in her womb. Julien's mother had declared:

'That woman there has killed as many little brats as she's brought into the world.'

But all were wrong apart from Franciane, Eau de Café's mother, who, nobody knows how, had guessed her secret. Although normally dumb, as soon as Doris appeared on the de Cassagnac estate, her tongue would become unstoppable. Even the master, however familiar he was with her whims, had been amazed and had ordered her in vain to shut her mouth.

'What is it between those two devil women?' he asked all around, 'or between their mothers, do you know?'

He couldn't grasp the origins of such hatefulness between black folk, which his ancestors and he himself had helped to ignite, perhaps, as in the present case, without even the slightest intention of doing so. The black man doesn't need a sackful of reasons to hate the black man. Franciane stroked her bulging stomach and shouted to the assembled servants:

'That bitch wishes that God had granted her the same blessing as me. Look at the envy that's eating away at her eyeballs!'

The further her pregnancy advanced, the more aggressively Franciane would peck at her scapegoat. She was a veritable harpy. One day, she threw herself at the abortionist outside a hut where the latter had just been dressing the wound of a field worker who had been bitten on the thigh by a viper. Doris was still holding a packet of cure-all herbs as well as some yellow liquid in a phial, probably the poison that she'd sucked out with her own mouth and was intending to use to make antidotes. Franciane scratched her cheeks until she drew blood and the master himself had to intervene. Doris, normally so full of haughtiness towards all and sundry, had never flinched at the sarcastic onslaughts of her rival and on this occasion, too, said nothing in return. Her dress had been ripped on one side. The master gave orders that she be brought another one from among those belonging to his legitimate wife since he also had probably lost his sense of reason. Doris stared at Franciane, whom the master was carrying away in his arms, and said with deliberate slowness:

'Nee-gr-ess!'

Whenever she was on her way back to her home in Morne l'Étoile, she was forced to pass through the little valley of Macédoine. In the event of some storm breaking without warning, she could always knock at the door of someone or other. On the evening of the infamous day that Franciane had attacked her, Doris headed straight for the Thémistocle house and said as follows:

'Good evening, one and all! I wish to speak to Julien.'

'At this time of night, he's bound to be at the rum shop. What do you want from him?' asked one of the outlaw's many female cousins curiously.

'I've been given something for him from the de Cassagnac estate.'

'I see! Well look, leave it with me. I'll give it to him, it'll save you a journey . . .'

'No,' said the abortionist gravely, 'it's a message that he's been sent. His ears alone can hear it.'

She disappeared into the darkness. As she drew near to the rum shop, she called over a little fellow who was busy counting the stars and asked him to go and fetch Julien. Great hoots of laughter and the crisp sound of dominoes being slammed down on to tables reached her from the tin-roofed building brightly lit by three hurricane lanterns. She was afraid that Julien, to whom she had never said a word in her life, would refuse to interrupt his game, especially for a mere woman. And yet he came, accompanied by the boy, his hands shaking feverishly from having drunk too much. His mouth stank of cheap rum:

'Aha! So what does the devil's betrothed want with me, then?'

'I've . . . I've got something to tell you, man . . . Clear off, sonny!

Listen, I've just come from the de Cassagnac plantation and . . .'

'From the good *béké*'s place, ha, ha, ha! . . . So what's it got to do with me? I've never broken my back cutting the white's sugar-cane, even if it is as good as holy bread like your de Cassagnac's . . . ha, ha, ha! . . . I've got my garden at Bois-Cannelle and that's enough to fill my stomach. I don't need his job offers. The last time I was offered one, it led to a man's death.'

'It's nothing to do with that,' replied Doris, forcing herself to smile.

'Well, come on then, tell me quickly! You've interrupted a game where I was in the middle of fleecing my best mate, bugger it!'

She took hold of his arm and as it was the first time that such a thing had happened to him, he froze completely and utterly, having never suspected that a woman's skin could make him shiver so. They took several steps along the stone path. The crickets had started their sawyers' symphony.

'*Ou konnèt Fwansyàn?*' (Do you know Franciane?) asked the woman.

'Franciane who? The one from Fond Massacre who's only got one eye? The one who belongs to de Cassagnac?'

'Yes, de Cassagnac's woman, the one who opens her legs for the white and gives us every inch of her scornfulness . . .'

'What's it to me?' belched Julien. 'If she didn't do it with him, she'd only do it with some black man, wouldn't she?'

'Certainly, but she's going round telling anyone who wants to hear that you're not a man. She claims that she was there when you were born, by the side of the path to Fourniol, when your mother was on her way back from doing the washing at the river. She's making out that you've got nothing between your legs, that your two balls haven't appeared and that's why you're so afraid of women. "Julien's a queer," she's saying all around.'

'She said that?' he asked in a suddenly flat voice.

'She's been spreading it around since she began living with that *béké*. Before she was a girl like any other, brave and not at all malicious.'

'Her mouth dared to say that?' he repeated as if to let the idea sink in, no longer paying any attention to Doris. 'Her mouth said that, did it?'

He took the path towards his father's house, haggard and stumbling among the rocks, leaving his interlocutor there where she was. Or, according to other accounts, he went back into the rum shop without the slightest emotion showing on his features and began catching in mid flight the cockchafers that circled around one of the lanterns. As soon as he had grabbed one, he carefully tore off its wings and legs before tossing it into the lamp's burning glass bowl and watching it fry, a cruel laugh on his lips . . .

'When you see the torches lit at the market . . .' says Thimoléon, abruptly changing subject, but I stop him dead, without the slightest respect for his great age. I don't want to hear any more of all that drivel which has brought me nothing apart from sudden spasms of anxiety in my heart and bouts of insomnia that even cure-all herb can't treat. I'm leaving! It's decided and neither he nor Eau de Café can do anything about it. I'm leaving as I came, emptier than a drifting coconut shell as far as the unanswered questions that were blocking my life are concerned. Do I even know who is who now? Who said what? Perhaps I'd be better off throwing myself into the Grand-Anse sea to join the legion of women struck down by the curse of madness, who committed suicide one fine morning of their youth, the men who never found any compassion among others and preferred to embrace the depths of the water, the foetuses which if they'd lived could have given us some hero to save us from our tragic end, in short all those beings possessed by uncommon desires and thus, and only for that reason, discarded by the world. I want to forget, even if forgetting is cowardice. Forgetting is existential poverty. Disaster. Dilapidation. Dubious well-being.

'. . . When in the market you see the torches and hurricane lanterns lit,' says Thimoléon the carpenter stubbornly, 'you should henceforth steer clear of the dark corners, the dead angles formed by the empty drinks crates and stacked chairs. Stay under the bright light, with your back against the market's central pillar and play! Get close to the table with the fearsome stakes: fifty thousand francs! A hundred thousand francs! The one where the *béké* de Cassagnac, lord of the Séguineau estate, is toying with two or three bilious-looking mulattos and Ugly Congo's third son, the richest man among men here, who has built a fortune with his fighting cocks and black magic. A table of absolute equality (the dice are judges and masters) where all that is spoken is a sort of pungent, fierce Creole, made up of obscure words and 'ha!'s from the depths of their throats. There's no need for them to display their bank-notes, as trust and hatred reign supreme. The number, cast to the air, suffices alone. Ah! Don't sit in judgement on their cruelty, for what do you know about what goes on in their lives? What do you know about their waking dreams? Have you ever seen de Cassagnac wandering along the paths of his property, well before cock crow, talking to himself very loudly like Guinea blacks do, his hands behind his back, his head obstinately bowed towards the ground? Do you know the meaning of that bitter curl that he brings to his lips when he seizes the dice with his silky smooth fingers? And that's not to say that his people, those of his caste, understand it any more than you do. When he was an adolescent, his father was in the habit of taking him for a ride in the Tilbury through the countryside, pointing out the houses:

'There, they're my blacks . . . Over there, that plain is Millaud. It stretches all the way to Morne Cacao and all of it is mine and so will one day be yours. In my father's time, there was a distillery that made a rum which was the toast of Paris . . . I'll show you a letter from the Marquis de Cassagnac, with his coat of arms on it, which told us how proud he was to have such a prosperous branch of the family in the colonies . . . Now all that's just a memory. People don't recognize who's who any more. The black man goes around as proud as punch, not bothering to pass the time of day unless he's after a bit of work. In town, the mulattos treat us like ignoramuses, like savages. Ah! The destruction of Saint-Pierre was an utter catastrophe for us, that's what my father used to say to me. He also told me something else. He had a sort of adage: "My son, you must never let a day pass without kicking a

31

Eau de Café can read tomorrow in our dreams.

Last night she called me into her bedroom and gave me a packet of letters that Antilia had written to Émilien Bérard, even after he hanged himself, and said:

'Godson, if I should die, don't forget to send me under the ground in my blue poplin dress. It's under my mattress.'

I didn't have the heart to tell her that I am about to leave. In any case, she and Thimoléon will carry on swapping their soliloquies from another age without even noticing that I'm not there. For them, pouring out their share of words has become the surest means of putting off the day of reckoning. Everybody in Grand-Anse talks to and for themselves. They ruminate over unfinished dreams, simmer grievances whose cause is by now obsolete, insult the jinx that has tormented the black man since the curse was put upon the heads of Ham's sons, and make up extraordinary proverbs that will make their descendants laugh. They know there's no panacea for their ills. They know they're tied for ever to their sea. They've never needed my concern, the concern of one who went away and came back in search of an unlikely Grail. They're made of the same black metal as their sand. They're immovable.

I notice with great astonishment that Master Salvie is now the owner of a brand-new bus, of Japanese make, if I'm not mistaken, with mock-leather seats and the latest sort of hi-fi system, blaring calypso that's almost indecent for this time of the morning. Tells me that the Conseil Général has paid him a fortune for his bus, the 'Executioner of the North', to put it in a museum. 'My name's engraved on it, you know,' he swaggers as he puts our bits of luggage into the boot.

I'm the last to get on. The front is occupied by two tarted-up

black man's arse. That's the only way you can force them to show us respect."

'Hum . . .! Well perhaps that's not really possible these days. The world has moved on, but let me tell you something: watch out for the black man! He has more tricks in his head than we imagine. He's been watching us from day one and at your first false step he'll push you right over the edge! You'll understand when you take over from me . . .'

The young de Cassagnac hardly blenched at these words, enclosed as he was in a sort of dumb silence that perplexed everybody. Later, it was said that he avoided women, above all the mulatto girls who were plentiful on the estate, and that he regularly argued with his father over an alliance that the latter was burning to consecrate between his son and the daughter of the *béké* de Médeuil. And then, out of the blue, a young white lady was seen to disembark, who had the language and manners of France and who liked to run through the fields and bring back bunches of wild flowers. They were married. The patriarch and his wife passed away the following year. The de Cassagnac heir had a little girl whom he left in the care of an old negress who had been living on the edge of the estate since the end of the previous century, rebellious and mocking towards the whites. De Cassagnac refused without any explanation to hand over the education of his child to his wife. She, for her part, wasted away so much that all sorts of doctors were summoned to her bedside. Finally, Ugly Congo, the second of that name, decreed that she should be sent back to her own country as quickly as possible 'because death was on its way to take her there'. She had to leave. De Cassagnac took on a young black girl of sixteen to replace her in his bed once a month. He had several other children, mixed blood this time. When an uprising broke out on the banana plantations of the North, he declined to beat a retreat to Fort-de-France like his fellow whites. He wasn't touched. They said all around: 'He's a funny sort of *béké* all the same, that de Cassagnac!' So what do you know of his secret? Nobody makes a fuss of him or flatters him, but neither is he treated as an ordinary fellow. It's as if he belonged to a species apart from common mortals, neither *béké* nor black. When he puts down the sixty-thousand-franc stake, the two mulattos' eyes meet as they realize that they have to win the next throw if they want to carry on playing without losing face. A six and a four! A three and a five! A two and a five! It's all over for our two friends. A magnanimous de Cassagnac calls out: 'Let's play again.' Which means: 'I cancel everything, let's start again from scratch, gentlemen. It's not your money I need, as I already don't know what to do with all mine.' Ugly Congo smiles secretly to himself, certain that he'll be able to fleece these two bullshitters who have dared to sit at such a table. Between de Cassagnac and him has settled a sort of amused complicity of men who have seen everything, lived everything and are waiting for others to kindly give them the opportunity to express their opinion. By dint of living with his fowls, by preening their feathers, by applying lemon juice to their thighs, by making them peck in his cupped hands, the cock-master has taken on the appearance of a strange bird, half-cock, half-hawk, whose single eye quivers with hallucinatory swivelling movements. He is doubly familiar with black suffering, having been scorned by his Creole brothers on account of his father, who came from the Congo coast at the end of the previous century after slavery had been outlawed and who spoke only African. From him he learned the gestures and spells that destroy a life quicker than a flea's leap and force honour and respectation from one and all. His father also taught him hatefulness, that sort of hatefulness which has little by little sown the stitches of our society. A hatefulness that he, Ugly Congo, the second of that name, has been nurturing ever since with as much care and patience as he nurtures his fighting cocks. A hatefulness that puts a distance between him and others, so much so that nobody to this day has dared to confirm whether the greyish dice that he carries with him from village fête to private party across the whole island, are loaded. You shouldn't think that suspicions don't plague his adversaries because they mutter behind his back, once they've been fleeced: 'I'm prepared to bet everything I own that that pig has put a spell on his dice.' So it's that fellow who

288

will welcome you with his broad smile, the one that he reserves for special occasions and you, you'll have to take up the challenge by trying to block his dice. You must throw your own on to the table and shout something provocative such as: 'Play with mine if you're all that good, Ugly Congo my friend!' All those gathered around expect no less from you, and if you fail, you can give up the idea of becoming one of them again, of being reborn and refinding your place in Grand-Anse. Look at Chief Bérard, all puffed up with pride since the white archaeologists told him that his first name, Anakalinoté, was in fact a Carib phrase, '*Ana Kalina hoté*', which means: we alone are the real people. Such glorious ancestry won't allow him to accept the slightest weakness on your part. As for de Cassagnac, the unfaithful descendant of white slavers, he'll just give a sardonic laugh. From which you have to conclude that he's admitted you to his gaming table. Now, let's get back to serious matters, men. Seventy thousand francs! Eighty thousand! The night is half-way through, it's time we finished.

289

and overdressed girls with a vacant look and by schoolboys, who are quietly revising some lesson. I find myself next to an old-timer, very dignified in his grey lounge suit, and some market vegetable women, whose hair is pulled together under Madras headscarves. They reply with a mere nod to my 'Good morning' and take no further notice of me. Front Street is empty and wan under the light cast by the street lamps. The red, white and blue flag is swaying gently on the front of the town hall. I close my eyes so as not to show any emotion when Master Salvie pulls himself up on to his seat and yells:

'Passengers, non-stop down to Fort-de-France! If anyone doesn't like it, get off now, dammit!'

Everywhere it was just one huge exclamation of holy terror: *'Lanmè-a ka monté anlè nou!'*(The sea's swallowing us up!) The town was taking in water in every direction as it had been thoughtlessly built on shifting sands gradually reclaimed from the sea. The streets had disappeared as had the pavements and doorsteps. Legions of rats were casually paddling in Schoelcher Street, nibbling at the pages of hundreds of books floating by, suddenly liberated by the flooding of the bookshops. The tragic face of Lamartine glowered defiantly at the sky under a foot of water. A gorgeous woman who had gone deliriously mad was skipping, naked and desirable, on the corner of Victor-Hugo and République Streets. She was shouting rhythmically: *'Koké mwen, doudou, woy Annou, koké mwen!'* (Fuck me, darling! Come on now, fuck me!) and trying unsuccessfully to remember the tune of a carnival favourite.

'Even the end of the world can't be dignified in this country!' bellowed someone (possibly devil's Son in Person, the hard man of Terres-Sainvilles) at the very moment that, with a terrible groaning, the outside walls of the Fort Saint-Louis gave way and collapsed. Inside the houses you could hear nothing but the bang-bang of saucepans being beaten to invoke the gods of Guinea or the banks of the Ganges which we'd forsaken for centuries of time. On the ornate balconies of pseudo-Moorish design, ladies of a certain age were trying to pose as priestesses of doom but only managed to look like consumptives who'd been allowed out or escaped from the sanatorium despite their lavish dresses decorated with shawls and Creole jewels.

From time to time, the town's carcass staggered under the sea's blows, the walls swelled violently, cracked apart and then collapsed, sometimes revealing the suicide of an entire family, reluctant to face the onslaught to the bitter end. The sky was wrought with spasms of multicoloured flashes over the whiteness of its dead eye. The municipal siren was wailing tragically while the police helicopters were trying in vain to land on the roof of the *préfecture*, which had come to look pathetic in its Greek temple garb.

Abandoned children were floating aboard the remnants of chairs or sideboards, cheerfully rowing with planks and joyously splashing each other. Tins of food, bottles of Coca-Cola and Johnny Walker whisky, half-blind television sets, imitation crystal candelabra, blond wigs, complete sets of clothes still on their hangers were all bobbing around the streets as if they innately knew where they were going. A transistor carried on crackling out messages from fathers of families to their offspring left behind in the country, calls of help from women on their own, anguished screams from old men deserted in cowardly fashion to face their torment. Then, after a brief musical interlude, the presenter's voice was cut off dead; the transistor had crashed down under the weight of an enormous whiskered sewer rat. The hoarse voice of a left-wing politician asking all his right-wing counterparts to join with him to dam the forces of evil hardly had time to be heard.

Goldmouth was masturbating at the foot of the statue of the Empress Joséphine, perched on a half-emptied chest of drawers in which you could make out – and how incongruously – a stack of porcelain plates (which had probably never been used). At the moment when the whitish spume of his orgasm shot from his member, he yelled:

'Die, all of you, you band of idiots! You've fornicated with your own mothers, you've buried your yam fields under concrete lava, you've prostituted your wives and sisters, you've sacrificed the language patiently constructed by your ancestors, you've dropped your trousers day after day, so now die! . . . This town was a wart on the face of the earth, this island a purulent canker on the back of two oceans: good riddance, bugger it! The cataclysm I predicted on the day of Tricentenary is here. It's here! Oh yes, I can see your mocking smiles of suit-and-tie bank clerks, hear your final word of schoolteachers so sure about multiplication and conjugation, your empty bullshit of shopkeepers desperate to sell some imported trash, your filth of old tarts on heat always ready to get screwed for a pair of Pierre Cardin socks, your sadism of illiterate *békés* thirsty for mystic power and determined to exploit any being, living or dead, your dreadful speeches of mayors and deputies, swine and swindlers, your laughable dotage of *Négritude* scribblers and so on and so forth. So drop dead all of you, now!'

A baleful blast of wind ripped off all the roofs in town and smashed down the most hermetically sealed doors. Fort-de-France is henceforth wide open, but there won't be any looters. The last survivor, Goldmouth, doesn't want to be around to bear witness, like Siparis in his underground prison in Saint-Pierre after the eruption of the Mont Pelée volcano. He looks at our corpses floating about aimlessly in the water and sniggers, smoking with great puffs what's left of his ganja. He can't be bothered to strike a heroic pose, which wouldn't have made any sense in the midst of this mess of water, rubble and comedies. He intends, in all honesty, to follow suit and meet his end just as shabbily as anyone else. 'You die like you've lived,' he used to say philosophically. 'In any case, the nigger, you can tell, will end up in hell.'

In the morning (18th November 1999) on Radio France-Inter broadcast from Paris, Professor Jean-Yves Dupeux had solemnly demonstrated that an as-yet-unexplained fracture in the Atlantic fault line of the earth's crust, together with a violent eastwards shift by the continent of Africa, had brought about a tearing of the tectonic plate, which in turn had caused the island of Martinique, France's last overseas territory, to be engulfed, and all in the space of two days.

'And yet I had warned the French authorities as well as the UN,' said Professor Dupeux indignantly, 'but nobody, apart from the CNRS and Society for the Protection of Animals, would take my warnings seriously. I had demanded the immediate transfer of the 320,000 French inhabitants of Martinique as a matter of urgency to some under-populated area in the centre of France, but there again nobody would listen to reason. With the result that our civilization has added another colonial crime to the others on its conscience . . .'

Goldmouth tries to shout louder than the monstrous cracking noise coming from the ground. The air is nothing more than an incredible grey-blue vapour that masks the sky, the sea and what is left of the land. A prostrate man manages to cry out:

'And to think we were only two months away from the year 2000, for God's sake!'

'The nigger, you can tell, will end up in hell!' retorts Goldmouth before collapsing.

Someone is shaking me unceremoniously by the arm. A hand that's both hairy and rough to the touch.

'Hey, what a bloody good sleep you were having, my friend!' says Master Salvie, 'and on top of that, you talk when you're dreaming. That gave the market ladies a good laugh. It's not often they get that, what with how hard life is these days.'

Croix-Mission is full of an unusual joyousness. Cayenne roses stand out resplendently among the vegetable baskets unloaded tirelessly from buses that have come from all around the island. Haggling is under way amidst a deafening hubbub that wakes me up once and for all. I walk up the side of the Rich People's Cemetery, where the outside wall has been repainted in pearly white. Looking round to make sure nobody's watching me, I throw my notebooks as well as Antilia's letters to Émilien Bérard into a gutter where foul-looking water is trickling lazily along. A hooting car horn makes me jump and so quicken my step along the La Levée Boulevard. Suddenly I change my mind, retrace my footsteps and pick up my papers, wet and muddy now, which I put into my satchel.

The world is a perennial see-saw is the thought (from Montaigne) which suddenly crosses my mind and puts a tuppenny-halfpenny smile on my face.

La Carrière Vauclin
Martinique
(June 1986–September 1989)